MMF Bisexual Ror

D0847058

BECOMING DEREK

By

Nicole Stewart

ISBN: 978-0-9975675-0-2

PART 1

CHAPTER 1

DEREK CORNWELL DEJECTEDLY threw his hands up. "Ah, c'mon! Not today, Brittany," he groaned. His eyes scanned the packed hotel ballroom before coming back to rest on his date, Brittany the Bridesmaid.

"No, today feels right, Derek," she lisped. It was a quirk he had learned to overlook. It wasn't her fault she talked like her nose was perpetually plugged, but that nasally voice launching into a diatribe against him was too much irony. "You're a sweet guy. Just...well, maybe it's time for us to focus on bettering ourselves. Wait, why am I sugar-coating this? That's part of the problem; everyone goes easy on you. Derek, *you* need to focus on bettering yourself. It's time we went our separate—"

He desperately clutched her shoulders. "Please, for the love of god, get me through the rest of this wedding reception, and I promise we can break up in style tomorrow morning online like normal people. I've got everyone and their gam-gam looking for another reason to call me a failure right now, and you are seriously not helping my cause!"

It was his little sister Heather's wedding day. Dressed in a fashionable tux, his short to medium length sable hair carefully whipped into submission, Derek was trying to look as 'functional adult' as possible, and this breakup scene was subverting his act. Family members had already harassed him with unsolicited advice about how to get his life together so he could find a good woman, to which he had

4

responded that he already had a girlfriend. Had he spoken too soon?

There had to be a rulebook against kicking a man while he was down. Brittany unleashed, voice rising despite Derek's attempt to shush her, "I have tried mightily to be on your side, Derek, but that's hard to do when you sabotage yourself! All you care about is utter bull-crap. God, if I hear one more word about video games and anime—kid stuff—I am going to scream! When will you grow up?"

"No." He held up a finger to stop her. "A-anime is not kid stuff, and keep your voice down!" he hissed. People were starting to look in their direction. Derek snatched a flute of shimmery champagne from a passing server to calm his nerves and tossed it back with a grimace before chuckling humorlessly. Of course, today.

She marginally lowered her tone. "You think life is a joke. Nobody's laughing with you. They were laughing at you, but the punch line is getting older, and it's not funny anymore. You're the punch line, Derek. It's sad because you have so much potential! You happen to have a great job, to have a lot going for you! You just don't apply yourself."

He tuned her out and closed his eyes, envisioning a train rushing headlong off the edge of a cliff—the howling horn, engine chugging aimlessly, passengers puking, pissing and shitting themselves in panic. That summed up his pathetic love life in a nutshell. A half-smile tipped his lips.

"...need to get your own place. I mean, no woman wants to be with a thirteen year-old boy trapped in a man's body, living in his parents' basement. Look, I only dated you as a favor to your sister, but now that Heather is married, I doubt she'll bother with her brother's *short*comings any longer."

"Shortcomings? Well, did you ever think maybe your *expectations* were a little too *deep*, Brittany? Because, I happen to know my comings are average, thank you. Maybe you should try Kegels."

"Ha! Right there, that's what I'm talking about. To think I thought I could help you. Laugh on, loser. I wish I never met you."

"Mutual." He raised the empty champagne glass in a toast. She flipped him off and stormed away, presumably to catch the bouquet and ruin some other sod's life. Derek loped over to the open bar because, fuck her. "Double shot of Jack," he muttered to the bartender. With his drink in hand, he sank into a moody, thoughtful haze, as he tried to make himself invisible to discourage conversation.

He was in the middle of contemplating how much worse his life could get when his best friend Owen entered the ballroom. Derek groaned as he wrestled with a desire to be left alone, and the knowledge that his gregarious bud wasn't about to let that happen.

As usual, Owen Henderson looked perfect, dressed in a scarlet shirt and tailored gray suit that obviously wasn't a rental. The jacket molded to his broad shoulders and tapered to a narrow waist, and his trousers hugged his taut bottom and ended just above the ankle, exposing brightly colored argyle socks. The light of the chandelier glinted off his wire-rimmed glasses, as he flashed smiles left and right at other guests on his way across the ballroom. He looked like a care package, like God's gift to women. Plus, he had a beard. A thick, unruly, manly fucking beard.

He was making a beeline for Derek, who was wondering how the debonair pharmaceutical salesman made it all look so easy. A sea of women leaned in toward him like high tide reaching for the moon. Conversely, Derek would've had to fall flat on his face to command that kind of attention. He watched his own mother stop melodramatically swiping fake tears to wave Owen down for a hug. Just the other day, his mom had asked him why he couldn't be more like his best friend. He blamed his parents. They should've given him better genes.

Owen greeted him with a salute and a grin. "Bartender, give me a Grand Ginger, please. Derek, my man."

"How do you do it?"

"What?" Owen was taken aback by the question out of the blue.

"Make it look so effortless. I live in the basement of my parents' house. You own a house. I drive a used car. You have a late model sports car. I'm working my dream job, and I hate it. You stumbled upon a career and you love it. And, I just got dumped by Brittany. Do you even get dumped? I can't see that happening."

The bartender delivered Owen's drink, and Owen swirled his cocktail thoughtfully before saying, "For one thing, I don't spend a lot of time making useless comparisons."

Derek laughed. "Hey, when you're the cream of the crop, why bother, right?" He wasn't envious. Okay, maybe a little envious. But,

Owen was his best friend, and he didn't wish ill on him for being Mr. Amazing. He just wanted in on the good life.

Owen's wide mouth split in a grin. "I'm flattered. Really. But, stop denigrating yourself. If you don't think you're the shit and a half, then who the hell else will? Listen, successful people don't undersell themselves. Modesty will get you nowhere. They have one weapon in their arsenal that trumps all." He swallowed a sip of his Grand Marnier cocktail and eyed Derek.

"So, what's the secret?" Derek rubbed his hands together in anticipation.

"Ego." Owen replied, "Successful people get the best. And, everyone else knows it. Whether they deserve it or not, it doesn't matter. Successful people go after the best. That's why they get it."

Derek made a fist with his hand next to his temple and spread his fingers in a simulated explosion. "Mind blown. Why on earth have I been going through life with subpar desires? Know what, I'm gonna go out right now and say I want a Lamborghini. Better yet, a whole fleet of Lamborghinis. Why settle?"

"You have to admit you haven't exactly always gone after the best in life." Owen chuckled, a melodious tenor rumble, and patted Derek on the back. His gaze swung pointedly to Brittany over in a circle of frumpy bridesmaids, looking like the She-Woman Man-Hating Club. "Also, the key words are 'go after.' It's not enough to want something. You have to know exactly what you want, and you have to go for it. Take the lady at the end of the bar, for instance."

Derek snuck a glance at the woman in question, and his eyes widened as the drink he was sipping lodged somewhere in his windpipe. He sputtered, coughing. His eyes watered and he turned away to keep from spraying Owen with liquor. As Derek pulled himself together, he got another look at her.

One strappy stiletto tapped the footrest of the barstool; the other was planted on the floor. An expanse of honeyed calf swung back and forth hypnotically, leading up to her muscular thighs barely covered by a little black dress. She was leaning against the bar. Thick, wavy hair flowed over her shoulders down to the middle of her back, which was exposed by the backless dress. He spied artful tattoos trailing down her arm, and exposed side boob. The dip of her spine slid his gaze down to the swell of her sexy derriere. His eyes swept back up, and she happened to turn, to look at him. Derek dropped his gaze.

When he got the balls to look back up, he saw some guy stroll over to her and murmur something in her ear. He got a sinking feeling in the pit of his stomach when a tiny smile flitted across her lips, as if she was interested. Then, she flipped her long hair over her shoulder and dramatically rolled her eyes, effectively dismissing Mr. Whisperer, who stood there for an embarrassing second waiting for her to acknowledge him, before finally drifting away.

Owen had a teasing look on his face. "You want to talk to her, don't you?" he asked.

And be ignored like the other guy? "Pfft. Nah. She's not my type," Derek lied.

"You do. You're just scared, and that's what holds most people back. A try beats a fail, any day." Owen raised his glass. "Here's to wanting the best and going after it. Come on."

With his pal dauntlessly heading toward the striking stranger, Derek stared after him in shock. He gnawed on a nail as Owen made his approach, and rather than ignore him, she was giggling and talking in no time. "Typical," Derek muttered testily. He motioned for the bartender to bring him another Jack. He figured he might as well enjoy the show. Owen might be able to walk up to any hot chick and instantly charm her, but that wasn't Derek's talent, and surely the most successful people knew when not to push their luck.

But, after several minutes of the two of them talking at the end of the bar, Owen gestured for Derek to come join him. Derek arched a brow and shook his head. Owen beckoned more insistently, headed back toward Derek with a look that brooked no argument. "Shit, shit, shit," Derek breathed in a panic. He nervously set his empty shot glass on the bar and prayed the liquid courage stayed in his veins long enough to carry him through an introduction.

"You asked me how I do it. This is how it's done," Owen whispered out of the corner of his mouth when he finally had Derek at his side. "Adelaide, this is my friend Derek Cornwell. Derek, Ms. Adelaide."

"Hi." Derek swallowed thickly, unsure of what to say next.

Up close, she was even more stunning. Lustrous dark blond hair framed her oval face, fine features aligning symmetrically. She had almond shaped, deep brown eyes and a plush mouth. Her complexion was exotically bronze, deeply tanned. She flashed a self-confident smile that disarmed Derek completely.

"Cornwell. You must be related to the bride! I used to know her new husband."

"Steve? Oh, yeah. He's a great, great guy. How, uh, how do you know him?" Derek stammered.

"Actually, I was telling Adelaide more about you, that you worked in graphic design as an ad man. She was interested in knowing more about that," Owen prompted.

"It's really nothing," Derek said uncertainly. After all, he'd probably not have that job much longer. Brittany was right; his portfolio sucked. He'd been working at Ad Ent, Inc. for five years without a single raise or promotion. Probably time to chalk that one up as a loss.

A dry, stale moment descended. Owen stared at Derek like he'd grown a third arm for not engaging more. Derek shrugged helplessly. Adelaide sipped from a straw, looking at the both of them. "This is fun," she mumbled. Losing interest fast.

"Um, you like games?" Derek interjected with the only topic he was adept in maintaining. Video games.

"Oh, I do, actually," she brightened. "Drinking games are the best. When I was in college, we used to play this one called I Never where you had to say something you'd never done, and then if anyone else had done it, they had to take a drink."

"Fantastic," Owen said with a smile. Her eyes lingered on his mouth. "Though, I've got one better—drinking not involved since I have to drive tonight—called Would You Rather."

"I've heard of that one," she replied, interest piqued.

Derek's eyebrows were a question mark above his clear blue eyes. Weren't they talking about video games? "I don't think I've ever heard of Would You Rather. I'm more into video…"

"It's an easy game. I say two things and ask you which one you'd rather do. Derek, you can go first. Would you rather talk about RPGs, or talk about something that actually appeals to this beautiful vixen, here?"

Derek opened his mouth to say something, but changed his mind, nodding. "Point taken." Owen high-fived him.

"Wait, what's an RPG?" Adelaide asked, chuckling.

"Not important," Derek and Owen said at the same time. They started laughing, and she giggled along. Derek promised to tell her later. It felt good to say that, like there'd be a later.

Owen ordered another round of drinks for everyone. They continued with the game. Without even realizing it, Derek relaxed and went with the flow, like he would have if it was just him and Owen. Adelaide proved to be down to earth and funny. She fit right in with them as if they'd been friends for years. He didn't bother to analyze whether that was a good thing or a bad thing, considering there wasn't anything flirty or romantic about the encounter.

Would you rather be held hostage with the potential of getting killed, or hold others hostage with the potential of killing someone? Would you rather eat fire ants, or slugs? The choices got more and more creative. A couple of other guests kept looking in their direction as the group burst out laughing every couple of seconds at what one or the other said.

It felt…normal.

Owen held up his hands for silence as he thought up another set of choices. "Alright, I got one. Last one," Owen said, staring at Adelaide. "Would you rather take your pick of one of us—me or Derek—or have the both of us at your disposal for the rest of the evening?" Derek stared at Owen in disbelief.

Adelaide peered over the rim of her cocktail glass at him. Her dark brown eyes slid to Derek. She seemed to be weighing out her choices. "Hmm, that's a tough one. But, explain exactly what you mean by 'at my disposal'."

"I mean, completely at your mercy to do whatever it is you want us to do," Owen responded casually. He cocked a brow skyward in challenge, leaving the ball in her court.

"So, let's say I need somebody to help me move. Two would be better than one, right? And, the deal is I get you for the rest of the evening?"

"The rest of the evening," Owen conceded. Derek nudged him in the ribcage. He totally was not about to help some random chick move in the middle of the night. Owen nudged him back. She totally was not about to leave with some random guys just to get help to move in the middle of the night.

"Your decision, Addie?" Owen quizzed her.

"Wow, no one's called me Addie in years. That's cute. Okay, I have my final answer. If I had to choose…I'd say the both of you. And, if I can have you both for the rest of the evening, I know exactly how I want to spend the night."

Derek laughed, thinking the situation was entirely hypothetical but it sounded a little serious. "Whoa! Where are we going with this, exactly?" he asked.

"My place or yours?" asked Addie.

CHAPTER 2

ARRESTED AT THE entrance to Owen's bedroom, Derek was more voyeur than participant.

The black dress dropped to the floor with a quiet swish. Adelaide wore no underwear underneath; there was just naked body and allure. Derek sucked in a breath at her sexiness. With a body like hers, Photoshop wouldn't have a thing to retouch. He hadn't even known women like her existed in real life until now.

Derek watched from the door as Owen stepped up behind her and dropped his hands to her outer thighs. His best friend made a slow exploration with his fingertips, sweeping up Adelaide's sides, around to the front where the globes of her magnificent breasts filled Owen's palms. Owen squeezed the pillowy orbs with an appreciative grunt and eased his hips forward to press against her, expletives flying past his lips.

"Sweet fuck! This is what I'm talking about," Owen murmured.

"Mmm…" Derek's cock thickened and lengthened in his trousers in response.

"Yes," Addie hummed with anticipation. *Yes, indeed,* Derek inwardly echoed.

Though less experienced in the bedroom than his counterpart, he easily recognized she was eager to be pleased. She rolled against his best friend's lower body insistently. But, it was the look in her eyes that told the story plainest. They stared at each other, Derek and Addie. She licked her lips wantonly. Derek suddenly understood the archaic phrase 'come hither'. She had a look that called him by his very manhood. He discreetly readjusted his erection. Owen, nibbling at the soft skin of her shoulder, made her wriggle with pleasure and they broke eye contact.

Owen brushed his nose along her long, slender neck. Derek moved closer, close enough to smell her, too. Her perfume was heady—orange peels and jasmine. Her head lolled back to rest on Owen's shoulder, and tendrils of glistening dark blonde hair clung to his shirt. Derek gulped as his eyes strayed back down to her exposed breasts. With twirls of his fingertips, Owen was making her nipples harden to fine points.

"What else would you rather do?" the pharmaceutical salesman growled. Owen shrugged out of his blazer, simultaneously unbuttoning his shirt. His upper body bare, he looked like a sex god. He cast a glance at Derek and nodded encouragement for him to get in on the action, but Derek tugged at the collar of his shirt self-consciously.

Addie flashed Owen a smile. "I'm waiting on you guys," she said. Owen paused, stopping long enough to kiss her. Owen lingered at her lips, and Derek tried to imagine how she tasted—probably as sweet as maraschino cherries. Her bare breasts rubbed against Owen's bare chest, enticing him to taste other parts of her. He rained kisses down her neck and chest.

"You heard the woman. She's waiting on us," Owen coaxed.

"You can play, too. Don't be shy," she purred.

Derek wasn't sure how to proceed. This was a novel situation for him. He watched his best friend pet and fondle the unequivocally sensual Adelaide, wishing he had the nerve to sample what was on the table. No strings attached sex with the sexiest, most sensual woman he'd ever met. Jesus H. Christ. "I'm n-not shy."

"Take your clothes off," she whispered.

"Promise I won't peek," Owen said with a grin. He sat back on the bed with her standing before him. Her full breasts at mouth level, he curled a tongue around a light brown nipple and sucked her into his mouth. She inhaled sharply, which caused her lush breasts to jiggle, and Owen grabbed each one to massage as he licked and suckled. Addie leaned forward to press Owen into the oversized bed, with her heart shaped ass in the air.

Derek fumbled with his belt, feeling like a novice. When he got his pants off, his erection sprang from the opening of his boxers, and he was glad she couldn't see how very much she affected him. He squeezed his eyes shut, hoping he wouldn't climax too fast. Jesus-God, she was unbelievably sexy.

Kicking aside the tuxedo pants, Derek took off his shirt and looked down at himself. An anxious groan threatened, but he could do this. Then, he looked back up. Adelaide was kissing a trail down Owen's washboard abs. Once she made it to the waistband of his trousers, she unfastened Owen's pants and wrapped her slender fingers around his massive hard-on. As if the action was as much a turn-on for her as it was for the gentleman receiving and the one watching, she reached down to touch herself. From behind, Derek had a clear view as her middle finger slipped and slid over her dewy lower lips.

She explored herself, spreading her petals open wide, and the entrance to her pleasure beckoned. Her skin glistened with arousal. She stuck a finger inside of herself, prompting Derek to clutch his rigid cock with a lusty groan. "Damn, Adelaide..." He sucked in a breath. Before he realized it, he was jerking off.

As she touched herself, she rubbed Owen's swollen shaft up and down, leaning forward as if part of the tide that couldn't resist his moon. Each time she did it, Derek was sure she was about to swallow his friend's penis whole. She licked her lips, mouth slightly agape, but she didn't do more than touch. She seemed torn between letting go and playing the proper lady.

Owen said with a soft chuckle, "You don't have to stop yourself from doing what comes naturally." He ran a hand through her thick hair.

"You caught me," she said sheepishly. Rising to her full, impressive height, Adelaide stopped masturbating Owen, and turned back to Derek. "I thought you said I could get the both of you."

"You can, but ummm..." Derek reluctantly sat down next to Owen. The room was semi-lit by the light of the master bathroom, the door partially ajar. Derek cast a quick peek at Owen, whose eyes were hooded and glazed. The only thing keeping Derek from bolting for the door was the fact he had enough alcohol in his system to be more curious than reticent. "What do you want me to do?" Derek murmured.

"Promise not to judge?" she asked in a small voice. Derek looked into her glossy brown eyes and realized she was only half-joking. She might be fun-loving and uninhibited, but he also saw raw vulnerability there.

"What happens between us stays here," Derek replied. "Besides, who are we to judge? We're all in this together, right?"

Owen added, "I assure you, there's only one of you. There are two of us. We can be doubly wicked. There's nothing to judge."

She dropped to her knees at the foot of the bed. Her greedy mouth given permission, Adelaide closed her lips first around Owen's cock and sucked hard and fast, her hand clasping his erection, counterturning with each wet slurp. Owen let out a loud gasp and moaned, "Oh, fuck!" Derek's eyes widened in shock. Derek reached out to hold her hair back so she could keep going, and Owen reflexively grasped Derek's wrist, squeezing. With a pop of her mouth, she released Owen and went to Derek, who could do nothing but stumble back and let her have her way.

His cock rammed the back of her throat. Derek grimaced, groaning. He was overwhelmed by the hot rush of ecstasy that came with her skilled mouth. Higher and higher he climbed. His hips strained forward to stuff his thick member past her receptive lips, and she clutched his cock in hand to masturbate him as she sucked him off. "Addie! Addie—wait!" he tried to slow her. Derek knew he was about to blast off. He couldn't let that happen. Not yet. She felt too good to pull out fast.

She wouldn't stop. "Let me taste you," she pleaded. "I just want to taste you." She made sounds of pleasure as she bobbed up and down. She followed his backward scoot up the bed, climbing up on her hands and knees when she had to. Using one hand to hold him steady and add to the mayhem of her mouth, Addie stroked Derek's swollen shaft as she sucked his quivering tip.

His hips moved to the ebb and flow of her oral sex. Sweat beaded along his forehead. Derek had never—

"Please, baby, please! Slow down. I'm about to—"

—had never experienced anything like the expert pull of her mouth. He vaguely registered Owen move from beside him and heard his friend rifling around in a bedside drawer, but Derek couldn't open his eyes. She was taking him to nirvana. She slowed down. But, the teasing flick of her tongue over his throbbing cock was as titillating as the rapid suck and blow. Butterflies flurried in his lower stomach. His breaths came out in desperate pants as he tried mightily not to explode.

Derek spied Owen positioning himself behind Adelaide. A guy like him had no shortage of willing sex partners, but a woman like Adelaide had to be one in a million, even to Owen. The way she went at it as if her very life depended on giving a man pleasure! Derek could tell she was enjoying herself as much as the boys. Rather than wait for her to get back around to sucking him off, however, apparently Owen preferred to be proactive.

Owen unwrapped a condom and carefully slid it over his erection. "Your turn," he whispered to her. When Owen rammed his meaty shaft home, Derek felt her body quake and quiver with aftershocks. "Hell, yes!" she cried out. She arched her spine, and Derek witnessed her creamy wetness coating Owen's shaft. Owen put a hand to her lower back and thrust harder, faster.

Derek wanted to look away—it felt wrong somehow to stare—but the sight of his handsome best friend plowing into Adelaide was as much a part of the thrill as what she was doing to him with her mouth. If he thought she'd get distracted by what was happening behind her, he was wrong. Adelaide returned to pleasing Derek with her hot little mouth. Her breasts swayed against his thighs, and she expertly rippled her tongue along the base of his penis. She slipped her mouth down to his balls to suck and fondle them, too.

Derek lifted his hips in surprise, letting her mouth explore further and further back, until her devilish pink tongue found his sphincter. He let out a sharp cry of pleasure as she swirled her tongue around *there.* "What are you doing?" he gasped.

She masturbated him to silence. He felt it. He was about to come. The combination of her licking and teasing his asshole while she massaged his cock was too much. Waves of ecstasy assaulted him. A spasm went through him. A geyser of copious jizz erupted. Gasping and moaning, Derek stiffly seized as more and more ejaculate spilled. Adelaide closed her mouth over his messy erection and sucked the last drops free, and the silvery cum clinging to her lips made her mouth look delectable.

Meanwhile, Owen let out a groan as he pumped into her. Derek's racing heart struggled to slow down after his climax. All he could was lay back and watch the show. Adelaide rose up on her knees and bounced against Owen, who wrapped his arms around her. She pulled Owen's face to hers for a kiss, and his tongue slipped into her mouth.

He squeezed her breasts, eliciting a cry of pleasure from Adelaide.

The two of them together were an erotic tableau that he couldn't take his eyes off. Owen's dark brown brows were knit together in confusion, mouth open in shock. Owen tangled a fist in Adelaide's long hair, and she leaned her torso away from him for better leverage of her lower body as she fucked him back. The wet, lusty sounds of their bodies pounding were a turn-on. Derek started to swell again.

His cock sprang to life as Adelaide rolled over onto her back, and Owen positioned himself between her legs. From that angle, Derek could see his friend's massive erection pulsing in and out. The frenzied pace rushed them to completion. Suddenly, Owen trembled and pulled out of her. He ripped off the condom. Derek groaned as he saw Owen's thick, long shaft, so tumescent the veins stood out in relief. Adelaide—furiously rubbing her clit, writhing with ecstasy but not quite at her climax—screamed, "Unh! Yes, Owen! Come for me!" Growling with release, Owen jerked off and a powerful blast of ejaculation arced to her flat stomach.

When he was milked dry, Owen slumped back, spent. "You...oh my god, you're amazing." He tapped Derek's leg with a weary chuckle. "Finish her," he joked. Addie giggled, the laughter turning to a moan as she continued to masturbate. She looked to Derek. He reached for a condom of his own and put it on, already hard enough for another round.

"Can you handle more?" she asked with a smile. Derek swallowed. She came toward him and sat astride his lap, his hard cock sandwiched between their bodies. Owen stroked her back. She leaned toward him and kissed him. Derek looked away, suddenly feeling uncertain. Could he give her the satisfaction she deserved?

"Wow," he breathed. "I have never done anything like this before. I just want to put that out there."

"Me neither," she confessed. "It's fun, though, isn't it?"

Owen slipped his hands beneath Adelaide's ass and lifted her up. As she came back down on Derek's manhood, Owen kissed down her back, nibbling at her hips. She squirmed and whimpered softly. Her sounds of pleasure were less frantic now. But, Derek marveled at how wet she was. He slipped inside her silky sheath easily, though her tight snatch fit like a glove around him. "Holy shit," he whispered slowly.

"Taste these," Owen suggested, fondling her breasts. He squeezed them, and her nipples jutted toward Derek. Adelaide moaned. Derek licked his lips with a hungry groan, then tentatively licked her nipples. She moaned again, louder. He closed his mouth around the left one, and she started to move up and down his shaft. Her kitty gripped him in response to the pleasure he was giving her. Derek sucked her breast harder, more confidently. As his swollen member eased free of her hold, she moved her body to squeeze him tighter. As he surged back up and into her, her body softly enveloped him. Contracting and releasing him, she controlled him.

Her fingers toyed with the wavy hair at the nape of his neck. She wrapped her arms around his shoulders and rolled her body against his like a dancer. It was such a fluid movement. Derek instinctively met her thrust for thrust, as Owen kissed along her neck and squeezed her nipples. Owen surprised him with a hand to his lips, boldly pushing his forefinger into Derek's mouth. With the wet fingertip, Owen gently reached between their bodies to rub around and around her engorged clit. His knuckles bumped against Derek's stomach. She was sandwiched between the two men. Their eyes met, Derek's and Owen's. Owen gave a small smile. Derek smiled tremulously back before his eyes squeezed shut and he emitted a tortured groan.

He vaguely registered that Owen rose to his knees and moved around to the side of the erotic pair. Addie obligingly took his hard shaft in hand to suck him off as she rode Derek. Derek tried not to notice that Owen was keeping his eyes on him, watching the expressions of lust and desire and completion flit across his face. Having never been part of group sex, Derek told himself not to think anything of it. Besides, Owen's avid interest in what Derek was doing to Adelaide seemed to arouse the blonde beauty even more.

Derek watched her watch Owen, as Owen watched him, and Adelaide's perfect mouth divinely sucking his best friend's cock sent his own arousal level up several notches. He felt her body tense with excitement. Felt her grip him with more purpose than before. Felt her steamy heat unleash like a summer rainstorm all over his rigid shaft. It made him let go. As the second orgasm powered through him, Owen reached the finish line at the same time. Adelaide convulsed and cried out and squeezed Owen's dripping cock in her free hand, as she raked her nails down Derek's back.

The three of them collapsed to the bed in a tangle of bodies.

Derek couldn't remember ever having been so turned on, so expertly gotten off in his life. His chest heaved as he tried to make sense of what had just happened. Then, Adelaide snuggled up to him and laid her head on his shoulder. Owen tucked his arm around Adelaide from the other side of her. None of it quite made sense to Derek, but it didn't seem to matter to the other two. They had done it. It'd been good. That was enough for him.

Adelaide murmured sleepily into his ear, "Can we do it again?"

CHAPTER 3

DEREK WAS AWAKENED by the whisper of cotton sheets sliding against his bare skin. He cracked his eyelids open and saw Adelaide's long, bronze legs beside him, standing next to the bed. She had her back turned. He watched her shimmy back into the black dress. She shook out her hair and stretched, sighing languidly. She sought out her handbag, and stepped into the bathroom where he heard water running, the toilet flushing. Derek watched through slits seconds later as she snuck out of the bedroom. A part of him wanted to hop up from the bed and chase her down.

Flashbacks of the night before assailed him—her silky body moving up and down against his, her soaking wet pussy clutching him tighter, her climax as the muscles within rippled and contracted and sent him back over the edge—vivid images he'd be hard-pressed to ever forget. A lucky break had allowed him to have sex with a gorgeous woman, with no strings attached. Funny that he *wanted* strings. He wanted her number. He wanted to call her later in the day, to go out with her again. She was witty, and entertaining, and unparalleled in the bedroom. It didn't seem right to let her walk out of his life uncontested.

Yet, his best friend Owen shifted in sleep, throwing his arm across Derek's torso, and the warm easy weight held him prisoner. Derek inhaled the oddly appealing mix of musky cologne and male sweat imprinted into Owen's skin, his friend's head tucked against his neck, his soft breaths stirring the hairs of his shoulder. The way they were sprawled in slumber, Owen's legs were twined with his, and a decadent urge to test boundaries surfaced. Derek put a hand to Owen's back and slowly, slowly slid it over his feverish skin, and taut muscles. Owen shifted in sleep again, nestling closer.

Derek hitched in a breath at the way his body responded, morning wood getting harder with desire. Only it wasn't for Adelaide. Owen, warm and inviting, clung to him in sleep. His sculpted lips begged for exploration. His hot body promised thrills unimaginable. Derek craved something he couldn't put a name to it, or wouldn't put a name to. It was crazy. He wasn't thinking straight.

At a soft flurry of snores from Owen, Addie looked back. Derek quickly shut his eyes. He pretended to be asleep, but he heard her leave. He didn't try to go after her. Derek pushed the stirs of arousal out of his thoughts and squeezed his eyes shut. Last night had been complicated, he reasoned. No wonder he was having wayward thoughts. But it was still dark out, barely dawn. He needed to sleep a little longer. With a little rest, he'd wake up with a clearer head.

"What you need is a life coach."

They sat poolside in Owen's backyard. It was a lazy Sunday, hot and beautiful. A cerulean sky dotted with white fluffy clouds overlooked the two shirtless guys in swim trunks lounging on an outdoor sectional. Sunlight made Owen's toasted skin gleam, and Derek eyed his own dusky arms, wondering if he should apply more sunscreen. He noticed his muscles were decidedly less prominent in comparison to his friend's, shrugging at the comparison. He was trying to work on not doing that.

"My pockets have determined that is a lie," Derek quipped. "I can't afford a high-priced hack to come in and play guru. I need some practical advice on how not to continue being a screw-up."

Owen gestured in a circle with his free hand and sipped from a frosty *piña colada* with the other. "Get it all out. All the self-deprecating comments you can think of. I'll give you a minute. Go!" He popped a pineapple wedge into his mouth and chewed patiently, waiting.

"Cut it out," Derek said with a laugh and a shake of his head.

Owen stretched an arm along the back of the sectional, accidently rubbing against the back of Derek's neck. Derek sat forward and pretended he was just going for his drink on the coffee table in front of them. He took a small sip. He still had a headache from last night.

"I'm trying to give you the opportunity to bad mouth the hell out of yourself one good time, so I don't have to keep hearing this crap. Have at it," said Owen. His full lips curled upwards in a grin, but it was hard to spot through his facial hair. His dark eyes twinkled teasingly behind his glasses.

Derek examined him, the pale blond lashes and hollow cheeks, the sharp nose—general good looks. He tried to remember back to when and how they had become best friends. It was hard to say. They grew up in the same neighborhood, which created a sense of always having known each other. By middle school, they had most of the same classes. In high school, they carefully orchestrated their schedules to have more of the same classes. They even went to the same college together after graduating.

In the years of knowing each other, Derek had been the hard worker who never quite won the prize. He had a long streak of 'honorable mentions', but Owen had been the natural achiever. He didn't have to put in much effort to come away with first place. Eventually, Derek had taken the hint destiny was trying to throw him. Brittany said it best. "Laugh on, loser."

As time progressed, it seemed fitting their lives would work out the way they had. Considering Owen always coasted to the finish line without breaking a sweat, Derek figured he probably wouldn't understand his struggles.

"Okay," he tried. "Despite a thorough education and years of experience in my field, I sometimes feel like I'm winging it and nobody knows it but me. Soon the shit will hit the fan, and everyone will wonder how I got past grade school. I gained five pounds last week. None of it was muscle weight. I can't stick to anything. Not a workout plan, not even reading a full novel." He ticked off more bad traits on his other hand, finally rounding off with, "I get bored easily. I heard once that people who get bored fast are really boring. I think I'm boring."

Owen chopped a hand through the air. "Minute's up. Stop."

"I wasn't done yet."

"Something tells me you could go on and on about your favorite subject: Ways you think the worst of yourself. Hate to tell you this, but your failures aren't nearly as interesting as you think," Owen chuckled. Derek punched him in the side, and Owen doubled over, still laughing. Once he sobered, he eyed Derek speculatively. "There's hope yet. I wasn't talking about you hiring some hack. I was talking about you and me working together to shape you up."

"Ah! So, *you'd* be the life coach?"

"Precisely. You could do worse. You could be saddled with someone who doesn't know you, or care about you. I happen to be two-for-two on both counts. I know you, care about you and respect you, and I want to see you be successful as much as you want to see you be successful. In fact, I've been giving it a lot of thought all morning. What's the one thing we could do to instantly make you see yourself in a different light? And, you know what occurred to me?"

"That I need glasses? I've tried to pull off wearing them before, but I either come out looking like a nerdy intern or a near-sighted research assistant. You, on the other hand, rock the hell out of a pair of specs. Are those custom?"

"You need a wardrobe change."

"Wait, what? What's wrong with my wardrobe?" Derek looked down at the swim trunks with flame patterns inching from hem to waistband.

Owen smiled tightly. "Remember the other week when I stopped by your job? You had on a pair of trousers that were a size too big, and a shirt with a stain on it."

"I spilled coffee on myself. Shit happens."

"You also need to learn the benefits of the mantra, 'Be Prepared'. You should always keep a spare shirt. As I recall, you had a meeting later that day and I was appalled to even think of you walking into a boardroom with a stained shirt. Now, I propose we go shopping, but, don't worry, the cost is on me. I need to show you how to mix and match some style essentials to present your best face forward."

"You know, my only problem with your suggestion is changing how I dress doesn't change who I am."

"Yes, but you'd be surprised at how much it changes how you think of who you are, *and* what other people think of you when they see you. Do you want my services or not?"

23

To begin with, they had to go to the Cornwells. Derek used his key to let himself in. At the sound of the front door closing, Lydia Cornwell peeked her head out of the living room. "Is that you, honey? Oh, I was worried sick when you didn't call or come in last night. I saw you drinking at that reception, Derek. You had no business driving." She wagged a finger fussily.

"Give the kid a break, Lydia," his Dad, Frank, called out.

"Yeah, relax, Ma."

Owen interjected, "I drove last night, Mrs. Lydia. No danger there."

"Aw! Owen, my responsible boy!" Lydia dragged Owen into a hug. Derek and Owen shared a look over her shoulder. Derek shook his head, smirking. Owen shrugged and grinned. Frank stepped into the foyer and waved the paper at them to shoo his wife off.

"Let the boy breathe, Lydia. For goodness sake, you're like a cougar sometimes."

"Pish posh, Frank," she said, giggling. "He knows I mean nothing by it." She winked at Owen, who discreetly wiped the lipstick smudge from his cheek and followed Derek through the front hallway to the door to the basement. "And, you still should have phoned if you were going to be out all night, Derek," she called after him.

"Next time, Ma. I will." Derek slammed the door and locked it with a disgruntled sigh. "She babies me so much."

"You like it," Owen teased. "Alright, where's your closet?"

Derek gestured to an overflowing clothes basket. His mother had done his laundry and folded his belongings earlier in the week, but Derek had rifled through the basket a time or two. The clothes were now a rumpled mess. Owen held up a pair of jeans with a hole in the back side. "Really?"

"What? Don't judge me. Those are my yard work pants."

Owen balled them up and tossed them aside. He went through a few more things before pronouncing the entire basket a loss. "The situation is worse than I expected."

"I know. I should be ashamed of myself," Derek deadpanned.

"Nope. You should stop with the 'woe is me crap' and take control of your life. Let's hit the mall. I know I can help you. I consider it a challenge."

"I'm not sure if I should feel good or bad about that statement,"

Derek said with a laugh. They hopped back in Owen's car after saying goodbye to his parents, and headed straight for Owen's favorite clothier.

As they strolled past well-dressed mannequins and a shoe section with price tags that made Derek blink in amazement, Owen said, "Like it or not, if what you told me about your conversation with Brittany last night is accurate, your ex had some good points."

"Whose side are you on, traitor? What do you think of this ironic combo, by the way?" Derek stepped around a rack and came back holding up a Star Wars t-shirt and a pair of rainbow suspenders. Owen's face went blank with lack of amusement. Derek frowned and shoved the t-shirt back on the rack. "Fine. What were her good points?"

"I'm sure she's not the first person to tell you to grow up," replied Owen. He took his time examining different styles of shirts, blazers, and vests. He ambled over to a row of suits and picked around, guestimating Derek's sizes. "Now, I happen to know a lot of women who find a child-like man appealing, but there's a big difference between holding onto aspects of childlike innocence and awe, and just flat-out being a stagnant adult. Here, try this on."

Derek rolled his eyes and grabbed the outfit Owen put together and extended to him. Owen pointed to the dressing room. Derek called over his shoulder as he went, "I'm beginning to wonder if anyone has ever told me the truth about myself. All of a sudden, all this negative shit is coming out."

"We tried subtle," Owen replied, a smile tickling his lips. "I told you Chuck's didn't go with trousers, but you insisted."

Derek shrugged out of his shirt and pants, standing there in his boxers. He posed before the full length dressing mirror and studied his reflection. He was thin but rangy, with corded biceps and a ripple of abs at his stomach. In the yellow light, his olive complexion looked sallow or exotic, depending on the critic, a throw-back to his Armenian ancestry. He also had his ancestors to thank for his thick head of wavy black hair and his strong bone structure. His face was put together pretty well. He had a penchant for frowning, not with his lips but with his thick brows and piercing blue eyes. He wondered how Adelaide had seen him. How had Owen?

Derek didn't have a particularly colorful sex life. His pursuits could best be described as vanilla, meaning plain but decent. His experience with orgies and group sex was limited to categories of porn. When it came to power moves, he was used to putting it in, moving it around, and praying he hit the spot. And, he wasn't used to having an audience. All of that had changed last night.

Addie had clearly climaxed, (evidence he hit the spot.) He definitely had had an audience. He'd finally been initiated into the group sex club, and he didn't know how to feel about it, other than wowed by the experience. It was waking up naked next to his best friend that had put a slant he hadn't expected on things. Derek tried to get the mixed emotions out of his head—the inexplicable arousal, the feelings of self-loathing for having a 'gay' thought for a second—they were getting in the way of progress.

He had a life coach, someone who would help him become the man his parents, his sister, and his long list of exes wanted him to be. But, if one thing could change how he viewed himself, that thing was what happened last night—wardrobe be damned.

When he was fully dressed in the clothes Owen had handed to him, the slate gray shirt un-tucked to better fit his style, the black suit hugging his physique nicely, and dark blue loafers standing in for his usual tennis shoes, Derek stepped out of the dressing room to model the ensemble. Two ladies helping a teenaged boy pick out a tie nearby stopped what they were doing to stare. Derek overheard one of them say, "See George, that's how you set standards."

Owen applauded slowly, a bright smile breaking through his beard. "Now, that's what I'm talking about. How do you feel?"

"Like I'm playing dress up," Derek replied. He held up his arms, stretched, shook out the jacket. He did feel a little like a kid trying on his father's clothes, but he also felt a bit more impressive. He could imagine himself heading in to work dressed as he was, instead of in whatever wasn't dirty at the top of the clothesbasket in the basement. The office had a loose dress code, and Derek had never been big on fashion. He just hadn't seen the point. However, he could wear this. He could wear it and enjoy it. "I think I like it," he said uneasily.

Owen came over and checked the fit of the suit, tugging at the waistband and adjusting the lapel of the jacket. "Mm hmm, looks good on you. A full wardrobe makeover only requires a few staple pieces, like this classic black jacket and trousers. I see you left the shirt un-tucked. That works for a casual day at the office or if you're going out on a date. But, you can easily dress this suit up with a more serious pair of kicks and a tucked white shirt."

"Okay, okay! Enough," Derek brushed him off, annoyed at being fussed over. "I never pegged you for a fashionista."

Owen chuckled, holding out his arms. "Who did you think dressed me?"

"Some chick," Derek replied honestly.

"Go figure. I thought your mom got you ready." Owen blocked the faux punch Derek fired his way.

They finished out the afternoon perusing store after store, until Owen felt Derek had a sizeable bulk of clothing to choose from to begin his life anew. In the food court of the mall, Derek treated them both to a late lunch. Owen sipped a protein shake as he pulled out a notebook and a pen. "So, here's your homework for the next week."

"Let me just say, I like the fact that you're taking this unpaid job so seriously."

"Well, thank you," Owen replied sarcastically. "I hope you do, too. It's time for you to come into your glory, my friend. I know how great you can be. You just have to realize it. Otherwise, you're wasting both of our time. Now, where was I? Oh, right—your homework for the next week. I want you to break in your new wardrobe and start introducing and referring to yourself as 'Mr. Cornwell'. I want you to also practice placing the title in front of the names of others you respect, even if you have a fairly casual relationship with them."

"Dude, this gets weirder and weirder," Derek replied with a grin. He doused his fries in ketchup and chewed thoughtfully. "Alright, I'll bite, Mr. O. Why add the Mister?"

"Because, Mr. Cornwell, it's time you let the world know they can take you seriously. You'd be surprised at how the words we use and ways we internally describe a person go on to frame our perspective of others. And, hey, no more nicknames. Bob is Robert now. Jennifer isn't Jen or Jenny. You're no longer on the playground. Time to put on your big boy name."

"This is grown man shit."

"Precisely.   By   the   way,   *Mr.*   *O*??"

CHAPTER 4

"BABY D, MR. Clancy left a message for you," the graphic design floor secretary announced, when Derek stepped out of the elevator the next morning.

"That's Mr. Derek Cornwell to you, and thanks, Ms. Sullivan," he murmured pleasantly, accepting the handwritten message. Her eyes widened when she looked up from the Sudoku game she was playing and actually got a glimpse of him. Derek nervously smoothed a hand over his three piece suit and flipped back the wavy hair that fell into his face. It seemed everyone in the office stopped what they were doing to watch him cross to his cubicle and take a seat.

He tapped his keyboard, and his Mac powered on. Derek wondered why his supervisor was leaving messages for him, of all people. He unfolded the scrap of paper the secretary had handed him and deciphered her messy handwriting. Meeting at nine. "Great," he muttered. On the plus side, he hadn't spilled any coffee on himself yet; but, if he did sometime between now and nine, he had a spare suit in the car.

When he looked back up, everyone was still staring at him. Derek cleared his throat and picked up a pencil. He bent over a graphic he had been drafting on a sketchbook last week, for an ad they were working on for a new men's cologne. It looked a lot like previous work he had submitted, unimaginative but safe. It was the sort of work everyone in the office agreed Mr. Clancy favored.

At nine o'clock, no coffee breaks later, Derek pushed back from the busy work and forced confidence into his stride. Shoulders back, head up, he approached Mr. Clancy's door and knocked.

"Come in."

He stepped into the quiet, inner sanctuary of the head of design and stood wondering what to do next. Mr. Clancy didn't deign to look up. "What do you want?" the supervisor asked, a hint of boredom in his tone.

"It's Mr. Derek Cornwell, sir. You requested a meeting?"

Bertrand Clancy was pushing seventy. His dark hair had gone mostly to white, and he didn't bother concealing it. He wore it slicked to the side, always wore a nice suit, looked every inch the accomplished businessman. He was a dinosaur—especially for this industry—but he was still around because he had an intuitive gift for finding the best and brightest, and getting them to put out *their* best and brightest work. He was notoriously hard to please because he knew his stuff better than anyone else at the company. Everyone respected him, especially Derek. He had studied him in college; the guy literally wrote the book on ad design.

"Mr. Cornwell," Mr. Clancy repeated with a chuckle. "Well, sit down. We need to go over a few things, and I don't have all day."

"Of course, sir. We're both busy." Derek hurriedly took a seat, breathing a sigh of relief that addressing himself as Mr. Derek Cornwell to Mr. Clancy hadn't sounded as pompous out loud as it had in his head.

"Some of us busier than others, by all accounts. Now, you're working on the Wonder Man ad team, right? Peer Reviews were turned in last week. Derek, I'm not going to beat around the bush. You got some of the lowest scores to ever come across my desk."

"E-excuse me, sir?" Derek swallowed.

"Allow me to read a few direct quotes, if you will. 'Derek Cornwell is consistent. He consistently keeps mum during brainstorming sessions. He consistently does the bare minimum required to be considered a part of the team, and he consistently turns in his work several hours late, thereby putting the rest of us behind.' Oh, here's one I personally liked. 'Derek can go fuck himself.' Anonymous source. Care to explain yourself?"

"I d-don't know why they don't like me, sir. I do my job."

Mr. Clancy leaned forward with a stern expression. "Did you

know I handpicked you from a stack of other equally talented graphic designers? I chose you because your portfolio, while not as robust, had a unique quality I thought would imbue this company with new blood. Instead, you've been here five years and never rocked the boat. I'm disappointed in you."

Derek didn't bother to stammer that he thought the goal was *not* to rock the boat. He was still stumbling over the idea that Bertrand Clancy had handpicked him based on his portfolio. "I, uh, I'll do better, sir. I'm sorry."

"Yes, you are. I took a second and looked over every project you contributed to in the past five years, and it was sorry, sorry work. I'm going to have to let you go."

"No." The answer blurted out of its own accord. Derek smashed a hand to his face in shock at his own audacity, but he meant it. No, he wasn't about to let himself get fired. He needed this job. He forced his hands together in his lap. "I want another chance."

"Why should I give you another chance? Do you deserve it?" Mr. Clancy cocked his head to the side and examined his sweaty employee. He had seen Derek around the office, had never seen him suited up, had never seen him stand up for himself. Derek recognized he had some social hang-ups that likely accounted for a lot of the bad reviews, and Mr. Clancy was probably aware of that too, considering he'd apparently been following his work. But, they were also both aware that being part of a team required overcoming personal hang-ups.

Owen's words replayed in Derek's head—"*Whether they deserve it or not...successful people go after the best*"—and he struggled not to look as terrified and undeserving as he felt. He wanted this job. It was the best thing that had ever happened to him. He was keeping this job.

"Sir, I am brimming with new ideas that, well, I think can rejuvenate our department. When I initially tried voicing these opinions, I was told to stick with the status quo and I ignorantly complied. I'm taking the blame for that. But, if you allow me to show you what I can do, I promise I will not disappoint."

"You've had five disappointing years. You still haven't given me a good reason for why you deserve a second chance," Mr. Clancy sat back with a sigh. He held up a handful of papers. "These reviews alone justify letting you go."

"Undeserved or not, I want two weeks to change your mind,"

Derek replied, quietly defiant. He steeled his jaw and refused to back down. His blue eyes stared into Mr. Clancy's. "Two weeks."

After what felt like an eternity, the supervisor dropped the reviews and tapped his chin speculatively. "Alright, two weeks. What do you suppose you can do to change my mind, Mr. Cornwell?"

"I want full control of the Wonder Man ad."

"I'd be stupid to do that. You'll continue as part of the team, but I'll allow you to use your downtime to create an advertisement of your own for Wonder Man. In two weeks, both spreads can be presented. Keep in mind, I'm judging you on your personal design, as well as your work within the team. You're only competing with yourself. This...should be interesting."

Derek left the office wondering how the hell he was supposed to squeeze in the extra work. And, what else he could do to engender his apparently disloyal team to him. "Fuck," he muttered into his hands as he stood outside the closed office door. "Want the best. Go after the best." He had covered the first half of that. Now, it was time to go after what he wanted.

Back at his desk in his cubicle, as he wracked his brain for ideas for his personal project, Derek forced kinky thoughts of his weekend out of his head in order to focus. He grabbed his sketchbook and crossed his ankle over his knee, leaning back in the office chair. Page after page, he scribbled potential ideas for the full page advertisement for the cologne. Without the multidisciplinary team, he had to think outside the box because there were certain aspects of the ad he couldn't tackle on his own—like the photography. He sucked at photography. On the other hand, he knew some great photographers. He just had to figure out what he wanted to convey.

An hour later, he threw his pencil down and popped his cramped knuckles. There was graphite along the side of his palm. His vision blurred and his eyes burned. He scrubbed them with the back of his hand. When he looked up, he was surprised to see the secretary standing next to his cubicle. "Hey, something's different about you," she whispered.

"Um...new haircut?" Derek joked.

"I dunno. It looks good, though." She licked her lips with a secretive smile, and leaned in so no one else could hear what she said next. "Harold told me to wait until sometime after lunch and pretend like I forgot to give you the message, but they're planning a brainstorming session at one. He wanted it to look like you weren't on top of your shit."

Derek arched a brow in surprise. "Thanks. Thanks for telling me."

"Don't mention it. Just so you know, I gave you a good peer review, alright?" She waved her fingers and strutted away, her pencil skirt hugging a nonexistent behind. She had never given him the time of day before.

Derek scratched his head, wondering at the extra attention. He had caught several women in the office giving him appreciative glances all day. Maybe Owen's advice was right. Who knew the clothes made the man? Derek shook his head wryly and glanced back down at his sketchbook. His cellphone vibrated on his desktop, and he reached for it. He had a text message from his best bud. "Meet me at the bank at six for the next phase of #ReshapingDerek."

He chuckled briefly before sending a confirmation back to Owen that he'd be there. The text message got him thinking about the weekend again... thinking about Adelaide. It was hard to believe any of it had happened. Derek could have kicked himself for not making a bigger effort to get some type of contact information from her before she left. As it stood, he had no way to get in touch with her.

"Except," he murmured, a light bulb going off overhead. "She was at my sister's wedding." Before the thought was fully processed, his fingers were fumbling for his phone again. Derek quickly scrolled through his contact list for Heather's number. He knew she and her new husband, Steve, were already back from their honeymoon because the young couple could barely afford a trip. They'd gone two towns over and stayed the night in a pricey hotel. His parents had footed the bill.

Heather picked up on the second ring. He could hear some of her clients in the background where she worked as a hairdresser. "Hey, Derek! I heard. Oh, honey, I am so sorry Brittany dumped you. She told me all about it, and I can only imagine how heartbreaking that had to be on my big day! How could she do that to you?"

"Yeah, don't worry about it. Listen, I know you're busy, and I'm kind of in the middle of something, too. I just had a quick question for you." He bypassed what might've ended up being a lengthy Dr. Phil moment and cut to the chase. "There was this woman named Adelaide at the wedding. I figured she had to be one of your friends. Do you, by any chance, happen to know how I can reach her?"

"Adelaide?" Heather's normally chipper tone turned frosty. "That skank? Ugh! She's one of Steven's ex-girlfriends. I can't stand her! She crashed my wedding and, let me tell you, if I knew how to get in touch with her, she'd be a missing person by now."

"Yikes! Sorry I asked." Derek couldn't picture his bohemian little sister hurting a fly, but she definitely had venom in her voice for the wedding crasher. He tried to picture a boring accountant like Steve bagging a woman like Adelaide. He couldn't picture it.

"Why'd you want to know, anyway?" Heather asked suspiciously.

"Um, for a friend," he lied.

"Who, Owen? Oh god, tell me he didn't fall for that tramp. Hey, I gotta go. Can we talk about this later?"

"It's not a big deal. Talk to you later, sis."

Derek hung up the phone, feeling dejected about the lead turning into a dead-end. He had no other options. It was probably time to give up   the   infatuation.

CHAPTER 5

"I'M JUST SAYING. Some people can't afford to save. You know how expensive it is to be broke? And, I'm probably going to need that three hundred I just transferred out of my checking account back in a few days." Derek and Owen strolled out of the bank on Main Street. Derek dug his hands deeper in his pockets and wiggled his fingers around, feeling nothing, not even spare change.

Owen quirked a brow. "Can't afford to save! Are you kidding me? Maybe if you're juggling some real household expenses—a mortgage, insurance, taxes, utilities—and, even then, it's not impossible. Just complicated. People can't afford not to save money, actually."

The two men flowed along with the rest of the pedestrians filling the city sidewalks. The starless sky overhead was illuminated by the lights of the business district.

"I know you're right, in theory. It's putting it in practice I'm worried about." Derek complained, but he was secretly pleased his bro had taken the time to connect him with a financial advisor. There were some things everyday people were expected to just know, things that were never fully explained, and the only way to learn them was to screw up royally. It helped if you had a guiding hand.

"Look at it this way. Job security is all about knowing you'll have a paycheck. Well, financial security is all about knowing you'll have money in the bank, whether you have a paycheck or not. Now, there's no way I can promise you you'll never go broke again, but what I can say is with the right planning you can survive if you fall on hard times for a while." Owen stopped him, placing his hands on Derek's shoulders. "Do you trust me?"

"I trust you," said Derek. "I don't have to like it, but I trust you." Owen's gaze swept over him. Derek self-consciously smoothed a hand over the pumpkin orange shirt and dark blue blazer that made his pale blue eyes pop. Their gazes met. Derek felt a surge of pride knowing, for a change, he didn't look out of place next to his well-dressed friend, and a surge of something else, which he ignored. He stepped out from under Owen's touch.

"Atta boy," said Owen, looking at the time on his oversized watch. "Oh, shit, I gotta jet. I double booked myself. It's a wonder I had enough time to help you get everything done, especially opening up that secured credit account. You'll be needing that. I've got a date with a hot chick from this clinic where I made a delivery earlier."

"What? Dude, do you have to pick up women everywhere you go? I wanted us to go out for drinks together this evening, you and me, my treat." Derek pouted, but Owen pulled a face.

"Rain check?" He was already walking backwards to his sports car parked curbside.

Derek thought back to when they were younger, when it was easier to make impromptu plans to hang out. With Owen's career taking off, he was either too busy with work or too busy with women to spend much time with Derek. Most days it wasn't a big deal, but he wanted to celebrate tonight. He had a lot of positive shit going for him now. That was cause for a few beers, some good laughs. Derek waved him off. "Yeah, yeah. Hit me up tomorrow."

They got into their dissimilar vehicles and went their separate ways, Owen to some nightclub in the city, Derek to his parents' house. In the beat up used Mazda, Derek tried not to think of it as his best friend having a good time without him. They weren't kids anymore. They had their own lives. Still, it sucked ass.

It was getting dark out. When Derek pulled up to the house in the middle class hamlet where his parents lived, he felt an awkward sense of displacement. He couldn't put his finger on what caused it, couldn't quite name it, but the feeling was there. He looked up at the clean white siding and pale gray roof, the entryway overhung by a portico. Shrubbery and green leafy plants filled flowerbeds to either side of the door. The narrow windows gave the house a boring face.

This place he had called home most of his life belonged to his parents. That was the rub. Now that he was an adult, the house just didn't fit him. Derek unlocked the front door and went straight for his basement hideout. In the small room downstairs, his twin sized bed—the same one he had slept in since childhood—took up much of the space. The other half of the basement was cluttered with the accumulated junk of middle-aged parents. He straightened his rumpled blankets and threw his tired body down onto the lumpy mattress, staring at the wall instead of the mess.

Closing his eyes, Derek rehashed his day. From the early morning meeting with Mr. Clancy to the surprise afternoon team brainstorming session, he knew he hadn't been himself today. 'Himself' was normally the last person to voice a suggestion, but he had voiced opinions left and right at the meeting with Harold and crew, simply to piss them off. He couldn't believe they'd all given him bad reviews.

Hell, then again, it wasn't that hard to believe. Derek barely knew most of the people in his office. No wonder they felt no sense of camaraderie with him. He could change that. He had to, if he wanted to keep his job. Clancy was judging him on his team performance and his personal project. It was time to come out of his shell and shine.

Derek reached under his bed, patting the dusty concrete floor underneath until his fingers landed on his journal. He pulled it out and opened the heavy book half-filled with crisp, blank pages on his lap. He couldn't remember the last time he had used it. The book boasted mostly doodles, some rambling musings, but one section in particular was home to his early ideas from when he started at Ad Ent. Maybe he could find something to inspire him with the Wonder Man ad.

"Derek, honey, dinner's ready!" His mother's voice cut through the nostalgic flip through pages.

Derek slammed the book shut and shoved it back under his bed. He called out, "I'll be up in a second, Ma!" Derek undressed and laid his new clothes neatly on his bed to be hung up later. He ducked into the cramped basement bathroom where he turned on the shower and watched the cubbyhole sized room fill with steam. Stepping under the hot spray, he washed away his day and re-dressed in lounge pants and a t-shirt, which he was certain someone would point out wasn't suitable dinner wear. Unfortunately, Owen had thrown out most of his old stuff.

The lounge pants had to suffice.

By the time he made it up to the dining room, his parents were already eating. "What took you so long," Frank griped. "Your mother puts a lot of effort into getting dinner ready for when you and me get off work. I make it to the table on time. What's up with you?"

"I had to stop at the bank this evening. Owen was helping me take care of some financial stuff."

"God, don't tell me you're borrowing money from him, too." Lydia's sweet voice wrapped around insulting commentary made him cringe, even though he knew she was speaking from a place of parental concern. "Please don't mooch off your friends, baby. It's embarrassing. Do you need a little extra cash?" Derek quickly waved the suggestion down.

"No, I wasn't borrowing money, and I don't need you to give me extra cash. Not yet, anyway. Hopefully, not ever again. He was hooking me up with his financial advisor. Owen's giving me pointers on how to build wealth."

Frank shared a look with Lydia. "Don't that beat all," he grunted.

Lydia nodded agreement as she handed Derek his fried eggplant, lamb chops, and quinoa. The fact his mom still fixed his plate was a depressing reminder of his status in life. Derek tried not to look ungrateful. He was grateful for everything his hovering, overbearing, overly attentive parents did for him. Just as he suspected though, new clothes wouldn't fix his situation.

Lydia prattled on about her day as the Cornwell men said little while they ate. Derek briefly wondered what Owen was up to wherever he was, and then his thoughts turned to Adelaide. The dinner table wasn't the best place for his wild imagination to conjure up a tactile memory of her expert fellatio. Derek blushed and tuned back in to the chatter. "...and, Heather called me. Did I tell you that, Frank? She wanted us to know they enjoyed the hotel room."

"She called to tell you *that*?" Frank gagged, wiping his mouth with his napkin.

Lydia tittered. "That's usually what people do on their honeymoons. Enjoy themselves."

Derek grimaced over his parents alluding to his sister and her new hubby having sex, *enjoying* their hotel room. He took a sip of wine and muscled down another bite, but his appetite was already shot before he sat down to dinner. All he wanted was some time alone, so he could mentally see his way past the problems at work, and float on fantasies of Adelaide some more. He was itching to call Owen and get his take on their weekend romp, but he didn't want to come off as the giddy noob he felt he was. Owen was being cool about it. He probably had threesomes all the time.

Lydia got his attention. "She also told me, Derek, that you and Brittany broke up at the wedding reception?"

Derek choked. His father gave him a whopping thump on the back that made him sputter even more. "Jesus, Derek! She did that big of a number on you? Get a hold of yourself," Frank mumbled, chuckling. Derek rolled his eyes and managed to catch his breath.

"Bah, hush, Frank," Lydia fanned aside his comment. She gave Derek's hand a sympathetic squeeze. "Of course, she did a number on you, my poor guy. Did that girl lead you on? Why didn't you tell me that you were having problems with her? I could've helped." Derek wriggled his hand away. He felt smothered, and he felt like a cad for feeling that way about his mother, but that's what Lydia Cornwell did. She took over a situation and 'helped', whether you wanted her to or not.

"Well, for one thing, Ma," he said, "what I do with my girlfriend is personal. It wasn't Heather's business to talk to you about it, either. For another thing, we weren't having problems. We just kind of agreed it would be best if we stopped seeing each other. An amicable split. You know, like those celebrities do."

Lydia shrugged, perplexed. "I don't see why you always hop from relationship to relationship. You break up so fast, before I even have time to get used to your little lady friends. Don't you think if I got to know them, I'd be better able to steer you to a good match? You're a handsome boy. You've got a lot going for you. You just need a push in the right direction."

Frank dropped his fork on his plate with a *clank*. "Oh, tell it like it is, Lydia. He's clearly not ready for a relationship. He barely has his own shit together. Any woman takes one good look at him, she hightails it for the hills. No offense, Derek. Just calling it like I see it." He threw an apologetic smirk at his son. Derek noticed his father's words echoed Brittany's. It stung to know he wasn't living up to everyone's expectations. Also, for people to talk about him like he wasn't present.

He cleared his throat loudly. "Look, I know I've had some problems in the past, but just know you'll see a whole new me in about two weeks, and don't say I didn't warn you. I've got some irons in the fire, some game changing stuff. And, either I'll get the advancement I need at the office, or I'll find a job that fits me better. As for a girlfriend..."

Derek tugged his cellphone out of his pocket. He could get in touch with Steve, Heather's husband, and find out how to reach Adelaide. "If you'll excuse me, I need to see a man about a horse."

He pushed back from the table, leaving his parents staring after him with confusion written on their faces. Derek overheard his mom repeat what he'd said. "See a man about a horse?"

"He means a prostitute, Lydia," Frank supplied, teasing.

"Oh!" she wailed.

Derek laughed as he ducked into the basement and locked the door. He had Steve's number saved in his phone. The trick was to make sure Heather wouldn't find out what they were talking about, meaning he couldn't just flat out ask about Adelaide. Heather would pitch a fit. Thinking on it, he carefully crafted his message and crossed his fingers, waiting for a response back. "Hey Bro—Owen & I wanna welcome you to the family, proper. Drinks Friday night?" It took a half hour before Steve finally replied, a laconic affirmative.

Derek sat up in bed with an excited hoot and instantly dialed up Owen to let him know the plans for the weekend, only to remember his best bud was out. Owen answered anyway. "In the middle of something. Wassup?"

"Why'd you answer? I was going to leave a voicemail. Didn't mean to bother you."

"I thought it was something important." Owen sounded strained.

Derek joked, "Totally forgot you were likely getting laid right about now."

"Close. Getting there," Owen hitched in a breath and let out a throaty groan. "Motherfucker," he sighed in ecstasy. "What, Derek? What do you need?"

Derek covered his face, groaning enviously and then chuckling with amused disbelief. Only a friend like Owen would answer a phone call in the middle of getting head, on the off chance it was something important. "Nothing that can't wait. I'll hit you up tomorrow. Or, send a text. I should've texted." He heard the tell tale sound of a woman doing dirty deeds with her mouth, and got a boner just thinking about it. Owen's labored breathing and barely suppressed moans made Derek fidget with nervous energy.

"…yeah, t-text me later."

Derek ended the call and stretched in bed, staring up at the ceiling. His hand aimlessly drifted down to his crotch. "To be that guy," he muttered, smiling.

CHAPTER 6

AFTER THE ABBREVIATED chat with Owen, his thoughts turned lustfully back to Adelaide, and then he couldn't stop thinking about her. It was probably thanks in part to overhearing Owen's shenanigans on the phone, but it was also because he was so close to finding out where she had disappeared off to. If he could get Steve to open about Adelaide, he might be able to finagle him into giving up her phone number or address.

He could admit it was slightly stalker-ish to go about it the way he was planning, but he didn't have any better options. How else was he going to find her? It could take forever to go through Heather and Steve's friends lists on their social media pages to find her. Derek closed his eyes and replayed scenes from the threesome, getting randy at the vivid images his mind's eye conjured. His thin body twisted and tangled in the sheets of his too small twin bed, as he slipped from drowsily wondering how things would be if they linked back up, to dreaming.

Adelaide throws her body on the bed. It's Owen's bed, only his best friend isn't anywhere around. Before Derek has time to wonder where Owen is, Addie peels her black dress over her shoulders and head with a swish of her dark blonde hair. Her voluptuous breasts spill free with a bouncy jiggle. Dusky nipples point skywards. Her hourglass body glows bronze in the dream light. She spreads her shapely legs, still wearing her heels. Then, she gets on her hands and knees with her pert bottom in the air and crawls enticingly to Derek, whose standing at the foot of the mattress with a raging erection.

He gets a whiff of her citrusy, floral perfume. The sight of her slender fingers wrapping around his shaft makes him tremble with anticipation. Her hand feels like silk. A husky laugh rumbles in her throat as she smiles up at him. "Do I turn you on?" she asks needlessly.

"Infinitely." He cups his hand over hers in answer and guides her to stroke his manhood. She doesn't need any help. With deft fingers, Addie reaches a hand between his legs to gently massage his testicles. At the same time, her mouth closes around his member with the same shock of ecstasy as the night the three of them were together. She doesn't rush.

She drives him to the back of her throat, pulls back slowly. A silver string of saliva clings to her sensual lips as she takes her mouth off his cock to look up at him with her bedroom eyes. She licks it free and goes back at it, plunging him in and out of her mouth with growing frenzy. She uses her hands, her tongue, her lips and teeth to rub, suck, and nip at him until he feels like he's about to let go.

"Hold it," she whispers, lips directly against the tip of his erection.

"I'm trying," he gasps. Derek squeezes the base of his cock and wills himself not to come yet.

"Tell me what you want me to do," he murmurs. She guides him down onto the bed and positions her nubile body in a sixty-nine with her stilettoes inches from his face.

"I want you…" She groans as she sucks him back into her mouth from the new angle. He clutches handfuls of the sheets. Thrills of pleasure zing through him. Derek sucks in a breath, hips rising of their own accord. "I want you to satisfy me. I want you to win my heart," she whimpers as she laves a silky, wet trail up and down his shaft. "Mmm…it's so hard. So hard for me. Make me love you."

Derek wraps his arms around her lower body and drags her saturated pussy to his face. He buries his nose and mouth inside the flower of her womanhood, his tongue spearing into her entrance. She quakes in his arms, and he keeps doing it, fucking her with his tongue. He squeezes her closer. Drawing her clit into his mouth, he flicks his tongue around in dizzying circles. He feels her clitoris throbbing against his lips as she stops giving him head and whines in excitement.

Then, he sucks and nibbles—all the things she did to him.

"Ah! You're gonna make me do it," she moans. Whipping her hair over her shoulder, she takes him in hand again and continues fellating him. Derek growls as he thrusts up and into her mouth. She grinds against his lips, as if riding his face. The entire act makes him want to shower her with his desire.

Adelaide pushes up off of him, leaving his face glazed with her sweet cream. "Don't stop," he begs, wiping his mouth.

Her hands sweep up to her breasts, and she fondles herself, making her nipples pebble. She stares at him with her deep brown eyes. "You're gonna make me do it, aren't you?" she whispers. Her hands ease down her curvy torso to the V between her legs. She climbs back on top of him like a reverse cowgirl. With her heart-shaped ass resting on his pelvis, Derek watches as she leans forward and teases her dripping wet vagina with his swollen cock, swiping up and down with the tip against her clit. It's as much torture for him as it is for her.

He closes his eyes and exhales shakily. "You feel like liquid silk," he observes. Her tight pussy comes down around him by degrees, inch by inch. With each slow drop, her sounds of ecstasy get louder. Her vocal cries drive him to clasp her hips and finish impaling her with a swift upward thrust.

"Derek!" she screams as her climax catches her off guard.

A gush of female ejaculation splashes around his shaft. "Yes, yes! Fucking squirt for me, Addie," he growls. He splays his hand at the base of her spine in amazement at the X-rated sight. Derek's eyes roll back as his body experiences the euphoria of her snatch soaking him and stroking him at the same time. She begs him to fuck her, harder, deeper. He does his best to comply. She leans forward and writhes up and down his pole like a dancer, derriere bouncing with skillful control. She swirls her ass around, and his cock in her tight pussy spasms at how wet and wicked it feels, like he's drowning in pleasure.

He has to take control. Derek struggles to sit up, and he wraps an arm around her waist to drag her off of him, down onto the bed. Addie lands face down in Owen's pillows with her perfect ass poked in the air. Derek smoothly re-enters her. "Satisfy me, baby," she commands again.

"I will," he swears. Successful people go after what they want, right?

Derek grasps her hips, his thighs and pelvis slick with her wetness and only getting wetter by the second. He hammers her wanton body down to the mattress. In the heat of the moment, she hooks a foot around his calf, and her stiletto digs into his leg. But, Derek doesn't notice the pain. All he feels is the pleasure of her silken sheath constricting around him. Waves of pleasure assail him with every move. He hums as he feels her inner muscles ripple, ready to release again, the tension between them building to a snapping point.

Then, his frantic pounding stills to one last deep, hard surge as they both skyrocket to bliss at the same time. His cock pulsates within her climaxing pussy. Derek reaches around to grab her chin and pull her face around to kiss him. As her lips meet his, suddenly Owen enters the room.

"My turn," he says softly.

It was still night when Derek woke up, expecting to be in Owen's bed. He was in his own, and it was lonely as hell without his plus-twos. The dream resisted fading into wherever dreams go to be forgotten. "Make me love you," she'd said. It was a figment of his imagination. His subconscious mind was telling him what he wanted to hear. In reality, she probably wouldn't have two words to say to him; after all, it was Owen who had caught her attention first. Derek just happened to get lucky.

On the other hand, she had picked the both of them. He wondered which one she would've chosen if she could only have one.

"It's about presence." Owen pushed his shopping cart down the breakfast aisle and headed straight for the produce section. It was Tuesday evening, day three of Operation Reshaping Derek. It felt good to have something to do with his evenings after work, because otherwise he'd be sitting through another tense dinner with his parents. As it was, Derek had let his mother know in advance he'd probably be late all week, and not to hold dinner for him.

"Presence?" Derek repeated.

Picking up a cantaloupe and testing its ripeness, Owen nodded. "Presence. Like stage presence, only it's life presence." He handed the cantaloupe to Derek to put back and strolled along. Derek tossed the out of season melon back on the pile of fruit to follow him. "You can have the attention of every important person in the room if you have a certain presence, even if you retain their attention only briefly. All you need is an opening. People formulate impressions in seconds, and having a strong presence is the way to make a strong impression."

Derek was taking notes as they strolled through the grocery store. Literally, he had his tablet in hand, scrawling Owen's suggestions so he could go back over them when he got home. Monday had been a success, with the exception of almost getting fired. With Owen as a life coach, he'd managed to hold onto his job, get the attention of damn near every woman in his office, and had the courage to try to find Adelaide. It was the single most productive day of his adulthood.

"You can create presence, even if it doesn't come naturally to you. Ever wonder why women like to be fashionably late? It's a nifty trick. While everyone is arriving *en masse*, no one pays particular attention to who's walking into a room. But, if no one is crowding the entryway, think what a perfect frame it makes. All eyes on me."

Derek laughed. "Oh, no! Don't tell me that's why you showed up at the reception late."

"What? No," Owen protested, laughing. "I'm just using that as an example. Hey, look around this store and tell me who you see that stands out the most."

Derek looked around, spotted an elderly gentleman dressed in his Sunday best. He was carrying a walking stick and smiling at every pretty lady he passed, young and old. Derek pointed to him. Owen nodded. "He stood out to me, too. You know why? In a sea of sameness, there's something different about him. His clothes are different. The fact that he's smiling and speaking is different. He's engaging. He's setting himself apart, and that makes him eye-catching."

"What's the hack for this one?" Derek asked peering at his device, stylus poised.

Owen sighed and took away the tablet. He put it in the shopping cart. "Look, you don't need to take notes. You just have to observe the world around you. Be present. Now…the first lesson is you need to walk to the beat of your own drum. Even if you have no clue where you're going, the hack is to avoid seeming directionless. Do you know where the bread aisle is?"

"*Pfft*, no. I never shop at Whole Foods. They're too overpriced. Do *you* know where the bread aisle is? This is your store."

"You should invest in your health. It may cost more, but it pays more, too. Anyway, I don't remember where the bread aisle is. But, I can roam around, scratching my head, looking lost and hope someone asks me if I need any help. Or, I can stride boldly ahead, head up, eyes open and know that I'll find it soon. It's a supermarket. There's bread somewhere. Why look lost?"

"Wait, I'm confused. I thought we were talking about presence. Like, having a presence when you enter a room."

"We are. It applies. If that gentleman you pointed out had seemed lost and confused, would you have been as impressed by his sense of style, the beat of his drum? It's a rhetorical question. You wouldn't be. You might empathize with his plight, but you certainly wouldn't look at him and think he's got it all together. You can create presence by becoming *present*. Not allowing anything, not even anxiety over where you're going, to get in the way of you getting there. Understand?"

When they got back to Owen's house, he modeled it for him to help Derek see what he meant. "I want you to step into the kitchen," said Owen. "Then, walk out of the kitchen into the living room."

Derek lifted his arms and dropped them. "You really want me to walk from there to here? That's like, five steps." Owen hit him with a stern look. "Fine. How do you want me to do it?"

"Tell you what. I'll show you what I'm looking for, and then you do it. Watch me." Owen walked into the kitchen, waited for a bit. He paused at the threshold to the living room and made eye contact with Derek, flashing an easy smile. "Hi, how are you?" he spoke in a midlevel voice—not too loud, not too soft—and enunciated his words clearly as he breezed past Derek with a confident stride. "Your turn."

Derek stepped into the kitchen and fixed his posture. Shoulders back, head up, he stepped out. He hesitated at the threshold, but he had already forgotten to pause, so he kept walking. "Hi, how are you?" he said through a false smile. His words sounded tight because of it.

Owen stood with his fist pressed to his chin, unimpressed. He shook his head. "Do it again. This time, walk less like you're constipated and smile less like a serial killer."

CHAPTER 7

A TEXT MESSAGE alert chimed, and Derek looked up from the computer. He had spent the majority of the hump day morning working on his part of the assignment with the team that didn't want him. It was a welcome interruption. Derek picked up the phone and eyed the time, noting it was time for his lunch break, as he opened the message from Owen. His hunger rumbles disappeared when he looked at the text, eyes widening in surprise. "He didn't mean to send me this," he mumbled to himself, chuckling at the error. He almost hit delete, but his thumb wouldn't follow through on the action.

He stared at the picture of a shirtless Owen in pinstriped boxer briefs and trouser socks sprawled on a leather lounge chair with a high ball glass, cigar in hand. He had shaved his beard, but the facial hair was nicely growing back. His glasses gave the sensual photograph a philosophical bent, and there was a quote: "You have to learn the rules of the game. And then you have to play better than anyone else," attributed to Albert Einstein.

Derek barely read the accompanying message. He couldn't tear his gaze away from Owen's seductive, spread-legged stance. The boxer briefs molded to his crotch, showing off an impressive package. It wasn't the first time he'd seen it. Of course, he had taken a peek the night the three of them were together, but this was different. This wasn't peeking. This was staring.

Derek went so far as to enlarge the photo so it filled the entire screen of the phone, and he cupped a hand around the device in case

47

any nosy coworkers passed nearby. Derek cast a searching glance left to right. Then, he reminded himself it was probably better if he didn't ogle a half-naked man in his cubicle. It was his lunch break, anyway. Time to find some grub.

"What the hell has gotten into me?" he muttered with a self-deprecating laugh as he rose from his desk. He meant to shut the phone off. He had every intention of tossing it aside and forgetting about it while he ran out to pick up a bite to eat. Clearly Owen had sent the picture to the wrong party. But, he didn't put the phone away. Derek found himself strolling purposefully toward the elevator bay, and he tucked the phone in his pocket en route. He got off the elevator in an older part of the building where many of the offices had been converted to storage rooms, and there was no one around to watch him stealthily make his way to an isolated restroom. Derek shut himself in so he could pull himself together, and finally get past the nonsense in his head.

It was one thing to wake up in a warm bed next to somebody and not want to get up because the bed felt so comfortable. It was something else entirely to get a thrill out of looking at his best friend's half-naked picture.

Away from prying eyes, he stared down at the phone in his hand, and the voice of panic loud in his mind told him to look away. Yet, there was a rebellious streak encouraging him to explore the forbidden desire he'd been suppressing ever since the erotic ménage with his best friend and the audacious Adelaide. As his eyes roamed the digital expanse of Owen's bare chest, he wondered idly if the act had subconsciously caused him to link the two people in his head in some twisted sexual way.

"What am I doing? What am I—" He let loose an abbreviated snort and covered his mouth, shaking with unprocessed emotion.

He was alone in the single-occupant restroom, the one almost no one visited because it was dank and dark. There were updated facilities closer to the offices. Here, he was sure there wouldn't be a knock or impatient jiggle of the doorknob. But, just in case, he hurried over to check (to double check) the locked door.

With trembling hands, he balanced the phone on the back of the sink where he could get an unobstructed view of the image filling the screen: Owen. Derek braced himself up with his palms against the countertop, but his reflection looked back at him. Derek desperately hit the light switch to hide from himself. No one would know. No one would find out. It was all in his head, and his thoughts were his own to deal with, nobody else's business. He squeezed his eyes shut tighter, as if the locked door and darkness weren't enough.

He would never have characterized himself as gay. He didn't have a problem with gay people. He simply couldn't see how one man would want another to...

Owen presses him against the cool tiles of the bathroom wall, one strong hand gripping the back of Derek's neck and the other at his belt buckle. At first, it's like a wrestling match—pushing and pulling, fighting to get closer or to get away. Derek can't tell. Adrenaline pumps through his veins, and he's sweating. He's panting. His senses are on overdrive. He smells that erotic mélange of male sweat and cologne—Owen's smell. He hears distant echoes of sex sounds, grunts and moans that don't sound like fighting much at all. He wants to be taken.

Owen's fumbling fingers release Derek's throbbing manhood, and the first touch is a shock. Slightly rough fingertips, neither work tough nor girlishly soft, just right. Owen fondles him. Derek gasps as his cock surges with unchecked desire, so engorged a thick droplet of pre-cum swells to the tip and spills over Owen's fist. He hears a husky moan in response, and in this place the feeling is unquestionably mutual. It's safe to say:

"I want you." (The words hovered in a darkness as blue as the screen of his phone.)

Owen breathes into his ear, an ethereal sigh, "I want you, too."

The kiss. Owen comes at him, and their mouths collide with a gentle click. "Oh," Derek whispers against his mouth in awe. Stars. He sees stars light up the darkness, coming on one by one with each fluid kiss. And, the stars ignite a burning glow in his groin. Owen's silky tongue flows into his open mouth to flick against his own, and he sucks the plush bow of Owen's lower lip. They nibble, parry, thrust, wrestling again.

Owen's strength makes Derek feel heady with a need to be dominated. He fights back harder just to be pushed more authoritatively against the wall. A rush of arousal travels from his toes to the crown of his head, like a liquid heat that leaves Derek breathless

49

and prickly with goose bumps. The heat below his pelvis burns through his turgid cock until he can barely stand to not have it soothed. His heart pounds faster with terror and desire. He can't stop himself. He threads his fingers through Owen's thick dark hair, drawing his head down to his chest.

Owen bites his nipple, and Derek cries out in a strange mix of pain and pleasure. Kisses rain down his stomach, leaving him quivering for more. Owen, on his knees, strokes Derek up and down in strong, quick pulls of his hand. He knows exactly how to please a man, and when to stop teasing and put his mouth where his libido is.

But, Derek weakly protests, "You shouldn't. We shouldn't." Even in his dreams, reality threatens to intrude. Derek tangles his fingers in Owen's hair, pulls his head back and bends forward, unable to resist kissing his glistening lips.

Owen passionately kisses him back. "Why shouldn't we?" he asks. In the impossible darkness, his eyes are glossy with need. The need to taste, to devour, to satisfy.

His searing hot mouth closes around the head of Derek's cock as his fingers form a ring at the base of his shaft. He slides his tongue down to the hilt and slowly licks to the tip, swirling a wet trail. His fingers follow the journey back from tip to base, masturbating Derek while he sweeps his tongue from side to side beneath the underbelly of Derek's purple thunderhead, leaving Derek shaking with need.

"Fuck, yes," Derek whimpers, whispers, tries not to say. Owen swiftly takes all of him into his mouth. "Oh, god!" he moans. In and out, Owen sucks with his lips wrapped tightly around Derek's shaft. Derek desperately clutches the sides of his friends face to stop him, but his own body betrays him. He urgently thrusts into Owen's mouth. With a hoarse cry, he achingly draws out. Owen holds still...let's Derek fuck his face. Derek grunts, unable to stop himself. Again, in and out of Owen's mouth until Owen resumes control, massaging Derek's pulsating cock with a throaty moan. Owen unabashedly continues sucking him off. Derek moans appreciatively when Adelaide steps forward out of the dark and tenderly kisses his lips while Owen finishes the job.

The cellphone buzzed again, a soft vibrating whir to signal a call coming through.

Derek's lust dazed mind didn't process the sound as he continued tugging to the fantasy, but he answered anyway—answered as fantasy Owen made him gasp and stammer, as his corded dick spewed hot, sticky jizz in a shower that seemed endless. Staccato bursts of rapture made him swear, "Oh, shit! Oh, god!"

"Bad timing?" Owen's very real voice poured through the phone.

Derek blanched in the darkness, heart dropping to his feet when he registered the phone pressed to his ear. "H-hello?"

On the other end, Owen laughed out loud. "This is payback for last night, isn't it? Touché. Alright, have fun, tiger. I'll call you back."

"No, no, I wasn't—I mean, I was just," Derek tried to catch his breath and get his thoughts together.

"Hmm…well, I was just calling to see what you thought about the lady porn I sent you. I'm thinking about posting it to my blog, but I wanted to know if it was too risqué."

"I-I got the text. I was just going to text you back and tell you I liked it a lot."

There was a pregnant pause. "How much is a lot?" Owen asked teasingly.

Derek hit the light switch and bright fluorescent light flooded the restroom, blinding him. He blinked and rubbed his eyes, caught sight of his blushing reflection. "No, not like that. Jeez, Owen."

"So if you weren't…you know," Owen replied curiously, "then, what *were* you doing?" Derek heard the smile in his voice. Owen was getting a kick out of this.

Derek gnawed nervously on his bottom lip, wondering exactly what his friend was over there assuming. He should've just let him go with the assumption that he was getting 'afternoon delight' from one of the buxom broads in the design department. Owen was always telling him he should go after one of the sexy, accomplished women he worked with at Ad Ent.

"Hey, let me call you back," Derek said suddenly. He didn't have an answer for what he was doing. No one was supposed to know what he was doing. The last thing he'd expected was Owen to call right in the middle of him fantasizing about—

Derek cut the thought short. The lights were on and he was back to reality. Owen responded, "Yeah, call me back and let me know what you thought about the pic." Derek hurriedly ended the call before he could launch into any more questions. He looked down at the mess he had made of himself. In his enthusiasm, he hadn't taken any precautions, but his luck had held out. His pants showed no evidence of what he'd just done. Most of it was on his hands and the floor.

Derek sheepishly washed his hands and used paper towels to wipe down the scene. He glanced at his watch and saw he still had a few minutes left of his lunch break, much needed time to compose himself. Back in his office, however, even with the sexual frustration released, Derek was hardly composed. He worried over Owen reading too much into the phone conversation. He fired off a text to say he did think the picture was a little risqué for a motivational blog, but that the female fan-ship would love it. Owen didn't respond back immediately, and Derek puzzled over the lack of response. He tried to tell himself to stop worrying.

He wasn't gay, and Owen didn't think he was gay. Years and years of close friendship, and Derek had never once thought of Owen sexually. All of this was because of that one incident with Adelaide.

He tried to convince himself of that as he furiously threw himself into his work, cutting short his lunch break for fear of what else his muddled mind might entice him to do, but the more Derek tried not to think about it, the more he realized he couldn't just blow off the question of sudden bi-curiosity. The truth was he had always found Owen attractive, intelligent, and fun to be around. And, while that didn't necessarily make him gay, the lines were blurring as to whether he wanted to be *like* Owen or be *with* Owen.

A long banished memory resurfaced. Owen was the first of the pair to get a serious girlfriend back in high school. Derek remembered feeling cast aside, being very upset about what he felt was an infringement on his friendship. He remembered being jealous. In fact, if he was honest with himself, anytime someone or something else had Owen's attention, it bothered him. Was that a sign? Did he feel more for his buddy than merely brotherly love?

Derek wearily ran a hand over his face. "What does any of this mean?" he muttered, clueless.

"Hey, you!" Derek jumped, startled. His pencil hit his desk with a *clack*, and he instinctively covered up the draft of his personal ad design. When he looked up, he saw the secretary standing next to his cubicle. Libby Sullivan leaned in with a bright smile, her red lipstick too saturated for her sallow complexion. "Heads up, another secret brainstorming session, this time after hours. They left the memo about it in your inbox, knowing I don't deliver inbox content until the morning"

"Thank you, Ms. Sullivan. I appreciate the help. Um, can I ask you a question?" She leaned closer, eyes widening. "Why *are* you helping me like this?"

Libby tucked her tongue behind her teeth with a coquettish smile. "Oh, it's nothing personal. Mr. Clancy wants me to make sure you get a fair shot is all," she replied. She dropped a hand on his shoulder and added, "But, between you and me, I'd have done it anyway. You're growing on me, Mr. Derek Cornwell."

With a wiggle of a wave, she sashayed away, glancing back once to catch him staring after her. Derek hummed speculatively at the news Mr. Clancy was still pulling strings on his behalf. He took a closer look at the work for the Wonder Man ad. He had to wow him. He had to blow him away. He had to make it worth his while, and he suddenly had an idea of how to do exactly that.

In bold print, Derek scrawled at the bottom of his sketch of two suited men and a woman in an evening gown. "Make 'em wonder."

CHAPTER 8

DEREK WAS FULLY aware that Harold, the team leader, was trying to sabotage him. The clock ticked closer to quitting time, and he struggled with the question of what to do about it. He could continue showing up to meetings, despite the fact he wasn't exactly invited. At least, until Harold wised up and stopped telling Libby Sullivan all his dirty little secrets.

On the other hand, he could let Mr. Clancy know what was happening and have him nip the shit in the bud. The chances of that backfiring on him were bigger than the odds of Harold wising up, though.

If Mr. Clancy resolved the matter, there'd be grudges held. This unspoken war could last years. Harold was one of the top performers in the department, and it didn't pay to get on the bad side of someone who could potentially be your boss one day.

Derek sighed and powered off his desktop. If he didn't show up to the meeting, he might jeopardize his job. It was clear he was at the top of Mr. Clancy's hit list. He thought about firing off a text to Owen to get his friend's advice, but he was still iffy about talking to him so soon after the lunch break fiasco. Instead, Derek tried to assemble all the micro lessons Owen had doled out in the past few days.

Successful people wielded their egos to get what they wanted, whether they deserved it or not, and people gave it to them because they knew that's what they were after. He had to look the part. He needed to have the kind of presence that made people stop and look in his direction. It all seemed incredibly superficial, like the most basic advice.

Yet, as he collected his things and got ready to clock out, he considered the underlying message: Take charge. He suddenly realized none of the options he had considered were very confrontational because he wasn't a very confrontational guy, but this problem wasn't going to go away by ignoring it, or by getting someone else to handle it. He had to tackle it head first.

The gray corridor to the boardroom where their brainstorm sessions were held was quiet and empty by the time he stepped out. Derek adjusted his black skinny tie and made sure his white shirt was tucked into his royal blue slacks. His black leather shoes barely made a sound as they whispered across the carpet. He tugged on the sleeves of his matching blue blazer and swiped his fingers through his chaotic mess of wavy black hair.

He knew what he wanted this time, which wasn't just to do his job on the team. He had to win the team. He paused outside the boardroom door and glanced at his watch. Rather than being fashionably late, he was a little early. When he walked in, the room was empty. The old Derek would've taken his seat and waited patiently for the entire shindig to be over so he could skulk off to his Mazda in the parking garage and shoot home.

New Derek had to think outside the box. It was late evening, and his stomach protested skipping lunch. He had a thought. He pulled out his cellphone and ordered out, enough for all eight members of the team. "We'll get your delivery to you in a half hour or less," said the chipper woman at the restaurant.

"Thanks, much," he said with a smile. Nothing brought people together like food.

Instead of sitting tight on what he had worked on for the project until somebody asked, Derek opened the files on his tablet and had them cued up to show off upfront. Harold breezed into the room while he was going back over his work, and his stunned expression was priceless. Harold's face twisted in a perplexed smile. "Ah, so you got the inbox?"

Derek stared him down as Harold took his seat and several other members of the team filed into the room. "I certainly did, although it was odd of you to announce the meeting by afternoon inbox when everyone knows Ms. Sullivan makes her deliveries in the morning. Luckily, I periodically check my box throughout the day. I'm curious to know, though, how the rest of the team members managed to get the message." He watched as people tried to avoid his gaze. A small smile tickled the corners of his lips.

Harold Gensler nervously tapped his laser pen in his palm without an answer. One young woman piped up, "I, uh, heard about it from somebody else on the team."

"At any rate," Harold cleared his throat, "everyone's here and accounted for. Let's get started. I want to bring everyone's attention to the drawing board where I personally made a mock-up of the ad design we discussed earlier this week." He beamed proudly as he powered on the projector. His beady eyes skimmed over Derek, and his smile wavered. Derek had his hand raised.

"You know, I was giving it some thought, and I wonder if we're moving in the right direction with this. We went with a super hero theme because, who doesn't want to be a super hero? I mean, it's called Wonder Man. At the same time, have any of you guys paid close attention to the product description?"

"Oh, come off it, Derek. We don't have time for your contrarian ways. What is it with you, lately? I think I liked you better when you sat quietly through these sessions," Harold quipped. A round of soft chuckles erupted.

Derek pointed to one of the men in the group that he knew stayed on top of the fine details that Harold liked to blow past. "Brian, you're a master at picking apart a generic product for something that makes it one of a kind. By any chance, are you familiar with the fragrance notes in Wonder Man?"

"Of course. This product actually makes it easy to find something that sets it apart. Most men's fragrances are woodsy or spicy. This one is smoky, with hints of patchouli and white ambergris, base notes of rose. It's a gutsy combination for a men's cologne," Brian replied.

"Thanks, Brian," said Derek. Someone knocked on the boardroom door. It swung open and the evening shift security officer held up two big bags of takeout.

"Somebody ordered out?" she asked.

"That would be me," said Derek. He hopped up to accept the package, nodding his appreciation to security as she left. All eyes were on him. Derek felt a tiny tremor in his hand, but he forced himself not to succumb to a bout of nerves, especially not right now. It just reminded him so much of being the awkward kid giving away his candy so people would like him. He forced himself to recognize he was working from a more strategic (adult) standpoint now.

As he unpacked the bags and brought out a stack of paper plates and utensils, he used the floor to push his idea. "I took the liberty of ordering out. This session might get lengthy because I had a game-changing thought earlier today that I wanted to present to you guys."

"Uh, excuse me," Harold interjected indignantly. "You don't come in here and take over things on a whim! The rest of us have worked hard on this design, and that's what I'm presenting. You can save your idea until the end of my presentation or the end of time for all I care."

Derek paused opening food containers and handing plates to everybody. "I'm sorry. I didn't mean to interrupt you, Harold. I know everyone is interested in seeing how our ideas came together."

A woman in a red suit rolled her eyes dramatically. "Honestly, I don't want to be here all night. Harry, we've all seen your presentation in one form or another. It's standard. Let the guy tell us his idea so we can get out of here."

As more voices added to the clamor to let Derek continue, he felt a subtle shift in the room. He knew it by the way Harold glared at him as if he had made a fatal error. It wasn't his goal to get any further on Harold's bad side, but he'd have to work on getting the truculent team leader to warm up to him some other time. Right now was about connecting with the rest of the team.

Derek boldly disconnected Harold's tablet and wirelessly connected his own to the projector. He explained before he showed his work. "When you look at those fragrance notes—patchouli, rose—that doesn't scream superhero, action man to me. It's softer, more subtle. What comes to mind for you guys?"

"Hippie," someone muttered with a chuckle. That got laughs.

Things loosened up as someone else said, "Well, when you pair up patchouli with the word wonder, I think of imagination, whimsy. I mean, it's a smoky scent, right? Smoke isn't tangible."

Derek nodded his approval. "That's exactly what I was thinking, too. I think we're going in the wrong direction marketing a scent like this to the he-man, alpha males of the world. This is a more refined aroma. It's for the poets and the dreamers. We need an advertisement that appeals to the gentle man."

And, with that, the super hero ad design was unanimously (save for one person) voted out. They spent two hours overtime working up a new plan and plotting how to get it done in time for their deadline at the end of the next week. Derek sat back and watched as his input took shape and became one part of a bigger whole. For the first time ever, he had a sense of belonging to the group.

Harold scowled at him, and Derek lifted a brow. With a barely perceptible lift of his chin, he signaled Derek had bested him this time. There was a challenge in the man's eyes, but Derek was no longer intimidated. It only inspired him to prove why challenging him wouldn't be an easy fight.

◇◇◇

Owen broke the surface of the water and flipped his wet hair back, grinning at Derek, who sat poolside still dressed from work. It was late in the evening, thanks to the afterhours brainstorming session, but he wasn't ready to go home. So, he had stopped over at Owen's. He wanted to feel like there was more to life than the office and his parents' house.

"So, tell me how this week has been different for you so far, now that you're implementing my strategy?" Owen climbed out of the pool and strolled to the outdoor sectional. He was dripping wet with the slant of late evening sun turning the water droplets into glitter on his buff body. Owen grabbed his towel from the coffee table to wipe his face clear before turning to stare at Derek.

"I told you about the second chance to make a better impression on my boss, right?" Derek asked. Owen looked at him askance. Derek couldn't remember if he'd mentioned it. His mind had been such a mess the last few days. "Yeah, he called me in for a meeting and told me my peer reviews sucked. He was about to fire me."

"Seriously?" Owen frowned. "What'd you do?"

"I told him to give me two weeks to prove he should keep me." Thinking about it, Derek smiled. It was a ballsy move, but he'd made it happen. "Basically, I made him an offer he couldn't refuse."

"You didn't let him refuse, and that, my friend, is the secret to success. Hell, yes! You're a fast learner, *Padawan*! I'm proud of you." As Owen sipped from a tall glass of sweet tea, his eyes probed Derek's. A rush of butterflies flurried in Derek's stomach. He glanced away.

"Thank you," Derek murmured modestly. "Speaking of going after the best, I've been trying to track down Adelaide, too. What do you think of that?"

"Oh, really?" At that, Owen appraised him coolly. "How's that going for you?" His guarded question for a question was telling. Derek studied him, trying to see why tracking down Adelaide was a problem for him.

"We'll both see soon enough, if you're free Friday," Derek shrugged. "I convinced Steve to have drinks with us. Turns out they used to date. I made the mistake of asking Heather about her, and she nearly bit my head off, saying Addie had crashed her wedding."

"Ouch!" Owen made a face. "That could get ugly. You're sure you want to go through with finding her? Let's say you bring her home to a family dinner. Heather's sweet as pie, but people like that are the ones you usually have to worry about. I'm telling you, heads will roll." Owen chuckled and Derek shook his head, although he agreed. He'd never heard his sister as angry as she'd been on the phone talking about Adelaide.

"Dude, she's all I've been able to think about since, like, the night we spent together." It wasn't quite the truth, but it was close.

Owen nodded in agreement, finally flashing a genuine smile. "You have a point there. I've met a fair amount of interesting ladies, but she has this *je ne sais quoi* quality. Hard to resist, hard to forget. I don't blame you for hunting her down. I'd have already tried, if it had occurred to me there was a way to get in touch with her." Owen's eyes got cloudy, as if he was lost in thought.

Derek had an unsettling hypothetical question crop up. What if Owen was as into her as he was? He had naturally assumed a womanizer like his best bud would see Adelaide as another notch in his belt, nothing more, nothing less. Odds were, if Owen was interested, he'd be the winning man. That was just how things worked between them. Derek stared glumly at the pool, eyes skating from the manicured back lawn to the split level house.

He shrugged. "Hey, don't let me get in the way of you getting to know her, if that's what you want. Like I said, we can both meet with Steve, find out how to get in touch with her."

Owen smirked. "Funny. You know, I can't picture a man like Trump telling some other real estate mogul, 'You can have this one, if you want it.' In fact, somebody else wanting it would make him go after it harder."

Derek quirked a brow. "What are talking about? I wouldn't do that to you. We're friends. That's cutthroat, man."

"I'm not suggesting you shaft me," Owen laughed. "I'm just saying, remember what I taught you. Successful people go after the best. They don't voluntarily step down. Besides, what would I look like trying to build a relationship with one woman…committing this hot looking body to one woman?" Derek burst out laughing, knowing he was joking. Owen didn't have a conceited bone in his body, but he exuded self-confidence. Derek much preferred it to brash cockiness.

Still uncertain, he decided to take Owen at face value. "So, you weren't into her like that? It was just sex for you?" he queried.

Owen twisted his lips, deciding how to answer the question. "No, I wouldn't say it was just sex. That shit was somewhat spiritual, the way it went down. Wasn't it for you? I'm talking transcendental! I learned some things about myself." He chuckled. "Adelaide, she's a stunner. Put it like this, if I was looking for a relationship, she'd be a perfect fit, but I'm not ready to settle down. So, go for it."

It wasn't exactly the answer Derek wanted to hear—he wanted something closer to a flat out 'I'm not interested'—but, it was as good as he figured he'd get. Owen had never cock-blocked in the past; then again, they'd never been interested in the same girl in the past. Derek supposed only time would tell if being with Adelaide caused problems in his friendship, and if it did, he'd drop her in a heartbeat.

He held up his iced tea glass and clinked it with Owen's. "Just know, I love you, bro. I'll never let a woman come between us."

Owen made a sound half way between a snort and a laugh. "Never doubted   that   for   a   second," he   replied   confidently.

CHAPTER 9

FRIDAY COULDN'T HAVE come soon enough for Derek.

After his helluva work week, he nearly sprinted out of the office Friday evening. He raced his Mazda across town to Owen's place, and they took Owen's swanky ride to a sports bar downtown that offered a guy-friendly atmosphere where Derek was sure his sister would feel comfortable with her husband hanging out, mainly because Heather didn't frequent sports bars. Aside from big screen TVs strategically positioned around the restaurant, men came there to watch barely legal waitresses maneuver around in short skirts and tight t-shirts with plunging necklines. Steve had suggested the place.

"What's he like? Is he cool, or whatever?" Owen quizzed him. Owen whipped the wheel and eased into a parking spot in front of the building. Amber light illuminated the windows, and the place looked packed. Derek spied several different games playing on the various televisions.

"Who, Steve?" He shrugged. He hadn't really made a point to get to know Steve. His little sister dated him for nearly a year, but Derek had assumed she'd realize she was too young to get too serious, which showed how much he knew. "I thought he was some casual romance. To tell you the truth, I didn't get a good look at him until the wedding."

"I saw him there. He damn sure didn't look like her type."

"Gotta have a great personality is all I can say," Derek joked. They climbed out of the car and ambled through the glass double doors. Owen gestured to three empty barstools, but Derek shook his head.

"We might want a little more privacy if the conversation gets personal."

Owen laughed. "Exactly how much are you planning on telling your new brother-in-law about our one night stand with his ex?"

Derek crinkled his nose, annoyed. "I hate it when you call it that. It was more than a one night stand. Why do you think I'm here? To make it *more* than a one night stand." They were taken to a table, and shortly after sitting down, a pretty coed with sparkling blue braces and cute glasses skipped over. She wore a t-shirt with the local university logo and a pair of tight shorts. "Hi, my name is Hannah, and I'll be your server for the evening," she announced. "Can I get you boys anything to drink?"

"Hi, Hannah. Let me get a cognac and coke, please." Owen was all flirty smiles while Derek was distracted by the prospect of having a handle on Adelaide soon, if he could finesse the information out of Steve. "What do you want to drink, dude?" Owen asked.

"Huh? Um, Jack Honey. You guys have that?"

"I'll check with the bar!" she said helpfully.

Owen flirted, "How very proactive of you! Most people I know would say 'I dunno.' You say you'll check with the bar. I'd pay to have you come work for me. Fantastic!" The waitress blushed a becoming shade of pink and giggled girlishly. "How old are you?" Owen asked her.

"I'm twenty. I'll be twenty-one in a few months, though." She said the last with a promising lilt to her voice. Hannah took the drink orders down in a small order booklet, and she peeked at Owen from under a thick fringe of lashes.

Ignoring their pointless small talk, Derek tapped his phone to see if Steve had texted him back. He was nervous the guy wouldn't show up. If Steve didn't have or didn't want to tell them what they wanted to know, Derek would hit yet another dead end. "You know what," he interrupted the thirst session. "A regular Jack will do. You don't have to check with the bar."

"Are you sure?" She dropped her gaze back to her order book at his stiff expression. "And, did you guys want to order appetizers while you wait for your friend to get here?"

"No, thanks," Derek answered brusquely. She blinked big blue eyes at him but kept her smile in place.

"I'll be right back with your drinks," she said.

Owen nudged him. "Hey, relax, buddy. Why are you so wound up?"

"You have this thing you do where, if an attractive woman comes around, you instantly turn into Casanova. It's annoying. And, it's insincere. I bet she'll be itching to give you her number when we get ready to go, but you're not interested. I see it all over your face."

Eyebrows raised in amusement, Owen asked, "What do you see?"

"You had a half-smile when the two of you were talking. Your arms were crossed, and you were looking over your glasses—like this—like an old man. You were humoring her, rightfully so. A wolf like you with a pretty young thing like that? Danger. I can see you're as bored as I am, waiting for this schmuck to show up. She was just gullible enough to buy it, and she was too damn chatty, by the way. What happened to prompt service?"

Owen's shoulders bounced with quiet laughter, his eyebrows clashing together. "Okay, don't be a dick about it," he laughed. "She was chatty, but who knows? That little interaction a minute ago might've made her day."

Derek blew out a breath. "Right, I forgot. You're the savior of lonely women."

"You better act like you know," Owen quipped. "Don't hate me because I'm beautiful, Derek."

Derek absently flipped him the bird. "Watch out, here he comes. He just walked in." Owen slightly turned his head for a quick look. Derek's eyes darted from Owen to Steve and back. He gestured in a circle with his fingers. "C'mon. Act like we were talking about something super interesting so when he gets over here it doesn't seem like we were idly waiting for him. It can't look like I invited him out simply to talk about Addie." He nervously picked up the menu and flipped through it.

"Well, then, stop looking so suspicious," Owen hissed back as Steve drew closer. Owen started in the middle of a story about a competing antipsychotic coming on the market. "...good results in clinical trials, but I wouldn't count on it being around for long. Those studies were funded by the makers of the drug."

"Hello," Steve barged in, sitting down heavily in the chair between them. "Sorry I'm late. I promised Heather I'd pick up her favorite ice cream on the way over."

"Oh, hey, Steve," said Owen. "Anyway, some of the stuff they try to pull is unethical. I stay as far away from the bad shit as possible. That's why I'm thankful I have a job at Arex and not some other place where nobody gives a damn."

Derek replied, "`Won't it melt in the car?"

"What?"

Steve shifted. "Oh, yeah, no. I went to the supermarket, and then I thought about that—it melting in the car—so I came on over here to meet up with you guys. Howya doin', Owen? Good to see you again. Hey, Derek."

"Look at me, rambling," Owen said sheepishly. His eyes met Derek's. "Steve, you've got to excuse us. I promise we'll talk some bachelor stuff so you can live vicariously through me and Derek." Steve chortled.

Derek stammered, "Yeah, w-we were talking shop. You didn't miss anything."

The waitress came back with Owen and Derek's drinks, and Steve put an order in for a cherry coke. A less chatty Hannah left with, "You guys can flag me down when you're ready to order your entrees." She flashed a quick smile at Owen, who raised his glass to her, and then she darted off.

"Whew! Boy, she was cute," Steve commented.

Derek struggled not to be judgmental. Sure, the man was his sister's new hubby, but he needed to befriend him to get around to discussing Addie. "That she was," he replied guardedly. "So, Steve, how's married life been treating you? You miss being single?" Steve whistled and held his hands up defensively.

"Hey, I was just complimenting the lady."

Derek forced a smile and said, "What? No, I wasn't accusing you of anything. I meant, in general. How's married life?" He took a slow swallow of his Jack Daniel's and eyed him over the rim of his glass.

Steve's defensive look morphed into a rueful grin. "You guys are fucking with me, aren't you? You called me here to give me the big speech about if I hurt your sister, you'll hurt me, right?" Owen barked out a laugh.

"Why the hell would we need to do that?" Derek asked, amused. "You already know *that*. Seriously, we just called you here so you can start hanging out with us, you know, let us get to know you better. Heather told me you're a car salesman. Join the club. We're all salesmen of some sort. Owen's in pharmaceutical sales. I do ad work."

"Yeah, I heard you were working at Ad Ent. I used to know this redhead who worked in advertising. Man, she had the biggest melons." Steve crudely gestured with his hands before his chest. Owen smiled tightly. Derek was positive he was thinking Steve wasn't the sort of guy to let into their inner circle.

"Means to an end," he whispered out of the corner of his mouth to Owen. Owen pretended not to hear him, and Steve really didn't hear him, but Owen nodded almost imperceptibly a few moments after he said it.

Owen supplied, "I admire married men, but I can't see it for myself. You get used to dating around. I like to leave the field open in case one of my exes wants to go for another round."

A toothy grin spread across Derek's face. "Yeah, Owen, your crazy exes would still come out of the woodworks, probably crash the wedding if you ever decided to get married. This guy is a real womanizer, Steve. Watch him."

"I'm harmless," Owen demurred. "What about you, Steve? You have those kinds of problems?"

Steve glanced aside, shaking his head. "I don't really like to talk about my exes. Leave the past in the past, I always say."

Derek anxiously coaxed, "But don't you have—"

"I have to admit, Derek, I can't see a straight laced man like our buddy Steve, here, being caught up with a crazy ex. His type is probably more predictable, stable, dependable...a little bit boring, if you ask me. But, we're two different kinds of guys. Guys like me enjoy our cars and our women fast and a little dangerous. Trust me, you haven't fully lived until the one you love has almost killed you." Owen's lips curled up at the corners. He smoothed a hand over his beard, as if to further drive home the point. Manly man.

Steve patted his paunch of a belly and shrugged self-consciously. "Eh, well, don't get me wrong, I've had my share of excitement," he was forced to say. Derek's eyes bounced from Steve to Owen. He marveled at how Owen was meticulously steering the conversation, and Steve didn't even realize it.

"Well, yeah, even good girls get a little freaky for us," Derek chimed in.

Owen nodded encouragingly. "Personally, I prefer my women bad. And, blonde."

"Okay, that does remind me of this one woman I used to mess with, and you guys aren't gonna believe this, but she crashed my wedding."

"What?" Derek feigned surprise.

"No way! Steve, you're holding out on us, my man!"

"I know, I know. Most people take one look at me and think, 'Look at him, chubby, not that cute, poor guy.' They don't know how many really stunning women like my homely looking ass. I pull chicks. Used to, anyway."

Owen waved his hands to cut him short. "No, no, no. You tell about the wedding crasher. You don't get to gloss over that so easily." He smiled jokingly. Derek clenched his glass in his hand so hard, the liquor sloshed a little as he took he sip. He set it back down before he spilled it all over himself.

A contrite Steve stole a glance in his direction. "Just for the record, I did not invite her to come like Heather thought. Did she talk to you about it?"

Derek touched his chest, shaking his head. "Heather and I solemnly swear not to dive into each other's personal lives."

"What? She talks about *your* personal life all the time," Steve retorted, chuckling. "I'm kidding! I'm kidding! Anyway, the ex…Adelaide."

"Silence the friggin' lambs!" Owen exclaimed. "Addie? Adelaide with the honey blonde hair and the bangin' body?"

"You know Adelaide?" Steve frowned.

"Ah! Man, I know her. Small fucking world! I met her at the reception and got to talking to her," Owen gushed.

Derek snapped his fingers twice. "Oh, I know who you're talking about. You mean the sexy woman in that black dress by the bar? I saw you with her, Owen." A jealous gleam darkened Steve's eyes, but he quickly covered it with a surprised laugh. "Huh! I guess everything happens for a reason," he said. "Hey, maybe you distracted her from giving me a headache. That chick used to be into me so hard it was damn near frightening. Calling, texting, wanting to meet up. I was like, I'm only one man!"

Owen talked over him, "Yeah, we hung out a bit after the party, but when she put her number in my phone, I forgot to hit save and lost it. Steve, you mean to tell me *she* crashed your wedding? Wow…there's always the one that got away, huh? Did you dump her or did she dump you?" Owen paused for affect. Derek was on the edge of his seat.

"Take it from me, buddy. She's not worth the hassle. We dated for half a year right before I met Heather, and the whole time I was with Adelaide, I had to deal with her constantly running around on me. Late night booty calls from other men. She'd say she was meeting me someplace, then get dropped off by a 'friend,' as she called 'em. I caught her sexting guys online and stuff. The woman loved sex, and you could tell. Not, like, in a normal way, but in a compulsive way. She just wasn't worth the hassle."

Owen pulled his cellphone out anyway. "Which part of I-won't-be-getting-married-anytime-soon and I-like-to-play-the-field did you not understand, my friend, Steve?" he asked with a lecherous grin. "There's no hassle to no-strings attached. Do me a solid and give me her number. You don't need it anymore, and I won't tell her you gave it to me. I just can't wrap my head around never talking to her again after that glorious goddamned night." Owen said the last like he meant it. Derek absently nodded, knowing exactly what he was talking about.

Steve chuckled. "You dirty dog, you already bedded her, didn't you? Yeah, that's Adelaide's M.O., alright. She was a wild one. Know what I think? I think she's a real live sex addict."

"The number," Owen repeated.

"Sure, I'll give it to you. Long as you know what you're getting yourself into." Steve took Owen's phone and begrudgingly keyed in Adelaide's number. "There. You can keep her off of my back," he added. Derek squinted, trying to see why a woman like Adelaide would've gotten involved with the portly, boyish-faced little man.

Derek lifted his glass to flag down the waitress. She came back to refill their cups, but Steve declined. "No, thanks. I'll be heading out in a minute."

Owen rushed to protest, "You got here a handful of minutes ago. Don't tell me Heather has you on such a short leash you can only be away from the house a handful of minutes."

"Eh, it's married people stuff. Guys like you wouldn't

understand," Steve turned the table. "When I'm away from my wife, I miss her. I like having her around. It's a lot more interesting than having to keep up with a bevy of women because I can get to know all of her instead of spreading myself thin. That's the joys of holy matrimony."

Derek poked a finger down his throat and pretended to gag. "That's a pretty speech, Steve. I'll be sure to tell my sister you were on your best behavior tonight." He grinned broadly. Steve chuckled, finally loosening up. "You'll have to hang out with us again sometime, man." Derek and Steve smacked hands in a handshake. Steve reached over and shook Owen's hand, too.

"Alright, fellas. I'll be seeing you!"

The same way he eased in, Steve eased out, leaving Derek and Owen to finish out the stag night alone. Derek stared at Owen's phone, innocuously placed in the middle of the table. Owen glanced down at the phone and back up at Derek.

Owen slid his phone over. "Mission accomplished," he said. "You have her phone number. Now, what are you going to do with it?"

"What else would I do with it? I'm going to call her," Derek replied. "I'll hit her up and let her know we had a blast, and I'd like to hang out with her again sometime."

Owen cupped his chin in his palm and stared at him. "So, none of what Steve-O told you changes your mind? I'm not one to kiss and tell, but he made a strong case against not getting romantically involved with her. Something tells me your 'hang out with her again sometime' isn't strictly sexual. What are you doing, Derek? If you're looking for a loving, long term relationship, this might not be the way to go."

"This is me ignoring you," Derek replied, keying the phone number into his phone and saving it. When he glanced back at Owen, Owen was smirking. Derek threw his hands in the air incredulously. "Seriously? You expect me to take Steve's word? He has every reason to lie. I bet he exaggerated half the story, probably including the part about being heavily involved with her. Could you picture a woman like Addie with a guy like him?"

"No, I can't. But, probably not for the reasons you think. Derek, I strongly feel the need to tell you this. It was a great one night stand, and that's all it has to be. Okay? I hate that you've built this woman up in your head, because if she doesn't live up to your ideal, you're going to be hurt. Not to mention it'll be a tough sell to the family if Heather doesn't like Addie."

Derek swallowed, wondering if he was being dauntless or foolish. "I know what I want. And, I'm going after it," he said quietly.

Owen squirmed uncomfortably, finally backing off. "Alright. Look, it doesn't matter what I think or what Steve says. If you want to go for this woman, then go for her. I support you."

A slow smile spread across Derek's face. "Support me enough to call her for me? Technically, he gave you the number."

"Uh-uh, nope, no way. I have women literally queued up to ride this train." Owen hiked his thumbs toward his chest. "I have no need to call her. You want to talk to her, then talk to her. I've given you the tools you need, Padawan. The force within you is—"

"What do I say to her, Owen?"

"You say, 'You might not remember me, but my buddy and I shagged you after my sister's wedding a few nights ago, and I want another round with your sweet ass'. Honesty is the best policy," Owen improvised. "No, don't say that. That sounds misogynistic and degrading, and I think I've had too much to drink. Waitress? Can I get a seltzer water, please and thank you."

Derek laughed as he swallowed the last of his drink. He gestured for the waitress to bring him another whiskey. Derek and Owen stayed in the bar for another hour, talking shit and shooting the breeze. There was plenty to catch up on. Derek regaled him with Harold's underhanded office politics and how he had trumped him at his own game. Then, the conversation grew less coherent with more expletives than verbs, and a lot of giggling and chuckles, and flirtatious passes at the beautiful serving girls who took it in stride. After Derek's fourth drink, Owen threw an arm around his shoulders and squeezed him in a half hug.

"You look sufficiently wasted. You ready to go home?" he asked.

Derek heaved a sigh. "Hang on a minute. I've gotta do this while I've got the balls," he slurred. He fiddled with his phone until he got his text messages open to compose a text. A drunk text.

"Give me that," Owen suggested. He took the phone and keyed in a quick message. When he was done typing, he showed it to Derek before he sent it off for him.

"Hi, this is Derek. Would you rather get to know me better or not?" Derek read aloud. "Sounds legit."

"Thank me when you're sober," Owen mumbled. They climbed to their feet and headed out of the restaurant. When Derek stumbled slightly, Owen grabbed his hand to steady him, and he didn't let go. Derek distantly pondered why in some cultures male affection was welcomed and in others it was considered taboo. He welcomed the warm fingers clasping his, helping him stay balanced. Anyone seeing the two men meander through the parking lot to the souped up sports car would have their opinions about their relationship, but Derek didn't care.

"Ay, Owen," he mumbled. Owen leaned in with his ear close to Derek's mouth. Derek giggled in amusement. "Holy fuck, I was about to say something drunkenly sappy. It's allowed when you're this drunk, but I can't now 'cause you just got way too close for that shit to not break the Man Code."

"Ha! Let me back up then so you can shower me with affection at will," Owen replied with a soft laugh. He opened Derek's door and Derek folded his lanky body into the car and put on his seatbelt. Looking up from the buckle, he noticed Owen still standing there looking at him. Finally, Owen moved around to the driver's side and climbed in. "I love you like family too, man. I want nothing but the best for you," he said.

Derek rested his head on the headrest and closed his eyes. The very necessary disclaimer—'like family'—put boundaries in place that had always been there, that Derek had only recently begun to push. He wondered what his friend would say if he told him, plain and simple, that he didn't love him like a brother or a cousin. He didn't love him like family. He cared about Owen in a very different way. He wanted him intimately.

Owen had said it best. It was a one-night stand, and that was all it had to be. With him, too. Derek clenched his cellphone in his fist in frustration. He wanted them both, but that wasn't how life worked. But, if he had a choice, he would rather…not choose. He dismissively tossed his head back to clear his thoughts. The view beyond the windshield doubled. "You know if you take me to my place, my mother is going to flip out," Derek commented. "Dude, I'm fucking shit-faced."

"That you are, my friend. Primetime for another lesson. Always know your limits," Owen replied with a grin. Derek blew a raspberry, giggled again, and dropped his hand on top of Owen's. He rubbed his thumb along the soft skin between Owen's thumb and forefinger. His best friend didn't move away. They locked eyes.

Derek replied, "I want you...I want you to take me home with you."

PART 2
CHAPTER 10

"I WANT YOU to take me home with you...but, dude, it's a fucking Friday night!" Derek said to his best friend, Owen. "I'm drunk. I'm pumped. And, it's far too early for two good-looking bachelors such as ourselves, to call it quits."

Owen let out an amused chuckle as he gripped the steering wheel of the sleek black Camaro and sped along the highway through the sparkling city night. Derek sat beside him in the red leather bucket seat, wearing a loopy grin and slurring his words, after just seconds ago holding his hand and staring dreamily into his eyes—things that happened after way too many drinks.

Owen shook his head with a grin. "Uh, uh. No way I'm letting your drunk ass keep me out all night. You need to get somewhere and sleep it off."

"Ha! Always, always the responsible party, my friend. That's why I love you, man," Derek cracked. And anyway, there wasn't anywhere else he wanted to go or anything else he wanted to do. He hadn't spent bro-time with Owen in a while, so he was content to call it a night if it meant hanging out somewhere other than his own basement apartment at his parents' house. He leaned back on the headrest and closed his tired eyes, making a mental note that it was high time he found his own place.

They had just rounded off an evening of drinking with Derek's new brother-in-law, Steve, and the night was wearing on. Derek peeked down at his phone and reread the text message he had sent to Adelaide back at the bar. Steve had gone home early. Of course, Owen had stopped drinking before getting too shit-faced, and Derek hadn't. So, when he got the bright idea to pour out his heart in a drunk text, Owen had saved him from himself. Instead of a rambling, incoherent mess, the text simply read: 'Hi, this is Derek. Would you rather get to know me better or not?' He smiled and shoved the phone back in his pocket. Mission accomplished.

Now, his best friend was graciously taking him to crash at his place, rather than leave him wasted on his parents' doorstep. "I just have one favor to ask of you," Owen stated. He looked over at Derek with a semi-worried frown.

"Oh, yeah? What's that?"

"Please, please, don't barf all over my bathroom like you did last time."

Derek guffawed. "Oh, shit! I forgot about last time. Don't worry. I gotcha covered," he said, giggling. Owen winked and grinned, his fears allayed, at least for the time being. They had so much history together that Derek knew even if he did toss his cookies again, Owen would just hand him the cleaning supplies to clean his mess up. Shit was like that when you were as close as they were.

They cruised to a halt in front of Owen's house, and Derek peered up. There wasn't a moon in the sky, but a faint twinkle of stars swam dizzily overhead. The split-level home was in a cozy residential neighborhood where recycling bins stood next to trashcans at the end of long, paved driveways. Nice cars were parked out front. The lawns were so well kept, they appeared fake. It was a far cry from Derek's basement apartment in his parents' house, not to mention a lovely getaway when he didn't want to stumble in drunk.

Derek fell out of the passenger side of the sports car. With a grunt, he pushed up from the ground and whipped his dark, wavy hair out of his eyes. Chuckling at his lack of coordination, he slurred, "I'm fine. I'm alright."

"No, you're not." Owen let out a wheezing laugh. He strolled around from the driver's side to give his best bud a shoulder to lean on. "I've got you. Watch your step." His tenor rumble stirred the air near Derek's ear, as he set him to rights and ushered him in the direction of the front door.

"You're my best friend," Derek sang. He threw out an arm, which

Owen gently eased back down to his side, making shushing sounds. "I'm sorry, I'm sorry. I don't want to wake your neighbors," Derek stage-whispered, giggling. Owen rolled his eyes. "And, I promise I'll grow up tomorrow. This is the last time you'll have to drag me, drunken and disoriented, into your humble abode."

"Derek, my friend, what would my weekend be, if not for nights like this? I live vicariously through you," Owen fibbed.

Derek giggled, hiccupped, and focused on putting one foot in front of the other to the stone steps that seemed to dance in his hazy state. Owen dug the keys out of his pocket and hit the alarm on his car, before sliding the key to the front door home in the lock with an audible click. It swung slowly open without a sound. A tropical scent wafted from inside the house. Owen was big on smell-goods and homey stuff like that. Derek stumbled in, sniffing appreciatively.

"You know where your room is. I'll hook you up with a sobering smoothie. How's that?" Owen suggested.

Within no time, Derek was showered up and more coherent, sitting in Owen's kitchen continuing their aimless conversation started at the bar. He was dressed in a pair of his bud's lounge pants and one of his t-shirts. He felt comfortable, more at home in this place than he ever felt at his parents'. The décor was era-appropriate. There was soft indie rock playing in the background, and Owen had mixed him up a batch of his soul-sobering 'Kill the Buzz' smoothie—an exotic, less-than-yummy blend of bananas, coconut water, egg yolks, and asparagus.

"I dunno, I guess I'm more reluctant to ruin a good thing," Owen replied. "Adelaide is a one of a kind girl, but it doesn't take long for the novelty to wear off and all the bad faults to come to the light. Given Steve's unsavory account of how it was to date her, I wouldn't waste time trying to pursue something serious."

"You said you support me in this. Don't be a butthead about it. Just remember, life coach, I'm not on your therapy couch right now," said Derek. "Or, should I say lumberjack." He smiled broadly as he looked Owen over. The hipster beard fit the red flannel pajamas Owen had changed into for bed, and he did look a lot like a lumberjack.

"Cute." Owen smirked, leaning against the kitchen counter with a mug of hot tea in hand. A tiny dimple showed at the corner of his mouth when he grinned back. "I'm just saying. I liked her, too. Not enough to get fucked over, though."

"If she turns out not to be the woman of my dreams, I know how to break up. I've been dumped enough times to know the script by heart. Trust me. Anyway, she might not even text me back. Fingers crossed." Derek held up both middle fingers and crossed them one over the other, and Owen did it back. They had had come up with this move back in high school.

"Fingers crossed." Owen said absently, sneaking a peak at his watch. He lifted his eyebrows at the lateness of the hour. "Man, time flies. What do you say we turn it in? You feeling a bit more sober now? I'm beat."

Derek couldn't suppress a yawn as the words cleared Owen's lips. He was just about to say he wasn't tired, but he was. It had been a trying week. It had been a great night. "As nasty as this shit tastes, I better be sober after drinking it. Get you some rest. I'm going to finish this and head up, but if you don't hear me coming up to bed in the next few minutes, it means your concoction finally did me in."

He listened to Owen's laughter recede as he ambled out of the kitchen and up the stairs to his bedroom. Derek finished off the last sip of murky green smoothie, and drank some tap water to wash it down. He sat at the kitchen island, thoughtfully ruminating over the risks associated with tracking down Adelaide, and the risks of not doing it.

According to Steve, Adelaide was a wild child with a touch of nymphomania and a penchant for infidelity. She might look like a lady, but she was no shrinking violet. He recalled their one night together, and all the ways the sexually skilled seductress had taken him and Owen through the throes of ecstasy. His body aggressively responded to the memory. She was just that good; the mere thought of her brought on an erection. He sheepishly adjusted himself as he made his way back to the guestroom. He turned on the television to play in the background, and he climbed into bed.

Derek knew she was more than a pretty face and a sweet body, and he preferred to believe his infatuation wasn't simple lust. The brief game of Would You Rather at the wedding reception (that had led to the threesome) had given him a hint of her wit and self-assurance. He wanted to get to know her. (He wanted another chance to experience the thrill of her body.) He couldn't see himself never talking to her again. (Or, never sleeping with her again.) It wasn't just about the sex, he told himself.

He was wide awake two hours later, staring with glazed eyes at the blue screen of the television. Quiet canned laughter played in the background of a sitcom. Sleep eluded him. Derek tossed and turned in the guest bed, even though the Memory Foam mattress cushioned his body like a dream. He was significantly less drunk than earlier, but not entirely sober, which left him in a mix of restlessness and contentment.

It wasn't hard to envision what it would be like if he and his best friend were roommates. What if Owen was in his room right this minute, lying awake, too? Nights like this, they could crank up the game console and play until their eyes slammed shut. In fact, he decided to peep in and check, because wiling away the time on a video game sounded much more exciting than staring at the ceiling, waiting for Adelaide to text him back.

When Derek stepped out of the quiet guestroom into the deeper silence of the hallway, it seemed nothing was stirring. He was turning to go back into his room, thinking Owen had to be sleep, when he heard a muffled, lusty moan. Then, he *knew* he should go back to bed, but curiosity got the best of him. Derek tiptoed up to Owen's bedroom door, which was slightly ajar. He peeked past the crack.

The television was on in there, and the moan had come from the TV, not Owen. Owen was stretched out on top of his covers in bed, watching what sounded like porn. Derek stepped back in embarrassment, and his footfall caused the floorboards to creek. He froze in panic when Owen's dark brown eyes skated lazily to the partially open door. When Owen didn't immediately get up to check out what had made the sound, Derek's racing heart gradually slowed to an almost normal tempo.

He swallowed thickly. He felt several degrees hotter. He knew he shouldn't look, but it was like the day Owen had sent him a half-naked text to get his opinion about using the picture for his blog. Derek had found himself in an isolated restroom at the office where no one could peek or pry into what he was doing. He had locked the door, checked it twice, and…since then, he had tried his best not to think about what he'd done next.

But, this was just like that. He squinted as Owen started rubbing his burgeoning erection through his flannel pajama pants, his inquisitive fingers gliding idly along the shaft, back and forth…back and forth. The TV in the background made wet, sexy sounds and cast flesh-toned light across his reclining form. A woman's voice cooed with pleasure. Owen's burly hand gripped his penis in a tight squeeze with a long, slow stroke, and the outline of his impressive member was clearly visible.

Derek couldn't un-see it. Nor, could he calm his erratic pulse at the sight. It sent a lurch through him. Owen began to ease his flannel pajama bottoms down. Derek recoiled at the realization his palms were sweaty and his stomach was doing flip-flops, and the recognition that he was so damned *aroused* by watching his best friend masturbate. Yet, he didn't want to look away, and he was no longer scared of getting caught.

As Owen's pants slipped lower and lower, a length of pale inner thigh was exposed, black boxers, and then bare pelvis. Derek's mouth suddenly went dry with unspeakable desire. It sent chills through him just to imagine what it felt like. To be touched. To touch. Meanwhile, Owen kept his gaze directed at the television and reached a hand into a side table to retrieve a small tube of lubricant. Oozing the clear substance onto the head of his semi-rigid penis, he continued to pleasure himself.

Owen made a ring with his thumb and forefinger, moving his hand up and down near the bulbous head of his shaft. His lubricated manhood glistened and gleamed in the dim light. His fingers danced a little faster with pressure, enough to make him wince with pleasure as he glanced down at himself, mouth slightly agape. His deep-set eyes were hooded and half closed, and he licked his lips, clamping his teeth down on the bottom one. Derek, staring, heard him gasp with satisfaction and thought Owen masturbating was one of the most erotic things he'd ever seen.

The sounds of steamy sex coming softly from the television provided the appropriate score for the scene. Owen dropped his head back on his pillows and, closing his eyes tightly, began to pump his massive manhood into his hand. With each hard thrust, he clenched his abs, and his powerful hips rolled up a fraction off the bed and slowly lowered. Derek watched the muscles ripple in his thighs. Owen moaned and hummed with pleasure.

Derek clapped a hand over his mouth to keep from breathing a sound of his own desire. He shifted and his cock throbbed against his leg, which caused him to blush fiercely. He had convinced himself the sexual attraction was a fluke brought on by that one taboo sex act. He hadn't felt the same since the threesome. This simply wasn't the way things were supposed to be. Not for him. But, here he was, staring. His eyes stung. He couldn't blink.

Derek squeezed his eyes shut and willed his dick to get with the program. Unfortunately, Owen picked that moment to hiss out a breath, coupled with another guttural groan that sent need spearing through him. *One last peek*, he told himself. Owen had lifted up his legs and was intermittently rimming himself with a moist fingertip while he bucked in ecstasy, jerking off. It was so unexpected that Derek inhaled sharply.

With a raw cry, Owen shivered and his meaty cock spewed a stream of white jizz all over his muscled stomach. It took a minute for him to recover. He lay back, breathing heavily and shaking the cum off his fingers, back into the puddle pooling near his navel. Then, his brown eyes turned back to the door. Something in the satisfied half-smile that touched his lips told Derek his friend knew he was there. He couldn't know, though. There was no way he could see into the darkened hallway, right?

CHAPTER 11

DEREK CREPT BACK to the guestroom. He had to get away. The down comforter offered refuge, but he couldn't hide from his thoughts, nor his raging erection. He hadn't had sex since that night with Owen and Adelaide. His frustration was mounting, and Derek didn't want self-gratification. He wanted to screw. He wanted to plow his stiffness into someone's eager body and take them both over the edge.

"That's the liquor talking. Go to sleep," he desperately negotiated with himself. Huddled beneath the covers, he forced his eyes to shut and his excitement to simmer down. He didn't know if it was the unrestricted nature of his thoughts or the fact he was doing things he'd never done before that gave him such a thrill. Derek half wished he could put the same-sex lust to the test—just get it out of his system. "Don't be crazy," he muttered. His brow furrowed. He finally went to sleep.

"Shed your inhibitions," Adelaide whispers in a sultry tone. "Let's take care of each other..."

Derek opens his eyes, and he's standing next to Owen. The both of them are naked. Adelaide is on her knees between them, and it's a rerun of the wild night after the wedding. He stares down at her as she expertly swallows Owen to the hilt, drawing away patiently until his corded erection pops free, and Owen hitches in a breath. "That's it," he breathes, dropping his head back with his eyes closed. Giggling, she flicks her tongue along the tip. Owen gently holds her by the back of her head and guides her.

Derek looks around in a daze and realizes they're in his best friend's backyard by the pool, but the landscape is an impossible palette of hyper-saturated colors. The water is phthalo blue. The sky is the same translucent tint, and the grass is a blinding green. Owen's chiseled body glistens in the white sun, covered in a sheen of water from the pool, and Adelaide on her knees is a nude, golden goddess with strands of copper in her flowing, dark blonde hair.

She turns to Derek next, and seductively sucks his throbbing erection into her mouth, sliding her velvety tongue over his sensitive skin and using her lips to stroke along its length. All the while, she looks up at him with doe-like eyes, at once worldly, and innocent. Derek wheezes with arousal as silky saliva dribbles down his shaft in slow-motion, gasping at the mesmerizing roll of her tongue curling along the undersurface of his swollen member to lap it back up. As she sucks, she touches herself.

"This is the way it's supposed to be," she purrs. Her voice echoes, reverberating through the dreamscape like it's spoken from everywhere. Derek nods in agreement. Yes, this is how...

He tensely cups her head against his lower body and eases into her mouth, drawing back out slowly and deliberately. He does it again, and her cheek expands as his hardness pokes inside. Her lips squeeze around him, and she makes greedy, lusty sounds to accompany Derek's grunts of pleasure. He caresses her face and makes love to her mouth with his rigid cock, while down below, her hand moves furiously between her legs.

Suddenly, Adelaide stands up and drags Derek down to her pelvis. As she thrusts her tantalizing womanhood to his open mouth, she lets out a fierce moan, and Derek realizes she's brought herself to climax. He grips her plush, round, ass cheeks to spread her wide, baptizing his face in her glistening dew.

Whimpering with ecstasy, she places her hand to the crown of his head and rides his face with a sexy roll of her hips, the evidence of her gratification collecting on Derek's lips, cheeks, and chin. He drags his nose over the petals of her womanhood, and licks into her crevice to taste her. Her X-rated squeals of pleasure make him throb painfully with need. Derek closes a fist around himself. He's caught off guard when Owen's hard-on grazes the side of his face. Derek pulls back and looks up to see his friend beating off right next to him, watching

Adelaide reach completion.

"My turn," Owen growls possessively.

He grabs her by the waist and lifts her up. Owen smoothly deposits her onto his own swollen junk, and holds her while he strokes up and into her. Her legs dangle over the crooks of his arms.

"I wasn't done yet," Derek interjects with a raspy chuckle, wiping his lips and smiling. But, he stands back as Owen takes control, and Adelaide clutches his shoulders with a tremulous whine for more. She sensually arches her back and lolls her head to the side, and her satiny hair trails to the top of her ass. Derek studies the graceful sweep of her spine, her shoulder blades like abbreviated angel's wings. Her heart-shaped ass bounces against Owen's pelvis.

It's too enticing to resist. Derek boldly steps forward, sandwiching Adelaide between the both of them, to stroke his swollen member against her pillowy ass. Derek gasps against the back of her neck as he masturbates. He taps his turgid erection to her soft skin. She reaches a hand back to assist as she passionately kisses Owen. Derek reaches around her to rub her clit while she cups her fingers over his and strokes him tighter. The sensation is exquisite.

Then, Owen lets his lips graze Derek's over Adelaide's shoulder.

It's a butterfly kiss, possibly even an accident. Given permission, however, Derek's mouth closes over his best friend's, and the kiss becomes a passionate tangle of tongues. He wantonly pulls Owen closer, as Owen clasps the back of his neck to kiss him harder, with Adelaide's back pressed against Derek's chest.

"Yes," Derek breathes. "Ah, god, yes!" Her hair flutters against his face, and Adelaide jerks her skillful hand up and down his shaft between them. With her touch and Owen's kiss, he feels himself about to let go.

"Do you think about me the same way I can't stop thinking about you?" Owen whispers fiercely against his lips. "Do you?"

Before Derek can respond, Adelaide tenses with a sharp cry, and she drops her head back against Derek's shoulder as a powerful orgasm sweeps through her. He helps to hold her up while Owen clutches her lightly by the throat and continues pounding into her until the final wave of pleasure sets her free. Derek looks down over her heaving chest, down her flat, quivering stomach to the place where Owen enters her. The evidence of her completion soaks his thighs and covers his glistening shaft. At last, she slips weakly from Owen's arms, leaving only the two men standing.

They stare wordlessly at each other for a brief eternity. Then, Owen shyly tugs Derek by the hand and guides him to the sectional. Derek winds up half-sitting, half-reclining on the cerulean blue pillows of the wicker furniture. Adelaide, quivering and sated, lying naked on the sun-warmed pavement next to the hyper-blue pool, watches them with desire-filled eyes and a satisfied smile as Owen slowly, slowly... bends at the waist, and puts his mouth to Derek's steel pipe.

"Ah!" Derek hisses in shock.

Owen's hot mouth works swift magic, his tongue sliding expertly into the slit at the tip and gliding back down to the base of his erection. For a brief moment, it's like simultaneously watching the show and experiencing it. The tableau is a titillating scene—fit male bodies in their prime, naked against a lush paradise backdrop.

Owen's ash brown hair ruffles in disarray as Derek clutches a handful, his head bobbing vigorously up and down at Derek's groin. Sounds of excitement escape his mouth around Derek's erection. Wet, slippery sounds of oral sex are heard, and quick, sharp gasps and throaty moans of pleasure come from Derek. Owen, with his heavy, tumescent erection in hand, masturbates while he sucks, until his well-primed tool shoots gushes of hot, silky ejaculation in his excitement.

Derek's dusky skin is flushed and sweaty, his face a mask of abject bliss, and there's the beautiful, nude Adelaide rubbing a hand between her legs with guilty pleasure as she observes. He surges deep into Owen's mouth and...

"BEEP, BEEP, BEEP!"

His cellphone alarm blared. Derek's eyes snapped open, and he squeezed them shut with a disoriented grimace. He swatted at the phone until it hit the floor and quit its incessant beeping. Knuckling sleep from his eyes, Derek finally sat up.

"Shit," he exhaled.

He looked down at his impressive morning wood, and remembered snatches of the very realistic dream. His cock felt well-fucked, and he knew he must've been masturbating or somehow stimulating himself in his sleep. Derek slinked out of bed to look around for his clothes from the day before so he could get cleaned up. That's when he saw his cellphone on the floor had a text message alert.

"Adelaide?" he exhaled hopefully.

The message was brief but promising. "Would you like to hook up and maybe hang out today?" she had responded. He read it again and again between getting showered, getting dressed, changing Owen's sheets, pretending like he hadn't had the most exquisite wet dream the night before. It was Saturday morning, and the sun slanted through the blinds with cheery light. He heard his friend somewhere downstairs in the kitchen, assumed he was cooking breakfast. The smell of bacon and toast confirmed the suspicion. Derek padded down the stairs and made his way to a stool at the kitchen bar. "Morning, sunshine," Derek greeted.

Owen stood over the electric range flipping fluffy yellow omelets, and using a fork to poke at crispy strips of bacon. Wheat bread was toasting in the oven. The addictive smell of fresh-brewed coffee permeated the air. Owen pulled down two plates and began fixing breakfast for them. Derek poured up two mugs of coffee. They moved over to the breakfast nook to eat and talk about how the day would go.

"Any trace of a hangover?" Owen lifted a brow, already knowing the answer. Hangovers didn't stand a chance against his smoothie concoctions. Derek smiled and shook his head, shoveling forkfuls of food into his mouth. "Good," said Owen. "So, what's on our agenda for the day? Movies? B-ball? Video games? I've got the whole day free."

Derek pushed the phone across the table and watched Owen read the text message he'd received from Adelaide. Owen studied it, saying nothing. Derek sighed. "So, what do you think? Should I tell her yes? Should I go out with her?" he asked.

Owen shrugged. "I don't see why not." He looked unenthused. In fact, he wore a slightly disappointed expression—eyebrows pinched, lips downturned. It occurred to Derek that, in a role reversal, this time it was Owen with plans for them to chill together and him asking for a raincheck. It made him feel uncomfortable because he didn't want his bro thinking he preferred Adelaide over him, but…well, shit, he wanted to see her.

"Hey, why don't you come, too?" he impulsively invited, but Owen adamantly shook his head.

"No, no, no. We've been over this before. Chasing after Adelaide is your thing. I figured we'd do a little more with Operation Reshaping Derek today. Now that I think about it, a date is the perfect hands-on lesson. I can give you some pointers, like get your car cleaned up and select the right type of cologne, but we can start by getting you dressed. You game?"

"Admit it. I'm your real-live Ken doll, aren't I?" Derek joked.

Owen cocked a brow in amusement and smugly ran a hand over his beard, which was growing back nicely since the last trim. "My boy, I have all the naked dolls a man could want, and they're all of the feminine variety—big, gorgeous tits, womanly hips and tender pink lady bits down below," he replied loftily. Owen lifted his coffee mug in salute.

"Ha! That's my idea of a playdate," Derek replied nervously. Yet, the comment brought flashbacks of the dream—of Owen sucking him off and nearly making him explode with ecstasy. There was no way something like that would happen in real life, no matter how much the idea piqued his curiosity. Derek shook his head to dispel the images, and took a shaky breath. Owen picked up on the swift mood swing, eyeing him with concern.

"You okay, man?"

"Huh? Yeah, no, I'm fine," Derek answered too quickly.

He needed to see Adelaide. Perhaps she was the cure to his ridiculous new preoccupation with homo-erotica. Or, maybe she was the catalyst and it was too late to be redeemed. Derek didn't know. It just seemed unfair to want a man as badly as he wanted his best friend, and not be able to tell a soul, not even Owen.

Owen didn't ask any more questions, and Derek didn't volunteer an explanation, but the men had been friends for too long for the tension to go unnoticed. Sooner or later Derek would have to say something if this didn't go away. He just didn't know *what* would end up being said. Derek sighed glumly and finished off the rest of his coffee.

CHAPTER 12

BY LATE AFTERNOON, he was climbing into his used car. He had taken Owen's advice and run the Mazda sedan through a carwash. The interior was nice and clean too, with one of those cardboard scented trees hanging from the mirror. It was pretty surprising how much a wax job transformed his vehicle. Likewise, Derek had polished up for the date.

He had basically gone shopping in Owen's closet, and his best friend hadn't told him what to wear this time. Owen had left it up to him to come up with something 'fetching'. Thus, Derek was in cropped khaki cargoes and a white Henley shirt with red sleeves. He had on comfortable sandals. A straw Fedora was perched jauntily on his head. He couldn't tell if he had nailed the look or totally botched it, but he was discovering having Owen as a life coach didn't mean the guy would hold his hand every step of the way.

It had been only a week since Owen had taken on the daunting task of helping Derek morph from born loser to walking success story. Already, there were signs his friendly advice was working in Derek's life. He used to think of himself as having perpetual bad luck no matter what he tried, while Owen seemed to go through life with a fistful of four-leaf clovers. Once upon a time, Derek had looked on his best friend's great career, beautiful home, and bevy of attractive bed partners with a touch of envy. Now, he didn't have to feel that way because his fortunes were looking up. Especially, when it came to romance.

Derek had made arrangements with Adelaide to meet her at a local amusement park called The Whole Dam Family. It was a public place, a fun place. It was the kind of place where if things went south and he needed to disappear, all he would have to do was blend into the crowd. As he came around the curb to the parking lot, the sun glinted off of rollercoasters, a Ferris wheel, and other thrills beyond the gaily-painted tall wooden fence that encircled the property. At the entrance, there was a huge sign boasting 'Good times galore' with the park's cartoon mascot, a plucky looking beaver, grinning maniacally. He found a spot in the crowded parking lot, and once the car was parked, he sat in the front seat drumming up his nerve.

The rearview mirror showed him a guy with wavy black hair finger-combed carelessly to the side. He grabbed the Fedora off the passenger seat and slapped it on. Thick black brows came together over ice blue eyes, and his shapely mouth practiced smiling. He had a five o'clock shadow growing in, which made him look more…sophisticated. Satisfied that there wasn't anything embarrassing stuck in his teeth or hanging from his nose, Derek climbed out of his car and headed inside. She was waiting for him.

He found her by the cotton candy machine. She looked carefree, unabashedly nibbling at a big ball of pinky fluffy sugar on a white paper cone. Her almond-shaped eyes sparkled with merriment, as her gaze followed the passage of a colorful clown carrying a bright bouquet of balloons. One of the balloons escaped and floated up into the sky, and she shaded her eyes to watch it ascend with a smile on her lips. Derek paused, enthralled by the sight of her.

Her tall, statuesque body filled out a pair of dark denim skinny jeans and a thin white blouse with quarter-length sleeves. Leather cowboy boots kicked at clumps of sawdust that covered the well-traveled ground. The late summer breeze lifted her long blonde tresses, turned a sandy hue by the afternoon sun. She stood out in the crowd. Adelaide Ingles was exactly as he remembered her, if not even more striking. Derek recovered his senses and hurried over to greet her.

She didn't see him or hear him at first, too busy watching the balloon drift away in the sky. He weakly cleared his throat. "Adelaide?" When she turned, her full, pouty lips parted in surprise. Her eyes flew over him, widening slightly.

"So, you actually showed up." Her voice was the same haunting mezzo-soprano, deep in a feminine way, but sultry without even trying to be. It sent a spark through him.

He stuck his hands into his pockets, shrugging self-consciously under her scrutiny. "Derek Cornwell, here. Remember me?" he said lamely.

"How could I forget you?" She crossed her slender tattooed arms, and sassily rested her weight on one hip. The stance drew his gaze from her artistic face to her enticing body, but she put a finger under his chin to bring his eyes back to hers. "Now, let's talk about how you got my phone number," she replied archly.

Derek gulped. He had hoped the subject wouldn't come up, but of course she would ask. "A mutual friend?" he replied. He stopped short of telling her he had weaseled it out of Steve, although it was easy enough for her to guess. She probably wasn't too happy her ex was doling out her contact info. "I...I hope that's not a problem," Derek stammered.

At his utterly disconcerted expression, her sternness dissipated, replaced by free-spirited laughter. Addie had an infectious laugh. "Boy, are you uptight! Are you always like that? You're going to have to loosen up with me. Look, if I didn't want you to have my number, I wouldn't have responded back to your text. I'm a pro at the silent treatment."

Derek breathed a sigh of relief. "Well, I'm glad you took a chance instead of ignoring me. Honestly, you don't know how cool it was to see that you texted back. I really, really...really wanted to see you again..." Derek clamped his mouth shut. *Three really's?* He internalized a groan of shame that almost escaped his lips. Could things get any more awkward than the overexcited drivel he was rambling? "Um, do you want to get some tickets so we can...you know." He gestured to the rides.

She flashed a disarming smile that made it hard to breathe. "Actually, I already got my own," she replied, holding up an all-day pass. "I'm kind of used to taking care of myself, but I'll let you play the old fashioned gentleman for the rest of the date, if that's what you want. I'll walk with you to get yours."

She had no qualms about grabbing his hand as they headed toward the ticket booth at an unhurried pace, moving to stand in line as they silently sized each other up. Adelaide drew the eyes of every male in the vicinity and some of the women, too. For Derek, it was like suddenly being initiated into the popularity club, because those same staring people shot envious looks in his direction for being with her. She caught Derek studying her and playfully elbowed him in the side. He tugged at a strand of her hair in retaliation. She stuck out her tongue.

"Welcome to The Whole Dam Family where your whole *darn* family can have good times galore. How many?" Derek looked up and noticed it was his turn at the ticket window, and the attendant behind the glass was staring with a bored look at the two of them play-fighting. He adulted-up and bought his tickets, and they meandered off through the park. There was so much to do that he had a hard time deciding where to begin. He was standing indecisively in the flow of foot traffic, when Adelaide took charge and pulled him aside.

"Can I say something right upfront?" She wrung her hands, the first sign of nervousness he'd seen from her so far. Derek leaned in and gave her his full attention. She took a deep breath and said, "It would be great if you can let your sister know that…I apologize. At first, I was like 'whatev', but then I felt like a bitch for not taking into consideration how popping up at her wedding would make her feel. It was a tasteless joke."

"Of course, I can," he replied. Actually, it would be his pleasure. He had a feeling under better circumstances, Heather would've loved Addie. Adelaide smiled appreciatively. Derek waited until they were suspended high above the amusement park on the Ferris wheel a while later to ask, "By the way, why did you crash the wedding?"

Addie rocked forward and back to get the carriage to start lazily swinging as the ride climbed toward the sky. "This is fun," she gushed, peering over the side at the people, tiny as ants down below. Her bubbly laughter made him smile. He thought she wasn't going to answer his question—he was admittedly prying into something that was none of his business—but she finally shrugged nonchalantly and explained.

"Right after grad school I met Steve, and we dated briefly. When we broke up, he took it extra hard. I almost had to put a restraining order on him. I guess meeting your sister mellowed him the hell out because he finally stopped harassing me. Then, I found out he was spreading rumors that I was the one stalking him. Can you believe the prick?"

He swallowed queasily. "That guy is a character. Yeah, I figured it was something like that. C-can we stop rocking, please?" Derek gripped the safety bar and willed himself not to throw up.

"Oh! Sorry! Are you alright?"

He waved off her concern. He was fine—about five more minutes of rocking would've changed that prognosis significantly, but with the carriage slowly coming to a standstill—he was fine.

Adelaide carried on, "...Anyway, when I found out he was getting married, I decided to show up and watch him panic. I could have told everyone what a liar he was...but I didn't. Now, your turn to answer a question for me. Why did you go through the trouble of finding me?"

"Look at you! How could I let a woman like you walk out of my life completely, huh?" He grinned.

"You didn't have too much of a problem with it the morning after," she teased. "How's your boyfriend, by the way?"

"Whoa! Not my boyfriend. Owen and I are real cool friends who grew up together. That's all." She looked skeptical or maybe she was still teasing. He couldn't decide. He gazed at her quizzically.

When the Ferris wheel descended and Derek asked her what else she wanted to do, she threw her arms wide to encompass the entire amusement park. "I want to do everything! That's what you'll learn about me if you stick around any real length of time, Derek Cornwell. I'm all about new experiences, making memories, and being wildly spontaneous. Can you keep up with that?"

He couldn't have been more different. "Try me and see," he replied. Derek found the idea stimulating, but pieces of Steve's warning tried to resurface. His brother-in-law had mentioned Adelaide wasn't the kind of girl to stay in one place (or one man's bed) for long. He wondered if her need for new experiences and admitted rash impulsiveness had anything to do with that, but he told himself they'd cross that bridge when they got there. So far, so good.

"Are you afraid of heights?" she asked minutes later.

They were climbing up a sky-high stairway to the top of a curvy, swooping slide with a bunch of kids and teenagers. This one was Addie's pick. Derek was rapidly discovering that she was more of a dare devil than him, but he was gamely keeping up with her, like he said he would. Adelaide missed a step and stumbled. Derek quickly steadied her. He tried not to look down. They were a dizzying height from the ground.

"Watch out," he cautioned. "I don't want anything to happen to you on my watch. I'd never be able to forgive myself."

"That's what I get for wearing cowboy boots to a park. Ha! You're a sweetheart, aren't you? The kind of guy who fancies himself a romantic—chivalrous and protective. Jeez, I thought guys like you didn't exist," she laughed. "This song that's playing? It's one of my favorites. I love country music." To Derek's dismay, she purposefully let the rails go and danced her way up the next few steps. He put a hand to the small of her back just in case.

"Country music is okay," he called up from behind her. "I'm more into indie."

"Could you guys get a room?" an obnoxious preteen boy quipped from behind them. Giggles erupted from other kids close by.

Addie flashed them a mischievous smile, waggling her eyebrows humorously. Derek ducked his head, blushing but smiling, too. He remembered being that age. Maybe coming to a park wasn't the best of ideas, he thought. But, when Addie let loose a loud, gleeful shout as she zipped down the slide just ahead of him, he changed his mind. Coming to a park wasn't all that bad. He reached the bottom and found her waiting for him. "C'mon, c'mon!" she called excitedly. She grabbed his hand again and dragged him to another ride.

They went from carousel to coaster to funhouse, standing in long lines, surrounded by the mouth-watering smell of funnel cakes and other assorted fair foods. The music was loud, and he didn't recognize half the songs, but it was entertaining. The patrons of The Whole Dam Family were a mixture of young adults like them looking for a good time, families of bored parents and squawking kids, and bands of teens prowling the grounds for trouble.

Addie kept the conversation going, and the usual first date gambits were covered, as well as stuff he'd been warned never to speak of with friends. They talked about politics and religion, current events, and every hot button topic out there. Derek found himself being candid because she made it easy for him to be himself. He was the conservative to her liberal.

She was a ball of energy, a bubbly twenty-something with the spirit of a little kid. She could wax poetic and be profound one minute, and the next she would giggle at an off-color joke. Derek had been entranced by her sexual prowess the first night he met her, but after spending a whole afternoon with her, he was completely taken with all aspects of her personality.

"You're nothing like I expected," he murmured as they moved away from the rides and started looking for something else to do.

"Well, what did you expect?" she asked, chuckling. "You barely had anything to go on."

"Right, right. But, I guess I just built you up in my head as this—I dunno—different woman." It felt good to be getting to know her.

"Like build-a-girl? Nice."

Derek snorted in response and affectionately gripped her hand tighter. She squeezed his hand back. He pointed to a carnival game booth where participants could throw darts at balloons for a chance to win a massive teddy bear. "Oh, that looks like a good one. You'll find that my work as a graphic designer gives me...excellent hand-eye coordination."

"Let's see what you've got," said Adelaide.

He bought in, received five darts, and took his first throw. When the small metal projectile bounced harmlessly off a round, red latex balloon without popping it, Addie covered a laugh. Derek grumbled incredulously, "Son of a—that was a fluke. Here, let me try again. So, what do you do for a living, Addie?" He frowned with determination, queuing up for another throw.

"Ahem, I'm a party planner. Concentrate," she ordered.

"I am. Stop looking at me. You're making me nervous." Derek flashed her a smile and then refocused on the prize. He steadied his dart and prepared to throw.

"A little higher," suggested the carnie running the booth.

"You're gonna miss if you don't stop shaking," Adelaide said in a sing-song voice.

Derek chuckled. "No, I'm not going to miss. Stop looking!" He fired again. This time he got one.

"Hey! Way to go!" Addie clapped.

Derek threw his arms up with a hearty shout. "Yes!" He had four more tries to go for a total of three balloons. He picked up another dart.

"A party planner, huh? I can see that fitting you. What exactly does that entail? Like, do you hook up with a bunch of college coeds and get dirty with jello in a kiddie pool?" The image popped in his head, vivid and sexy, of Addie in a bikini sloshing around in lemon jello with equally hot babes.

She tossed her head with a laugh. "No, it's nothing like that. I work predominantly with families of children with disabilities to give them the best social get-together possible, given the constraints. It's more like I hook up with a bunch of happy, grade school kids and get dirty with paint and playdoh. I, uh, have a degree in childhood development…and a Ph.D. in special education."

His eyes bugged. He missed the balloon. Derek turned to her, blown away by the admission she had a doctorate. "That's pretty cool. I never would've guessed."

A half-smile curved her lips. "Why? Because I'm too sexy to be very smart?" She laughed good-naturedly at his flustered protest that he hadn't meant it like that. She sobered and answered, "It's cool. I get that a lot. It used to bother me, but now I simply sit back and wait for the 'wow'."

Derek sheepishly smiled. There were all sorts of dumb blonde jokes, but Adelaide was definitely proving not to fit the stereotype. He turned away from her and mouthed, "A doctorate?" Derek vaguely wondered if he could even be considered on her level.

He won the huge pink teddy bear and gave it to Adelaide. She cuddled it close, and it had all of her attention, right up until they passed a mobile food cart and she caught sight of the yummy junk food on display.

"Look, Derek, look! Candy apples! Ugh, I have a weakness for sweets, and you choose to meet at a damn amusement park! My diet is shot to shit," she exaggerated, laughing at herself.

Her favorite food was candy, Derek surmised. She was a dichotomous mix of oddly responsible and unapologetically immature. "Aww, I didn't know it'd be such a temptation. I'll make it up to you. Do you like to work out? I'm not much of a gym rat, but maybe we can get together sometime and—I dunno—jog or something," he suggested, grinning.

Adelaide clapped a hand over her fist and nodded. "I'll hold you to that. I happen to love my daily morning jog. I hope you can get up and keep up, though. I start at the crack of dawn, and I can keep going and going until you beg me to stop." She said the last in a sultry drawl with a flirtatious wink. Derek chuckled at the double entendre.

"You are…nothing like I expected," he repeated. He reached in his wallet and bought her a candy apple. She led him to a vacant bench and picked at the hard red shell, nibbling each sticky morsel like it was ambrosia. Her eyes closed, and she sighed dreamily.

Derek glanced at his watch. The afternoon was approaching evening, and the crowd was thinning some. Derek knew as the day deepened that a rowdier set would be out, fewer families and more teenagers. He wasn't ready to end the date, but they had already spent a few hours together. He didn't want things to get tedious. Better to leave her wishing for more than wishing for less.

"Well, my friend, I am having the time of my life, but I think we'll have to reconvene this at a later date. I have some work I need to get to, and you, Ms. Ingles, might tempt me to shirk my responsibilities if I let you. Do you like coffee shops?"

Chewing on another crunchy bit of candy coating, Adelaide made the so-so gesture with her hand. "They're too quiet and depressing." She looked at the time on her cellphone and agreed it was time to get a move on.

Derek replied, "Quiet is good for talking and getting to know each other." She smiled over the round hill of apple. Derek smiled back. "I want to take you out again. How does next weekend sound?"

"Hmm, I don't know what my schedule looks like. How about you call me midweek and we'll see?" she said evasively. Derek would've preferred an affirmative answer, but he took what he could get. He'd be happy to call her midweek.

"And, I can pick you up next time. I promise I won't kidnap you. I'm not a psycho or anything," he said, rising to his feet.

"You never know these days," she said breezily. "I might be."

Derek chuckled softly and puffed out his chest. "I'm not worried. I can handle myself." She stood up and stepped closer, and he peered into her cat-like eyes. Adelaide brought her lips to his and gave him a friendly peck. It didn't quite classify as a kiss. So, why did the mere touch of mouths send electricity zipping through him? Her inky brown eyes left his cool blue ones to stare at his lips, and she kissed him again, this time more intimately.

"But, can you handle me?" she asked seductively. A slender eyebrow arched.

Derek dropped his gaze to her mouth. He boldly traced his tongue along the vermillion border of her sensual bottom lip, tasting the sweet candy. He cupped her face and rubbed his thumb along her cheek. "I don't want to handle you. I don't want you tamed," he replied softly. The statement brought heat to her eyes.

Adelaide stepped away and put some distance between them. She reached for her teddy bear and bit into her candy apple, back to her playful vibe. "Next time, coffee shop it is, then. Let's go," she directed. She gestured ahead with her apple, and Derek walked her out of the amusement park to her car in the confusing maze of the parking lot.

Before he could say good-bye, she threw her arms around his neck and hugged him tightly, as if she didn't want to let him go. Derek shyly smoothed a hand down her back. "Can't wait to see you again," he murmured. She nodded. Adelaide gently disengaged. He stood back and watched her get into her car and drive off. It had been the perfect date.

◇◇◇

Lounging on the couch together, Owen listened to the recounting without much input. "Are you sure you want to keep going with this?" he asked when Derek got done telling him about the day. Derek threw his hands up in disbelief. After everything he'd said about how amazing the woman was, his best friend still had doubts? Derek sighed, tired of repeating himself.

"I'm definitely not backing down just because my brother-in-law gave her mixed reviews, man," he spat.

"Well, you sound like you know what you're doing, so..." Owen looked away.

The sportscaster on TV talked over the awkward tension that descended. Derek wanted Owen to be happy for him. He had never begrudged Owen any happiness. The guy had a big house, a fancy car and all the sexy, freaky girls he could ask for. Yet, he didn't want Derek pursuing a relationship with Adelaide.

Owen broke the stalemate with another question. "Did she at least ask   about   me?"

CHAPTER 13

MONDAY MORNING DEREK dragged his old journal from under his lumpy, twin sized mattress to accompany him to work at Ad Ent, Inc. The book was his repository for secret musings during some tough times in the not-so-distant past, and inside were ancient sketches and doodles, scribbles of poems, random brain junk. Ideas aplenty. He needed those ideas to jump-start the revamped Wonder Man ad. Derek tucked the bulky leather-bound book into his shiny, new briefcase—the latest addition to his wardrobe—compliments of Owen. Carrying a briefcase made him feel more prepared.

Derek dashed out of the basement apartment, almost barreling into his mom in his rush. She was coming to his bedroom/apartment door with a basket of freshly laundered clothes. "Whoa! Sorry!" He steadied her and gave her a fleeting kiss on the cheek before he skirted around her.

"Oh, look how nice you look! Will you be home in time for dinner?" Lydia Cornwell called after him.

Derek paused on the way out the front door. "Probably not. Got some important stuff to handle at work, so you don't have to wait up for me. But thanks, mom."

He escaped into the mild, late summer morning, sweeping the door shut behind him. "Be careful on your way to work," he heard her yell through the door, always concerned about him. With a wry grin at her caution, Derek hopped into his Mazda. It was still gleaming from the weekend wash. He zoomed out of the sleepy, aging neighborhood where his parents lived, cruised to the wide open highway, and slowed to a crawl on the congested surface streets.

By the time he made it in to work, he felt ready to take on the world. Derek breezed out of the elevator and headed straight to his cubicle. He didn't pause to socialize, even though the design floor personal assistant, Libby, looked like she was about to fall out of her chair trying to follow him with her eyes. "Good morning, Mr. Cornwell," she purred in greeting. He flashed her a brief smile, waved, and kept walking.

His confidence was at an all-time high since the weekend date with Adelaide, which was perfect, because he needed every ounce of self-assurance to tackle his problems in the office. Just one short week ago Mr. Clancy had called him in to give him his walking papers, eventually giving him a second chance (or just enough rope to hang himself with.)

He was given two weeks to create his own ad to prove he had the out of the box thinking his supervisor wanted to see. That was the easy part. He also had to use that time to work with a team that didn't want to work with him, creating another ad for the same product, and he was down to the last five days before both presentations were due.

Derek threw himself into the fray and spent the better part of the morning on his computer making his drafts come to life. "Now, if Mr. Clancy isn't completely satisfied with this, then there's no pleasing the guy," he murmured to himself. As he tweaked his handiwork, he saw it as analogous with the tiny changes Owen was helping him make. He was being similarly reshaped. From his love life, to his work life, to his personal well-being, Owen's crash course into successful adulthood was rebranding him.

After a while, Derek pushed back from his monitor and reached for his cellphone to check the time. He had a meeting with the team, and he couldn't be late. Holding onto his job required him to excel individually as well as within the group, and turning around their attitude toward him was where Owen's advice would come in most handy.

The six other group members on the Wonder Man cologne ad team, led by Harold Gensler, had conspired against Derek to get him fired with poor peer reviews and general bad-mouthing. When that didn't work, Harold resorted to calling secret team meetings to exclude him. Derek understood the initial diss. He could admit he had been unmotivated and disinterested after five years of producing the same-ole-same advertisements. But, now he had to repair the burned bridges. He didn't like to play office politics; unfortunately, he had to get on the good side of Harold and his team.

To that end, Derek briskly strolled into the boardroom Monday after lunch for another meeting Harold was hoping he would miss. He channeled his inner Zen with a purposeful stride, dressed in a dark blue suit to project a sense of trustworthiness and integrity. The outfit was pressed and fitted appropriately, giving him a polished, capable air. But, it wasn't just the clothes that were different. As soon as he entered the room, he connected with his team members with eye contact, a ready smile, and personalized greetings to show them he was fully present and ready to participate.

Derek took his seat. "How's it going, Mr. Cornwell?" Libby Sullivan, the secretary, whispered as she leaned in to fill his cup of coffee. Derek nodded, stopping her before she added cream and sugar.

"Thanks. It's going great, Ms. Sullivan. You know, I'm not sure if anyone's told you this, but these little things you do make working here that much easier," he whispered.

"Uh...thank you! Good morning, ma'am," she said, turning to Derek's colleague, her mood clearly brightened by the comment. The coworker seated next to him followed his lead. That set off a chain of sheepish murmurs of appreciation from the rest of the truculent set of designers, who were more apt to ignore staff assistants than to acknowledge them. Derek leaned back in his chair with an intrigued smile. Just a tiny gesture, but the effect was amazing. The secretary tiptoed back out of the boardroom with a thousand watt smile.

Harold snorted impatiently. "Alright, let's get started." The meeting commenced with the team leader taking center stage, and Derek zeroed in. He needed to show he could be an active participant without taking over completely. During the last meeting, he might have overstepped his boundaries a little. Having convinced the team to give up Harold's idea of using a super hero to push the new scent, Derek didn't want to risk offending the team leader any further. But, he was fully prepared to pick up where they left off, once the floor was open.

He had drawn up several variations of the gypsy, dreamer, smoke motifs discussed at the end of last week. When Harold finally gave others a chance to talk, Derek presented his contributions. He had created a collage of images from his journal. Most of the team gathered around him to help decide what worked and what didn't, throwing out other ideas, changes that would make things better. For the first time in a long while, the brainstorming session was a group effort rather than a one man grand stand. It wasn't long before they felt they'd hit upon a winner.

"Fine," Harold muttered tersely in conclusion. "Since everyone is in agreement that you'd rather go forward with this sissified dreamer b.s., I'll schedule the photo room so we can get this knocked up, hum? Alright, guys and gals, meeting adjourned. Excuse me, Derek. I need to speak with you privately."

The room gradually cleared of group members, leaving the two men still sitting at the table. Derek crossed his ankle over his knee and leaned back with his forefinger to his chin, waiting to see what else his nemesis had up his sleeve. He wasn't prepared for what Harold said next. "I think you need to recuse yourself from the group."

Derek let out a soft, shallow laugh. "Have you lost your mind?"

"Nope. I haven't. I think you know it's the best thing you could do at this point. I mean, let's face it. A last ditch effort can't make up for months of you slacking off." Harold lifted his brows and steepled his fingers, staring pointedly at him. Derek rolled his eyes and leaned forward.

"Listen, I understand you're upset things aren't going your way with the Wonder Man ad, and I empathize; but, the new concept is the better concept. And, as far as my past work is concerned, you seem to have forgotten that I'm the best graphic designer this team has. In fact, the only complaint Mr. Clancy voiced was the lack of innovation. That's what I'm trying to change."

Harold angrily slammed a hand down on the boardroom table with a loud *thwack*. "Goddammit, I'm sick of entitled millennials like you thinking you don't have to put in the same amount of effort as the rest of us! Yet, you still think you should get the same acclaim. Ten years ago if I'd pulled the same shit, I'd be out on my ass. Why the hell are they keeping you here, you little prick?"

"I can't speak for Mr. Clancy. That's something you'd have to ask him."

Harold scowled and flapped a hand dismissively. "Oh, to hell with him! Clancy thinks high maintenance, diva behavior is just a necessary evil of the art world. He's idealistic with his damned head stuck in the clouds, but this isn't a painter's studio, or a gallery. This is a business. I need professionals on my team, and you, Derek, fall short of that description." He aggressively jabbed a finger in Derek's direction.

Derek crossed his arms and stared unflinchingly into Harold's angry eyes. Things were going too far. He had to put an end to this madness. He suspected his work history wasn't really the underlying issue. "Regardless of how you personally assess me, I'm qualified to do my job. That's why I'm here, and you can't harass and intimidate me into stepping down. But, you can tell me what your problem is with me, and maybe we can settle this…like professionals."

Harold hissed out a long suffering breath, the type of exhalation that was characteristic of someone with a grudge. "I've already told you. You don't do your work, or at least you didn't. Now, you want to showboat like you're god's gift to the group. Well buddy, you're not."

"For my past lack of commitment to this group, I sincerely apologize; and, if you feel I've been showboating, you're wrong. I'm not trying to steal your shine. I'm not just doing this to keep my job. I'm honestly trying to connect with you and the other members of the team because I understand that by myself, I'm a great graphic designer, but with the rest of you guys, we're a real creative force. I need you guys as much as you need me," Derek humbly acknowledged.

"I see straight through you. You're trying to take over my team," Harold accused quietly.

Derek shook his head and stated plainly, "No, I'm not. What I'm trying to do is take us from the outdated advertising rut we've been stuck in since I started working here five years ago. You're the only one who can lead this motley crew of misfits, but we all have a part. *I* have a part in this—its success or its failure."

There was nothing more to discuss. Derek sighed and stood back from the table. Harold watched him walk to the door, some of the older man's discomfiture erased. He looked less harried but no less suspicious. Derek figured it would take baby steps, but he was bringing him around. He closed his hand around the door handle, pausing before opening the boardroom door.

"Dissention in the ranks undermines our creative process. Whatever your personal issues are with me, can we at least bury the hatchet until we get this ad for Wonder Man done?"

Harold nodded sharply. "Let's see how the final product turns out," he said resolutely. "Because if your bold, new ideas can't pass muster, I'm letting you know in advance that I'll be requesting you off of my team."

Derek smiled tightly. "Our team, Harold. Our team." He exited the room, easing the door shut behind him.

◇◇◇

As the business day inched closer to quitting time, Derek split the rest of the late afternoon between proactively researching the next product slated to be marketed by Ad Ent, and wrapping up the finer points of his personal design for Wonder Man. He was in the middle of an important call with his photographer to schedule a photo shoot for the ad when his cellphone buzzed on his desk with an incoming call. Derek shrugged his work phone from one ear to the other, leaning forward to glance at the caller ID. "Well, I'll be damned," he murmured in pleasure. It was Adelaide calling.

His photographer repeated his name for the third time. "Are you even listening to me?" he quizzed moodily.

"Huh? Yeah, Franco, I'm listening! Um, so, what are you thinking? Like, all CGI or live action interspersed or…" He continued the conversation and made plans to call Adelaide back after work. Any other day, he might have abandoned the tedium for a quick chat, but this wasn't any other day. Derek was proving himself. As much as he hated it, Harold had been right about his lack of professionalism. Owen's words came to mind: *If you don't like something someone says about you, but it's the truth, then don't get mad at them; change it.*

It was hours later when he clocked out and left, one of the last of the stragglers lingering around on the design floor. He strolled to the elevators, and once on the ground floor he paused at the security desk for a friendly chat. When he made it out to his car in the parking garage, Derek sat in the driver's seat without cranking it up, simply savoring the pleasure of sitting idle. This was the time of day he customarily called Owen, but their conversations were always brief, rarely about anything important.

"Hello?" Adelaide answered on the first ring. He had decided to call her, instead. Owen could wait. The hair on the back of his arm rose at the sound of her voice, and Derek found himself grinning like a lovesick teen.

"Adelaide, hi. I'm sorry I missed your call. It was a bit unexpected since you told me to contact you midweek," he gushed.

She giggled breathlessly. "I did, didn't I? Turns out, I couldn't wait to talk to you again." Derek lifted his brows. She amended, "Well actually, I'm bored with re-reading romance novels and playing on the internet, and I decided I needed some real-live human interaction. So, how's it going?"

"It's going great, now that I'm talking to you," he said. He clamped his teeth over his bottom lip and worked on not sounding too over the top.

"What?" she said with a smile in her voice. "I know it couldn't have been that bad. Talking to me should not be the highlight. Tell me about your job. What'd you do today?"

"Whew! More like what didn't I do," he chuckled. He gave her a brief rundown of the projects he was juggling, and she told him about how she'd been busy booking venues and scheduling entertainers for a series of upcoming events.

"I'm self-employed," she replied, "which people think means I'm basically free to do whatever I want on any given day, but it doesn't. It just means while others work nice, neat, eight to twelve hour shifts, my job is twenty-four seven. I'm still working, actually. Well, working and watching TV."

"Multitasking, I see." Derek heard the beep of a call trying to come through, but he ignored it. When he peeked at the caller, he saw it was just Owen. "What are you watching? Is it something good? I'm into documentaries, mostly."

"Ick! I hate documentaries!" She gave him a rundown of the reality show playing in the background, and Derek scrunched up his nose. She admitted it was a guilty pleasure. "Don't tell anyone, but it's like junk food. You know even the healthiest health nut sneaks a chocolate bar every now and then."

"Eh, I guess," he said skeptically, smiling.

"Headed home? My favorite time of the day used to be right after work, getting home and popping off this bra, dude. I bet you can't wait to get naked soon as you walk through the door. That's the only thing I miss about working a regular nine-to-five. Nowadays, I wear whatever I slept in the night before to work."

He pictured her in a sexy negligee. Derek chuckled. "Yeah, I have an apartment, but it's in the basement of my parents' house. So, there definitely won't be any getting naked in the foyer. I can't wait to move, though. I love my folks and all, but sometimes it's hard to live with them..."

"Can't live without 'em," Adelaide added softly. Derek noted the wistful tone in her voice as he maneuvered smoothly through traffic. "I was in foster care for most of my life, so I wouldn't know. I mean, I guess I would know what it's like to live without them, but not how to live with them, you know? I wouldn't know." She sighed and erupted with self-conscious giggles. "Oh gosh, pay me no mind. Enough of that stuff."

"No, don't clam up," said Derek quietly. "We can talk about anything you want to talk about. I'm sorry you had to go through that. I know that had to be tough, and it still makes you sad. I hear it in your voice."

"It's cool." She took a deep breath and didn't bother expounding on her past life in foster care, but he felt a kinship with the feeling her lengthy inhale conveyed—the feeling of trying to re-center, to pull it all together. Maybe the girl who seemed vibrantly blasé had things that made her feel off balance, too.

"What do you want to talk about, then?" Derek prompted gently.

"Oh, I remember what I wanted to ask you! What are RPGs? You and your friend said something about that, that night we hung out together. You told me you'd explain it later."

Derek held the phone away from his ear at the sound of another beep. He swore softly. It was Owen again. He hit the ignore button and kept talking to Adelaide. A smile touched his lips at Addie's reference to the night they met. "RPGs?" he replied. "Role-playing games. Well, not like in real life, but video games. I'm a real gamer geek."

He started discussing his favorite subject, which Adelaide surprisingly seemed to find interesting. It wasn't until he had made it home that he realized how long the conversation was lasting and that Owen had called a record seven more times.

"Uh, Addie, I don't want to end this wonderful chat, but I really need to call Owen back. He's trying to reach me. Something must be up," he said apologetically. "But, will you hit me up sometime tomorrow?" Derek climbed out of his car and locked the doors, shuffling to the house while he kept the phone tucked between his face and his shoulder, with his keys and briefcase in hand.

"Sure thing," Addie murmured. "Before you go, I didn't get the chance to tell you what a great time I had with you Saturday. I'm really looking forward to seeing you again this weekend."

"The feeling is decidedly mutual," Derek replied. He was still smiling to himself when he hung up the phone and opened the front door to go inside, but the smile slipped from his lips when he saw the text messages that had apparently come in between the back-to-back phone calls from Owen. His attention was diverted away from the texts, however, by the sound of raised voices coming from the living room. Derek paused on the threshold when he heard his name mentioned.

CHAPTER 14

FRANK GROWLED, "HE'S my son, too! You don't think I want the best for him?"

"Not if you want to kick him out on the street!" Lydia countered.

"Honey, don't be histrionic. Derek isn't a little kid anymore. He's an adult, and the only way he'll act like a twenty-nine year old is if we make him. We were already married with a baby by the time we were his age, and *we* got a late start."

"I understand that, Frank. You don't think I understand that? All I'm saying, is he just got out of school—"

"Five years ago."

"—and, he's not financially ready."

"Not financially ready? Heh! We're not rich people, Lydia. We never planned to take care of our grown offspring. We don't have the resources to keep this up! The added utility costs, food costs, the toilet paper, laundry detergent, cleaning supplies—that he doesn't use—and everything else, including this roof over his head, all adds up to a fat monthly allowance that he doesn't deserve!"

Derek wordlessly stepped into the well-decorated but outdated living room. In the crisp, blue suit with the mahogany brown briefcase in hand, and his silky black hair smoothly coiffured, he wasn't dressed for the scene. This was a conversation about a guy who sat around the house and binge-watched TV for hours on end. He wasn't that guy. He was a man who was actively working to be independent, but had a couple of bad breaks and needed a little more time to get on his feet.

He dropped his briefcase with a loud *thump* and his parents, who were glowering mutely at each other, finally noticed him. "Derek..." Lydia rushed toward him with her arms outstretched in motherly concern. Derek held up a hand to halt her.

"You don't think I deserve to be here?" Derek asked hoarsely.

He kept his eyes locked on his father. Frank Cornwell tightened his lips in a frown. He was standing stiffly like a linebacker in front of the fireplace, a bear of a man against the civilized backdrop.

"So, I don't deserve to be here?" Derek repeated angrily.

"No, you don't," Frank replied bluntly. "And, if I didn't pay the mortgage every month, the bank would tell me the same damn thing. Nothing in life is free, Derek. If you don't earn it, then it's charity, a hand out, not something you deserve."

"Hey, I go to work and bust my ass every day! You think I want to be here? You think I want to drain your resources? I have student loans, a car note, car insurance! Oh, did I mention student loans? I am *trying* to save up to buy a house, but I am drowning in debt! It's a damn endless gerbil wheel to nowhere."

Frank nonchalantly lifted his broad shoulders and dropped them. "You know what, I empathize. That's exactly what it feels like sometimes, but welcome to the real world," he quipped cynically.

Lydia sat down heavily on the edge of the buttercream couch, covering her lips in distress at the confrontation. She blinked away tears and glanced around with a lost look. Upon seeing this, Frank's furrowed brow smoothed. He sighed heavily and gestured at a chair. "Have a seat, son."

Derek didn't want to sit, but he did anyway. He took the other end of the couch. His father eased into his overstuffed leather armchair looking nonplussed, ready to have this talk that he'd apparently been holding back from having. Derek never argued with his parents. They had always been good to him. He couldn't understand why they would turn on him.

Frank stated calmly, "Son, I know the economy isn't the best, but you're not destitute. If you were stuck in a dead end job instead of the career you have now, I might not be saying what I'm saying. What you seem to think is that because you have bills to pay, we should support you. The thing is, for the rest of your natural life you're going to be juggling bills. What we're doing by pretending like we can shoulder that burden for you, is we're crippling you, and I won't stand by and let it continue to go on, because you can do better. We can do better."

Derek wanted to hang onto his anger, but what his dad said made sense. Of course, he'd have expenses from now on. He thought bleakly of his monthly income. With what he had left over after bills each pay period, he took home enough for a decent studio apartment, although not much else. Then again, his basement bedroom was nothing more than a glorified studio apartment anyway. It was just that Derek had always seen himself moving out of his parents' house and into a nice starter home.

"He's right, Derek," Lydia replied reluctantly. She sniffled and looked at him with bleary eyes. "But, you know we'll help you as much as we can. I could even do your laundry for you and stop in to help you keep things tidy. A-and, I keep a little purse money. I'll be able to give you a loan if you, you—"

Frank shook his head. "No we won't, Lydia," he stated firmly. "We won't let you starve, Derek. But, you won't get much else other than a hot meal that you'll have to come over here to get—'cause this isn't a delivery service. You need to learn how to take care of yourself. I already know you can do it. You only have to convince your mother here, and you don't want to let her down or she'll never stop coddling you." He gave a crooked smile. Derek's lips involuntarily turned up at the corners.

"Alright," he said gruffly. "I'll start looking at apartments and be out of here by the end of the week." He was stung about getting kicked out, despite understanding what his dad was saying. He crossed his arms and looked away.

Frank let out a soft chuckle at his son's stubbornness. "A week, eh? Well, I'm giving you a full thirty days. No sense in creating unnecessary hurdles for yourself. Sometimes it takes a while to find a place that suits," he replied.

Derek nodded, but he fully intended to be out within a week. He knew it was an ambitious plan. However, he couldn't see himself living there much longer, knowing his parents secretly felt he was draining their meager resources. He left them sitting in the living room and escaped to his bedroom in the basement. What was it he'd been about to do before the unexpected family powwow? Derek dug his cellphone out of his pocket.

The texts were from Owen. He peered at the last frantic message. "Are you okay? WTF Derek? Where are you???"

"This guy," Derek groaned and ran a hand over his face. He called him back. Owen answered in a panic with rapid-fire questions that made Derek scrunch up his face in bemusement.

"What happened? Where are you? I called your parents and neither of them answered—"

"Owen."

"—I called the hospitals. I called the jails—"

"Owen! I'm fine. I saw you calling me, but I was on the phone with Adelaide, and I couldn't take the call right then." The phone went dead silent. Derek thought the call had dropped and pulled the phone away from his ear to check, but the time-ticker was still running. "Hello?"

"Dude," Owen muttered tersely. "You had me worried out of my goddamned mind thinking something terrible had happened to you, picturing you in a car accident or some other type of medical emergency, all because you couldn't spare five seconds to put fucking Adelaide on hold and let me know you were alright?"

The vehemence in his tone made Derek bristle indignantly. "Hey, it's not my fault you let your anxiety get the best of you. Why would you think something was wrong, anyway? People miss calls all the time."

Owen ground out, "We don't ignore each other, Derek! I would never do this to you."

"Don't you think if something bad would've happened to me, my family would've gotten in touch with you?" Derek snickered dismissively. What the hell had gotten into him?

"Why would they, Derek? Think for a second. I'm not your spouse. I'm not a family member. I'm a friend. I'd be the last to know." He bit off his words, and Derek knew Owen was livid. His shoulders dropped as he imagined the amount of fear his best friend had experienced the hour between him getting off work and finally calling him back. If the roles were reversed, he'd be upset, too.

But, Owen was going a little overboard. Derek contritely responded, "Okay man, I'm sorry. I didn't mean to make you worry, and I'll be more mindful of it next time. I got so caught up talking to her. She's one of the most interesting women, seriously. You'd like her."

Owen blew out a breath with an angry growl. "Yeah, whatever. She sounds nice. I'm glad you like her."

"In other news, my parents are kicking me out."

"What?" Owen sounded disoriented by the rapid topic shift.

"Yeah. Dad's giving me thirty days. I told him I'd be out by the end of the week. So, do you know of any places that might be up for rent? Cheap, cheap places," Derek said, chuckling lightly.

"I don't know. Get one of those apartment guides from the kiosk in front of the supermarket. Look, now that I know you're okay, I have to go. I'll talk to you later."

Before Derek could respond back, Owen hung up the phone. Derek stared at his device, perplexed. "What the fuck?" he mused aloud. Derek didn't think their little spat was cut-the-call-short serious. He tried to call him back, but Owen didn't answer. Derek threw his phone onto the bed and laced his fingers through his hair. "Man, whatever," he complained. Owen would realize what a moody bitch he was being, and get over himself eventually.

He sat up wearily so he could take off his good clothes and get a shower. It seemed like his to-do list never shortened. To add to his work woes, he now had to find an apartment and fast.

◇◇◇

Derek scrounged around for something to eat. His mother hadn't held dinner for him. He imagined it was part of Operation Kick Derek out, but it didn't bother him as much now that the idea was firmly planted in his mind that he had to move out. He suddenly began to look at the prospect like a grand adventure. How many times had he said he wished he had his own place? This was the boost he needed. He spent the hours before falling asleep searching out properties online, putting in applications for some.

He searched until his eyes got too heavy to keep them open. When he drifted off to sleep, he found himself again in a familiar dreamscape...

They're in his best friend's backyard by the pool, but the landscape is an impossible palette of hyper-saturated colors. The water is phthalo blue. The sky is the same translucent tint, and the grass is a blinding green.

This time Owen kneels on the pavement before the brown wicker sectional. Derek reclines against cerulean blue pillows. Owen closes his beautiful lips around his swollen shaft, with his fingers caressing and massaging Derek's erection. His mouth is like warm silky honey. His dark, unruly beard brushes like a tickle over Derek's balls. He sucks in a breath and rakes his fingers through Owen's hair, drawing his hand down over Owen's cheek to drag him by the chin up to his lips for a kiss. Their mouths click and release.

Owen drops moist pecks back down his torso and puts his hand to Derek's chest as he lowers his mouth back to his cock. "Ah...Ah," Derek pants. He thrusts up into Owen's deep throat. "Ah!" Owen's head moves faster up and down, as Derek clenches the sides of the seat. Owen claws his nails down Derek's tight stomach.

Through a haze, Derek looks up and sees Adelaide strut toward him. She climbs up onto the sectional to ride his face while Owen fellates him. He closes his lips around Addie's pulsating clit, and sucks her throbbing erogenous zone in tandem to the way Owen sucks him. It's give, and take, and get. Derek trembles in agony and ecstasy. She squirms, crying out, grinding harder against his face.

The sounds of her quest for climax echo through the quiet outdoor landscape. She tastes like sweet summer rain. Derek clutches her hips and guides her over-excited body down to the sectional beside him, ready to give her the penetration for which she begs. He reluctantly pushes Owen's face away from his erection, and turns Addie around to make her lean over the sectional. He closes his hands over hers, admiring the way that she rests on her knees with her ass wagging salaciously as he positions himself behind her.

Owen daringly drags his hands over Derek's taut ass, as Derek pushes into Addie's saturated womanhood. She lets out a primal yowl of pleasure. She pushes her bottom back to envelope him to the hilt with her glorious-feeling sheath. He knows it feels good to her by the way her body begins to throb and pulsate around him. Her juices flow copiously over his shaft, as he thrusts in and swirls his hardness around, stroking every inch of her.

"Unh! Adelaide, yes," he growls. Gripping her by the shoulders, he stares down at the perfect dip of her spine, the way her bottom jiggles as he spears into her. When he glances over to his side, he sees Owen watching, waiting, stroking his stiff hard-on with powerful hands.

Then, he feels her thighs quake, and Adelaide throws her head back to stare blindly at the sun with wanton cries of abandonment. Derek fondles her breasts while he takes her. Feeling her rhythmically squeeze and release and squeeze his swollen cock in her inner grip makes him gasp her name hoarsely. Derek passionately grabs a fistful of her hair to draw her mouth to his, to kiss her as he pumps into her. Her moans pour into his mouth until he lets her go.

Owen, with an aroused sharp intake of air, clasps Derek's buttocks to make him plunge in and out of Addie even harder. He masturbates against Derek's outer thigh, and he gingerly collects a bead of pre-cum off the tip of his turgid cock and places it to Derek's lips. Derek sucks Owen's finger into his mouth, sucks as if he's returning the fellatio favor, sucks until Owen gasps with need. Owen tugs his wet digit out of Derek's mouth and erotically circles Derek's asshole with it.

Derek jerks, spasms in Addie's sweet, sweet body in response to Owen's touch. "Jesus, god!" he groans. He glances over his shoulder at his sexy male best friend repositioning himself behind him.

With trembling lips, Derek turns back to kiss Addie's neck, her shoulder, the column of her spine, but Owen possessively tangles his fingers in Derek's hair, and draws him around to kiss him instead. Owen plunders his mouth. Derek's thrusts become uncontrolled, frantic, ready. Growling with unchecked desire, he hammers into Addie so fiercely that she digs her fingernails into his thighs with growing excitement. Her tight vagina spasms again in a rippling wave around his thick shaft. Derek exhales and goes weak in the knees with indescribable pleasure, but Owen holds him up with a bracing arm around his waist.

Owen drops to his knees and drags his hands to Derek's hips to hold him steady, as he dips his moist tongue into the crease of Derek's buttocks. His silky tongue makes a wicked exploration. "Oh, don't stop," Addie coos urgently and Derek whimpers, overwhelmed with ecstasy as he gives her what she asks. He plows inside of her, reaching back to guide Owen's head.

But, Owen needs no guidance to lick and play. He sucks at the *winking hole and buries his tongue inside of him. Derek thrusts deeper into Adelaide and back out to meet Owen's tongue—in and out, licked and laved, penetrated and penetrating.*

Owen rises to his feet and presses his tumescent member to Derek's body, inch by inch, slowly muscling his entire, massive cock into his tight hole. The feeling of fullness surpasses anything he's ever experienced, making Derek grunt and moan tremulously, and fuck Addie harder as Owen fucks him. It's the most intense thing Derek has ever imagined. It takes a moment for them to get the swing of things, but when their thrusts fall in sync, it's like a dance he's known all along. Derek marvels at the ebb and flow.

He hears Owen panting against the back of his neck. Owen's sweat drips down the small of his back. Owen's hard, goddamned beautiful cock paints his insides with rapturous ecstasy. Each thrust into his body makes Derek feel closer to letting go, and the combined effect of Adelaide's silky, wet, tight womanhood massaging up and down his quivering manhood is the icing on the cake.

She starts to come with a tremor and a quake as Owen thrusts deeper, harder, faster. A series of loud cries of rapture blast from her mouth. Owen growls, "I'm. About. To. Come! Ah!" His nails dig into Derek's narrow hips as he pumps, pumps, pumps until he can move no more and his ejaculation releases into Derek's ass, adding to the wonder.

"Wait, wait, wait," Derek cries, unable to keep his own climax at bay. "Don't stop! I don't want to stop! Wait." But his protests can't save him from himself. Derek's climax strikes with such potency that he feels like his very being shatters. He lets out a long, hoarse wail with release...coming undone...coming un...done...coming.

Derek groaned as he rolled over and squeezed his eyes shut tighter. When he opened them, he stared bleakly at the rafters of the basement ceiling, lost in the transitional reverie between sleep and waking   life.

CHAPTER 15

SHE SENT HIM a selfie in her running clothes by text the next morning. It read, "Making up for the carnival food. WYA?" Adelaide was a heart-stopper in a snug pink halter top straining to contain her ample breasts, and black spandex capris molded perfectly to her round, sexy ass. It was a welcome wake-up call. Derek smiled sleepily as he composed a good-morning response, and then rolled out of bed with renewed determination. Not only did he have to put in a full day's work, he had to fit finding an apartment into his busy schedule. So, he didn't linger around shooting cute little emoticons back and forth. He told her he couldn't wait to talk to her after work.

He went about his usual morning routine and made it to the office with plans to complete his personal project, and start working on how he would present it to Mr. Clancy. The most surprising development was the turnaround of the attitude of his other team members. His email inbox was loaded with messages about the group ad, and it only took him a second to realize the reason; they had added him back to the email CC list.

Derek squeezed apartment searches in during his breaks, and he took note of the most promising prospects. By lunch time, he felt like he had done the work of ten men. He slumped back in his desk and peeked at his cellphone to see if Owen had called or texted. He smacked his lips in irritation when there were no new notifications.

"Good afternoon, Mr. Cornwell," Libby Sullivan whispered sexily. She had an arm draped over his cubicle wall and was staring down at him like a cat watching a mouse. Derek shifted in his office chair uneasily. Ever since his wardrobe change, she had been giving him the eye.

"Ms. Sullivan, what can I do for you?" He put professional distance in his tone so as not to give her the wrong idea. He could be polite, friendly even, but damn sure not flirtatious with a coworker. Clearing her throat and straightening up with a tug at the hem of her short skirt, Libby smiled nervously.

"I was just wondering if you'd like to have lunch with me," she said hopefully.

Derek rarely had lunch with anyone from the office. He liked to keep to himself, and he was about to tell her exactly that. However, it occurred to him that becoming a team player meant more than showing up at brainstorming sessions with his immediate coworkers. There was no harm in sharing a meal in the very public breakroom where she couldn't put the moves on him. If Mr. Clancy, their supervisor, happened to see him being less of a loner and a little more social, then that was even better.

"You know what, why not? I could use a break."

"Yes!" she enthusiastically squealed. He chuckled and clocked out, following the attractive, young secretary, who skipped ahead of him with pleasure at having her offer accepted. Derek reached in the chrome double-door community fridge and took out the turkey wrap he'd picked up from a fast food place on the way to work.

"Which one is yours?" he asked helpfully.

"The veggie tray. I'm on a diet. Gotta lose ten pounds," she laughed self-deprecatingly. Derek looked her up and down. The only place she could stand to lose any weight from was maybe her bouffant hairstyle.

"Here you go." He handed her the small tray she had indicated and sat down across from her.

The clunky breakroom tables were functional, cube-shaped sculptures, and had room for four chairs that fit snuggly into recesses like a puzzle. They came in muted pastels. The space had artsy light fixtures and frosted glass cabinetry, and the many houseplants suspended from hooks near the wall of windows and perched on top of the cabinets gave it a homey feel. There were a few other people enjoying quiet conversations and quick food alongside them. Derek figured he'd just have to deliver some small talk, some gregarious smiles, and he'd be home free.

Libby crossed her long legs and stared invitingly at him from across the table. Her high-heeled foot grazed the inner curve of his calf, and her lips curled upward. She nibbled on a bright orange baby carrot with her eyebrow quirked. "You know, you have really been turning heads, lately. You're the buzz around the watercooler."

"Humph! Is that so? I hadn't noticed. I've been, um, kind of focused." He pointed ahead with both hands. She kept smiling and dipped another carrot in Ranch dressing, then sucked the creamy whiteness off the orange tip. He looked down with an uncomfortable chuckle.

"Let me be the first to say, you are quite the catch," she replied coyly.

"Well, thank you."

"Any lucky lady in your life?"

Technically, no. "Actually, yes. Um, her name is Adelaide."

"Oh, is that so?" Libby pouted cutely.

"I don't want to jinx it, but we've hit it off pretty nicely. She could be the one." It was speculation, but not quite a lie.

Libby rolled her eyes melodramatically. She leaned in casually, dropping the sex kitten act, which made Derek inhale deeply with relief. "Well, what's she like? How long have you guys been going out? Does she work here? Do I know her?"

Her line of questioning was simple curiosity and nothing more, he deduced. Libby was the office gossip, not the office tart. He launched into a description of Addie as she nodded and asked more questions, raptly attentive. He chose his words carefully, but less than a half hour lunch break later, she had pried the whole story out of him and was ready to give him advice.

"So, you went out with her one time and she's already sending you good morning texts?" Libby put a celery stalk between her teeth as she shook her head. "She's got it bad for you, Mr. Derek. It's easy to see why, but...well, just watch out for girls who move too fast."

Derek quirked a brow. "Nah, she's harmless. I don't think she's moving too fast. She's just straightforward. Some guys are into the chase. I hate misleading games, so she's exactly my kind of girl."

"I guess..." Libby shrugged and gazed skyward with a hum.

"Take it from me, though. A lot of women have attachment issues, and those issues come out in *all* different kinds of ways—too clingy, not affectionate enough. Sometimes we miss the signs a guy is interested and don't connect until it's too late, and other times we connect way ahead of time. Don't get me wrong. Guys are like that too, but hell hath no fury like a woman scorned."

They put away their empty lunch trays, and Derek walked Libby back to the design department. "In my opinion, she's not moving too fast," he reiterated.

"Like I said, watch your back, Casanova. Talk to you later, Mr. Cornwell. Nice having lunch with you. We've gotta do that again sometime! And, good luck with your *lo~ove* interest," she said in a teasing tone. "Hmm, I just wish I would've gotten to you first." She grinned and poked him in the chest. Derek blushed. He waved goodbye as he left her at the front desk and hurried back to his cubicle.

He took a minute to see if Owen had tried to get in touch with him, and when he didn't see any missed calls or texts on his cellphone, he threw it back on his desk in frustration. He did, however, have a handwritten message for a missed call to his office line from one of the apartment complexes where he had sent an application. "Shit, I hate I missed that," Derek muttered to himself. He picked up the phone and quickly called them back. He didn't need to pass on any opportunities at getting a new place because thus far his search had come up dry, and he was running out of time.

When he got someone on the line, he found out there was a vacancy, a two bedroom townhouse at the upper limits of his budget but still reasonably priced for the amount of square footage advertised on the website. He figured he could cough up the extra money if the place turned out to be a keeper, and Derek made arrangements with the leasing manager to do a walk-through after work. No sense in letting someone else snatch it up. Deals like that moved fast.

He played with some numbers in his head to determine the feasibility of taking on the added cost, especially for space he didn't necessarily need. But, considering the small size of his budget, the place was a steal. Derek took another look at the site where he had found the listing. There weren't many pictures, which was disconcerting; however, the description listed all the basic amenities. It was worth a peek.

An hour before his usual clock-out time, he met up with his photographer and got the stills for his personal project. He was the last man standing when the lights went out over the main floor. Derek flipped on his personal lamp and finished up, and when Mr. Clancy happened to surprise him by strolling by his cubicle, he mentally applauded himself for putting in the extra work. "You're really impressing me, kid," Mr. Clancy murmured in passing with a smile. Derek nodded meekly and continued working. There was nothing left pending by the time he left the building for the Ad Ent parking garage.

Thinking of how proud he was for actually sticking to his goal to revamp his life, Derek used his hands-free device to call Owen and see what was up with him being missing in action. None of this would have been possible without his best friend. He realized that, and Owen needed to realize how much he needed him and stop being a dick.

"C'mon, pick up," he muttered. Derek hopped into his Mazda, listening to the phone ring and ring on Owen's end. He was about to hang up when Owen finally answered.

"Yeah?" Owen greeted Derek laconically.

"Yo! I thought you were avoiding me, or something. What's up? I know you can't be still mad about me missing your calls yesterday." Owen didn't respond. Derek blinked in annoyance. "O…kay…well, are we still doing this Reshaping Derek thing? Because, so far your life coaching skills have changed every aspect of my life, and I can't repay you for everything you've done for me if you're no longer talking to me." He smiled as he hit the highway. Visions from the dream the night before resurfaced. Derek gripped the steering wheel tighter.

"Yeah, you know what, I'm probably going to be tied up all week. Maybe after I free up some time, we can move forward. You don't need me, though. You never really did," Owen commented caustically.

Derek gnawed on his lower lip. He didn't want to point out how much his best friend was sounding like a spurned lover. He also didn't want to examine how that made him feel—all tingly with anticipation on the inside. "Alright, cool…well, hit me up when you get some free time," he mumbled.

"Yeah."

"Bye?" Derek prompted. Owen hung up the phone. Derek started to call him back and tell him off about this second time hanging up in his face, but he resisted the urge. He couldn't wait to talk to Adelaide about the rift in his friendship so he could vent and de-stress, but first he had to check out his potential new place.

The townhouse was located in a fairly new complex. The sun hadn't set yet when Derek parked his car and jetted into the leasing office for his scheduled meeting with the manager. "I was beginning to think you weren't going to make it!" she said when she answered the door. The property manager was a dowdy, middle-aged woman wearing a floral mu-mu and scuffed pink flats. The cloying odor of tobacco smoke clung to her, and she had an unlit cigarette clutched expectantly between two pink press-on nails. She patted her mousy brown curls and smiled at him.

Derek extended a hand in greeting. "I'm terribly sorry about being late, ma'am. I'm Derek Cornwell. We spoke on the phone about me taking a peek at a two bedroom."

"Of course," she said, turning aside to cough into her shoulder. She loudly cleared her throat, then gave him a once over. "You're not what I pictured. Ah, well, you better be glad you skated in before I left. I sometimes lock up early so I can get home before the worst of the evening traffic. I got my stories to watch, and what not. But, right this way, Mr. Cornwell. If we make it quick, I might not miss 'em."

The nameplate on her cluttered desk read 'Anna Ringwald'. Anna drew a bulky set of keys out of a desk drawer and beckoned for him to take a walk with her. They exited the cramped leasing office. Derek peered around to gauge his surroundings. There were plenty of cars in the parking lot, at least two of them sitting up on cinderblocks, unusable. He spied a rusty jungle gym and broken swings in a courtyard at the center of the property. But, the lawn was well kept.

Anna led him to a unit near the leasing office and used the big bundle of keys to let them inside. The first thing he noticed was the smell. It was a nasty perfume of dank mustiness and more stale cigarette smoke. There was an open floorplan, and from the door he could see the kitchen separated from the living room by a countertop with a marbled plastic veneer. The low ceiling gave the room an oppressive feel. Natty beige carpet with an old-fashioned shag weave covered the floor.

"And, is this the one that's vacant?" Derek asked fearfully. From his vantage point, there was nothing about the townhome that appealed to him. He prayed there was another unit, one that was more modern and didn't smell like regrets.

The property manager shiftily glanced to the left as she responded. "Well, we have units come available at all times. Your deposit will secure the size townhome you want—you know, one bedroom, two bedrooms, and whatnot. But, what everybody raves about is all this space. You won't find more square footage nowhere else with a rent like ours." Her smile was too big.

Derek peeked into the kitchen. He saw a stove, and a fridge that was canted unevenly to one side. There wasn't a dishwasher. He walked into the small room and looked around. His loafers stuck to the tacky linoleum. Someone had mopped with dirty mop water, and the residue was sticky. He frowned in distaste. There were grease stains on the backsplash behind the stove. Dust clung to the popcorn ceiling overhead, and an ancient sprinkler was caked in so much grime that it took him a second to realize what it actually was.

"Online you said all units are equipped with a dishwasher. I don't see any," he replied, looking around with distaste at what he did see. There was a large scorch mark on the plastic counter next to the stove. He leaned forward and peered down the dark hallway, reluctant to even step into the two bedrooms if the main living space room looked like this.

"Well, we haven't had the chance yet to update the stuff on that internet, but we had to take those dishwashers out of some units because tenants were complaining about them running up their power bills." Anna sniffed. Derek wondered if there had ever been a dishwasher in the first place.

He quirked a brow. "So, these aren't energy efficient appliances?"

"Well—"

"Never mind. I appreciate you taking the time to show me the townhome, but I think I want to keep looking around," he interrupted.

Derek forced himself not to run out of the dingy place. He speed-walked straight to his car, and when he got behind the wheel, he allowed himself a fleeting moment of disappointment before he cranked up and sped off. Well, at least Anna would get home early enough to catch her 'stories and what not' now. He had had such high hopes. "Back to the drawing board," he muttered to himself. He wasn't ready to give up yet. He couldn't. He had a point to prove.

CHAPTER 16

IT WAS MIDWEEK. With one major task out of the way, Derek was facing another uphill battle. His personal project and presentation for the Wonder Man ad were both ready to show Mr. Clancy, and the group ad was on schedule to be finished by the Friday deadline. It was the apartment search that was giving him fits.

Derek sat at his cubicle with his work phone pressed to his ear and a hopeless expression painted on his face as he stared blankly at the computer screen. Yet another property manager was telling him he didn't meet the qualifications. He blew out an exasperated breath. "Yes, but how do you expect people to provide a rental history if they've never rented from anywhere? I'm trying to create a rental history."

"We're sorry, Mr. Cornwell, but should anything change about the status of your application, we'll be sure to let you know. Have a nice day."

Derek slammed the phone into the cradle and covered his face with his hands. He had bitten off more than he could chew, but the only option was to swallow, and try not to choke. His dad had affixed a calendar to the refrigerator at home, marking down the thirty days, giving Derek all the more reason to want to be out sooner rather than later.

He was tired and cranky after staying up half the night talking to Adelaide, though he wouldn't have cut that call short for anything in the world. He closed his eyes and played it back as he sat at his desk. He had caught her fresh out of the shower, and she had sounded sultry as sin, telling him she was lying in bed thinking of him. When Derek voiced he was doing the same thing, thinking about her, she had taken the playful banter a step further and described in exquisite detail the kinky fantasies she was entertaining.

He pictured her dragging her fingertips over her pink pearl, the way she had described. He imagined her hair fanned out on her pillow and her beautiful face screwed up in a passionate scowl. He heard again her breathless whispers as she talked about it. How she told him she was so wet that the moisture was soaking through her cotton panties. How her breasts hurt so bad from needing to be sucked. Derek shook out of his reverie, but he was itching to see Adelaide again, so he could make her lusty promises of the night before a reality.

Derek had other things on his mind when he got off work and made his way to the parking garage. He was puzzling over how to fix things between him and Owen. Once again, he gave him a call on his way to his car, and Owen didn't answer. Derek sent him a text to let him know he was trying to get in touch with him, even though he knew Owen could see for himself that he wanted to talk to him. It was pointless to keep playing phone tag.

They had never spent more than a handful of hours not communicating with each other. This was a record—two days straight. He missed his friend, but he was determined to give Owen space and time to get over what Derek considered an overkill response. As always happened when he thought about Owen these days, his fickle brain turned back to Addie when he couldn't get through to his boy.

The conversation with her the night before hadn't been all phone sex. Before diving into dirty deeds, Addie had surprised him by candidly confessing, "You think I'm jaded, don't you?" As he sat at his desk, he could again hear her silky voice whispering through the phone last night.

"I wouldn't say that. Not exactly. I consider you pragmatic. It just takes some getting used to. I'm a little more idealistic."

"I used to be." She snorted, giggling. "I mean, like, as a kid or whatever. I guess I had a less than ideal childhood. Taught me early."

"What do you mean?" he asked, curious about her.

"I dunno. I was bounced around from one foster family to another. I saw enough to make me question human decency. I hate talking about it. Can we change the subject?" She chuckled nervously on the other end of the phone.

He shrugged and rolled over in the bed. "Sure, my beautiful cynic. We can talk about whatever you like."

"Ha! I'm not a cynic. I'm just saying. I witnessed these perfect potential moms and dads—who welcomed me with seemingly open arms—become something else entirely behind closed doors. I'm talking conniving wives, cheating husbands, shoddy parenting—the whole nine yards. Any cliché of the fucked up American dysfunctional family, I've seen it. Needless to say, I was thoroughly schooled in keeping up with appearances while hiding my inner demons."

He wondered if her description was how she saw herself—a beautiful monster. He had been warned of her fangs, but he hadn't seen them. Derek was beginning to believe she was simply misunderstood. If given half the chance, he might be able to show her she didn't need them. Not with him.

He dialed Adelaide's number as he hit the road. "It's midweek," he greeted her when she answered. Addie's infectious laughter poured over the phone.

"It is midweek. I guess you want to know how we stand on that coffee date. Well, what if I tell you I'm free tonight, and I want to see you."

Derek's eyes widened. "Hmm, I'd say that can be arranged. Where would you like me to pick you up?"

"Hang up. I'll text you my address," she murmured in an unmistakably inviting tone.

He couldn't hang up fast enough. It took him close to forty-five minutes to find her apartment. It was on the other side of the city, approaching the outskirts. Derek found her waiting for him outside her front door with a designer hand-bag on her shoulder, ready to go, and he suppressed a tiny, ungracious sense of disappointment at realizing she wasn't intending on inviting him up. The sentiment was soon replaced by pleasure at the chance just to see her, however.

She was standing there in a shirt-dress that fell mid-thigh, loose and flowing, the top buttons free to expose the hills of her breasts. Tanned legs extended what looked like miles. Her glistening honey blonde hair was pulled up in a careless top-knot with wispy strands escaping around her angular face, and her nose ring glinted in the setting sun. Her burgundy painted smile revealed gleaming, white teeth.

There was nothing not to like about her.

Powering down his window, he stuck his head out of the car. "Where to, hitchhiker?" he asked.

She grinned and ran around to the passenger door. Adelaide hopped in the car and spontaneously pulled him into a hug. Derek inhaled. She smelled like lemon grass and oleander. "Hey, you," she whispered. Derek pulled back before his libido pushed him to do more than hug her. "I've been craving ice cream all evening, but I didn't feel like going out. What do you say we find us an ice cream shop?"

"That sounds like a plan, and I happen to have cause to celebrate. Guess who finished the impossible in less than two weeks."

"Ooh, tell me more," she cooed playfully. "I love the sound of success."

"Well, it's nothing much, but…" She pulled on her seatbelt and directed him to the nearest ice cream place, as Derek regaled her with the latest goings-on at work, from the solidarity of his team members to his satisfaction with his personal project. "I have little doubt that my supervisor will be wowed by the presentation on Friday."

They walked into the retro looking ice cream shop, with its checkerboard floor pattern, and blue and pink neon lights tracing along its walls. A long counter boasted old-fashioned soda machines at one end, and toward the far wall were display cases filled with enticing flavors of ice cream. Derek and Addie ambled over and peered down at their choices. There were rows and rows of colorful, thick, creamy ice cream studded with fruit and candies. More sugary treats filled glass jars atop the display cases to be used to garnish the scoops. There were flavored syrups, whipped creams, nuts, and berries.

Adelaide was the proverbial kid in a candy shop, and her face registered bliss. "I think that success story deserves more than two scoops," she winked. "A gallon of lemon custard, please," she told Derek.

"A gallon?" Derek chuckled and moved over to the register to order the flavor she selected, but he turned to her and whispered, "Just know that I didn't tempt you with sweets this time. This is all your doing. And, how do you propose we keep a gallon of ice cream from melting while we're out and about, hm?"

"Oh, honey, we're going back to my place." The suggestive way she said it made Derek hum speculatively.

The attendant rang him up and slipped through a door marked 'Employees Only', returning a few minutes later with a lidded bucket labeled with graphics of sunny lemons. Adelaide clapped her hands together in delight. Derek made a mental note to bring chocolates the next time he came to see her, just to see how she'd react to that. He had once read somewhere that people who enjoyed sweets tended to be sweet. He could vouch for the statement as applied to Adelaide. She smiled and accepted their order, leading him out the door and back to his car with a seductive sway of her hips.

Derek hesitantly entered her apartment a few minutes later. He hadn't known what to expect, but Adelaide's abode was much like the woman herself—spontaneous and free-spirited. Bold red paint on an accent wall drew attention to a massive framed piece of art, beneath which a white leather sofa took up floor space. On the opposite wall was a mounted flat-screen. The floors were a dark hardwood, and a black rug covered most of it. There were two squat accent chairs facing a love seat that matched the sofa.

"Would you like a tour?" she asked. Adelaide ambled into her kitchen and popped on a light, and the apartment was illuminated. She pulled down two bowls and started dishing up ice cream.

"I don't want to invade your space," he said. He sat gingerly on the edge of the couch. "Your place is nice."

She returned and took a seat on one of the accent chairs, and she settled their bowls on the white coffee table in front of them. "Thank you. I've been here for a year, almost. When my lease is up, I'm thinking about moving."

"Well, if you hear of any vacancies, let me know. I'm in the market." Derek absently pulled his phone out of his pocket and checked to see if Owen had responded to his messages or phone calls. He hadn't. Derek sighed in frustration.

"What is it?" Addie asked curiously. "Am I cutting into someone else's time?" She smiled devilishly, as if she didn't care if she was. He shook his head with a grin.

"Not at all. I was just trying to see if my best friend, Owen, had gotten back to me. He hasn't. He's been, uh…kind of upset with me for the past few days. Ever since I started hanging out with you. We usually do everything together."

At that comment, she brightened with recognition. "Oh, Owen is the guy who was with you the night we met, right?"

Derek blushed a deep shade of crimson as he connected what he'd said and her response. He laughed good-naturedly. "Yeah, yeah. I've been telling him he'd really like hanging out with you, but he's…I dunno…he never gets serious about women. He's something of a playboy, which is kind of crazy because he's one of the most loving, nurturing guys. Real relationship material. You'd like him if you had the chance to hang around him. He has a great personality. Like, every chick I know digs him."

She smiled as she ate a spoonful of lemon custard ice cream, staring at Derek inquisitively. "Hmm. Well, you rarely talk about him. The night we met, I got the impression you and him were pretty *close* friends, but then I figured you must not be."

"What? No, we've been friends since we were knee-high, man." Derek leaned back. It was complicated. He couldn't explain why he refrained from mentioning Owen when he was around Adelaide. The way the two of them were tangled up in his fantasies, he was afraid she'd be instantly aware of the underlying attraction, and he couldn't have that. "I don't think guys sit around talking about their friends like girls do," he joked.

She shrugged. "I've always been better at making friends with guys than with other girls. Gah, women talk about the most inane stuff. Bestie this and bestie that. I keep a distance because if I haven't known you since I was ten, then we're probably not bestie anything," she said with a laugh.

Derek shifted uncomfortably, thinking about what Steve had said about her male friends. He tasted his ice cream. The lemon custard had a smooth, zesty flavor he instantly liked. He had never tried it before, and he told her as much. "I think this might be my new favorite flavor."

"Ah, god, yes! It's my all-time favorite. Next time we have to get the pistachio, though. Have you ever tried it? Mm, and when I get the chance I'm going to bake you my famous ooey gooey cake. Baking is one of my hobbies."

"So, about these mostly male friends of yours," he interjected. "Do you ever run into any issues with men you date when you tell them you have a lot of guy friends?"

"I don't date much," she confessed. She laughed. "Look at you, prying for information! First of all, I don't have a lot of guy friends. I said I find it easier to make friends with guys than I do with girls. But, rest assured, when I do date, the gentleman is usually mature enough to understand a friend is just a friend."

Derek narrowed his eyes and studied her beautiful face. As lovely as she was—independent, intelligent, and appealing as she was—it was hard to picture her single for long. "Why don't you date much?"

With a sigh, Adelaide drew her knees up, clearly contemplating how best to answer. She seemed hesitant to talk about it, and Derek figured he probably shouldn't have asked. He was irritated with himself for even caring so much. He knew he sounded insecure, at best. He just really, really…really liked this girl. *Three really's.*

"Derek, I have to be honest with you. I don't like to be tied down. You're…a very nice guy," Adelaide said soberly.

He groaned inwardly. "No, I wasn't trying to tie you down," he tried to say. She waved her hands to halt him.

"What I'm saying is, usually when we get to this point in the conversation, it's because someone is feeling the p-word."

"What?"

She whispered dramatically with widened eyes. "Possessive." Derek stared at her. She giggled and looked away.

"That sounds like a horror movie," he laughed.

"I know, right? It is!" she heartily agreed, chuckling too. "I tell people all the time, I'm a woman, not property. You cannot possess me."

He let out a low sigh. "Well, I'm not trying to possess you. Let's get that clear. But I take it what you're telling me is, I'm barking up the wrong tree if I'm looking for anything more than long talks, hugs, and fist pumps, right?"

She scrunched up her nose and canted her head to the side with a half-smile. "Not necessarily…when I fall, I fall hard. It's hard to get over. So, I just have to make sure that the guy I'm choosing to be with matches me best."

"We have nothing in common," he admitted.

A defeatist mood descended over him, as Derek told himself Owen had been right. It was a waste of time finding her. It would be so much more disappointing to lose her after spending this short time around her and becoming completely enraptured by her. Derek set aside the suddenly unappetizing ice cream and mentally prepared himself to enter the friend zone. In a few weeks, he'd be the guy she went to amusement parks with and talked on the phone to about the jerk who was getting the chance to screw her every night.

She surprised him when she said, "Having very little in common makes things interesting."

Derek settled back on her leather couch and watched her play with the rest of her ice cream. She swirled her tongue around her spoon. "You're looking for someone who matches with you, yet you're telling me having almost nothing in common makes things interesting. Can I just say that you're sending mixed signals?" he asked with a wry grin.

"Can I admit that it's probably because I haven't quite figured you out, yet? The night I met you, things were straightforward—wham, bam, thank you, ma'am."

Derek leaned forward, his eyebrows clashing together to protest the crudity of her assessment of what for him had been more like a spiritual experience. "No, it wasn't like that."

"Of course it was! It was a one-night stand," she replied pragmatically. "It went exactly as it should have."

"Wow. If you're looking for a best match, let me recommend Owen, because you two sound exactly alike right now."

"We're not talking about Owen right now. We're talking about you." She ran her bare toes up along his inner leg. Derek glanced down at her pedicured foot and back up to her eyes. "You know, I never expected you to reach out to me. I guess I was so surprised to see your text message that day that I simply reacted instead of thinking things through. Now that I've gotten to know you a little bit, however... I have no idea what to do with you, Derek Cornwell."

"I'm not willing to get my heart broken," she murmured.

"I'm   willing   to   risk   it,"   he   admitted.

CHAPTER 17

ADELAIDE VERY DELIBERATELY began unbuttoning her dress one slow loop at a time as Derek watched, mesmerized. Her plush breasts popped free of the loose cotton shift but were still encased in a black lace bra. She let the dress drop from her shoulders, swish down her hourglass torso and pool around her wide, womanly hips. With an inhale through clenched teeth, she stared at him from beneath dark, sooty lashes as she boldly took the cups of her bra in hand and drew them down so that her breasts were completely exposed. The bronze globes quivered deliciously.

She leaned back in the chair with her shapely legs spread and the tips of her toes touching the floor. "Do you think he's jealous because of me?" she murmured.

"W-what?" Derek stammered, her question the last thing he thought she would say at that moment.

Addie grabbed her bowl of ice cream from the side table and swirled her spoon around in the cold, milky treat, drawing a dollop of lemon custard ice cream to her lips. Adelaide caught a droplet with the tip of her tongue and let the rest dribble from the spoon in a careless ribbon of melted liquid crisscrossing her cleavage. She gasped at the chill, shivering erotically. Her dark gaze dropped sexily down to her body, then back up to Derek's eyes.

"You've been spending a lot of time with me lately. Do you think he could be jealous?" she repeated.

"Owen knows I'm not casting him aside. I hope he's not jealous.

I've p-put up with him standing me up to be with his girls in the past, so he should be able to handle the same." Derek tugged at the collar of his shirt. Things were getting hotter.

She tittered with amusement as she stroked the spoon down her stomach, pausing with the spoon at the waistband of her black satin panties. "No, silly. I mean do you think it bothers him that you got the girl! I mean, you both met me at the same time, but…you got me." She casually lifted her shoulder and gave him a sideways glance. A playful smile came to her lips. She naughtily slipped the ice-cold silver spoon into her black satin panties and swished it slowly across her clit. Derek watched her with baited breath.

"I…I, uh, hadn't really thought about…"

She beckoned for him. Derek moved abruptly from the chair where he was sitting, to the floor before her. He gazed up as she removed the spoon and placed it to his tongue. With a soft moan, he licked off a taste of ice cream and Addie. She lifted a dainty foot and put it on his shoulder, hooked it behind his neck and dragged him forward. Derek buried his face in the fragrant crotch of her panties and inhaled her enticing pheromones. He nipped at her through the thin fabric. His mouth closed over her mound. She rose off the chair in her passion to be devoured, and he drew her down onto the floor with him.

Derek shoved her dress up to her waist and stretched out atop her nubile, semi-naked body. Her feverish skin burned beneath his lips as he placed them to her throbbing pulse and sucked the side of her neck. He raked his teeth over her collarbone. She whimpered as he followed the trail of ice cream she had painted over her beautiful breasts, licking and sucking the sticky cream until there was nothing left. He left her aching with need. He suckled her pert nipples until her breasts were heavy and engorged with desire, while he ground his pelvis against hers. She clung to him, wriggling against his body impatiently.

"Wouldn't you be jealous?" she panted, tearing off his shirt. "Wouldn't you be jealous if you couldn't have me?" Her mouth flew to his chest. She sucked his nipples the way he had sucked hers. Pleasure like a trigger wire tightened from his chest to his groin. Derek groaned, pushing her back down to the floor.

Her thighs dropped open, and he ducked his face to the fount between her legs. Adelaide clawed at the floor. He steadied her bucking hips and closed his lips over her vagina in an intimate tongue kiss through her panties. He pushed the barrier aside. She tore at his hair as he hummed against her body, mouth wide, with his tongue flicking rapidly up and down her clit. Sweeping around and down into her slit, he lapped at her delectable pussy.

He fired a thin stream of saliva at her clit and closed his entire mouth over her most erogenous zone, to suck and nibble as she cried out. She was so fucking wet. She clutched the back of his head and bumped her throbbing pussy into his mouth, grinding and groaning. Adelaide fucked his face. The scent of her, the taste of her, the feel of her had his cock so hard he felt like he would burst through his own skin.

Derek pulled away to take off his pants and free his erection. He burst out of his boxers and closed his fist around his meaty shaft. Adelaide grabbed his member. He pushed her back and wedged himself between her legs. He snatched the panties down her thick thighs, and the satin ripped as he tore them off of her. He was stiff and so ready, and watching her writhe on the floor, begging him to put it inside her only heightened his need. He stopped, breathing heavily.

There was something missing. He squeezed his eyes shut and tried not to think about the wild dreams that had plagued him for nights on end. He could almost feel Owen's hands and lips, could barely picture having sex with Adelaide without him.

"What is it?" Addie asked breathlessly. "Do you need a rubber?"

Derek reached for his jeans and dug a condom out of his wallet, wrestling it onto his turgid member and hurriedly coming back to her. She was so eager, she could barely get his cock inside of her fast enough. He looked up as her head dropped back and she let herself go, accepting the pleasure with abandonment as he thrust himself inside of her pliable body. Derek ducked his head to her breasts and licked her round, dark nipples. Her mouth fell open in a loud moan.

Derek put his fingers to her neck and, gritting his teeth, plowed into her. She reached down to touch herself while he stroked in and out, savoring the dewy wetness covering his cock. She pulled her fingers away and shoved them in his mouth. He thought about Owen in the dream, wetting his fingers and fondling his ass so exquisitely it had made him want to explode.

"Addie," he gasped. Derek hitched in a breath and jerked his dick out of her grip. He had almost climaxed. He squeezed the base of his shaft, swearing softly. She felt so damn perfect, but it was the flashback of the dream that had almost done him in.

Adelaide shoved him off and took control, clambering astride his hips. He gripped her ass while she brought her tight snatch down around his swollen member, and the rain slick entrance tightened to a vise around his pulsating cock once she got all of him inside. He exhaled and his eyes fluttered with ecstasy. She felt better than a dream.

Her ass wiggled in a circle as she squeezed her inner muscles and fucked him so expertly, that his toes curled and his eyes rolled back. Her pelvis pounded against his, her clit throbbing against the hilt of his shaft. "Stop, stop!" he gasped. Addie let out a wail of protest as he threw her off of him.

He squeezed the head of his penis while he stretched her out and spread her wide. Derek tucked two fingers into her pussy and rapidly masturbated her. He jerked against her clit until she was squirming and screaming his name. Her breasts jiggled as her whole body was rubbed to glistening glory. She thrust into his palm, her juices dribbling over his fingers. Her found her G-spot and pressed hard circles into the ridged region. She cried out expletives and fucked his fingers, harder, harder, harder, out of control.

"Why should he have to be jealous?" he groaned. Derek put his mouth to her womanhood while he finger-banged her. He looked up and asked again, "Why…when you said you wanted us both?"

She let go and exploded with a gush of creamy white pleasure. "Yes!" she yelled. "Oh my fucking god, yesss!" Derek moaned as he swiped his tongue swiftly over her quivering clit while she poured into his mouth with exquisite release. Her sharp cry cut off with a satisfied exhale.

Derek rested on his haunches and Addie dragged her sex-weakened body up to return the favor. She closed her manicured nails around his hard shaft. She stroked up and down and sensually sucked the head of his engorged penis. He bit his lip and leaned back to rest on his elbows, moaning tremulously. Derek unleashed her beautiful hair and let it cascade over him in a silken blonde waterfall. He swept it back from her face to watch her as she sucked him off.

Then, he closed his eyes and pretended it was Owen. Derek arced up into her mouth. "Ah!" he groaned. "Ah, shit!" She gripped him tighter. Derek had to pull out.

"Are you saying you want me to fuck your friend?" she looked up at him from her sexy stance on hands and knees. Adelaide seductively flicked her hair over her shoulder and wiped her pretty mouth.

Derek grabbed her by the back of her neck and brought her lips to his. He kissed her fiercely, his nose pressed against hers. He cupped her cheeks and softened the kiss. He couldn't tell how she might feel about the request for another threesome, and he wasn't quite coherent enough to examine it too closely, delirious with pleasure as he was.

He moved up behind her and sucked her neck. Adelaide leaned forward, and Derek rose on his knees to enter her. The amazing feel of her body made him shout her name. She reached down to rub her clit and stroke and fondle his balls. Her breasts bounced and her flat stomach clenched as she tightened around him. Derek grunted with exertion and exhaled slowly. He laid back and let her ride him in reverse with her perfect pussy rocking up and down, taking him in and out. He held her waist and her hair tickled the side of his face. Then, she leaned all the way back onto his chest and let him pound up and into her.

With a hoarse exclamation, Derek tore his cock out of her body and ripped off the condom as fast as he could. His penis jerked in his hand between her legs, and he climaxed all over her mons, leaving her peach landing strip sticky, wet with his spent excitement. He couldn't stop shaking because the release was so intense. Adelaide whimpered, her chest heaving, her body taking a while to calm back down. She didn't move from her reclining position atop his body. Reaching down, she clasped his member and stroked the last drops free.

When she rolled off of him, he reached for his boxers and used them to wipe her clean of his spunk. Derek laboriously inhaled.

"I so needed that," she said breathlessly.

Derek chuckled. He turned on his side to stare down into her face. "I needed it, too." He swiped a stray wavy strand of hair from her face. "Are you pleased?"

"Sated…satisfied…What about you?"

Derek laid back and looked up at the ceiling. "I couldn't ask for more," he said with a soft laugh. He gripped her fingers in hand, and she let him.

"So…" She glanced over at him. "…about this fucking your

friend   thing…"

CHAPTER 18

"DON'T FORGET, TOMORROW'S the big day! Be on your shit, Mr. Cornwell," Libby said by way of a goodbye.

"Thanks, Ms. Sullivan. I couldn't have done it without you and your timely announcements of those secret team brainstorm sessions they kept trying to have without me."

Libby crossed her arms on top of her desk and smiled. "Well, you can make it up to me by taking me out to dinner one day. Oh, yeah, your lady friend can come, too," she added dryly.

Laughing, Derek tossed her a wave and headed out of the office building. It was the first day in weeks that he hadn't stayed late on the job. With both presentations complete and ready to be shown to Mr. Clancy in the morning, he was in a good mood. Spending the night with Adelaide contributed significantly to the glow.

Derek had come up with an excellent solution to the problem of Owen's and Addie's fears of a committed relationship, and his own barely elucidated secret need to have them both. He had toyed with the idea all day long, although it had initially occurred to him when he told Adelaide that Owen was real relationship material. Addie was the female version of Owen, granted with a lot rougher past. While Addie shied away from being possessed because she had seen the dark underbelly of false promises, Owen played the field because he simply hadn't met anyone who made him want to settle down.

They were both swimming away from deeper emotions to float in the shallows of gratuitous sex—not that Derek had a problem with sex.

But, as Adelaide had adeptly pointed out, he was a romantic at heart. He cared about Owen in a way that was hard to explain, and he desired more than physicality with Addie. So, the perfect way to handle the conundrum was to entice his friend and his lover into an unorthodox coupling, the likes of which Derek never would've considered if not for the threesome that had set it all in motion. He could see the perks of sharing.

Derek hadn't fully explained his plan to Addie yet, but he was crossing his fingers he could get her on board. It was Owen he was worried about.

Straight-laced, the type who played by the rules despite his playboy persona, Owen might not be down to become the missing line in the triangle of Derek's fantasies. Admittedly, he had no intention of telling his best friend about his before-now secret attraction. That was too fantastic of a proposition to make. Instead, Derek would ask him to play alternate. Anytime Addie needed a fix and couldn't get to Derek, she could have Owen.

He knew Owen would believe his tale. Owen already thought Addie was a damn sex addict, thanks to Steve. Derek knew there was no way to succinctly squeeze her into such a box. She was far too complex and dynamic to simply be a sex-crazed deviant. Instead, he recognized she was a woman in search of affection, uninhibited enough to fully explore her sexual self in the process.

Derek was so wrapped up in the idea that he completely forgot about the need to find an apartment. That is, until he got home to his parents' house and found his dad watching television in the living room. Frank looked up from the TV screen. "I thought you'd moved out on us when you didn't come home last night."

Derek dropped his briefcase by the entrance to the living room and decided to go in and have a chat with his old man. "I've been having a little trouble finding a place," he explained. "But, I'm confident that by tomorrow I can begin packing."

Frank arched a bushy eyebrow and chuckled. "You don't have a place, but you're ready to start packing. Well, alright then. Anything I can do to help?"

"Keep doing what you're doing, Dad. It helps."

"Sarcasm will get you nowhere, son," Frank chuckled, amused. "Here's an idea. Have you thought about asking your buddy to let you crash at his place for a while? You might be more comfortable there. He has plenty of space, from what I hear."

"You and mom are always thinking I'm mooching off of Owen. He's my friend, not my financier. I'm fine, Dad. I'll find an apartment."

"Oh no, I wasn't talking about mooching off of anybody. No, no. I was thinking you could split the expenses. You'd probably come out paying about the same as you'd pay for an apartment. You know, before I married your mother I had a roommate, and it just made things easier."

Derek hadn't thought about it, but considering the idea that had sprung to mind the night before, perhaps rooming with Owen might not be so bad. He had thought about it in the past. And, after the research he'd done into local rental listings, he knew his father was right about probably paying around the same amount. If he and Owen split the bills, he could be paying one bedroom apartment money and staying in a five bedroom house. He nodded his head appreciatively. It all depended on how Owen felt about it, but Derek thought it was worth a shot to ask.

"I'll keep that in mind. Thanks, Dad," he said with genuine appreciation. Frank shook his hand. He hadn't done that in a while. He looked up at his son with a slow smile.

"Keep up the good work, son." He patted Derek's hand and let it go.

Derek looked over his shoulder as he walked out of the room. His father was back to watching television. He shook his head and smiled, making his way to his bedroom to throw together an overnight bag. He was on his way back to Adelaide's house.

"Hey, I remember this place," she murmured with a sly grin.

"It's all coming back to you now, is it?" Derek laughed softly as he pulled into Owen's driveway. "I hope he's home. He hasn't answered my calls in the past two days. C'mon, let's see."

"Wait a minute, wait a minute! Are you sure he's going to be okay with me just showing up at his house? This is crazy, Derek. From what you tell me, he's not exactly a big fan of us being together, and you want to pop up on his doorstep with me?"

Derek leaned over and kissed her lips, silencing her. "Would you trust me and don't get your panties in a bunch?" he said, chuckling. He climbed out of the car and went around to her side to open the door for her.

"They're not in a bunch. I'm not wearing any."

She walked ahead of him up to Owen's front door, and Derek had to jog to keep up. He took a steadying breath and rang the doorbell, waiting patiently. It didn't take long for Owen to open up. "What the hell?" he mumbled.

"Hey!" Derek greeted him, pushing inside. "You remember Adelaide, don't you?" Addie waved her fingertips and followed him in. Owen turned around with one eyebrow lifted and his arms crossed after shutting the door behind them.

"To what do I owe this unexpected...pleasure?" he asked sardonically.

"Well, for starters, you haven't been answering my calls," said Derek. "I was so worried that I called your parents, the hospitals, and the jails looking for you."

"Funny," Owen quipped. He tapped his foot, trying to hold onto his anger. They looked at each other. Derek slanted his head and smiled. Owen shook his head and couldn't hold back a tiny laugh. "You son of a bitch, you know you pissed me off."

Derek dragged him into a manly bear hug and let him go, playfully jabbing him in the shoulder. "Get over it, dude. I'm fine. You're fine. And, Adelaide is..." He exhaled and whistled. Her girlish grin was super cute. Derek caught Owen looking her up and down with hooded eyes and a half-smile tickling his lips. "Adelaide is fine, too. So, what do you say we three fine ass people chill out poolside, and have a couple of beers?"

He held up the case of lagers he'd picked up on his way over. Owen laughed. "C'mon, since you've invited yourself on over." He led them out the glass patio doors to the fenced in backyard. Derek watched Adelaide gaze around.

"Impressive," she replied. Owen shrugged modestly.

"It serves my needs. Feel free to take a dip if you like."

"I think I will," she said.

Adelaide grabbed the hem of her t-shirt and drew it up over her head, revealing a white bra underneath. Owen looked to Derek with a perplexed expression and Derek smiled appreciatively. Owen averted his gaze when she shimmied out of the rest of her clothes until she stood there in all her bronze glory, naked as the day she was born.

"Don't mind her. She's all about new experiences and being wildly spontaneous. Where do you want me to put the brews?" Derek asked.

"Uh, over by the..." Owen very deliberately turned his back to Addie, and led Derek over to the sectional. Derek set the six-pack on the side table and cracked open two bottles, one for him and one for Owen. As Derek sipped on the refreshing, cool drink, his eyes followed Adelaide swimming like an exotic mermaid from one end of the pool to the other.

Her shapely legs swished through the water. Her plump derriere wiggled invitingly. When she turned over onto her back to float, her perfect breasts pointed to the evening sky like dusky mountains. Derek's cock tightened in response.

"I see things are going well with you and her, huh?" Owen hiked a thumb over his shoulder in Addie's general direction.

Derek shrugged ambiguously. "Actually, that's why I brought her over here. I wanted to talk about something. Something kind of serious. I'm not sure how you'll respond to it, though." He tossed his bottle back. Owen did the same.

Nodding, he said, "Fire away."

"You know how Steve was saying she's a sex addict?" Derek lowered his voice. Owen nodded. "I spent the night with her last night. Man, I feel like my body's been through boot camp. Every single fucking muscle aches! It's damn near impossible to keep up with her," Derek laughed.

Owen smiled and almost peeked over his shoulder, but he turned back at the last minute. "Is that right? She was pretty insatiable the night me and you, uh..." Owen dropped his eyes, embarrassed. "It's kind of weird talking about how we both smashed a chick you're trying to date seriously now, you know what I mean?"

"No, check me out. That's what I wanted to talk to you about. Addie and me aren't dating. We're just sort of friends with benefits, at this point."

Owen smirked. "Goddammit, Derek, you let her talk you into being her fuck buddy?" he hissed. "You know you like her. I see this going all kinds of wrong." He shook his head.

Derek chuckled. "Would you let me get out what I'm trying to get out? With Addie's passions, I don't want a repeat of what Steve described. What if *you* were her fuck buddy? That way, things stay no-strings attached, the way she wants. She won't get skittish about things getting too serious…and, I probably won't get too emotionally involved."

Owen had started to choke on his beer as soon as Derek had asked him to be Addie's fuck buddy. "What?" He swiped the back of his hand across his lips.

Derek nodded enthusiastically. "Don't look at me like that. I'm serious." Owen looked shocked but not repulsed.

Of course, Derek had woven an entirely different scenario for Adelaide. He had encouraged her to be friendly with his best friend so Owen would have no cause to feel jealous. It helped that Addie already had a favorable impression of Owen from the night they met. But, it had taken some creative improv to convince her he personally wouldn't be bothered if things got flirty or physical between her and his best friend. Derek had explained her impulsive nature was refreshing, and he didn't want her to curtail her behavior on his behalf. So, anything that happened would be entirely up to her (with a little coaxing on his behalf.) The ball was in her court.

"I want you to help me keep her entertained," said Derek. "It's a win-win, man. Adelaide—she likes sex. I mean, she really likes it. I can barely keep up by myself, but you and me, we're a great team! She was open to a ménage à trois once; maybe she'll be open to it again…as in, on the regular."

"You're talking about two different things, three people having sex versus three people in a sexual *relationship*. That's polyamory. No, that's fuckery! It's insane!"

"Keep your voice down! I haven't told her the particulars yet."

Owen's eyes widened in alarm. He quickly glanced over his shoulder to see Addie swimming languidly in his pool. "Well, what did you tell her?" he whispered back.

Derek shrugged, unsure if he should confess it to Owen. "That I was okay with her sleeping with my best friend." He squinted, waiting for Owen to lambaste him for offering up the girl he wanted to someone else, which went against everything Owen had been teaching him as his life coach.

"And, she was okay with that?" Owen asked incredulously, shaking his head.

"Well…" Derek wasn't sure how to answer that. If he said yes, it would make Addie seem entirely too easy. If he said no, it would seem as if he was pressuring her to do something she didn't want to do. He decided to be honest on at least this one count. "She didn't agree to anything. I just put it on the table that I wasn't trying to tie her down."

His eyes swept over Owen's handsome face, the wire-rimmed glasses, and thick beard, the wide shoulders and…He shook his head. It would be the only way he could safely explore this new aspect of his sexuality, or rather this old aspect he had always suppressed. Derek nervously gnawed on his bottom lip.

Owen said, "You're crazy, you know that?"

"C'mon, just look at her—that tight, sexy ass and those long, sexy legs. Do you really want to let me have that all to myself?" Derek joked. He looked at Adelaide, then looked at Owen. "Why don't you go talk to her? Ultimately, I brought her over here for you to get to know her better. This isn't a booty call, guy. You're not that special." Owen smiled.

Derek left him sitting on the sectional and ambled over to the pool. Adelaide swam from the deep end and smiled up at him. "How are things going with you patching things up with your friend?" she asked. The sunlight glinted off of her wet, glistening hair. She looked like a dream. He flashed her thumbs up and began taking off his clothes. Addie's eyes darkened with lust. He shoved off his pants and stood there in his boxer briefs. Derek removed those, too.

"Hey, Owen?" He looked back to see his best friend studiously avoiding gazing in the direction of the pool. Derek snickered. "Owen."

"Yeah, man?"

"Come join us in the pool, bro."

Owen laughed dryly. Finally, he turned around and lifted his beer in salute. "Are you sure you want me to do that?" he challenged. His eyes bore into Derek's. They had been friends so long that Derek understood what was going through his head. Owen was thinking things were different now that Derek had feelings for Adelaide. Could he really handle seeing another man having sex with her?

Derek nodded once to let Owen know everything was cool. With a splash, he submerged himself beneath the refreshing, blue water. Adelaide swam around him like a golden fish, and he danced playfully around her. She swam forward to kiss him gently on the lips. Derek exhaled and vibrant bubbles fluttered upwards. He swam up to follow them, cresting the surface with a deep inhale and shaking the water out of his eyes.

When he looked up, there was Owen standing naked and glorious right above him. Owen's wide shoulders tapered to narrow hips, his stomach was chiseled with abs, his thighs thick and muscular, and his manhood was unobscured. Derek didn't mean to stare. He didn't realize the expression on his face confessed much more than he could've put into words. He didn't know he had given himself away, until his eyes flew back to Owen's and his best friend squinted down at him quizzically.

Owen moved further down to the deep end, lifted his arms, and dove smoothly into the pool. As he swam to the shallow end to meet them, Adelaide turned to Derek with a lifted brow. "He's going to figure it out, you know," she said.

Derek gazed after Owen. "Figure out what?" he asked. When he turned to her, she wore a knowing smile.

"That   you   want   him,   too."

PART 3
CHAPTER 19

"HE'S GOING TO figure it out, you know," Adelaide said.

Derek gazed after his best friend, Owen, a man he had secretly lusted after for quite some time. Derek wasn't gay, and he didn't know why he felt the way he felt. He just did. "Figure out what?" he asked obliviously. When he turned to his new lover, Adelaide "Addie" Ingles, the blonde haired vixen wore a knowing smile.

"That you want him, too," she replied.

"Huh?"

Before Derek could formulate a better response to her surprising deduction, Owen swam up behind the lovely water nymph and playfully pulled her nude, lithe body underwater. Adelaide let out a squeal of laughter, kicking and splashing. She came up for air with twinkling eyes and a smile, and Owen grinned back as Derek treaded water. His heart pounded beneath his ribcage.

How did she know? He had been so careful to hide the taboo desires that didn't fit into his self-described heterosexual lifestyle. It was true, he had brought Adelaide over to hang out with Owen in the hopes the three of them might eventually form a polyamorous, friends with benefits relationship. Not that he had any concrete plans to get physical with Owen. He felt he'd be content with simply fantasizing about it while the two of them sated Addie's voracious sexual appetites together.

Now, it was clear that his attempts at keeping his homoerotic thoughts under wraps weren't as successful as he had imagined. Derek kicked off and dove deep to hide the play of emotions that flitted across his face. He was embarrassed that she had seen straight through him, but he was also a little bit relieved not to have to continue wrestling with his inner demons by himself. At least it was something he could talk about to someone else now.

But the problem was, Derek didn't want Addie thinking he was only using her to get to Owen. That wasn't the case. He was into her. He was just into Owen, too. He came up for air only a few feet away from them, and Derek swept the water from his face with a sigh. Why did this shit have to be so complicated?

He gazed across the rippling cool blue pool at Adelaide and Owen playing together. For all his reticence to play third wheel, Owen looked like he was enjoying himself. There was so much to talk about that Derek hadn't had the time to get into, but at least he could see Owen was giving his idea a try. What sane man would turn down the opportunity to sleep with a gorgeous woman like Addie, anyway?

Derek swam back toward them. "I was telling Owen he should really get to know you," he said.

"Yeah, I'm a nice person, Owen. And, I've heard so much about you. I feel like I know you already." Addie grinned, flicking water in Owen's face. He laughed out loud and flicked her back.

"Oh, I see we're going to get along just fine," said Owen. He looked from Adelaide to Derek, and his expression sobered some. "I'm only curious to know if we're all on the same page here."

"What do you mean?" Adelaide asked.

No, no, no, Derek was thinking. He hoped to god Owen didn't open his big mouth and tell Addie the story he'd told him, about her needing some variety of cock in her life to keep her faithful. He groaned inwardly. Derek had come up with the brilliant idea to have his cake and eat it too, by convincing his best friend and new lover to engage in an unusual relationship arrangement. After all, a ménage a trois session had brought them together initially. In his lust addled brain, it had seemed like a good idea.

But, Derek had gotten Adelaide on board by telling her he was cool with her letting loose and being sexually spontaneous with his best friend, because she thought Owen might be a little jealous about him dating her. If the two of them found out he had given them different stories, the plan might fall through. Nobody liked to be manipulated.

"Uh, I think he means about that thing we talked about," Derek hurriedly interjected, implying she already knew what they were talking about. That way Owen wouldn't have to explain. Owen nodded.

"Yeah, that thing."

Adelaide swam around the both of them with a seductive smile. "Oh, that *thing*. I wonder that, too. Why don't we ask the orchestrator? Are we all on the same page, Derek?" She swam into his arms and laid a hand on his chest. Her skin was cool and wrinkled from being in the water, but her body felt warm and appealing against his. Derek placed his hands at her waist, and their legs briefly entangled beneath the water.

"I think we're all responsible adults here. Why not do something different? It'll be like an open relationship, only an exclusive one. I won't sleep around. You, Owen?"

Owen's brows came together over his sharp nose, but he laughed. "That wasn't part of the plan you gave me, but alright. I'll go for it. I won't sleep around. What about you, Adelaide? Would you rather one of us or the both of us?" He alluded to the game they'd played together the night the three of them met. It brought back salacious memories.

"Two for the price of one, huh?" she said with a lift of her brow. "I'm game. Any sexual history of STDs I need to know about?" She swam away from Derek and meandered back between them so she could get a good look at them.

Derek grimaced. "No, but that's definitely not the thing I want to think about while initiating a sex deal," he said with a laugh.

"Twenty-first century problems," Owen remarked. "I've got a clean bill of health and the papers to prove it."

"Then, in that case, I'm all in. And, I'm on birth control." She dropped a hand on each of their shoulders as her smile widened. "Fellas, I think we have ourselves a workable plan. Only rule I'll suggest is if you want out, say the word and you're out. No hard feelings, no petty squabbles. Clean break."

"Deal," said Owen.

Derek nodded. "Deal." This had gone far smoother than he'd anticipated. "Shake on it?" he asked, glancing at each of them.

"Oh, I think a deal like this has to be cemented in a different way," Owen suggested.

Derek knew exactly what he was thinking. Adelaide's eyes

glinted amber with mischief, then dark with lust. She knew, too. "What do you have in mind?" she asked as her body undulated enticingly under the water.

Derek wrapped a hand around her elbow and dragged her close. Her impish smile lured him. His lips connected with hers. She chuckled and ran her hands down his bare chest. Then, she peeked over her shoulder at Owen. He came to her, too. "So, I see we *are* all on the same page," she murmured as she kissed him.

Taking a handful of both breasts, Derek squeezed and massaged, and Adelaide's head fell back at the pleasure he gave her, exposing the elegant curve of her neck. Her beautiful lips parted. Shiny, white teeth peeked from beneath. Dripping golden hair caught the sunlight, brushing against Owen's chest.

Owen placed both hands to the sides of her upside down face and kissed her. Slow, inquisitive, questing—his mouth slanted over hers, and she breathed a small moan. While he kissed her, Derek leaned down to suck her delightful peachy nipples. They hardened to pebbles beneath his tongue, and her pillowy breasts gave way to the pressure of his mouth as he sucked. She moved her hands up Derek's shoulders, moaning louder. The crescents of her nails bit into his pale skin.

It was happening. Like in his dream, the colors of the backyard landscape were hyper-saturated in the evening light, and everything had a magical feeling to it. Especially her. They moved to shallower water so they could stand instead of swim, and Adelaide turned around to face Owen as Derek kissed the side of her face. Owen brushed his lips across her forehead. She wove her slender fingers into his chestnut brown beard and brought Owen's mouth back to hers.

Owen mumbled against her lips, "I like a woman that takes charge." The evidence of how much he liked it bumped against her pelvis, his erection standing tall and proud. She covered it with both hands, using the water to make her slow strokes up and down, slick and inviting.

"Do you? Well, you'll love this." She bent forward and replaced her hands with her mouth.

Grabbing the curve of her hip, Derek stepped up behind her and rubbed his erect manhood against her exposed vagina. Addie let out a sound of surprise. She reached back and caressed him, then guided him to her entrance. Derek bit his lower lip in anticipation. He was hard, and long, and ready for her, and the situation turned up his arousal even more. She eagerly spread her legs and pushed her bottom back to take him in slowly.

Derek clutched the base of his engorged shaft with a breathy moan as he entered her. She was impossibly tight, and wet as a rainstorm on the inside, and his cock curved exactly right to fill her up. "Mm, I can already tell I'll never want out of this," he gasped. When he looked up, Owen was watching him, smiling. That sent a flurry of excitement through him.

"You're not the only one," Owen groaned as he laughed. Owen wove his fingers through her hair and guided her head down to his erection. She obligingly took his swollen shaft into her mouth. Moaning with pleasure, Adelaide worked her hand up and down along his length while she licked and sucked. His face registered the same ecstasy Derek was feeling.

Derek gazed back down to where his body met hers beneath the shallow water. Was this really happening? Because, it felt too good to be true. He couldn't stop the moans and sighs of pleasure that welled up and escaped. He saw bursts of rapturous light with each of her inner strokes. Adelaide was skilled at seduction and an outright expert at having sex. He'd do whatever it took to keep her happy, to keep this deal going, to keep all three of them satisfied.

"Ohh, shit," he hummed. He pressed into her and drew back out in slow strokes that made her vocal with her need.

"Fuck me," she whispered naughtily. She moaned around Owen's cock, and tightened her inner grip to hold onto Derek longer as he tried to ease out. She was a vision of loveliness with her hourglass torso vertical before him, her head bobbing up and down, and her ass jiggling with each impact. Riding her body was the greatest thrill he had ever encountered. Pumping into her felt like teetering on a high cliff above bliss.

Owen, Derek knew, had to be thinking the same thing. His best friend's brow was furrowed and his eyes were shut. He had gone from guiding Addie's head to tenderly caressing her face as she fellated him. Derek had never seen him so gentle. It was so right—all of it. This was exactly how he'd imagined it would be.

Adelaide dipped her fingers down between her legs to fondle her clit, as Derek's lust drove him harder and faster into her body. He could feel the tension in her thighs, and in the way she tightened around him. When her whimpers and moans of arousal escalated to panting, breathless sounds of ecstasy that made her have to stop sucking Owen, Derek knew she was close to reaching her peak. Owen stood back and watched. He had his hand around his moist erection, stroking swiftly.

"Oh, guys...guys!" she cried, close, closer. Adelaide reflexively straightened and pressed her narrow back to Derek's chest, quaking uncontrollably. Derek, grunting, wrapped his forearm across her torso and hammered into her with wet, sensual slapping sounds.

"Give it to me," he gasped into her ear through gritted teeth. "Come for me."

She sobbed with ecstasy, "Oh, fuck, yes!" Then, she came around his cock with an erotic ripple of her sheath. Pure pleasure rocked her from head to toe. Her plaintive cries filled the yard, and Derek covered her mouth as he pressed his face into her hair, groaning with the exertion it took to keep from releasing inside of her.

He eased out of her body. Derek and Owen made eye contact. Owen lifted a brow. *What next?* He seemed to ask. Derek had a few ideas, but none of them were things he could say out loud. Yet, it seemed that Adelaide read him loud and clear because at that moment she did the unthinkable. She took Derek's hand in hers...and she guided it to Owen's still hard dick.

Both men's eyes bucked wide with shock. "Do it for me," she whispered, when Derek prepared to protest. He glanced sharply at his best friend. Owen looked around, as if he had to be certain no one else was watching, and Derek just stood there with his heart in his throat. What would he think of this? Derek was close to panic. But, Owen didn't snatch out of his hand with revulsion or jump out of the pool with horror. That was a good sign, right?

She nodded, looking from Owen to Derek. "No one has to know," Addie   coaxed.

CHAPTER 20

NEITHER OF THE guys said a word, but Derek allowed her to direct the slow stroke of his hand. He couldn't believe this was happening. Owen's cock felt hard and heavy in his grip, and the engorged shaft pulsated with his turgid arousal. Owen breathed faster. Addie took Derek's hand to the tip. Derek licked his lips, closing his palm around the head of Owen's erection. Addie took Derek's hand back to the base. Owen grimaced as Derek tightened his fingers.

Before long, she didn't have to guide him. He followed the cues of Owen's body, as his friend intuitively flowed into his hand and eased back out, pumping his hips rhythmically. Derek thought about how he would please himself and applied the same technique. He varied the pressure of his grip and added the rotation of his wrist, and when he got the desired response—Owen swearing softly and growling with excitement—he grew more insistent with his masturbatory tug.

"Yes," Addie whispered. Derek's eyes flew to her. She was rubbing her slender hands all over her body. She was squeezing her breasts and touching down between her legs. She licked her lips and stared at them both from beneath hooded eyes. "Why does this turn me on so much?" she asked, speaking to no one in particular.

She moved forward and took Derek's steel pipe into her own hands. She brought it to Owen's. Derek boldly wrapped his fingers around both their shafts and was jerking himself off at the same time, eliciting even more arousal from Addie. She flipped her glistening, wet hair over her shoulder and leaned forward to run her tongue along their shiny, water-slick manhoods, taking Derek into her mouth, and then Owen. She went back and forth between the two of them, intermittently coaching Derek in masturbating Owen while she sucked him off.

Derek was afraid to look Owen in the eyes, but he could feel the tightness building in the other man's body. Suddenly, Owen gripped Derek's arm to stop his movements. "Derek," he ground out hoarsely. That was all he could say before his body did what came naturally. Or, rather, before he came—naturally. Derek couldn't help the sharp intake of air, as his own cock jerked in response to the sight of Owen ejaculating all over his hand.

Addie cooed with delight as she watched, vigorously rubbing her clit. "Umph!" she moaned, rubbing faster. "Ah!" She dropped a hand on Derek's shoulder and squeezed. Just like that, she was coming again as Owen's groans of pleasure got louder with each emission, though he tried to remain stoic. The pleasure was too much to keep contained.

Addie collapsed into Derek's free arm, sated. She whimpered against his chest. He could feel her still trembling. Pulling his hand away from his best friend's spent erection, he stared at Owen askance. "Y-you okay?" Derek stammered. As in, okay with what just happened. Owen avoided eye contact and looked kind of blown away.

"Uh, yeah, yeah…" Owen cleared his throat. He quickly turned away from them, and climbed out of the pool. "I'll be, um, inside if you guys need me." His words tapered off nervously, and he scurried away like he needed to put some distance between himself and the two lovers. Derek stared after him. He worried that he had drastically changed their friendship—maybe for the worst.

Adelaide giggled breathlessly and took a deep breath. She stretched in his arms like a cat and writhed against him suggestively. "That was *nice*. You're welcome, by the way," she whispered, when Owen was out of earshot.

She put her hands to Derek's chest and kissed his mouth achingly slow and sexy. Her devilish pink tongue dipped inside, and she sucked his bottom lip and flicked her tongue against it. All the while, Derek just kept getting harder and harder. He groaned uncomfortably. "I'll take care of you," she promised.

Those marvelous hands of hers hiked down to his pelvis, but he didn't want to be touched. He wanted to be inside of her, and Derek had to admit that what had just happened made him want to ravage her body until she was begging him to let her explode.

He eagerly hefted her up into his arms, carrying her to the edge of the pool and depositing her on the wet concrete. Her nakedness was heaven on earth, but he didn't pause to stare. He took his throbbing cock and forcefully speared into her, eliciting a wild cry from her lips. Derek felt like twice the man he had been before, and his powerful lust drove him to new heights of pleasure seeking. Wrapping his hand around her throat, he moved in and out of her.

Hoarse moans tore from his lungs. He kissed the side of her face, down her neck, bit her shoulder—pumping into her receptive body like a mad man. Adelaide's legs wrapped around him, and she dug her heels into the backs of his thighs as she gasped with ecstasy. He mastered her body with his probing cock, finding her erogenous zones effortlessly.

Pictures flooded his brain of the heated moment with Owen. That it had happened floored him, made him want to release his sexual gratification all over her beautiful, silky body. "Ah, god, Addie!" he groaned, pumping. She wriggled in his grasp as she met him thrust for thrust, which caused her to rise and fall off the edge of the pool. Her feet dangled in the air, and her thighs tightened around him.

"Ohh, yessss," she sang.

Throwing her head back, she emitted a sharp yelp that signaled her incoming climax. He squeezed his arms around her, his palms pressed flat to her back, and let her ride out the wave on his erection. The erotic ripple of her inner walls almost did him in, but he held himself in check. Adelaide shook with pleasure, quaking as the feelings subsided. Finally, she was still in his arms, and Derek knew it was his turn. He slowly eased into her as he gazed down at himself. He was slick with the evidence of her orgasm. He was hard enough to break glass.

She let out a small whimper, with her clitoris hypersensitive after the powerful release. Derek kissed the sound from her mouth as he eased back inside, and that was about all he could take.

He yanked out of her embrace just as his body gave up the fight. His abs tightened, and his thighs locked up, and his glutes squeezed as his body jerked. His release poured from his body, and he cried out at the exquisite glory of it.

It seemed to take him forever to come back down to earth, but when he did, Derek came right back to the problems he had temporarily left behind.

Gasping and breathless, he managed to say, "I have to talk to Owen." Addie nodded. He slowly climbed out of the pool on trembling legs. He still felt a little weak in the knees, which made him chuckle wryly. She was the only woman who had ever been able to do that to him. But, then again, he had never had a woman of Adelaide's caliber.

He cast one more longing glance back at her after he got dressed to go find Owen. "Wish me luck," Derek said.

◇◇◇

Derek found Owen in the kitchen, surrounded by the makings of a sandwich. Then he noticed that there were three plates fixed, and Owen was pouring up three glasses of wine. "Hungry?" Owen asked without looking away from what he was doing.

Derek sighed and leaned across the kitchen countertop with his elbows resting on the dark granite. "We need to talk," he stated.

Owen shrugged. "What's there to talk about? What happened, happened."

From his perch, Derek watched Adelaide through the kitchen picture window. She was still in the backyard, but she had finally gotten out of the pool and she was getting dressed. He admired the lines and curves of her perfect body, while he tried to figure out how exactly to broach the subject Owen seemed reluctant to talk about.

"I meant, we need to talk about our friendship. You've been acting kind of weird to me, man. Are we cool, now? Cause, my life made a complete one-eighty after you started helping me out, and I don't want that to get off track. Hell, that's kind of why I'm all for this joint casual sex thing." Derek blushed, thinking that wasn't the only reason he was into it.

Outside, he could see Addie now talking on her cellphone, and from the looks of things the conversation out there was as intense as the one indoors. He wondered who she was talking to, or what it could be about. Some perverse side of him wondered if it was another man. After all, his brother-in-law Steve—her ex-boyfriend—had warned him that Adelaide was a player.

"I just want you to know you don't have to be jealous of me being with Adelaide," Derek murmured distractedly.

"I'm not jealous of you being with Addie, Derek."

Derek turned to Owen, who watched him with a closed expression. He was sipping from a glass of wine thoughtfully and gestured with it as he replied, "Although, I have to be honest, it's gonna take a while for me to get used to you not being the old, always home and available to hang out best friend. Now, I see why you used to get the sad puppy dog face every time I told you I had a date." Owen chuckled.

Derek smiled and ran his hand along the back of his neck. "Well, you were the one to tell me to know what I want, and go after it."

"Exacto," said Owen. "That's why I salute you. You got the girl. She's bangin' hot. More power to you. Of course, we can pick up where we left off with me playing your life coach. I just missed being able to chill with my friend."

"I'm right here. You were the one who stopped talking to me," Derek replied.

"Yeah, well…" Owen looked contrite. "Catch me up. What have I missed?"

"Got a big meeting tomorrow at work. It'll either finish off my career or launch it."

"Right, right, I think you mentioned that to me. You ready for it?"

"Mostly." Derek turned his hand from side to side to show so-so. "I figure I'll put on my best Owen act and wow everybody."

Owen chuckled and shook his head. "I don't think you want to try that. Just keep those pointers I gave you last week in the forefront of your mind. Remember, it's about dressing for the job you want, respecting yourself and others by addressing them appropriately, and creating presence. If you do those three things, you'll be set."

"Well, nobody does it like you," Derek murmured wistfully. He didn't realize how the comment sounded—especially after what had just happened in the pool. He blushed as Owen chuckled wryly.

"That's what she said. Anyway, you already know the main rule to success. Know what you want, and go after it."

"And, speaking of knowing what you want and going after it…" Derek scratched the back of his head as he pondered how to say what he wanted. Owen crossed his arms, waiting. He decided to come right out with it, and hope for the best. "What would you say if, hypothetically, what just happened—you know, *out there*—um…what if I wasn't too freaked out about it? I mean, what if it h-happens again?"

Derek flinched, but there was no way to snatch the words back. The speech hadn't come out the way he had semi-planned on his walk inside to find Owen. He had intended to make light of the situation, just point out that they were pals, it was cool, and it wasn't gay at all—not by a long shot. It was, like, nothing to worry about. Instead, what had come out of his mouth amounted to a confession of sexual attraction.

He pictured a hole opening up in the floor right in front of him so he could politely leap his ass into it. A black hole, a swirling maelstrom of no space, and no time to erase what he'd said. Only the leap would last forever. Way too long to have to replay this awkward conversation over   and   over   in   his   head.

CHAPTER 21

BEFORE OWEN COULD answer however, the sliding patio door came open with a loud bang that made both men glance sharply in that direction. "Derek!" Addie sounded frazzled and upset as she rushed inside, out of breath.

"What? What is it? What's wrong?" Derek flew to her side because she was visibly shaken. He had never seen the carefree woman so worked up.

She pushed her hands through her drying blonde hair and stared at him with urgent eyes. "Look, I need to leave. Something's come up. Can you take me home? I really need to get to my car."

"Yeah, sure. Of course." Derek looked back at Owen. It was a terrible point in the conversation to leave off, but he had to take care of Adelaide. There was nothing he could do but mouth a soundless apology.

Owen nodded understanding. "Go on. Get out of here. We'll talk later," he said.

"Thanks, man. Call me." Derek grabbed Addie's hand and raced with her out the front door to his Mazda. He opened the passenger side for her to climb in, and he ran around to the driver's seat. "Can you tell me what's going on? Is there any way I can help?" he asked, as he stretched his belt across his chest and quickly latched it.

"No."

"You sure?"

"Just stop prying into my personal life, alright?" she growled.

Derek pulled back at her angry outburst. "Okay...I'm sorry. I was just...j-just trying to be a friend," he muttered, perturbed.

She shook her shaggy gold hair, which gave her a leonine look as it dried to a frizz, curling around her face. She dropped her head in her hands. "No, it's me. I'm sorry, Derek. I shouldn't be lashing out at you." Her voice was muffled. He heard her sniff, and Derek worried she was crying. He kept one eye on the road, as he reached across and rubbed her back.

"Hey, hey, it's okay. Don't cry, Addie." She removed her hands and wiped her eyes. Her fingers dove through her thick, long hair to push it back out of her face. Adelaide, the brazen vixen, looked more like a kitten right then. He wasn't sure what to do. "Look, I'm not prying. It might make you feel better to tell someone," he said quietly. She nodded, reconsidering the idea.

It took her a second to gather her thoughts, and as she did, Derek stole glances. The twilight angle of the sun sent the last rays spearing across the sky and alighting on her face just so. It was impossible not to want to cherish her.

"You know how I mostly talk about the bad things that happened in my childhood? Well, it wasn't all bad. The last family I fostered with actually changed my whole world as I knew it. It happened when I was sixteen years old, and I was transferred to live with this older couple. They were so nice." She hitched in a breath. Her voice got smaller. "And, I was so horrible to them..."

"Hey, at sixteen everybody's horrible to their parents," he tried to console her.

She shook her head again. "No, you don't understand. By that point, I was fed up with the whole idea of wanting to belong to someone. I was anti-affection, anti-family, just...just anti! So, no matter what they tried to do to make me feel welcome, I always threw it in their faces that I didn't want to be there. God, I said such terrible things. I told them they weren't fit to be parents and that's why fate had left them without kids."

"Has something happened to them?" Derek asked, seeing where this was going.

"Gloria passed away a few years ago," she said regretfully. Adelaide stared down at her hands, toying restlessly with the hem of her shirt. "I never even got to apologize to her. I was at college. Soon as I aged out of the system, I ran off and got a job so I could pay for it. As I matured, I had these grand ideas about showing up over at their house one day and saying, 'Thanks for everything.' They made me, you know?

"But, I never got around to it. Each time I tried to draw up the nerve to do it, I chickened out. They fostered a lot of kids over time. They probably wouldn't even remember me. That's what I told myself. But...now, George is in the hospital. He's had a stroke, they think."

"Babe, I'm so sorry this is happening to you," he interjected. Derek grabbed her hand and squeezed it tight, brought it to his lips. She smiled wanly at him.

"Do you know, even though I haven't talked to him in ages, he had me listed as his emergency contact? He remembered me," she whispered. "And, just then when I got the call, I couldn't help but think, that's so sad. Such a wonderful person with no one else to turn to. No one but my completely inadequate ass." She gave a self-deprecating laugh that was a half-sob. Derek kissed her hand again before she gently pulled away from him.

"It's going to be okay," he assured her. It sounded like empty platitudes even to his ears. He tried again, "Addie, you're more qualified than you think. There's no reason for you to feel inadequate in this. You'll get through this...and I'm here for you. Now, do you really want me to take you back to your place, or would you rather me take you straight to the hospital? It'll save you some time, and I want you to realize you don't have to face everything alone."

"No, I don't wanna inconvenience you."

"The only thing inconvenient about spending time with you is that I don't get to do more of it." He smiled when she found a wavering grin at his compliment. Adelaide sniffled and cleared her face of tears, nodding gratefully.

"I guess that'll be fine. Thanks, Derek."

He had to make a U-turn to head back toward the city. "I meant what I said. You're not in this alone. I'm not just sticking around you for the good times."

"I kind of figured...and, that's what I'm scared of," she murmured. He glanced over and was met with the back of her head. She was gazing out the window. Her reflection in the glass showed a wistful look on her face, thumb tucked into her mouth like a small kid.

Adelaide had a powerful knack for making a man want to take care of her.

"Scared?" he asked. "Why?"

She finally looked at him. "Because the bad can get really bad, and I don't want you to get hurt." She clamped her lips shut and didn't say anything else after that, but what she'd said was enough. He rolled the thought around, mulling it over.

"What's the worst that can happen with me getting closer to you?" he pressed.

"You might fall in love."

"Oh, yeah? You think so?" he chuckled. "And, what about you? Is your heart made of stone, or are you capable?" She giggled softly when he reached past the center console to tickle her side. She needed a good laugh. He was keeping it light, but he really wanted to know.

"Might be capable. But, I'm damn sure no good at it. Anyway, what's the point of pondering? Like I said, you'd get hurt. So...let's just drop it." She kept her smile as she spoke, and Derek got the sense she was doing that thing she did, being too free-spirited for cages like love and romance. He sighed pleasantly and turned his attention back to the road. It was a pleasure to be in her company, to be able to help. He had to thank god for small favors.

Not long after, they pulled up at the hospital, and as soon as the tires stopped spinning Adelaide shoved open the door and hopped out. "I appreciate it, Derek," she called out distractedly over her shoulder.

She slammed the passenger door shut, and Derek blinked. "Hey, don't you want me to wait for you?" he asked. She paused long enough to lean through the open window.

"I've got it from here. You're wonderful, friend." She reached across and pinched his cheek. An innocent gesture with no heat to it. After the evening they had shared together—the three of them—it seemed to Derek she could've shown him a tiny bit more affection. On the other hand, maybe he was leaping ahead when he should've been watching his step.

How many times did she have to warn him not to get too involved before he got it through his thick skull? She was bad news, dangerous, a heartbreaker. Except, Derek vividly remembered what he had said to her the other night at her apartment. "I'm willing to risk it." Heartbreak. It was in the air like an autumn chill. He felt it coming.

CHAPTER 22

SIGHING, HE PICKED up his phone to call Owen and let him know what was up with Adelaide. Owen answered with his usual swiftness. "Was she okay, dude?" Owen asked.

Derek pressed the phone to his ear and nodded. "Mm-hmm. I just dropped her off at the hospital. She had a family emergency." His gaze darted across the interstate at the low volume of traffic. He'd be home in no time.

"Gotcha. So…"

"So, about this presentation tomorrow for Mr. Clancy. Man, the ads turned out stellar. You should see them when you get the chance." Derek gripped the steering wheel and braced himself, hoping Owen would go with the flow of the topic change.

"I'd love to. But, you don't get to skip over the conversation you initiated, buddy. About what you said to me over here, an hour ago. About being okay with what happened this evening happening again. Did you really mean that?"

"I was being hypothetical. I was wondering where your head was at on the subject. It was pretty…weird, you know?"

"You said you weren't freaked out about it."

"Are you?" Derek asked.

"C'mon, we've known each other damn near our whole lives. I'm surprised we never did anything like that before."

"Wait, what?"

"Well, you know how it is," Owen said with a laugh. "It's like in fraternities and shit, where they make you do all kinds of gay stuff to get into the brotherhood. And, I know plenty of guys who jerked each other off at some point. So, I wouldn't read too much into it."

"Oh." Derek wasn't sure how to proceed. Was he hearing this correctly? That Owen was okay with it?

"…Hypothetically, if it happened again…Fuck it, we'll see, right?"

Owen's response was delivered lightly, playfully. Dare Derek imagine? Maybe even, *flirtatiously*. Derek cleared his throat and opened his mouth to speak, but not a single word formed. He could hear Owen's soft chuckle over the phone line.

"Um, okay then. I guess, hypothetically, we'll see," Derek replied, thinking that was the safest response.

"Alright, bro, I'll let you get home now. Hey, keep me posted on how Addie's doing, will you? The way she ran out of here had me kind of worried about her."

"Alright, yeah, I'll call you later if she gives me an update. So, talk to you later. Bye, dude." Derek pulled the phone away from his ear and hurriedly hit the end call button.

He was stuck between a rock and a hard place. Now Owen knew or guessed his secret desires, and Addie knew, but both were about as available as a hotel with no vacancies. Adelaide's last words drummed up an amalgam of expectant fear and resolution for what was coming. For the life of him, Derek couldn't turn off his emotions for either one of them. He could only hope his idiot heart stayed on the margins of love instead of falling in completely.

◇◇◇

Friday morning was The Day, and Derek had the look of a man who had it all together for his important meeting with Mr. Clancy—the meeting that would determine whether or not he still had a job by the end of his shift. Derek was dressed in an all-black designer ensemble with tinted glasses for effect. His flyaway black hair was combed back and parted to the side, very professional. He carried his briefcase, the one Owen had given him, and he wore his best cologne.

Leaning on the lessons learned from his best bud during Operation Reshape Derek, he walked into the Ad Ent building like his presence was a gift to the design world, and when he entered the boardroom for the big presentation, Derek commanded attention, drawing stares and whispers.

"Maybe Derek should present," someone suggested.

"But, I always do the presentations!" the team lead, of course, adamantly protested.

Derek modestly held up his hands and backed down. "Now, now, guys. Let the man finish," he said. Harry stepped up to the screen with his little laser pointer and Derek lounged back in the chair with his ankle crossed over his knee—totally relaxed—while everyone else clung to the edges of their seats, nervous as hell.

"This is the, er, Wonder Man, uh…" Harry opened and closed his mouth like a fish out of water. He broke out in a panicked sweat, patting his pockets for his cue cards, and Derek quirked a brow in subtle amusement. This had never happened to the team lead before. What was going on? Everyone looked to Derek for help.

Derek calmly stood up and eased to the front, whispering, "That's it, Harry, I'll take it from here." He confiscated the pointer and rescued the team with a stunning oration that left Mr. Clancy open-mouthed with wonder. His team members hopped to their feet afterwards, clapping and cheering wildly. Then, someone dumped the whole pitcher of ice water from the middle of the boardroom table all over Derek's head, and he just laughed and laughed.

He had done it! He had really done it…

Then he woke up.

Coming out of a dead sleep, the blare of his alarm clock sounded like a dull buzz, and Derek snuggled deeper into his pile of blankets with an incoherent grumble. He tugged his pillow over his head because there was sunlight slanting through the high basement windows, hurting his eyes.

Sunlight slanting through the basement windows…which meant the sun had to be pretty low in the sky…

His eyes snapped open. "Holy shit!" he shrieked. Derek scrambled out of the bed, almost breaking his neck when he slid on a slick shirt that had somehow made its way from his unruly clothes basket to the floor to trip him up. "I'm late!"

He yanked off the t-shirt he'd slept in as he simultaneously whipped off his pajama pants, stumbling to the bathroom. "No, no, no!" Derek groaned. The shower came on with a hiss, the sound of which made him remember he hadn't turned off his alarm. So, he left the bathroom to hurry and do that, hurried back to the bathroom to get relatively clean, and in less than a minute, he was halfway dressed. That had to be a record, but one look at the time on his cellphone convinced him he still wasn't moving fast enough.

Derek dashed out of his room but skidded to a halt when he encountered his Dad waiting for him in the foyer. "Today's the big move out day, isn't it?" Frank peered at him over the top of his coffee mug as he blew on the piping hot brew.

Fuck, Derek inwardly swore. He had forgotten he was supposed to be moving out. Today was *not* shaping up the way he had planned. He had promised his parents he'd be out by the end of the week, but that was before he realized how impossible it was to find an apartment on short notice.

"Can't talk right now, Dad. I'm running late."

Frank chuckled. "Don't get a ticket, in your hurry. You don't need that trouble on top of everything else you're dealing with. By the way, good luck on your presentation."

"Gotta get there first!" Derek threw open the front door, jogged down the steps, and across the lawn to his car. He backed out—straight into the mailbox. Frank leaned outside to glare at him and Derek cringed. "Sorry!" he mouthed. His father, flapping his hands in disgust, slammed the door shut.

Derek sped ten to twenty miles over the speed limit the entire trip, ignoring his father's warning not to be in such a hurry that he got a ticket. This was an emergency, dammit. Derek sweated and swore, his eyes darting repeatedly to the dashboard clock. He was officially five minutes into his shift.

He snatched up his phone to call in and have Libby, the design floor administrative assistant, cover for him. Unfortunately, as soon as he hit the call button, his phone died. Apparently, he had forgotten to charge the thing and letting the alarm buzz for thirty minutes straight hadn't helped.

"Could this day get any worse?" He shouldn't have asked.

Derek made it all the way to the street where he was supposed to turn off for work when he saw the blue flash of lights in his rear view mirror, and registered the faint sound of the siren that, come to think of it, had been whirring for a while. His one-track mind had blocked out the sound completely.

"Holy friggin' *fuck*! Are you kidding me?" he shouted. That was when he realized his old bad luck was back. The gods of mediocrity had slammed him with their mighty fists. Accomplishing greatness was not in the cards for him. Derek's face crumbled comically as he dropped his head on the steering wheel and listened to the horn honk without even attempting to sit up.

Tap, tap, tap! The officer had made his way to Derek's window. "Get out of the car!" Derek noticed the antsy policeman was calling for backup using the radio hooked to his shoulder.

He powered down the window with a brave face, considering. "Yes sir, officer?"

"Man, I have half a mind to drag your tail out of there," said the irate gray-haired old timer, but he said it with a smile. He peered into Derek's car at the briefcase in the front seat. "Lemme guess, important meeting and you're late?"

"You've got it," Derek replied with a tight, uncomfortable smile. "W-was I speeding?" No, shit.

"Were you speed——? You know how long I've been trying to pull you over, son?" The cop's bushy brows made question marks above his eyes.

"Umm…" Derek shrugged helplessly. He had no idea. He'd been lost in a panic. Hell, he still was. Every minute that passed was like another nail in the coffin of his career. "Can you just give me my ticket? I mean, I'm kind of in a hurry and…I'm just going right there." He pointed up ahead to the Ad Ent, Inc. building.

Officer Bushy Brows radioed in again to cancel the backup call. He shook his head and started writing. "I should take you in for that medium-speed chase you just put me through. I was behind you for about the last mile and a half. I didn't know *what* your fool ass was doing." Scribble, scribble. "But, I know what it's like to be a cubicle monkey. Used to be one myself, before I got the job of my dreams." Scribble. He grinned and plucked at the badge pinned to his chest. Derek refrained from gagging. The cop tore the ticket out and handed it to him.

"Thank you, sir."

"Now look, you slow down from here on out. Don't make me

regret going easy on you."

Derek peered at the slip of paper with sinking hope. Such a long stretch of time had passed since he'd felt this low, felt like nothing would turn out in his favor. He was late. It was the meeting that would save or end his career. And, to top it all off, here he was getting a speeding ticket.

"What happened to my good luck charm?" he groaned. As the officer walked away from his car, he made sure to use all the proper signals and ease out into traffic to hop and skip right there to the office. He could only pray some major cataclysmic business event had occurred to keep Mr. Clancy from being in that boardroom.

CHAPTER 23

"WHATEVER YOU DO, just channel the smooth," he whispered. It rhymed. Sort of. It made for a decent mantra, as he sped through the corridors to the elevator bay and up to the design floor. He intended to do exactly that, although if there were ever a day he wished he and Owen could switch personalities, today would be that day. Derek wasn't cut out for this kind of pressure.

Libby, the design floor secretary, flashed him a tight smile as soon as she saw him walk out of the elevator. "You're late!" the secretary hissed. Derek held up the speeding ticket as he hurried to his cubicle. He quickly clocked in and marched to the boardroom, with Libby dogging his steps. "Wait up! I knew you'd make it in soon, so I took the liberty of telling Mr. Clancy that you had called in to say you had car trouble."

Derek halted mid-run and squeezed his eyes shut. *Thank you, Libby.* He was so happy she had intervened for him that he turned to her and kissed her on both cheeks. Libby let out a girlish squeal and giggled. Winking, she said, "Go get 'em, tiger."

Derek punched the air and breathed a sigh of relief. Knowing she had bought him at least a little bit of time, Derek calmed his racing heart and channeled the 'smooth' he needed to pull off a late entry into the boardroom. He could still salvage this. He just had to channel as much of Owen's personality as possible.

The door eased open without any noise. From within, Harry could be heard going over the group presentation, and from the sound of things, he hadn't gotten too far into the presentation before Derek arrived. Derek shut the door quietly behind him and paused. *Make eye contact.* He looked around for Mr. Clancy, connected and managed to smile. Mr. Clancy nodded, but his expression was unreadable. Derek took his seat as unobtrusively as possible.

Harry certainly knew how to pitch a good sale. He was expressive, and his voice and inflection changed to draw emotions out of his audience. Mr. Clancy sat with his elbow on the boardroom table, and his forefinger thoughtfully on his chin.

"We started with the ad for Wonder Man, thinking super hero. But, we ended thinking, what if? What if we broke some gender stereotypes? What if Wonder Man doesn't wear a cape? He wears glasses and has a beard and writes poetry. Or, maybe he wears a suit, comes in to work every day and stares out the window at the clouds. A dreamer."

Mr. Clancy tapped on the boardroom table with his gnarled knuckles. The older gentleman pushed his rimless spectacles up his nose and peered at Harry. "So, whose bright idea was it to change from super hero to metro man?" He smiled sardonically.

Derek gulped. He didn't like the sound of that, and Harry had no trouble pointing him out. Derek sat up straighter in his seat. "It was…I, um…" He cleared his throat nervously, because his voice sounded too uncertain to his own ears. He wasn't Owen. He was going to flub this. His dream was premonitory, only Harry represented himself. This was his one chance to speak, and he couldn't even get his words out.

Suddenly, all the self-confidence he had shored up in the two weeks since allowing Owen to play life coach and meeting Adelaide, fizzled out like hot air. Derek slumped in his seat. He was going to lose this job, and maybe that was for the best. He was an ad man, but this high profile company had expectations that surpassed his comfort zone. He could give up now.

Or, he could stop trying to be someone he wasn't, and simply be the best Derek Cornwell he could be. The guy who got speeding tickets after being warned not to speed. The guy who had a crush on his male best friend, but didn't have the balls to tell him. The guy who had come up with the brilliant idea to change the ad from being He-Man-ish, to a gauzy walk through a fog-filled park. That was him. A lot of fails. Some success. Some was better than none.

"I brought it up, Mr. Clancy…" Derek sighed. "I came to the idea after a combination of market research and general brainstorming. What sort of image does today's man want to project? We live in an imperfect world, in an imperfect time. The dreamer is someone who recognizes that, appreciates it, and makes the best of it. To me, the Every Man can relate to this at least on some level."

"Who else contributed?" asked another superior.

Harry replied, "Oh, it was all Derek's idea, but we all contributed, Mr. Blanche. As team lead, I take full responsibility. I should've followed my first instinct, and I'm professional enough to admit that."

Mr. Clancy nodded indeterminately, and Derek mentally started packing up his desk. He had a houseplant on top of his hutch. He could probably leave that to Libby. She might like it.

The presentation was concluded, and the lights were brought back up. Mr. Clancy and the other design superiors shared looks. The supervisor took off his glasses and rubbed his eyes, letting the glasses hang from his fingertips to the side. "I love it," Mr. Clancy murmured, with a casual shrug.

"W-what?" Derek was shocked. He loved the presentation?

"Mr. Cornwell, I'm impressed. Now, if you ladies and gentlemen will excuse us, we have other business to attend to. This Wonder Man ad is definitely a go. Congratulations."

Derek could barely believe what he was hearing. The best critique anyone ever got from Mr. Clancy was usually 'Hmm' or 'Well, alright then'. Every single member of the group breathed one big collective sigh of relief, as a slow round of applause filled the room.

"I knew it! I knew you'd be on board, sir," Harry schmoozed. Derek discreetly rolled his eyes.

"Congratulations, team. This one's a success," said Mr. Blanche with a vibrant smile. A smile particularly directed to Derek. He was getting noticed. Wow.

"Derek, I just want to say, your work this round was phenomenal. Keep it up!" said one of the execs.

"Thank you, I will," Derek promised with a grin.

Mr. Clancy and crew exited the room, deep in conversation about another project. Just like that, the pressure was off. The joint project had passed with flying colors. After the higher ups had all filed out of the room and it was just the eight team members left, Harry clapped his hands together and looked around at the group expectantly.

"Now," he said.

Derek squared off in front of him. He knew what time it was, time for the final assessment. Just the other day Harry had told him he wanted him off the team. Derek wondered if the success of the ad had changed his mind. "What's it gonna be, Harry?" he asked coolly.

Harry looked at the other team members before swinging his gaze back to Derek. He didn't look happy about whatever conclusion he had come to. "I guess you're staying on the team," he grumbled. The disgruntled team lead strolled out of the room, leaving the rest of the team members to congratulate Derek without him.

Derek basked in the glow of success, but when he finally extricated himself from the congratulatory circle, he isolated off at his cubicle to tackle phase two of Operation: Impress Mr. Clancy. There was still the matter of his personal project to take care of. Derek knew he had made his mark, but this would seal the deal.

As soon as he took a seat and powered up his computer, however, his cellphone buzzed on his desk. It was Adelaide, and he rushed forward to catch it, hoping it wasn't more bad news. He had worried about her all night after dropping her off at the hospital.

"Addie? Hi! How are things with your Dad?" he immediately answered.

"Foster Dad. He's not out of the woods yet," she said with a sigh. "I've been here all night, and I haven't gotten a wink of sleep. I'm worried sick about him, Derek."

"Have the doctors told you his prognosis? I mean, how do these things work?"

"Well, they started him on tPA as soon as he was brought in, which is a good thing. I think it saved his life. Now, it's a matter of wait and see."

"Do you need anything?" he asked gently. He might not be able to leave work, but he could certainly send someone to deliver something if she needed it.

"What'd I tell you during our first official date, huh?" she asked. There was a smile in her tone. "I take care of myself...I only called to give you an update. You know, in case you cared, or anything."

"You're finding it hard not to fall for me, aren't you?" he whispered. His lips curled up at the corners. She giggled through the phone.

"Easy, Casanova. Don't spook me."

Derek chuckled. "Alright, Addie. Listen, I've got a busy, busy day ahead. I'm supposed to be moving out of my parents' basement, although to where I don't know. I've gotta figure some things out, so it might be late when I talk to you again."

"Got a moving van? If you need a hand loading everything up, I'm scrawny, but I'm strong," she said gamely. He pictured her buxom body muscling a mattress into the back of a truck. Oddly, sexy stuff.

"Pfft, I can handle it. Company would be nice," he replied.

"I can do that, too. Catch you later, then. Once I find out how things are here, I'll probably get an uber and head home for a shower and some sleep. I should be free when you're ready. I just want to make sure he's okay, you know. I held his hand through the night, and...he looks so different." She was getting choked up. He could hear it. Derek shushed her soothingly.

"Don't get yourself worked up, hun. We take it moment by moment. And, you keep your head up."

"Thanks, Derek." She whispered goodbye and hung up the phone. Derek wished he could clock out and run to the rescue, but he couldn't. He entertained the thought of calling Owen to see if he was free to go visit her at the hospital; but, on second thought, he might need to ask an altogether different favor of him.

Derek didn't want to shell out unnecessary money for a hotel. He couldn't picture living out of his car, and he damn sure wasn't going home to tell Frank and Lydia he'd need a little more time to find an apartment. He only had one other option, and that was to beg his best friend to let him hole up with him until something shook.

Derek grabbed his phone and hurried to the elevators to catch them down to the ground floor. He needed a break from the fluorescent lights and cubicles, and he definitely didn't want anyone eavesdropping on   this   call.

CHAPTER 24

"C'MON, PICK UP," Derek whispered, pacing back and forth outside the office building with his cellphone pressed to his ear. It was midmorning by the time he exited the boardroom, and Owen was at work doing pharmaceutical sales, but he really needed him to catch this call.

"This is Owen," came his mellow tenor voice on the third ring.

"Hey!" Derek breathed a sigh of relief. "What are you doing? Got a second to talk?"

"You're in luck. I'm between clients now. Wassup?"

"Oh, don't mention luck. You would not believe the morning I've had." He stopped pacing and braced his back against the wall of the building, putting his heel up to the brick.

"Uh oh. Trouble with the meeting?" The sound of Owen's voice made him smile involuntarily. But when he realized that's what he was doing, Derek straightened his face. He didn't need to get distracted with fantasies. He had a fifteen-minute window to take care of the problem of finding room and board, before he had to rush back inside and deal with Mr. Clancy again.

"No, the group meeting actually went swell. I still have to do my presentation for my personal project, though. I overslept this morning, had to speed to work, and got a ticket, all before facing Mr. Clancy and his henchmen. Talk about a bad scene."

"Yo, you need to find whatever gypsy has a hex on you and make it right, man," Owen said with a laugh.

"Ha! How about you just lend me your goddamn fairy godmother, you lucky prick," Derek replied. "I went into the boardroom trying to be like you and clammed completely up."

"Dude, I told you not to do that. When are you gonna stop comparing?"

"Today. I had to stop. I realized I couldn't pull off the classic Owen Henderson charm—"

"Well, duh. Nobody can," Owen interjected.

Derek snickered. "The Derek Cornwell tenacity won out in the end. For a change, all the hard work I put into this paid off for me. At least, so far. Fingers crossed on the personal project." He crossed his two middle fingers over each other and could picture Owen doing the same, like they had done since they were teens. He chuckled to himself. It felt good to be talking to his friend again, instead of Owen being too pissed to take his calls.

"But, that's not why I called you. I've got a major favor to ask." Derek finally got to the point.

"Wait, does this involve Addie?" Owen asked suspiciously. "Because, I'm still reeling from your last favor, when you asked me to play her side piece." He chuckled. "Luckily, that turned out better than I expected."

"Um, bigger than that, actually. Probably a little more inconvenient, too. I need a place to crash."

"For the night?"

"More like for a few weeks. Remember I told you my folks were kicking me out? Yeah, well, I kind of bit off more than I could chew when I told them I'd have an apartment by the end of the week."

His Mom and Dad had sat him down around the beginning of the week and told him he had thirty days to get out. It was harsh to hear, but their reasoning was sound. Derek was in his late twenties and had a great career. He was only living in their basement because his mom felt his student loans prevented him from moving forward.

Derek was under the same impression too, until he didn't have a choice in the matter. Once moving out was his only option, he wanted it done and done fast, so he had promised his parents he'd find a new place before the week was out. The week was out. He didn't have anywhere else to go.

"Yep. Jackass. I could've told you that was a bad idea," Owen teased. Derek rolled his eyes.

"You could have, but that was around the time you stopped talking to me."

"Ha! Point taken. You done throwing that up in my face yet?"

"Not likely. I, too, can hold a grudge. Mine is just more vocal," Derek quipped. "Anyway, it's the end of the week, and I don't have a pot to piss in or a window to throw it out of, so to speak. I am *not* going back on my word to my folks. The last thing I need is for my Dad to say, 'I told you so'. I was hoping I could crash with you a while and keep apartment hunting. The alternative is I sleep in my car."

"Sleep in your goddamn car? What are you, crazy? You know you can crash here anytime. In fact, I'll do you one better. Why don't you move in with me?" A pregnant pause descended.

After what had happened between them by the pool, Derek hadn't even bothered to broach the subject of being roommates, although his father had suggested it. Things could get complicated if they were living under the same roof.

Anticipation bordering on arousal unfurled within him at the very idea, however. He had stayed at Owen's recently, and his late night venture to play video games had led to him spying on his best friend masturbating to a porno. Derek colored at the memory, but it had been highly erotic, and prompted X-rated dreams.

"Move in with you? I've heard friends shouldn't live together. It ruins friendships," said Derek.

"Let me ask you something, and be candid with me. What's the worst that could happen?"

"Well, I mean, we'd split the bills fifty-fifty, so that wouldn't be a problem," Derek supplied.

"Uh-huh. I don't see that being a problem, either. Anytime you fall short, you know my income covers it."

"Yeah, but I'd still pay you back."

"See? Sounding better and better."

"What about cleaning habits? You know I'm a slob and you're a neat freak."

"Oh, trust and believe, I have absolutely no problem nagging the piss out of you until you clean your shit up. You'll get so sick of it that being a neat freak too will come naturally." Derek chuckled. That really wasn't a problem anyway. His mom might spoil him by doing his laundry for him, but Derek had no trouble keeping other people's things nice and neat. "Got anything else?" Owen pressed.

Derek inhaled deeply and let the air out in a whoosh. "I dunno. Those seem to be the two main complaints, from what I hear."

"In other words, we wouldn't ruin our friendship by moving in together. What are you really afraid of?" He asked like he knew. Derek rubbed his forehead, unsure if he should 'be candid' like Owen had suggested. He sighed again.

"Owen. I can't explain it, but there's something going on between us. I mean, I've got th-these crazy thoughts and feelings and…gah, I can't talk about this. Look, if I were to move in with you, I think this will get worse."

"Why does it have to be something going on between us? It's the same as always. I want you around. I don't want you sleeping in your car. I want you to move in with me. Simple as that. You're making this shit way too complex, dude."

"You know what I mean!" Derek exclaimed in frustration.

Owen blew out an exasperated breath. "Yeah, I do. But, you have a bad habit of talking around a subject. Just say it. What the hell's gonna happen if you say it, Derek? Know what you want and go after it. Stop being a goddamn—"

"I want you." There. He'd said it. Derek squeezed his eyes shut. He wanted to disappear once it was out in the open. He didn't know what it said about him, his sexuality, or the future of his friendship, but it was the truth. "I'm into you. I think about you all the damn time, and it's driving me insane. I can't…"

Derek sucked in a breath and slid down the wall to rest on his heels as he put his forehead to his bent knees. He heard Owen take a deep breath on the other end of the phone. Derek continued, "I can't turn it off. So, if I move in with you, something is bound to happen. Dude, I don't want to lose our friendship over this." His voice rose with anxiety.

"Chill. Derek, chill. We're cool. What time are you coming? Trying to move out today, right?"

Derek reeled at how easily Owen coasted over his confession. He sniffed and tried to get ahold of himself. He was close to a full-blown panic attack. At the same time, he felt like another tremendous weight had been lifted off his shoulders. Owen knew everything. There was nothing left to hide.

"Y-yeah, Adelaide will probably be with me. We'll come sometime around eight-ish? Is that alright with you?"

"I'll be here. Can't wait. I'll have the grill going, and we can celebrate with a few beers, or something."

"You have no idea how much this means to me. Thank you. I know I've said it a couple of times in the past few days, but you've really made an impact on my life, dude." Derek rose from his kneeling position and stretched out his aching joints. Glancing at his watch, he saw it was just about time for him to get on inside for the next meeting.

"That's what friends are for," said Owen. "See you later, D."

Derek managed a short laugh. "That's Mr. Derek Cornwell…and see you later, bro."

"Wait, Derek? I wasn't going to say this, but I've gotta get this off my chest so we can set the record straight."

"Yeah?"

"Your ass knows me well enough to know that what you just said should never have been that hard for you to confess to me. Maybe to somebody else, but not to me. Derek, you are my best friend, alright? I accept you. I don't judge you. There's nothing to judge."

"I swear I'm not gay," Derek whispered.

"Who gives a damn about a label? And, you know what else? We're close, Derek. In fact, we're so close that I saw this coming from a mile away. No surprise, there. You can't ruin our friendship by being who you are. That's what I wanted to tell you. Just do you, and the rest will take care of itself. Now, step away from the panic button and get your head ready for that personal meeting with Mr. Clancy. You've got this, bro."

Derek smoothed his hand down his face to wipe the wetness from his eyes. He was slammed by everything Owen had said. The outpouring of love and acceptance was phenomenal. "Stop being so goddamn perfect, and I might be able to get over you," he whispered, half to himself.

Owen chuckled on the other end of the phone. "Bye, Derek."

"Talk to you later, Owen." He hung up. He stared at the world around him as if seeing it for the first time. He felt a lot like he had come out of the closet, only he hadn't. There was no closet. He wasn't gay.

Derek ambled back up to his floor, lost in thought about the conversation with Owen. Owen's assertion that he already knew was surprising, since Derek was sort of just learning of it. He wondered how long Owen had picked up on the subtle attraction.

Or, was it really something new? Owen had told him to be who he was, and it occurred to Derek that he had always idolized and emulated his friend. It was easier not to examine himself because he simply wasn't built like Owen, the total package—a born success story. Derek had felt that if he could just be more like his friend, then his luck would change. Ironically, the best form of flattery was probably how Owen had figured out the attraction.

Now, there was no excuse for Derek to continue the mimicry. As of the meeting earlier with the group, he had received the validation he needed to know that Derek Cornwell had better stick to being Derek Cornwell. And, as of the conversation with Owen, he realized the stark contrasts in their personalities that made trying to be like him even more ridiculous.

Namely, Owen wasn't in the same boat with him. He didn't have these same feelings and hidden desires. He didn't want Derek.

CHAPTER 25

"MR. CORNWELL?"

He looked up. "Yes, Libby, my sweet friend. What can I do you for?" Despite his muddled thoughts, he beamed at her. She preened.

"Just coming to report that Mr. Clancy will see you now," she replied.

Derek inhaled deeply. "Wish me luck, Libby," he whispered. She flashed a thumbs-up as he strolled to the supervisor's office. "Ready or not, here I come." He channeled his inner calm, which to the outward observer could be read as self-assuredness. Derek wasn't even aware, but the 'presence' he'd been trying to muster up since that lesson with Owen, came effortlessly when he wasn't trying too hard.

He marched across the design floor to Mr. Clancy's frosted glass door, and he held up his fist to knock. The supervisor must've seen his shadow because he called him on in before his hand connected with the glass. "Here's the man of the hour. Let's see what you have, Mr. Cornwell." Mr. Clancy held his hand out palm side up, and Derek handed him the project folder.

He quickly set up his tablet to wirelessly project his displays on the screen against Mr. Clancy's sidewall. "Before we start, I just want to say that I took your critique into deep consideration, and...well, what I came up with may be far left of field, but if you'll take a look at the data in the folder, you'll see that I've thoroughly done my homework."

He was nervous. It showed. But, his work would speak for itself, Derek knew. He wondered again why he had ever imagined using

Owen as a template would be best for him. They were two completely different people. Owen's suaveness came naturally. Derek, not so much. He had to use what he had, and what he had was: Talent.

The presentation lasted a tense half-hour. When Derek was done, he sat and waited for his supervisor to make an assessment. Mr. Clancy mulled over the data he had presented—market research and projected impact on sales. He wasn't in a hurry to put Derek out of his misery. Derek guessed he should be grateful for that, in case the news was bad.

"This. This pushes boundaries in an unexpected way," said Mr. Clancy.

The older man peered at the ad spread with the handle of his glasses tucked between his lips speculatively. Derek sat stiffly in the chair across from him. He had unveiled the design with a brief slideshow presentation, and now his supervisor was taking a closer look at the hard copies.

In a stark white room, two incredibly attractive male models in white suits with brooding faces and dark hair took the middle ground. One was coming toward the viewer with a hand tucked in his blazer and the other walking away while glancing back at the viewer. In the forefront sat a pale woman with honey gold curls spilling over her slightly turned shoulder. She was in a vivid red dress and wore lipstick of the same shade.

The image was open to interpretation. At the bottom of the page was the bottle of cologne, the name of it—Wonder Man—and the catchphrase Derek had come up with that certainly added a slant to the advertisement: Make them wonder.

Mr. Clancy continued staring at it, nodding his head. "Well, what do you think?" Derek asked nervously. A small smile flitted across the man's face.

Mr. Clancy replied, "This is good. It's bold. It's millennial."

Derek clutched his chest and couldn't help the grin that spread across his face. "I took a chance. I wasn't sure how the message would be received, but I have reason to believe there is a market for this particular type of advertisement."

"Of course! Derek, this is why you were hand picked. You haven't disappointed." He folded his glasses and set them on his impeccably neat desk. "Two weeks ago it pained me to have to say I wanted to let you go, but I saw no choice."

"Sir, I am infinitely grateful that you gave me another chance."

"Consider your position here secure. I'm afraid I'll have to take you off of Harry's team, though."

"W-what?" Derek's eyes widened with surprise. So, Harry had asked that he be removed after all.

Mr. Clancy shuffled the hard copy images back into the portfolio folder Derek had brought in, and handed it back to him. "Yes, I don't think you belong with that group, anyway. Although, I must say your contributions to the group project really turned it around and made it something sellable. Now, what I want to do is…I want to give you your own team."

Derek was frozen to his chair, overwhelmed. This was the promotion he'd been hoping for. Mr. Clancy was telling him he trusted his creative vision enough to let him lead his own team. He didn't know what to say. He couldn't say thank you enough. Derek straightened up and reached a hand across the desk, taking the older gentleman's hand in a firm shake. "Sir, I look forward to the opportunity to lead," Derek managed to say.

Mr. Clancy nodded. "Good. Because we've got some newbies coming in next week, and they're going to need a lot of patience, and a lot of guidance."

Some of Derek's enthusiasm deflated. No one wanted to work with new designers. They were a pretentious, mistake-prone lot. However, this was still a great chance for him to show his stuff. "I'm ready for the challenge, sir. In fact, I preemptively began working on the next product we're slated to market. I spoke with the company only yesterday."

"Yes, I heard! Excellent of you. That's the initiative I want to see. Keep up the good work, Derek. I don't want to have to call you back into my office for slacking off, or the next time might not end so well."

"I assure you, we're past that," said Derek. He rose to his feet after being dismissed, and he quietly slipped out of Mr. Clancy's office. He had done everything he had set out to do two weeks ago. He had secured his job, shown his talent, and proved to Harry Gensler he belonged on the team. For all his hard work, he'd been rewarded with a team of his own.

Derek sat back at his desk, amazed at how everything had worked itself out. He'd also taken care of finding a place to stay. Operation

Reshape Derek had been a success. But, now there was another problem on the horizon. There was the situation with Owen. Adelaide came with some kinks, too. He had his business life in order, and now he had to clean up his personal life.

"This should be interesting," Derek muttered at he stared at the text message he had never deleted. The one of Owen shirtless. Tonight marked the start of a new phase of their friendship. Was he ready for it?

"So, how does it feel to be a team leader?" Libby asked Derek at lunch. They were in the artsy communal lounge, and she was munching on lettuce wraps while Derek scarfed down a turkey sandwich.

"Mmph." He wiped his mouth with the napkin, grunting a response. "I'm psyched. I didn't expect it, but I'm psyched."

"Word around the water cooler is Harry's pissed about the promotion. But he's gloating, because he knows you're getting a team of newbies."

"Hey Libby, how do you always get the inside scoop? You haven't even been to the water cooler since the news broke," he said, snickering.

She wrinkled her cute little nose and scrunched up her face. "That's classified," she giggled.

"Well, you tell the water cooler chatters that I'm okay with getting a team of newbies. This place needs some fresh blood. And, I don't know why Harry is upset. He didn't want me on his team, anyway." He picked over his sandwich and set it aside so they could talk.

"I'm pretty sure he sees you as competition."

"I don't compete. I'm just happy to be here."

"Ah, yes…happiness. Speaking of which, I met a new guy," she said, waggling her eyebrows. Derek pulled back with a grin.

"Whaaaa?" He was pleasantly surprised. For a brief while Libby had tried to put the moves on him until he'd told her about Adelaide.

"Yes! Ah, god, he's adorable. He's cuddly, and goofy, and approachable, and we're going out next weekend if all goes well. How are things with you and your sweetie pie?"

Derek twitched his mouth to the side. "Hmm, progressing."

"Uh oh, sounds like you hit a roadblock. That's a good thing. I was worried about you two moving so fast. That was a bad sign, man."

"Right, you said something to that effect. Why though, Libby? What's wrong with a woman knowing what she wants and going after it?"

"No, nothing's wrong with that. But from what you told me, you two barely knew each other. When women rush into things like that, it only means one thing. That they'll attach to any warm body who shows them attention."

Derek frowned. "It's kind of the opposite." She put her elbows on the table and leaned in, all ears. He shook his head, laughing. "I don't know why I even asked how you know everything that's happening around this place. You have an uncanny knack for getting a story out of a person. You sure you're in the right field? Seems like with your skillset you could be doing something other than personal assistant work," he teased.

"You'd be surprised at how much my little talent comes in handy for this job. Word to the wise, you want to get in good with the higher-ups? Just tell them something they don't know." She flashed a thumbs-up sign and winked. "Now, where were we? You said she's kind of the opposite to the clingy, any-guy-will-do type, huh?"

"Yeah, she grew up in the foster care system. Let's just say she doesn't trust love. With Adelaide, she's all for a casual sexual relationship, but anything more 'spooks' her. Her words."

"My poor guy. So, she's got mommy and daddy issues. Yikes. Good luck with that."

"You don't think I can win her heart?"

"Truthfully?" Libby sucked in a breath and sat back with a serious look. "You don't play with a heart like that. The kind of heart that's been broken too many times to count. In my opinion, stick to the casual dating thing with her. Unless..."

"Unless, what?"

"Unless, you're actually willing to put your own fears and doubts aside to help rebuild what's been broken. You know what that means, right? It'll be the battle of a lifetime, but if you win it, she's all yours. So, if you want her for realz? Take it from a girl. Don't fuck with her."

Derek sipped from his water bottle and smiled. "I'll keep that in mind." He finished his sandwich and stared out the window at the blue sky, lost in thought. Libby was content to leave him to his silence. He idly wondered why he had never noticed her before. She was a cool chick. He hoped the relationship thing with the new guy she'd met worked out.

Derek had been toggling back and forth in his head about his intentions concerning Adelaide ever since their first official date to the amusement park. The way he had met her—on an impulsive one-night stand with Owen after she had crashed his sister's wedding—had prepped Derek for an explosive hook-up style courtship. He had pictured them hanging out, having sex, keeping things probably exactly how Addie actually wanted things.

But after that date, he had seen a glimpse of her vibrant personality and knew he could fall for a woman like that in a heartbeat. What *were* his intentions? He knew he wanted something serious. Maybe there was a question of how serious, but he definitely knew that casual dating (leaving Adelaide a free agent to find some other lover) wasn't his thing.

Addie's clear rules against getting too close kept him on the sidelines, however, and Derek didn't want to waste his time. He didn't know how long he had with her, but he had figured inviting Owen to join their mix would keep her novelty-seeking brain entertained long enough for him to convince her that she could be happy with him. Which in effect meant...he was totally accepting her casual sexual relationship terms.

After the conversation with Owen, however, he wasn't sure if any of that was still on the table. How could Owen be comfortable sleeping with him and Addie if he knew Derek had the feels for him?

Derek sighed. "It's complicated, Libby. All I can say is, it won't be me who breaks her heart."

"Aww, you're worried she'll break yours. Yeah, probably. Sucks."

"Yep."

"Anyway, congrats on the promotion," Libby perked up. Derek grunted a laugh and toasted his water bottle to hers.

"Congrats on your new beau. Hope it works out for you."

"For what it's worth, I hope Addie doesn't break your heart. I'd hate to have to put it back together for you," she teased.

"Stop it, minx," he said, grinning. "Come on. Lunch is over. I've gotta get back to my desk and start showing Mr. Clancy I deserve the top spot he gave me."

"Kudos. Chat with you later, buddy."

They exited the break room, and Derek's long-legged stride carried him to his cozy cubicle. There was some research stuff he needed to do to be prepared for his team. Mr. Clancy had informed him Monday would be his new start. Derek placed some phone calls and kept himself busy, but his thoughts were far from the office.

In truth, the unorthodox ménage-a-relationship went against Derek's entire make up. He was conservative, played things safe, and accepted his lot in life. Or, at least, that's how it used to be. And, while he was confident he didn't have to pretend to be Owen to be successful anymore, Derek couldn't be certain who exactly he was these days. He was in a state of evolution.

He forced himself to seriously contemplate what he really wanted out of the situation. Never mind what was plausible. Owen's advice was, success came to those who knew these things, and having a vague idea didn't cut it. So, if plausibility were thrown out the window, then Derek would say what he actually wanted was a chance to give Adelaide the love she had missed out on growing up. Call it a savior complex. Call it whatever. He felt she deserved it, and he knew she didn't think she did. That's why she wasn't seeking it.

As for Owen, Derek wanted…to explore? To experiment? If he was being honest, he wanted that, and more. The thought of having what happened by the pool the evening before happen again, made his manhood prickle with anticipation. He desired him. And, the scary part was that Owen accepted him exactly as he was, which made it that much harder to keep his taboo lust under control. Plausibility aside, Derek would be perfectly content to sleep with Owen and fall in love with Addie.

Unfortunately, reality wasn't set up like that, and he needed to pick more realistic goals. Derek put his feelings for Owen out of the picture, knowing it would be better to focus on taking care of Adelaide. She needed him—he needed her, too. She was the reason he was evolving, and Derek was vastly improved by the change her being in his life had wrought on him. He could only hope to change her hardened   heart,   too.

CHAPTER 26

"DID YOU GET any rest? What time did you end up getting home from the hospital?" Derek asked. Adelaide slid into the passenger seat and pulled on her seatbelt. As promised, she was coming with him to finish packing and load up the moving van he'd rented. She looked like a dream in a thin yellow dress, although her eyes looked tired and her smile was less vivid that usual. He touched her face. "You look beat, cupcake."

"I don't even know what time I got in. I was so tired I went straight to my room and fell into bed, but don't worry about me. I did manage to catch a few z's, and I'm feeling refreshed enough to tackle this project. So, let's go for it."

He smiled at her, and pulled out of the parking lot of her apartment complex to head back across the city to his parents' house. She leaned her head against the headrest and closed her eyes, and he was content to let Addie relax after the long night she'd had.

"By the time I left, the doctors said George was doing much better."

"He's probably going to need physical therapy."

"Yeah, I'm sure. He was left with expressive aphasia as a result of the stroke. They're hoping it will clear, but they said there's no way to tell just yet. Some of the twisting of his face cleared up a little, though." She stared out the window. He wished she wasn't so guarded. Derek knew she needed a friend's support more than ever right now.

"Did you talk to him?" he asked quietly. She nodded.

"I told him what I had been up to, how my business was doing. He squeezed my hand. He recognized the sound of my voice. That felt so good to me," she said with emotion.

"I'm glad you had the chance to do that. Addie, have you ever thought about going to see a therapist? It might help."

She smiled at him and shook her head. "You're such a feelings person."

He laughed. "Yeah, I guess I am."

"Oh Derek, I've had my fill of shrinks, head doctors, and quacks," she chuckled. "No, the past is the past. My life now is great, actually. I have a pretty dope apartment. I'm an entrepreneur. I've got this sweet deal of a sex ring going on." She winked and grinned, moods changing like flowing water. He wanted to penetrate the rippling surface and swim in the currents underneath. What was she really thinking?

"What's your biggest fear, Addie?" Derek asked impulsively. He wanted to get to know more than bits and pieces she very carefully allowed him to see. "Because with a past like yours, I think maybe the always smiling, skipping, happy you has to be an act. That carefree spirit thing you have going on might really be a sense of not feeling anchored."

"Alright, how much are you going to charge me to pick my brain?" She giggled and bit the corner of her thumb, staring at him with a look that told him she wanted him to think of other things. Her full lips conjured memories of being enveloped by her perfect mouth. But, Derek didn't fall into the trap. He turned his eyes back to the road.

"Back to the question. You tell me yours, and I'll tell you mine."

"You first," she prompted.

"Alright. One of my biggest fears is that I don't have the necessary qualities to be anything but mediocre. Your turn."

"No, no! You said biggest fear. That means what's at the top of the list. You can't just list one of your fears." She smirked.

"I asked the original question, so I get to make the rules."

"Fine, then. One of my biggest fears is spiders." She nodded cheekily, and turned back to watching the scenery flash by. Derek playfully tugged on a strand of her long, silky hair.

He gave her another one of his fears. "I'm afraid that because I don't have the tools necessary, even if I do reach some level of success, everyone will see my shortcomings and realize I'm a fraud."

"Me, too. Next," she retorted.

"Hey," he complained.

Adelaide erupted with giggles and turned to him. "Oh, come on!" She rolled her eyes and smiled. "Are you serious? You *really* want to do this."

"Yeah, I *really* do. I want you to talk to me. What kind of friendship is it if all we do is sleep together?"

"A damned good one," she fired back.

Derek barked a laugh. "You are *such* a bad girl," he joked.

She shrugged one shoulder and looked down at her hands, suddenly solemn. "Can be," she said laconically.

"There. See? That's what I'm talking about. I want to know where your thoughts wander off to when your happy face drops. I want to know what keeps you from opening up to me."

She snorted softly. "Derek, you want to know my biggest fear? That I'll end up like George; that I'll be in my eighties in a hospital, surrounded by strangers, because I don't have family. I'm an orphan. I'm the person nobody wants to keep around. And, as for friendship? Pfft, friendship is a joke. Nobody has lifelong friends any more, and the way I see it, that's the only kind that's real."

"How did you become an orphan?"

He knew she'd feel he was prying, but he wanted to chip away at that thick shell of armor. They were in a car, and it was a long drive. She couldn't escape his questions. Adelaide crossed her arms defiantly. "What, are you writing a book about me? Are you a journalist, or something? Derek, seriously, drop this."

"Was it a car accident? Did your parents pass away?"

"Derek!" she shouted. She covered her face, and Derek feared he had pressed too hard. He sighed and touched her hand to pull it away.

"I'm sorry. You don't have to hide. I'll stop…I'm just…just trying to know you. I don't know what problems you face. Hell, I don't know your work shift or your girlfriends. I'm not part of your circle. I don't follow you on social media. I feel like—"

"A one-night stand? Well, you are, Derek. You're the one who looked me back up. I was content to leave it at that."

He whistled sadly. "Harsh," he muttered.

"No," she groaned. "Derek. I'm sorry. When I get angry, I lash out. It's a holdover from when I was younger and I had to defend myself a lot."

He nodded but didn't ask any further questions or initiate any further conversation. If she was mad and lashing out, then now wasn't the time to talk to her anyway. They drove on another handful of minutes in silence with still a thirty-minute drive to go. Derek sighed and turned his thoughts to other trivial pursuits. No point in wondering about what made Addie tick. She was firm on it. Unless she volunteered the info, it wasn't any of his business.

He thought instead about Owen. The thoughts loosened the tension of his clenched jaw, and smoothed his furrowed brow. His eyes took on a hazy look. Adelaide stole glances at him but mostly seemed like she was ignoring him. Derek drifted on a collection of erotic dreams and sensual memories interspersed with snatches of conversation. All day after the phone call, he had been trying to piece together when his feelings for Owen manifested.

Again, he had flashbacks of watching him change during gym class, admiring the way his physique gradually filled out over the course of their tenth grade year.

"What are you thinking about?" Adelaide broke the silence.

"Aha! So, I don't get to know what's on your mind, but I have to tell you what's on mine?"

"You don't *have* to do anything but die when your time's up," she said glibly.

Derek reached across and pinched her nose. "Snarky, Addie," he chuckled. "I was thinking about Owen...and stuff."

"You like him, don't you?"

"Adelaide, how is that more important than you unloading some of the things that get you down, babe?" He seriously wanted to know. "We can talk about what I have going on, but you clam up if we talk about you. That's pretty one-sided."

She huffed in frustration. "Geez, let's talk. How did I become an orphan? My mother had me when she was fifteen years old. Her family was Catholic, so they wouldn't let her get an abortion. They sent her away until she delivered me. Once I was born, they sent me to some other relative to raise as their own. Only they got tired of me before I even reached my second birthday, and gave me up to the state. Is that interesting enough for you?"

"Please, don't get upset. I don't want you to feel you *have to* talk to me. I want you to know that you *can* talk to me. Understand?" Derek noticed she was almost hyperventilating between the sentences of her rapid narration.

"I want to talk," she replied. "It's hard to do. I never know where to start. Derek, my history is a patchwork quilt sewn together from scraps of stories other people told me. The truth is, I don't really know all there is to know about me. I don't know if my father drank or if my mother smoked pot while she was pregnant with me. I don't know who I got my hair color or eye color from. I don't know."

"That's what makes you sad," Derek said gently. She was talking. She was ranting, but she was getting it out, and that was good. He could take her tirade.

"No, that's what makes me angry. How does it make you feel to have all those questions for me and me not answer? Well, that's what my life is, Derek," she said brokenly. Adelaide sucked in a breath and struggled for calm. "My life is a book of unanswered questions. Questions I will never have explained. Why did they give me up? Did I cry too much? Was I sickly? Did they have other kids that needed them? I don't know."

He reached for her hand, placing his palm up on the center console. She eyed it but eventually laced her fingers in his with a tired sigh and a shake of her head. Derek stroked her rose petal soft skin. He didn't throw any more questions at her. He didn't think she could handle any more right now.

"Thank you," he murmured. "I know that had to be tough for you. To live through, and to talk about. I won't pry again."

"You will," she replied with a sardonic laugh. "They all do. Men seem to think they can fix you, and they poke and pry until they break you even worse."

He squeezed her hand. "I won't pry again because I hope next time when you need to talk you do it willingly. Feels better to get it off your chest, doesn't it? And, I won't break you, Adelaide."

She blinked back tears and popped on the radio. "Whatever." She crossed her arms and turned away from him. Derek wondered how to get out of taking her home to meet his parents in her current mood. She didn't seem to want to be there.

She changed to a country station and turned up the volume. Derek let the windows down so the breeze could whip through her hair. She laid her head on the headrest with her eyes closed again. The music soothed. Even Derek found himself getting into it.

"You okay?" he asked after a beat. He saw her nod wordlessly out of the corner of his eye. "I can take you back home if you'd rather not hang out with me this evening," he suggested quietly. She shook her head. "Are you sure?"

"One rough conversation and you're ready to get rid of me?" She didn't open her eyes as she spoke but a small smile lifted her mouth. Derek chuckled silently.

"I'm just looking out for your comfort. I don't want you to suffer through hours of my presence if you don't want to be here."

"If I didn't want to be here, I know where the door is."

"We're driving," he said.

Her smile widened. "It'd be a damned fine exit, though."

They arrived at his parents' house a short time later, and Adelaide's sour mood seemed to have improved. She hopped out of his Mazda, gazing at the house with interest. "What are your parents like?" she asked.

"Um, Dad's a cantankerous old fart and Mom is a cougar in training. They're decent," he quipped. She giggled and took his hand shyly.

"I'm sorry I can be a mean ass," she whispered, as they made their way to the front door. Derek dug his keys out of his pocket, nodding.

"That, you can be," he acknowledged.

"Still want to get to know me? 'Cause I'm pretty good at keeping up the act. All smiles. Everybody's happy."

He gazed into her eyes before he opened the door. "A friend told me earlier to be myself and everything else would follow."

"Oh, yeah?"

"Mm-hmm. So, don't show me the façade. Give me your bad days, your sad days, your realness. Let me know what I'm giving up if I ever have to let you go."

She leaned in toward him with a questing look in her eyes. She licked her lips and gazed at his mouth. "I don't want you to have to let me go," she confessed in the quietest voice. He had to strain to hear. Derek closed the distance between them with a tender kiss. "But, you will," she finished.

"Don't push me away, Addie," he murmured. Derek buried his

nose in her hair and inhaled. "Just don't."

CHAPTER 27

SHE SLIPPED AWAY from him and took the lead, turning the doorknob and stepping into the cooler interior of the house. Derek bit his lower lip, yearning. He shut the door behind him. "Come on. I'll show you where I sleep. Not a thing is packed, but it shouldn't take that long to get it all together because I don't own much. I only rented a van so I wouldn't have to make three or four trips with my car."

He took her to the basement. His father had brought home some cardboard boxes from work earlier in the week, and left them down there for him. Derek snapped one into shape and started packing.

"How can I help?" Addie asked.

He pointed to his entertainment center. "Want to unhook everything for me?" Derek gathered up armloads of clothes and took a second to semi-fold them so they'd fit into the box. He pulled the sheets and comforter off his bed and folded them up neatly so his mom could put them back in the linen closet. Then, he located all his shoes to pack them away.

"Want to know more about my childhood?" she asked as she worked. Derek glanced over at her in surprise.

"Sure," he replied. "Tell me anything you want to tell me." Derek paused packing and rested his butt on the footboard of his bed. Adelaide leaned against the wall by the stack of boxes that were accumulating.

"Well. I learned how to fight because I got teased a lot for being slightly overweight."

"I can't picture you overweight," he retorted.

"I was! I was a pudgy little kid. I'd show you, but I don't have any pictures of me from back then. They might be in my case file, though. Anyway, so this one time when I was seven, I got in a fight with this boy who was a few grades older than me. He said 'Addie's got a fatty'. I was so insulted. It wasn't until I was older that I figured out the little dork was trying to compliment me."

"Aww, he had a crush," Derek said, snickering.

"Yeah, I didn't really get into the whole dating thing until I was in college, though. Like, I didn't have any high school boyfriends or guys I wanted to be with. My mind was on other stuff."

"Other stuff, like what? Hobbies?"

She looked him in the eyes. "Like chores, running a household, taking care of little kids. See, most people think folks foster out of the goodness of their hearts, but in my experience? They see foster kids as free labor. As far back as I can remember, every house I was moved into felt like enslavement.

"Granted, sometimes that was just the family's routine, and it wasn't so bad then. Say the foster family has two biological kids and two foster kids, and we're all on the same chore board and have the same responsibilities around the house. Then, that's fair."

"But, it wasn't always like that."

"Right. Mostly, I'd step into a house and know within ten seconds flat how hard my life was going to be by how spick and span the place was. Man, I clocked more housekeeping hours from the age of four to sixteen than a flock of maids during the same time span. All things considered, I guess the extra work kept me out of trouble, though. Like I said, I wasn't into dating because of it."

"I think I had probably the most regular teenage American life possible. I had chores, but I got an allowance. And, really my mom picked up my slack. She's always been Susie Homemaker."

"Gloria was like that. She was the sweetest little old ball of energy. She'd get up around seven in the morning, and start up coffee and breakfast for George. Then, she'd clean the entire house, top to bottom. That was one place I didn't have to do much."

"Can I ask? What had happened by the time you were sixteen to make you stop wanting a family?"

Adelaide quirked her lips to the side. "It's hard to explain. There was no 'one' thing," she said. "I think it was because I had spent my entire childhood holding onto the dream that I'd get adopted and someone would want me. Sixteen was too close to aging out. I felt like my time was up. No point in getting attached to some family. A year wasn't long enough to form a lasting bond, anyway."

"I can understand that," he replied. "But, why keep the same attitude with relationships? You're not going to age out of adulthood. You have time to get to know someone, and care about them, and let them care about you."

Adelaide crossed her arms. "I see where this is going," she laughed.

"Ha! No, that isn't a line to segue into a 'why can't we be together' speech."

Adelaide shook her head in amusement. "Funny how you know exactly what speech it is, though!"

"Seriously, I just wanted to know why you're opposed to the idea of a relationship. Not necessarily specifically with me."

She ambled over to the bed and stood up in the space between his parted legs. Adelaide smiled down at him, hair cascading around her face in a golden wave. "In other words, why can't we be together?" she teased. "Hey, I've been down this road before. I nearly threw my life away behind some chump promising forevers. I was eighteen and it was my first taste of love. Do you know what I'm saying?"

"First love is the hardest to get over."

"That's not what I mean. I said it was my first taste of love. Period. See, when you grow up in a normal, healthy family arrangement, you experience love almost infinitely," she murmured. Her voice had a storyteller quality, and her eyes danced, envisioning what for her had to have been a fairytale when she was a child.

"Your first taste is someone snuggling you close after you're born, feeding you when you're hungry, running to you when you cry. And, in that moment you know in your little baby mind what love is. Love is this god figure that takes care of you. By the time you're preschool age, you learn love buys you things and makes you feel special. It appreciates your accomplishments and doesn't hurt you when you do something wrong. As you get older, you just keep adding to the list of good things love can be.

"So that by the time you meet your first heartbreak? Well, you already know that wasn't love because that's not how love makes you feel. And, you go on your merry way, mending up and looking for love again. You know love is a list of good things."

"But, when you don't know," Derek supplied, "your first heartbreak takes away all hope."

Addie slowly nodded. "That's right. Your short list might be filled up with wonderful things. Love makes you feel sexy in the rain on a warm summer day. Love holds your books for you while you walk across campus. But, you'll accept a crap-ton of terrible things on the list, too. Love calls you names when you make it mad. Love sleeps around. Love doesn't call at all some night.

"By the time you get your heart fully broken in half, you're sick of love, anyway. Love is a slow poison that isn't worth dying for. That's what I learned." Adelaide drifted away from him and started packing again.

"That's what you feel now?" Derek questioned.

"No," said Adelaide. "But, old habits die hard. When you've believed in something for long enough, your mind keeps it, no matter how illogical you might come to understand it is. I think I know that love isn't all bad. People wouldn't work so hard at it if it were. Yet, even if love found me, I don't have enough experience to show it back. I told you that before. Have you ever been in love?"

Derek pushed up from the footboard. "I've been in 'used'. I've been in the friend zone, and I've been in 'severe like', but I can't say that I've ever been in love. I was the ungainly teen with the zits and bad hair. My dashing good looks came later," said Derek. "Also, my shitty luck in the romance department pretty much nixed any chances of it happening, even after I grew out of the ugly duckling phase."

As they continued chatting, Derek made note of everything that was staying and what was going. There were about eight boxes stacked against the wall, and he wanted to make sure to take his television and game system. As he had predicted, all of his worldly belongings were boxed up and ready to go within less than an hour.

"I want you to hang out down here while I run these up to the truck," he said.

Addie shook her head. "I can help."

"I hired you to keep me company, not to mouth off," he joked.

"I know this really nifty trick where I can walk and talk at the same time," she smirked.

"Really?"

She grabbed a box and followed him up. "Yep. Cool, isn't it? Walking and talking."

"Hey, Derek?" Lydia called out from somewhere in the house.

"Is that your mother?" Addie whispered.

"Yeah. You want to meet her? I'm coming, Mom!" he called back.

"No! I don't want to meet anyone! Parents tend to think things are serious when they get to meet someone," she hissed.

"Oh, they'll take one look at you and know we're not serious. I could tell them flat out that I'm going to marry you tomorrow, and they wouldn't believe me."

"How do you know?" she asked, snickering.

CHAPTER 28

"HOW IN THE Sam Hill did you pull a looker like her?" Frank breathed in amazement.

Adelaide blushed. Lydia fluttered around her like a magpie. "Don't embarrass her, Frank," she said. "Adelaide, is it? What a lovely name! Derek, did you offer her something to eat? Or, something to drink? Don't just stand there. Be a good boyfriend."

"Uh, we're not official," Addie interjected. Derek chuckled.

"I don't know what that means," said Lydia.

Frank grinned mischievously. "It means they're just sleeping together."

Lydia gasped, and wagged her finger at him. "Dirty old man," she said with a laugh. "Ah, well, it's nice to meet you, Adelaide. I hope to see you around with Derek more often. He could use a beautiful woman like you to help him grow up."

"Lydia," Frank muttered.

"What?" she asked innocently.

Derek sighed. "At any rate, Addie and I will be tracking in and out for a bit while we take these boxes out. Wanted to give you a head's up before we got started."

"Oh, oh, Derek, you just made me remember. I was calling you because I need you to take these things I've wrapped up for Heather out to the garage. It's her old baby stuff that I kept to pass down—booties, and adorable blankets, and sweaters. Addie, do you knit?"

"Actually, I do know how to knit," Adelaide impressed Derek by saying. "I work with children with disabilities, and for some of my autistic kiddos, knitting is perfect for getting them still and focused."

Lydia met Frank's eyes and all but clapped with glee. "She's a keeper," she intoned. "You better not mess this up, Derek."

"Lydia," Frank admonished dryly.

"Alright, alright! I'm going. Derek, don't forget to take those things out to the garage for your sister."

"I'll get them," Frank pushed up from his armchair. "You kids load up the van. The sooner you're out of the basement, the sooner I can have my man-cave."

Adelaide waited until they were outside to say, "Your dad is amazing. Your mom, too."

Derek shrugged and grinned. "They'll do," he replied.

"They remind me of TV parents. When I was a kid, I always wanted a TV parent. Someone who says all the wrong things but at the right time, so it's funny as hell."

He laughed. "It sounds like you've pegged them right!"

They dropped off their load and went back down to get some other stuff, carrying on the conversation as they worked. "I bet you had a fun childhood."

"I can't complain. Owen and I used to camp out down here playing video games together."

"Ah, yes, your…*crush*," she said. She wore a teasing smile as she moved past him to grab another box. Derek set down the box he was holding and shook his head.

"It's not like that."

"What do you mean, it's not like that? I've seen the way you look at him. You get hard for the both of us just the same."

Derek grabbed her by the waist and spun around, leaning her over the box that he had just put back on the top of the stack. The tower of moving boxes ended at her pelvis, the perfect height to have her at the angle he wanted her. "What are you trying to say?" Derek murmured heatedly. He let his fingers drift up to her breasts and caressed her through the thin fabric. She wasn't wearing a bra, and her hardened nipples were obvious.

"That you're bisexual, Derek Cornwell. Deal with it." Adelaide giggled softly as she seductively wagged her ass from side to side against his growing erection. Derek tried to remember if the basement door was locked because he wanted her. He wanted her then and there.

"Bisexual? No, I'm not into men at all. You've got me all wrong, Addie," he whispered, biting his lower lip with lust as he stared down at her swaying ass. He put a hand to the small of her back and glided it up along the length of her spine. Clutching her shoulder, Derek pulled her up so that her back dipped and her bottom poked against his lower pelvis. "I'm into women. Rather, a very particular woman. You. And, I can prove it to you." She chuckled as he kissed the side of her face, fingers splayed against her throat.

He nudged against her bottom with his cock. Adelaide pivoted around in his arms with an eyebrow quirked and her full, sultry mouth fixed in a smile. "Oh, I didn't say you were only into men," she replied as she dropped her arms over his shoulders and locked her fingers together behind his neck. "I said you're bisexual."

"Shut up, Addie," he whispered. Derek picked her up and carried her to the wall. He pressed her up against it, kissing her lips with a ferocity that came out of nowhere. He wanted to believe she didn't know what she was talking about, but all the signs said otherwise. He was into his friend. It was true. Maybe that made him bisexual. It didn't matter, because Derek only fantasized about Owen.

Despite what Owen had blithely said earlier on the phone, Derek knew there would come a day when his adventurous, spontaneous friend got tired of the novelty of messing around. He wanted something more with Adelaide, something concrete, and he intended to get her to see that.

The dress she was wearing was made for easy access. It barely reached mid-thigh but was loose and airy. He fluffed it up to her hips as he quickly unbuckled his pants. "What are you doing?" she said with a laugh. "We can't have sex at your parents' house!"

He laughed, feeling like a randy teenager. "Yes, we can. We just have to be quick. And quiet. Wrap your legs around me." Then, his erection sprang free, and her eyes glazed with desire as she looked down at him, doing as he commanded.

"Oh, my!" Addie feigned surprise. She wrapped her long sexy legs around him and rested against the wall as he positioned himself to thrust inside. Her body was slick and moist with all the talk about sex, and Derek sighed with anticipation as she sank around his sword. She wriggled in his arms to get comfortable, her cleavage jiggling in his face.

Derek made a sound of appreciation as he grazed his nose from hill to hill. She smelled like candy apples. He loved making love to her sweet body.

"You don't need to try to convince me of your heterosexual maleness, Derek," she said mockingly. Tightening her thighs, she squeezed him with her vaginal muscles and hissed with desire. Derek groaned and thrust harder and faster. She covered his mouth with a kiss to hide her moans of excitement.

As he clutched her hips and plowed into her, visions of the erotic session with Owen tried to surface, but Derek blocked them out. He didn't want to think about his homoerotic infatuation. If he and Owen were going to be living together, then that would have to be a thing of the past. Because the more he considered it, the more he realized nothing could come of acting on his lust. Owen was a smooth ladies man. Derek wasn't his type.

His cock was lathered with her juices as he pounded her deepest spot. Adelaide's tiny gasps and soft moans filled his ears as he squeezed her closer, reveling in the pillowy feel of her statuesque body. This was what he wanted. This woman right here. She was about to climax, and he could feel it along every inch of his erection as she clamped down with her pussy, stroking him, and milking him for more.

"That's it, that's it," he crooned. "Come for me."

"Yeah," she whimpered. "Ah, yes!" She dug her nails into his back as she climbed to the top of ecstasy. Adelaide shuddered and sighed as the orgasmic storm swept through her. She sucked in a breath and moaned his name over and over, as he kept going until the very last tremor subsided.

Adelaide needed someone to show her love and affection. Derek pressed his forehead to hers and stared into her half-closed, dreamy eyes that reflected nothing but satisfaction and pleasure. Her lips were slightly agape. He rubbed his thumb along the corner of her mouth before kissing her, and she smiled in response.

He gently eased out of her body and let her feet slip to the floor. Adelaide sighed and shook out her hair, dropping her dress back to her thighs. She touched her vagina and hummed with sated amusement. "I didn't even realize how much I needed that," she said with a laugh.

Derek chuckled and led her to his closet-sized bathroom. He dug out a clean towel and had her stand in the doorframe with her legs spread, as he gently wiped her up. "There," he murmured. "Now, that that's done. We can stop this foolish talk of bisexuality. Alright?"

She crossed her arms and shook her head. "Look, I don't know what you're so worried about. In case you haven't noticed…" She strutted up to him and used the same cloth to wipe his still semi-hard cock. "I happen to like it," she said with an eyebrow lift.

He suppressed a groan as she stroked the towel along his manhood. He had purposefully held back from trying to get off. That session had been about her. Only, now it would take a minute to desensitize and let his brain know he wouldn't be climaxing just yet.

Derek took the towel and playfully pushed Addie out of the bathroom. "Well, I'm sorry, Ms. Ingles. But, you're going to have to get your gay kicks elsewhere. I'm not about to ruin my friendship with this, and that's exactly what will happen if I let you have a say."

"Oh, yeah? What makes you think that? I have a feeling it might bring the two of you closer together."

Derek snorted as he shook his head. "You don't understand. That's not how it works." He picked up two boxes to take upstairs.

She shrugged. "If you say so, but now I see why you wanted us both together," she said with a wink. She grabbed one of the boxes to follow him out to the moving van.

CHAPTER 29

DEREK AND ADELAIDE marched back up the basement steps. Only a few more boxes to go, and he'd be half way to his new home. The sound of their playful banter preceded them, so when they got to the top of the stairs and were met with a wall of silence, it was tense. His sister and her husband, Steve, had just walked into the house. Steve, as in Adelaide's ex-boyfriend.

Addie dropped her gaze and muttered, "Uh oh."

"Heather," Derek said in surprise. Suddenly, he remembered that he had forgotten to tell Heather that Addie wanted to apologize for crashing their wedding. Now here they were, face to face, and his bohemian butterfly sister who'd never hurt a fly looked like she wanted to claw the blonde beauty's eyes out.

Derek envisioned the bloodshed, the horror, the tragedy. And, of course, then he'd have to destroy Steve for setting all this into motion in the first place. "Shit," he muttered, shaking his head. This might not end well.

"What is *she* doing here?" Heather asked caustically.

She glared at Steve. Steve shrugged helplessly, looking like the dowdy car salesman that he was. *Why doesn't this car have a steering wheel? D'uh, I dunno, but check out the engine in this bad boy!* Derek tried to change the subject. "Sis! Uh, I didn't know you were coming over today. Sh-she's just helping me with some packing, and we'll be out of your hair soon. But, how've you been? How was the honeymoon?"

Derek laughed nervously. Heather didn't bother to answer. She put her hand on her hip and stared in challenge at Addie. "I'll take this out to the truck and wait for you there, Derek," she whispered. Adelaide pushed past Steve, but before she could make it to the front door Lydia stepped out of the living room.

"Is that you, Heather? Ah, yes! I got your text, and I have that stuff you wanted all wrapped up in the garage. Frank can take it out to your car for you. Frank!" Lydia yelled. She smiled at Steve and Addie before frowning down the hall for her husband. "Frank!—Oh, Heather, have you met Derek's new girlfriend, Addie?" She moseyed over to Heather and pulled her into a hug, gesturing for Adelaide to come be introduced. But, Addie self-consciously shrank away.

"Derek's new girlfriend?" Heather growled. "No, he didn't tell me about her. But, I guess she's all in the family now. She used to date Steve, too." She hiked a thumb at her husband, and Lydia looked confused and appalled.

"Did she?" Lydia gasped, scandalized.

Derek rolled his eyes. "Technically, they weren't really in a relationship, and that was a long time ago. So—"

"Yeah, but, Derek!" his mom scolded. Lydia's eyes flashed from him to Addie, and she frowned. She didn't want to fuss in front of company, Derek knew.

"Geez, it's not what you think." The one girlfriend he'd brought over to meet his mom, and this news had to come out today, didn't it? Derek groaned. Adelaide looked completely embarrassed, like she wanted to disappear into the floor. Derek recalled the black hole that he'd wanted to climb into back at Owen's house the other day. He put down the box he was holding and moved supportively to Adelaide's side.

"What is it, then?" Heather harped. "Why would you bring her here, knowing she did everything she could to sabotage my wedding? Derek, how could you?" He was upset at her for being rude, but he was saddened by the fact his sister looked genuinely hurt.

"Heather," he tried to explain, "I don't think you know the whole story, and I don't think now is a good time to talk about it." His gaze darted from her to their mom. Heather calmed down marginally, but she was still shooting daggers in Adelaide's direction.

"I know everything I want to know about that skank."

"Young lady!" Lydia said sharply. Heather had the decency to blush.

Adelaide made a sound of disgust and swept the door open, marching out to the moving van alone. Derek wanted to run after her, but he couldn't let his sister continue thinking Steve was Addie's unwitting victim. It was the other way around.

"Know what, Heather? Why don't you ask Steve about it? I'm sure he has some lively stories to tell, right, Steve? Tell us about how you two dated in college. That whole *stalker* business," Derek jibed.

The truth had come out as he had gotten to know Adelaide. Steve had spread rumors that she was a clingy ex who didn't know when to leave well enough alone, but in reality he had stalked her to the point of nearly incurring a restraining order.

Knowing his brother-in-law had lied about her once put everything else Steve had ever told him into question, too. That was the reason Derek was willing to give a relationship with Adelaide a go, even though Steve made it seem like she was a tart. She wasn't. She was a sweet, smart girl who had some tough breaks, and she didn't deserve to have to put up with crap from people like Steve.

Steve's fleshy face produced an innocent smile. "Hey, guys, let's not do this. Alright? We're all one big happy family. I'm sure none of us want to fight, and this isn't something we should discuss in mixed company." Derek didn't miss the leer the other man cast after Adelaide. Her retreating back showed off a delectable derriere, and he wanted to punch the bastard in the face for staring.

At that moment, Frank shuffled out of the kitchen with a bottle of bourbon and a tumbler of ice. He took one look at the three adults in the foyer—the scowls on faces, Steve's flummoxed expression and Derek's balled fists—and smirked. "Guess I better get two other cups, then. Looks like you fellas could use a drink. Come on, boys. Leave the womenfolk be and let's go have cigars, eh?"

Derek's eyes bore a hole into Steve. But, his Dad was right to quickly diffuse the situation, because he wanted to ring his brother-in-law's neck. Why couldn't he just tell the truth, and let Heather know that Adelaide wasn't the bad guy?

"Yeah, Derek. How 'bout we get a drink?" said Steve, patting him on his shoulder.

Derek flinched his arm away and followed his father to the

kitchen for more glasses, so they could hang out on the back porch and breathe. Would've been better if Steve didn't tag along, too. Unfortunately, like he'd said, they were all one big happy family now.

"What was going on out there, son?" Frank asked as he settled in a wicker chair on the back patio.

Derek sipped the cold liquor and shrugged. Frank glanced at Steve for answers. He piped up, "Turns out Derek's new girlfriend and I used to date. Heather's not too happy about seeing her here."

"Well?" Frank probed.

"Okay, first of all she's not my girlfriend, and she wasn't yours, either!" Derek glared at Steve. "Second of all, dude, you really need to start being upfront with my sister. You lied about Adelaide. You made it seem like Addie crashed your wedding because she couldn't let go of you, when in reality she only showed up to set the record straight."

"Look, man, I don't know what she's told you, but you shouldn't trust a word she says. That girl gets around. I tried to warn you, but you wouldn't listen."

Derek pushed up out of his chair, chest puffed. "Son of a bitch, you stalked her!" He jabbed a finger in Steve's face. Steve cringed. Frank set his glass down with a thumb and stood up between the two young men. He put his hand to Derek's chest and gently pushed him back.

"Hey, calm down, boy. This is your brother-in-law you're talking to. I don't think your sister will take too kindly to you smashing his face in. Now, let's just talk like grown men and leave the teenage hormones out of this."

Derek backed down reluctantly. "You need to stop bad mouthing her, Steve. You have no idea what she's gone through, and you have no right."

Frank chuckled and shook his head. "So, she's been around the block a few times, huh?" Derek scowled. "Take it in stride, son. From what I saw a while ago, she seems like a nice enough girl, and you can't judge a person by the skeletons in their closet, since most of us have quite a pile-up in our own."

Steve snorted. "Yeah, Derek. No one's judging you." Although he clearly was, out of some sense of jealousy. Derek could easily imagine why the other man would be so upset. Losing Adelaide had to be the biggest regret of Steve's life. She was sexy as fuck and an expert in bed. He couldn't picture the dense bastard appreciating her intellect, however. He probably didn't have the sense to do that.

"And, you." Frank wagged a finger at Steve. "You need to haul your meddling ass in there and make sure you haven't upset my daughter with this load of crap. Seems like a guy with your history wouldn't worry too much about other people's pasts. I'm pretty sure Heather won't be happy to hear you fudged the truth on that stalker story."

Steve didn't bother denying it. He nervously looked at Derek, who still wanted to go twelve rounds behind Adelaide's honor. Then, the portly man got up and padded back inside. Derek was sure his mom and sister were somewhere slut-shaming and man-bashing. He sank into his chair with a dejected sigh.

"Don't look so lost. It's been a good day for you, more or less," said Frank. "You got a promotion. You're moving out. You've finally got a damn girlfriend."

"That guy pisses me off," Derek spit angrily.

"What's this about her getting around? You know anything about that? I'd hate to see you in a bad situation with a beautiful woman. Those are the hardest to get out of."

"Adelaide may have some attachment issues, but it's because she grew up in a bunch of different foster homes. She's not promiscuous, if that's what you're getting at. She's just not looking for love."

"Even more dangerous. 'Cause you seem like you're in deeper than the Pacific."

"In love?" Derek laughed. "Nah. I care about her, that's all. I don't want to see her name smeared by some low-life like Steve. We all have some unorthodox behavior, and it's nobody else's business. I mean, how would you feel if some lout came to you exposing something personal about my life?"

"I'd probably have to weigh it out against what I know about you before I jump to conclusions. But, heck, for the longest, I pegged you and Owen for a couple. That's about as unorthodox as things can get! And, had anybody run to me with tales, it wouldn't have bothered me any. I'd love the both of you just the same."

Derek stared down at his hands. How the hell had his father picked up on the underlying attraction between him and Owen? He shook his head. It felt good to know if the truth came out, he had a supporter. Felt better than good, actually. He looked up at his dad. "Thanks, Dad. I needed to hear that."

Frank swallowed the last of his liquor and gestured with the glass as he spoke. "Damned glad you're not gay, though. I want grandkids one day. Keep that Addie girl around. Where's she at, by the way?"

"Waiting for me in the truck," replied Derek.

"Well, what the hell are you doing out here? Get your ass out there to her!"

Derek stood with a laugh and put aside the glass he was holding. "I'm gonna go ahead and get this stuff over to Owen's place. I told him we'd be there by now. Can you let Mom know I won't be coming back here tonight? Anything I've left, I'll probably just pack up tomorrow."

"Will do." He saluted his son, and Derek hurried back inside to grab the last box and meet Addie at the truck. Mission accomplished. He was officially moved out.

CHAPTER 30

OWEN HAD SALMON steaks on the grill by the time they arrived. He opened up the door to let them in, holding up a set of jangling keys for Derek. "Your official pass to the kingdom," Owen said.

"Oh, wow! It smells amazing in here. Where's the food?" Adelaide stepped inside and hugged Owen. Derek blinked in surprise. Then, Owen shook his hand and pulled him into a hug, too.

"Back patio," said Owen. "I thought you said you'd be here around eight-ish."

"Ran into Heather," he explained.

"Oh. Ohhhh. How'd that go?"

"She hates me," Adelaide said with a casual shrug. She walked through the house like she was right at home, out to the back patio where Owen had the table set for three.

"Need me to help you unload things?" Owen gestured out the front door at the moving van.

"Not tonight. Tonight, we celebrate." Derek held up two bottles of champagne.

The mini-party kicked off with Latin music and Owen dancing the samba while Adelaide doubled over with laughter. Derek swept her onto the dance floor to give her a whirl. The fun lasted deep into the night when they transferred the festivities indoors.

"I'm thinking we should all camp out in here in the living room tonight and watch movies," Owen suggested.

"Yay! Sleepover!" Adelaide threw her hands up and danced

around. "Wait, I didn't bring a travel bag." She pouted like a cute kid.

"Just do like Derek and borrow my clothes, which he never gives back." Owen lifted his chin toward Derek, which was guy-talk for, 'you're pathetic, bro', and Derek flipped him off.

"So, showers and night clothes for everyone, and then we meet down here?" he asked.

Addie high-fived the boys and raced upstairs to be the first to use the guest bathroom. Laughing, Derek stopped at Owen's bedroom so his friend could give him something for Addie to sleep in. Derek had brought up his suitcase and planned to hop in the shower with her to save time.

But, two tipsy, excited adults in one shower spelled desire. Seeing her naked body under the steamy spray reminded him that he was desperately in need. Derek hadn't gotten off earlier when he had pushed Adelaide's buttons in his basement apartment.

"Well, well, what have we here?" Owen strolled into the guestroom moments after Derek had carried her from the shower to the sheets. His plaid lounge pants were slung low on his hips, and his chiseled torso gleamed in the wan light of the lamp on the nightstand. "I thought we were watching the movie."

Derek was standing at the foot of the bed and Adelaide was lying in a puddle of submission against the cool comforter where Derek had placed her. The sight of his friend halted his conquest of her body. She sensually drew her legs together and swung her knees around to sit up. She had on nothing but a towel, which hugged her curves like a mini-dress. She eyed both men with a tiny smile tickling the corners of her lips and whispered, "You can watch."

He had dreamed of moments like this; yet, he wasn't sure what to say or do to initiate the script he had memorized so well. All the pieces were in place. Derek had only to act on his desires. In his fantasies, it was always Owen to make the first move. And, the last time Adelaide had guided his hand, teaching him how to masturbate Owen. Derek's hand flexed to touch him at the memory. Owen eased closer to the couple but stayed out of reach, and he hitched his thumbs on his hips as he stood to the side.

"Alright, then. Just here to observe," Owen clarified.

"Or...you can participate..." Adelaide giggled sexily as she dropped a corner of the towel that was covering her lush body. She let it slide lower and expose the curve of her right breast, and she flipped her thick mane of hair to the other side. Holding her head back, she ran her hand down the curve of her sexy neck as she stared seductively at Owen. He looked at her from beneath hooded eyes and started untying the drawstring of his pants.

Derek's wavy hair swished damply around his face, but he shook it out of his eyes. When his vision was clear, he saw Owen climbing into the bed with Addie. She reached for him, and Owen flowed into her arms. Their mouths collided. It was so sexy it made his manhood stiff with anticipation. He ran a hand over the bulge in his boxer briefs.

Owen dragged Adelaide's towel down her body and she thrust her breasts forward to be sucked. Soft whimpers flew from her lips as her hair spilled across the bed when she fell back. Owen groaned, settling between her legs as she kicked up her heels. Derek grabbed her slender foot and stuck her pedicured toes into his mouth. Her skin had a clean taste and satiny texture. Sucking gently, he elicited squeals of delight from her.

At the same time, Owen squeezed her thighs and drew his hands up to her hips to pin her to the bed as he rolled his pelvis against hers. He was still wearing his lounge pants in his haste to get to her. She tore at the cotton fabric with her sharp nails, trying to take them off of him. He swept his mouth back up to hers in a passionate kiss she broke away from with a gasp.

As he stared at Owen grinding between her legs, Derek rubbed his hand down his cock and closed his fingers loosely around himself with a sharp inhale. There was an urgency to the way the two of them petted and groped each other, and the sight of it made him want to join the fray more than anything. But, he had to tread lightly.

Owen knew his secret now. One wrong move and it might put them both in an uncomfortable situation. Keeping his eye on Owen's muscular back, Derek eased Adelaide's bare foot from his mouth, down his stomach to his boxer briefs, and she curled her toes around his erection. "Mmph…" he moaned. Derek jutted his hips forward to rub his cock up and down her heel. He cupped her foot against his manhood and rocked side to side.

"It tickles," she giggled against Owen's cheek as she watched Derek over his shoulder.

Owen grunted with need. "Yeah? Well, this aches," he murmured into the hollow of her throat. He tore himself away to take off his pants. But in his absence, Derek filled the vacancy between her legs to satisfy her. He was already mostly undressed. He had only to ease his swollen cock out of his boxer briefs and inside of her. "Wait," Owen said to Derek. "I wasn't done yet."

"I can't wait! Mm," she whined. She clung to Derek's face and ran her fingers through his black hair. Caressing his cheeks, she drew his lips to hers. Derek sipped at her moist lips as she took his cock and eagerly worked his erection into her body.

When the silk of her sheath closed around him, Derek shuddered with arousal. She was hot and lusciously soft. She clung to him with her knees and hands and writhed and danced beneath him with each long, slow stroke. His thrusts plowed into her receptive body, inspiring abandoned cries of ecstasy. Derek gritted his teeth at the exquisite joy of fucking her.

"Addie, ah, Addie," he groaned deliriously.

He had forgotten Owen was behind him until his best friend daringly leaned over his back while Derek made love to her. He was shocked to feel Owen beating off, Owen's erection grazing his ass. Then, Owen gently tugged a handful of Derek's hair and pulled his head back slightly so he could access Adelaide's lips. He kissed her as his body rubbed intimately against Derek's. Owen didn't seem to care that each pump of his fist made his cock poke harder against him.

Derek groaned at the torture of skin contact. He couldn't resist the impulse. He turned his face and interceded the kiss, and when his lips met Owen's, stars slid across the sky as his world tilted. Heady with desire, Derek felt weightless. Owen's grip on his hair relaxed as he cupped the back of Derek's head, and their lips gracefully slid over one another. Owen's tongue boldly darted into his mouth.

Derek moaned, weak in the knees. He had never been so sexually aware. Owen's beard tickled his face in rough contrast, but his mouth was pure silk. His tongue was velvet. Derek drank in his masculine scent with a sigh and splayed his hand against the other side of Owen's face to kiss him deeper.

Deeper. Adelaide worked her inner muscles to coax him to rapture. Derek gasped and ended the kiss, fearing Addie would make him explode if he didn't stop her. He wasn't ready to tap out. Not after Owen's kiss and the possibilities yet to be explored. So, he eased out of

Addie's embrace, despite her protests. She begged him not to stop, but Derek needed to pursue this.

"Come here," he said, turning to Owen. Boldly placing a hand to the back of Owen's neck, Derek pulled him close and stared him in the eyes with all the fire locked within. Derek breathed harshly, wanting to move forward. His fear stopped him.

"What are you afraid of?" Owen whispered, with a wry grin. He clasped Derek's face and dragged him slowly in. Their lips met again, fire and ice vying to destroy with ecstasy.

They were two dragons circling in an azure sky. Their chests met. Their erections touched. Owen shyly reached down to bring them together like Adelaide had in the pool the day prior, and he tentatively worked his hand around them both, up and down, thrusting against Derek's pelvis. Their hard bodies battled for release.

"Unh, fuck!" Derek grunted. "Ah, god, I want you!"

Owen cupped his face and looked him in the eyes. "Have me...*take* me." Owen squeezed his eyes tight as Derek dropped to his knees and drew Owen's cock to his lips, lapping circles around the tip.

Owen swept Derek's hair back from his face to watch. "Oh, shit," he sputtered. He laughed in amazement, but quickly the laughter turned to a hoarse moan. "Oh...Oh, *fuck*!" Owen grimaced, breathing heavily.

Derek's mouth raced back and forth along the track of Owen's erection, the massive shaft disappearing into his mouth. His throat instinctively relaxed to take him deeper. Derek groaned as he sucked, reveling in the taste of Owen's skin, in his scent, in his responses. It was like nothing Derek had ever done before, but it felt so right. Owen moaned uncontrollably now.

Watching his face told a story of shock and awe as Derek drew his tongue up and down along the shaft and jerked him off at the same time. He wanted to keep going and going, but Adelaide interjected herself into the equation.

"I need it," she whimpered. "Now!"

Both men glanced over from where they were standing and saw the woman with the hourglass figure sprawled across the guest bed with her thick, sexy thighs spread and her beautiful womanhood completely exposed. Two red-nailed fingers disappeared inside her vagina as she plunged them in and out, rubbing and stroking her clit at the same time. Her breasts heaved in her pursuit of ecstasy.

Owen clasped Derek's chin and drew his face back up, making him stand. Their lips connected briefly. Then, he led him to the bed, and they both moved to Adelaide. Owen faced her, and Derek molded his body to her back. She pressed her ass in Derek's erection. Groaning, he held himself between her cheeks and toyed with her sensitive anus. Adelaide went wild with excitement at the feeling. "Yes," she screamed. "Ohh, yes!"

Owen held her quivering legs open and plunged into her. Derek kissed her shoulder and reached around to squeeze her breasts, fondling her nipples. Owen caressed her buttocks, and his hand grazed Derek's manhood. But, instead of pulling away, Owen reached for him. Derek watched, stunned, as his best friend willingly began to masturbate him.

Derek closed his eyes and laid his forehead on the back of Adelaide's shoulder as his body was stroked back to excitement. Owen tugged Derek's cock like he was trying to ignite the fuse on the explosion that had threatened to happen all evening. Derek gasped, trying not to cry out. His breaths came out in small pants and moans while Adelaide sang with pleasure as Owen speared into her with powerful, hammering thrusts.

She eagerly clung to Owen, her plaintive cries filling the room. Derek ran his hand down to her clit, and her saturation made both their bodies glisten. The slick nectar of her womanhood poured over Owen. Through Addie as conduit, Derek could feel Owen speed up the pace with shallow, swift thrusts that he alternated with deep, hard plunges. Owen's mouth fell open without a sound as his eyes fluttered shut, but he shook his head, as if powering through the urge to climax.

"Make me come," Addie pleaded.

"Let go, honey," Owen whispered. His hand tightened reflexively around Derek's shaft as her body went tense between them. Her climax unfurled powerfully, and Addie wailed three times, each one louder than the last. "Ooh, fuck!" Owen moaned at the sexy sound. He had taken Addie to her peak, but now it was Derek's turn. Owen was close to release, and in his ecstasy, Derek felt him center his attention around the top of his cock and roll his palm around as if juicing an orange.

The pleasure was too much. Too much. Derek hummed excitedly and braced himself to orgasm. Whimpering, Derek bit into the soft flesh of Addie's neck, which made her cry out at the pleasure and the pain. Derek bowed his head, his face against her shoulder blades. He felt her body wracked by bliss as Owen continued to make love to her.

"Tell me how badly you want this," Owen taunted Derek.

"Ahh," Derek whined softly. "Ah, fuck!" Derek drew Adelaide's face back, nibbling at her jawline as he stared into Owen's eyes. His hips moved forward and back, pumping into Owen's hand. His ass tightened as his body prepared to fire away, making him quake against Adelaide's back. He was about to explode all over her.

But, Owen stopped.

"Ahhhh," Derek let out an agonized exhale, falling back onto the bed to stare up at the ceiling as his cock jerked spasmodically, the orgasm cut short. Owen positioned Adelaide on her side and moved to take her place facing Derek.

"Tell me," he commanded sultrily. He stared from beneath thick, dark brown lashes. Derek's chest rose and fell rapidly as he tried to catch his breath. He was so aroused that it hurt. "How badly do you want this?"

"I need you…"

Owen closed his hand back around Derek's cock and slowly lowered his lips to Derek's chest. He shyly flicked his tongue over Derek's nipple. Derek jerked in pleasure. Owen's hand slid to the head of his erection and eased back down. Now sated, Adelaide came closer to watch, a smile on her face. Owen kissed down Derek's chest and explored the rolling landscape of his abs. He tipped his tongue into Derek's navel. Spirals of pleasure swirled behind Derek's closed eyes.

"Yesss," Derek hissed, sucking in a breath.

"You want to try more, don't you?" Addie asked Owen in a soft, raspy voice. Derek's eyes slid open and watched the interchange. She sounded sexy, and well-fucked. She swept her hair out of her face and cupped the back of Owen's head. "All you have to do is give it a go." She gently pressed the back of his head to guide him to Derek's pelvis. Derek held his breath as Owen dipped lower. Owen chuckled nervously, but didn't stop her. He slipped out his tongue to draw it along Derek's skin as he went down.

"You taste…like…"

"Hunh!" Derek groaned as Owen's lips skimmed over him. "Stop teasing me…please…" He exhaled shakily, ready to pop with need.

"…Mmmm, adventure," Owen finished with a speculative hum. He turned his face to kiss Adelaide's wrist.

"Doesn't he?" she giggled softly. Addie caressed Owen's face and ran her hand over Derek's erection.

"Please!" Derek begged.

Owen's bearded cheek brushed over Derek's shaft, and Derek let out a sob as Owen parted his lips and swept his velvety tongue over him. He cried out again, as Owen closed his mouth over his erection with a hungry groan and sucked, exploring the head of his cock with his tongue. Derek shook as Owen took him deeper. "Owen!" he cried out, as Owen slipped his hand to Derek's testicles and squeezed enticingly.

It happened just that quickly. He shoved his friend away and clutched himself, as his seed rained out on the bedspread. Derek stammered with release, bursts of ejaculation shooting from his body as he doubled over on his side. It felt so amazing. So unbelievable. So unreal, but this wasn't a dream.

He looked back at Owen with stunned, sated eyes only to see his friend in a similar predicament. His eyes flew from Owen's spent cock to his face. Owen wore a wry grin. "Wow," Owen mouthed. He had gotten so aroused by the act of giving oral sex that he had climaxed, too. Addie stared at them both like the sight turned her on enough for another round. Owen and Derek shared a look.

"I think," said Owen, "I'm going to like having you as a roommate."

PART 4
CHAPTER 31

LATER THAT MORNING, Derek padded into the kitchen of his new shared digs, and peeked into Owen's cabinets to rustle up breakfast while Owen and Addie remained peacefully asleep upstairs. His thoughts were a jumbled mess. He knew he should be ecstatic about the turn of events—or at least, the fact that his X-rated fantasies about Owen were finally coming true—but he wasn't sure what it spelled for his future. He could easily envision himself getting more emotionally involved with both his best friend and his new lover, which was completely the *worst* idea possible.

Owen was an emotionally void womanizer. Owen, Derek was used to. Adelaide had enough baggage to fill a U-Haul—not that Derek minded. He was perfectly okay with her baggage. He was hoping to teach her how to talk about her past and get beyond the pain she was hiding with her carefree, bubbly personality now. But the bottom line was, as his coworker and close friend Libby had pointed out, with hearts like that, you either had to take it all, or leave well enough alone.

And, Derek hadn't quite figured out which of the choices he'd take. Well, maybe he had. He had slept with them both last night.

"Ugh...how do I get into these kinds of fixes?" he muttered to himself.

Derek rubbed his face and stared, bleary-eyed, at the strips of bacon sizzling in the skillet. The coffee machine was brewing on the kitchen counter, and the aroma of gourmet java filled the room. He inhaled deeply, exhaling with a sigh. There was nothing for it but to keep plodding onward until he hit a wall built of the bricks of a broken heart and mortared with tequila.

His cellphone buzzed on the kitchen counter, stirring him out of his gloomy resolution to suck at life. Derek stared at it, wondering who could be calling so early on a Saturday morning, and he thought about not answering. There was only so much he could deal with at one time. When he finally grabbed it on the fourth ring, he groaned as he saw the contact info of his nemesis from work, Harold Gensler.

"Hello," Derek answered dryly.

"Congratulations," Harold Gensler replied in a smug tone.

Derek rolled his eyes and snorted. The guy who had worked diligently to get him fired was calling to congratulate him? He paused before responding, flipped the bacon in the skillet and bracing his back against the edge of the counter to figure out if this call was the olive branch it seemed not to be.

"Well, good morning! This is an unexpected call. Anything I can do for you, Harold?"

Harry chuckled. "Nope, not a thing. Just calling to tell you I got the email from Mr. Clancy this morning stating that Wonder Man was going to use both ads. Glad that ended well for the both of us. You know, back when you were on my team, I didn't want you on my team. Now that you're off, I'm pretty sure we're solid! Simple, really—"

With furrowed brow, a half-smile touched Derek's lips. "*Not* that simple, really. I don't think I'll ever understand why, even after I showed you I was willing to put in the work necessary to make that team great, you still didn't want me around. I dunno, Harry. Smacks of insecurity to me. What do you think?"

"C'mon, you should know by now this is a dog-eat-dog industry. As long as you were on my team, you were a threat to my supremacy, but you're head of your own team from here on out."

"That right?" He turned back to the stove and cracked some eggs to make an omelet. Derek wasn't very interested in hearing anything Harold Gensler had to say, but he'd humor him.

"Oh, you're about to learn firsthand how cutthroat things can be, and somebody else can gun for your position, like you were gunning for mine. So, congratulations! You succeeded in becoming my equal. The real fun starts now," said Harry. "Monday morning you'll be meeting your rookie team, and I have no doubt karma will do a spectacular job of humbling you."

"Ah, so you called to gloat," said Derek, understanding better now. "Can't wait to see me fail. Again, you smell that? Smells like some old fart getting stagnant. Tell you what, Harold. Why don't you take care of your end of the business and I'll take care of mine? There's no need for either of us to get in the other's way. I have nothing against you at all."

"Ha! Gloat, give you a heads up, whatever you want to call it. More importantly, I called to tell you that Mr. Clancy isn't done messing with us. Check your email. Just so you know, this is the official gauntlet thrown. You see, it doesn't always end with a new team being formed. Sometimes what happens, is the old head has to be chopped to make room for new growth. You'll not only be competing with my crew and me—you'll be competing with your own. Have a blast!"

Harold hung up the phone before Derek could say anything else. He was left staring at his cell and scratching his head. Sounded like 'interesting' summed up how things were about to get on the job, as if Derek needed any more hassle in his life. He thumbed over to his email inbox and, sure enough, he had a message from his boss.

I think the healthy competition that began with your last assignment while you were a part of Harold Gensler's team motivated you to levels of creativity that even I didn't know you could attain. Job well done, Derek Cornwell. On this next assignment, your team will be working on the same project as Harold's. This time, there can be only one chosen ad. Put your all into it.

Derek read and reread the message again, hoping he wasn't seeing what he was seeing. It felt exactly like Harold had said—Mr. Clancy was messing with them, pitting them against each other for the benefit of the company. It was a dog-eat-dog world, but Derek felt like they should all get a bone rather than having to fight for scraps.

"This is utter bullshit," Derek groaned. He ran a hand over his face and shook his head. On the plus side, he had already begun building a connection with the company of the razor ad they were supposed to be working on. The big problem was that while Harold had a team of experienced personnel, Derek would be working with mostly recent college grads—kids who had been interns last summer. It was like gearing up for a little league game against professional baseball players.

His consolation was that if Mr. Clancy had orchestrated all this, he had done it in full confidence that Derek could handle the challenge. At least his career wasn't at stake this time. The day prior, he had faced down the threat of losing his job and come out a conqueror. The reward? He'd been put in charge of his own design group. Happy joy.

Derek still had a few kinks he wanted to work out in his professional world, and if Harold's heads up was any indication of what he could expect, it was too early to celebrate his 'win'. To be clear, he owed the recent turnaround in his life of failures, to Owen.

Owen, as his life coach, had given him pointers on how to project a powerful presence and gain the right attention, and his advice had stood Derek in good stead. Maybe Owen could direct him on how to proceed, now that Harold was throwing down gauntlets and shit.

CHAPTER 32

"I WOULDN'T WORRY about it," Owen replied blithely. "If he's calling you, he's the one who's worried. Don't let the office politics get to you, buddy. Remember, strong presence, go after what you want and respect yourself. You're already ahead of the game."

Derek handed him a breakfast plate. "That's what I keep telling myself, but this getting noticed crap is all new to me. He sounded like he was gunning for me, and Mr. Clancy's email didn't make me feel any better. Can't I just coast under the radar a little longer?" He shivered overdramatically. Owen poured three glasses of orange juice. Grinning, Derek looked at the other two people at the table, and he felt like this was 'family'. If this was what being out on his own was going to be like, he'd take it.

"He's just miffed at the attention you're getting. It's a distraction tactic to keep you too preoccupied worrying about him to do your job."

Addie chimed in, "That's my take on it, too. You know, that's why the corporate world isn't for me. My employees are on the same team. None of us are in competition with each other." She held a strip of crispy bacon above her face and dropped it into her open mouth. Morning sunlight came through the picture window and left her aglow. Tendrils of her wild hair floated around her beautiful face. Derek could stare at her for hours, days. He tore his gaze away.

"She'll eat us out of house and home," he said teasingly to Owen.

"*Us* already? And, you haven't even been here a full day yet. See, told you we'd do fine as roommates," said Owen, pushing his glasses up his nose.

Derek laughed aloud. "Yeah, well..." He didn't want to mention that *exactly* what he had warned Owen would happen had happened last night.

Owen had invited him to move in after hearing that Derek's parents wanted him to grow up and get out. Faced with the prospect of living together, Derek had come out of the closet and exposed his unorthodox attraction to his best friend. He was sure he wouldn't be able to hide it from Owen and knew it could lead to some sticky situations, as it had.

Owen didn't seem bothered in the least about it, however. That was what had woken Derek up early that morning and been on his brain ever since. But, why was Owen okay with the gay? It seemed totally unlike him, or Derek didn't know his friend like he thought he did. Where the fuck was this going between the three of them? Stealing glances as he ate, Derek pondered that question above all.

Derek noticed Adelaide didn't seem as uptight as before. Owen dropped his aloof façade and showed his true, quirky personality. They chatted amiably over breakfast as a comfortable rhythm was set. The joking and bantering rounded the table, and Derek felt included in a private club. Had anyone told him this was what having a multi-party relationship would be like, he would've scoffed. Yet, here they were.

Or, something like that. It wasn't a relationship, per se. Curse his silly heart. Derek heaved a sigh. "Alright, since I cooked breakfast, who has dish duty?" he asked. Owen quickly raised a hand.

"I'll do it. This was delish. Prop your feet up, chef." Wiping his mouth with a napkin, Owen glanced at Addie. "Oh, by the way, I'm very particular about how I keep my cabinets. Addie, you want to help? I can show you my system so that next time..." He laughed playfully at the insinuation that he wouldn't play the gracious host forever. And, why should he? They were all cool like that, Derek reasoned, smiling. Again, it struck him how easily the three of them segued together.

"No problem," she muttered, rolling her eyes. "Although, I personally didn't volunteer to do the dishes, and probably never will. *I* have a dishwasher at home."

"I'm sure I can come up with some kind of reward system you'll find satisfying for doing the job." Owen nudged her with his elbow and blew a kiss her way as she gathered her plate and rose to her feet, pouting playfully.

They left Derek at the breakfast nook and moved over to the kitchen sink while he finished his orange juice and watched them. He shook his head and smiled to himself. "You know, I feel like we've known each other for, like, a very long time." It was the same feeling he had gotten the first night they'd met Adelaide, like she belonged with them.

She peeked over her shoulder at him. "It does seem like that, doesn't it? Hey, how did you two become friends? What was it like growing up together?"

"Video games, video games, and more video games," Owen huffed.

Derek laughed. "Admittedly, I was a bit of a geek as a kid. Owen could've been way more popular than he already was if he hadn't wasted time hanging around with me, but I appreciated his friendship. I was socially awkward."

"And, I was socially unavailable. I'm not shy, but I'm not as gregarious as people think I am. I just know how to turn on the charm when necessary."

"And, you're in pharmaceutical sales?" Addie asked. "Personally, I think you're great with people. Selectively great, I should say. But, why the social isolation?"

"I'm particular," Owen tried to explain.

Derek pointed his last strip of bacon at him before taking a bite out of it. "Not particular. That's putting it mildly. He's *picky*. That's why he's still single."

Owen chuckled. "No, I'm still single because…" He hesitated. He shrugged. He didn't have an answer.

Adelaide studied Owen and looked to Derek. "The consummate lover boy is speechless. Owen, I'd say you're probably single for the same reason I'm single. We know better." She winked.

Derek, the hopeless romantic, disagreed. "I think you're both single because you simply haven't met better yet."

"Better is subjective," Adelaide pointed out.

"What do you say we three go out on a date?" Derek changed the subject. They could kick it around Owen's place all day, but things might get redundant if they didn't get out and see the world. He was having such a relaxed time with them that he didn't want boredom to set in.

Owen arched a brow and nodded. "That's a novel idea." He ran the skillet under the running water and dunked it in the suds to scrub away at it while he considered the proposition.

"Like, a date-date?" asked Adelaide.

"I, for one, have nothing in particular to do," Owen replied.

"I'm not in a hurry to get home," Addie said. And, for Derek this *was* home now. What better way to get to know each other than to get beyond the bedroom? He shifted in his chair, warming to the plan. He couldn't quell the urge to see just how far he could take this wonderful stroke of luck that he found himself in the middle of.

"Yeah, dinner and a movie type shit. Old fashioned," Derek said. "Opening doors, pulling out chairs."

"Hey, hey, we talked about that. I can open my own doors, thank you very much," Addie teased from over by the kitchen sink.

Owen cut in, "I personally like Netflix and chill, elitist prick." He set aside the skillet he was washing and went on to the rest of the small stack of dishes they had used for breakfast. Adelaide diligently put them away where Owen quietly instructed. To Derek he added, "But, a nice, fancy restaurant might not be all that bad. What do you say, Addie? You want to be seen out and about with us two?"

Adelaide ruffled his lustrous dark brown hair, and he smiled through his thick beard. "A little shaggier than my usual," she giggled. An unexpected frisson of jealousy arced through Derek at the familiar way they played together, but he didn't say anything. If he had to bet on it, Addie and Owen would make a more compatible couple, but he wasn't betting on anything. So, his anxiety aside, his friends looked cool together.

Derek rose from the table and approached. "Yeah, Addie. What do you say?" There was subtle tension underlying the unassuming request to go out together. He was aware the original sex deal didn't include relationship goals like dates. There were boundaries that couldn't be crossed, but as of yesterday the lines kept getting re-drawn, and Derek didn't think any one of them was sure of what was allowed and what wasn't. They were all winging it.

Adelaide's face dropped as she remembered something. Derek wondered if she had found an excuse to turn them down, but instead she said, "Oh, I do have an event later today! I almost forgot about that.

Ugh! I wish I could stick around for the weekend, but if we do go somewhere, we'll have to be back before five so I can make it to work."

"We'll get you back in time," Owen assured her. Derek and Owen shared a look. In Owen's gray eyes was acceptance of the direction Derek was taking things, which made him breathe a quiet sigh of relief. It was nice to know Owen wasn't just going along with things to keep from being openly contrary. He genuinely seemed like he wanted to go out—the three of them. What would that be considered? A triplet instead of a couple?

CHAPTER 33

"KITCHEN DUTY DONE," Addie said pointedly. "You owe me."

"I do, don't I?" Owen grabbed her arm and spun her around so quickly that her golden hair whipped around in an arc. He eyed Derek, who slid between her and the countertop. Adelaide smiled up at him. "Make it good," she whispered.

Derek's mouth crushed hers, swallowing the sound she made next—half-moan/half-sigh. She gasped into his mouth as Derek sharply tugged her pajama bottoms down. Owen's hands glided over the smooth hill of her bottom. He squeezed and lifted her butt cheek to probe her heated vagina. Owen groaned in anticipation as he pulled his cock out of his drawstring pants and stroked it along the same trail his hand had just taken.

Derek took his kiss from her lips to her nipples poking against the thin cotton of her shirt. He lifted the t-shirt out of the way. His tongue curled around the areola and licked silkily over her skin. Adelaide ran her fingers through his hair as she sucked in a breath. Two men at her disposal were infinitely better than one. Derek provided the foreplay; Owen raised the stakes.

She gripped the edge of the countertop as he forced her body to bend slightly forward so he could access her swiftly saturating pussy. When Owen speared into her, a ragged cry escaped. Derek lifted his head, sucking her chin in his haste to get back to her mouth. Her fingers fumbled at his growing erection.

There were no words necessary. They moved together like three parts of a whole. She masturbated Derek while Owen's body slapped wetly against hers—plunge after plunge of steel perfection. Groping and touching, they were all feels. Derek's cock jerked in her grasp. Owen gritted his teeth, holding onto her shoulder, pounding. "Ah," he hissed.

He yanked out of her pussy as he came too close to completion. Derek swiftly took over where he left off, grabbing Addie by the waist and turning her around to sit her on the kitchen counter. He dropped her onto his swollen cock like she belonged there. The sharp penetration made her scream his name. Her nails sank into his shoulders, but Derek didn't feel it. All he felt was the magical sheath closing around him, and gripping him in a warm embrace.

As her legs closed around his hips, he rolled his pelvis forward to ease in and out. When Owen's kiss caressed the back of his shoulder, Derek didn't even still this time. His frenzied pace became more frantic as Owen sucked the side of his neck. Owen crept a finger into the crease of Derek's ass and pushed gently inside of him. "Oh, fuck," Derek groaned, biting his lower lip. He squeezed his eyes shut, but Addie forced his chin up to look at her.

"You like it?" she cooed. "Uhn!" She threw her head back as her breasts jiggled and bounced in his face. Strong arm wrapped around her lower back, Derek held her up as she jostled around on his ready-to-bust cock. The combined effect of being inside of her and having Owen's finger inside of him, would send him over the edge.

Suddenly, Adelaide pushed him away. She dropped down off of the counter to her knees as if what she wanted to do next was too important to wait. Mouth open, she greedily sucked Derek's pulsating shaft. He weakened, doubling over with a throaty moan. It was all the opening Owen needed. He replaced his finger with just the tip of his dick, and a primal sound growled from Derek at the explosion of tension that shot through his body.

But, Owen didn't stop. He bent forward to drop a slick dollop of saliva into Derek's ass. It lubricated his steel pipe, and he pressed a fraction of a centimeter deeper. There was no way to focus on the discomfort with what Addie was doing with her mouth. Swallowing him whole, she worked her tongue in ways Derek had never experienced. His erection reached levels of hardness unheard of. It was enough to make him see stars.

And, before he knew what had happened, Owen popped past the toughest stricture, gaining access. What Derek experienced was sheer bliss. It wasn't anything like he had expected. The pleasure was intense and unending as erogenous zones he had only read about got touched in ways nothing but this could come close to.

"*Ah, god*," he sobbed. His fingers dug into the slick marble surface of the counter as his heart pounded in his chest. He had butterflies in his stomach. He had swallows and sparrows and sparkles and stardust. "*Ah!*"

Adelaide popped his penis out of her mouth and stroked it along her soft cheek, staring up at him with glistening, wide-open eyes. Her lips parted in wonder as she watched his faces of ecstasy. She eagerly went back to sucking Derek off. Her slender hand strummed his shaft, with her beautiful mouth following up the stroke.

Derek tangled his hands in her hair, mindless with excitement. He pumped in and out of her mouth as Owen hammered in and out of him, and the other man's jubilant sounds of pleasure accentuated the moment. This was it. This was it! Derek's legs began to shake, but Owen gripped his hips and thrust harder. He couldn't hold it back. He was coming. He was a rocket, a ship setting sail to the edge of the universe.

Owen opened his mouth and moaned Derek's name so poignantly, that the hairs on the back of Derek's neck stood at attention. The unexpected feel of molten ejaculation seeping hotly into his anal cavity shocked Derek's senses. At the same time, his cock jerked with a spasm and poured. The last thing he saw before his vision went dim was the result of his climax spilled across Adelaide's beautiful face.

Then Derek stumbled forward, barely catching himself before he fell. Addie slowly rose to her feet. Owen's limp dick escaped the tight hold of his ass. Derek felt stretched and completed in ways he had never been before. He couldn't slow his racing pulse. He didn't know what to say next, or how to move forward. In fact, he wanted nothing more than to bask in the afterglow of the wickedly naughty thing that had just happened.

But, Adelaide looked like her body was still afire, and something had to be done. As Derek slid slowly to the floor, he grabbed her hand and pulled her with him. She came willingly, stretching out like a fallen angel. It took all Derek's strength to position his face between her legs, but when he managed, he was glad for the effort.

Her aroused sex exuded a womanly musk Derek buried his nose into, before nibbling at her clit. Addie's hips bucked from the floor as she grabbed the back of his head and pressed his face deeper. She grinded against his lips, accepting the sweep of his tongue like she would die if she didn't get it. Owen dropped to her side to squeeze and toy with her breasts while Derek worked his cunnilingus skills.

She tasted sweet and ready. Her juices flowed copiously into his mouth as his face grew slick with her anticipation. Sobs of pleasure were uttered. Owen leaned forward and covered the tip of her breast with his mouth, suckling to add to the torment Derek was causing between her legs. She thrust against his tongue as her chest rose to fulfill Owen's quest as well.

The two men coaxed her over the precipice, and Adelaide had no choice but to drop. "Ohhh," she crooned as the climax struck. Pleasure like a riptide snatched away her control, and her body shook of its own volition. She writhed against them both. They petted and stroked her feverish skin until the last of the powerful orgasm had taken its toll. In the end, there were three people on Owen's kitchen floor, struggling to catch their breath and coming back from the rapture.

A tremulous giggle came from Adelaide. Her chest heaved. She drifted tired fingers down her flat stomach to cup her vagina. Derek's head rested on her inner thigh, and Owen's face was on her shoulder. She sighed deeply. "Wow," she whispered.

Derek had fewer words than that to describe what had just occurred. He was sore, and satisfied, and awestruck at the same damn time. He dared a peek at Owen and found his best friend watching him from beneath hooded eyes, studying him as if he was trying to figure out the same thing.

What had changed? When had this happened?

Derek was sure that after having this taste of fulfillment, he'd never be able to get enough. Owen turned his eyes away, and the threat lifted. In those gray orbs was too much promise. Derek knew better than   to   trust   a   word   that   wasn't   said.

CHAPTER 34

DEREK AMBLED INTO the upstairs guest bathroom and turned on the shower, standing under the steamy spray and reliving the ecstasy of thirty minutes ago. Eyes closed, Derek could remember the feel of Owen's lips against his skin. He could feel his hands. He plunged into a vivid replay of Adelaide's nubile body writhing gloriously against his as he pounded into her. Then, Owen pounding into him...

Derek groaned and dropped his head. He braced his hands against the walls of the shower and just stood there, trying to keep his mind blank. He didn't need reminders that he was in deeper than he had anticipated when he had initiated this habitual ménage stuff. It was shit like what had happened down in the kitchen that could get him caught up in obsessive thoughts.

Derek had been blown away by the magnitude of the pleasure Owen could give him. Prior to that, even his fantasies had been mostly safe. Now, he knew. He needed. He craved. One time wouldn't be enough. A few weeks would be a teaser. When Owen got over this novelty phase, Derek would be left with feelings he couldn't do a damn thing with, and none of this would matter—not the sex, not the camaraderie, not feeling like they were one big New Age happy family—none of it! Sighing, he shook away the flashbacks and finished up in the bathroom.

Once he was done, he trekked over to Owen's room with leaden feet. Derek had only a towel wrapped around his hips but was still a little surprised to see the appreciative gleam in Owen's eyes as he looked him over, even after what they had done together. There was heat in the gaze that had previously been cool, and Derek blushed, not daring to think Owen could reciprocate the attraction. It had to be a trick of the light.

Better to imagine that the homosexual urges were reserved for the bedroom—well, for sex, at any rate.

"Yo, um, I was just wondering what I should wear for this. Got anything spiffy?" Derek padded over to the closet to avoid looking at him.

From inside, he heard Owen say, "Have a look in there and grab whatever you like. I'm going casual. It's too early in the day for dinner wear." Derek chose casual slacks and a pullover from the expansive array of clothing choices.

When he came back out, Derek gnawed his bottom lip nervously as he stood by the side of the bed and surreptitiously, quickly dressed. "About what this whole mess…" he dared to broach the subject. Owen, cleaning his glasses, looked down. Derek looked down too, losing his nerve. "You don't mind Adelaide staying over every now and then, do you? I don't want to break any unspoken rules of living together by having guests over on the regular if it bothers you."

"What? No, I'm fine with Adelaide being here anytime she wants. She's really something else," Owen said breathlessly, chuckling. "I like her company."

Derek looked up sharply. Yeah, Addie was something. She was *his*. Kind of. He suppressed a groan. This was complicated. He couldn't extricate how he felt for Adelaide from how he felt for Owen, but he damn sure didn't want the two of them taking to each other so much that they cut him out of the picture completely. Stranger things had happened in his life. It didn't seem so farfetched, now that he thought about it.

Owen straightened his bowtie and smoothed a hand over his shirt as he peered at his reflection in the mirror. He caught sight of Derek's downcast face through the glass. "Why so solemn?" he asked with a grin. "C'mon, in a little while we're going out on a date with a beautiful woman and getting the chance to hang at the same time. What could be better than that?"

Derek tightened his belt buckle, shrugging. "I dunno. I'm just wondering if maybe you and Adelaide make a better pair than me and

Addie." He didn't dare say *than me and you*. "Remember how I asked you if you were jealous that I got the girl?"

"Derek," Owen groaned.

"No, hear me out. Dude, I would like nothing better than to know you've hooked up with a woman that matches you in every way. I mean, we're not getting any younger. At some point, people start thinking about love and marriage, right? Adelaide could be the one for you, but if we keep up this whole ménage thing—"

"Okay, stop. I don't want to hear another word of your existential angst right now, buddy," Owen replied, with a tense laugh. He turned away from the mirror and pinned Derek with a stern look. "Listen, all I want to do is go out with two great friends and eat some grub, drink some early beers, and shoot the shit. I'm not looking for a wife. Everybody doesn't think like you do, Derek."

"All I'm saying is, I don't want to be the reason you miss out on what could be a wonderful relationship," Derek finished uncomfortably. He threw his hands up in surrender and got ready to walk out the door. He didn't know if he was advocating for the two of them to nix him, or if he was testing the waters to see if Owen took to the idea. At this point, Derek didn't know anything anymore, other than that both scenarios made him feel like crap. What he wanted was Addie…and Owen…both of them.

"Derek, I'm developing feelings for Addie. Yeah, it's true. I didn't think it was possible, but she's kind of *impossible* not to love."

"Right," Derek muttered, closer to his escape. Owen rushed across the room and grabbed his shoulder, turning him around to face him.

"Right, but I care about you, too. You think I don't know you're already neck-deep in love with her?" Owen scowled.

"That's not the point."

"The point is, I think all three of us need this *friendship* more than we need anything else, and I don't want you to ruin it for us by getting caught up in your feelings."

Suddenly, Adelaide stepped to the half-open door. She tapped unnecessarily, and both men shut up. Pushing into the room, the bubbly blonde's smile shifted a little when she noticed the tension. "What'd I miss?" she asked. "Are we not going out now? Is something wrong?"

"No," Derek replied gruffly. Owen shook his head and drummed up a smile that didn't quite reach his eyes.

"Everything's fine. You ready?" Derek looked her over. She was still wearing her pajamas. "Changed your mind?" Owen frowned. She shook her head and held up her clothes from the day prior.

"We didn't think this through," Adelaide said with a laugh. "I have nothing to wear. I was wondering if I could borrow one of your shirts to pull-off as a dress."

An hour later as Derek and Owen waited downstairs, she came down in a pumpkin spice orange shirt—one of Derek's—cinched at the waist with a skinny belt. She had transformed completely, with her rich golden curls piled atop her head in a messy bun, and a few loose tendrils curling around her face.

Both men looked up from the video game they were playing with exclamations of wonder. "My god, you clean up nicely," Owen said with a grin.

Derek pushed up from the couch and moved to her side. He couldn't resist cupping her face in his palm and staring down into her eyes before gently kissing her lips. Owen had told him to keep his feelings out of it, but that was hardly likely. They both made him feel. He didn't have a choice. He guessed someone would have to pay for it. Eventually.

"All set?" he whispered against her lips.

She nodded slowly, smiling up at him. "You know what? You're going to make me do even more things I shouldn't do...like really like you."

"You can do that," he said, pleased. She shook her head.

"In my experience, hearts can't be split in two unless they're broken," she murmured pointedly. Her eyes turned to Owen, and Derek felt his heart tremble at the words. She was right. There wasn't enough room for more than one of them.

CHAPTER 35

THEY PICKED A quiet restaurant tucked off on a tree-lined street. It was in a part of town that had a lot of character, with historic buildings and well-tended gardens. In the late morning sunlight, Adelaide looked striking against the backdrop of bright, colorful flowers, and verdant greenery. She let Derek open the door for her this time. The three of them found a table near the back beside a wall of windows.

The restaurant had a zesty, tomato smell. Derek inhaled appreciatively. "I thought I wasn't hungry, but I think I found my appetite," he smiled. Addie grabbed a breadstick from the basket on the table and bit into it heartily.

"You ever been here?" she asked.

"I haven't," said Derek.

Owen replied, "I meet with clients here, occasionally."

"Excellent! What's on the menu?"

As she was reaching for the menu the server had just handed to them, Derek happened to look up and spot a couple walk into the restaurant arm in arm, looking very much in love. Derek stilled with his wineglass half way to his lips. Owen followed his gaze and so did Addie. Derek swore softly.

"Wow," she muttered, turning away and shaking her head. "Told you."

Derek couldn't believe what he was seeing. It was Libby. And, she was with his brother-in-law, Steve. His sister Heather apparently hadn't been invited to the party.

"She's my coworker," he muttered. It was Libby. Was Steve the guy she was talking about when she'd said she met someone new. "Man, what the fuck…"

"She's a looker," Owen gave him that. Derek swore again and set his cup down with a thump.

"Wow," Adelaide said again. Derek felt a surge of anger and pictured himself heading straight over and confronting the jackass. He was just afraid if he got his hands on him, things would end with bloodshed. He was thoroughly sick of seeing Steve's dark side. Was there any gem of goodness to the man?

"I'm not going to do it," Derek talked himself out of getting up. He grabbed his glass up and set it back down abruptly. "I'm going to do it." He had almost risen out of his chair when Owen placed a steadying hand on his arm.

"Hang on a minute, Derek. Let's see the lay of the land first. No sense in rushing over and exposing that you're here. He hasn't seen us yet, which means we have the advantage here, so give him enough rope to hang himself with."

Derek settled down in a huff. "I can't sit idly by and watch him cheat on my sister."

"Well, you don't know for certain that he's cheating," Owen replied. The waiter was headed back in their direction. Owen shook his head slightly, deterring her. They needed to remain incognito.

The pretty brunette smiled and mouthed, "I'll come back later."

"No, no, I'm certain of it," Derek said hastily. "You see, Libby is the secretary at Ad Ent, and last week at lunch she told me she had met someone new and had high hopes that he could be the one. I'm ninety-nine percent positive she was talking about Steve, which sucks ass on so many levels. Libby is such a sweet girl. She doesn't deserve this."

"Aw, I hate that. She looks like a sweet girl," Addie replied. "But, the Steve I know would definitely do something like this. So, what are you going to do, Derek?"

The three of them watched Libby and Steve take a seat across the restaurant. Libby wore a floral dress, her red hair flowing over her delicate white shoulders. Her lips were a vibrant red, and she smiled so hard that her cheeks blushed. She was beautiful. Next to her, Steve looked like the lucky shmuck that had won the lottery. He made a show of opening her napkin for her and placing it on her lap. He kissed

Libby's cheek.

Derek pointed discreetly. "You see that? It's exactly what it looks like. He's cheating on my sister! I'm going to figure out how to put an end to it, one way or another. Heather needs to know. Libby needs to know. Steve needs to get lost. To think he tried to make Addie out to be the bad guy."

It was Steve who had told him and Owen that Adelaide was an ex-girlfriend/stalker who had crashed his wedding because she wasn't fully over him. Derek had never believed a word of it, and knowing what he knew now of his brother-in-law, what worried him most was that Steve probably had. He was the kind of liar who believed his own stories. So, what on earth could he be telling Libby right this very second? She was vulnerable enough to eat up whatever came out of his mouth.

"What do you think we should do?" asked Owen skeptically. "Go beat him up? Call and tell Heather?"

Derek grimly shook his head. Letting his sister know they had seen her husband out with one of his co-workers wouldn't do. With Heather pissed about him being with Adelaide—especially since his sister took her crashing their wedding personally—she wasn't liable to listen to anything he had to tell her about Steve.

"He'll just say it was a business lunch or something, and I don't want to bring anything to Libby until we have definitive proof," he said.

"You want my suggestion? Leave it alone. Knowing Steve, he's not savvy enough to keep something like this under wraps anyway. The truth will come out," Adelaide provided. Adelaide held her phone up and began to record the interaction going on at the other table.

Derek looked confused. "I thought you said we shouldn't do anything."

She smiled wickedly. "Well, you're right. It doesn't hurt to have evidence, but I'm thinking you should hold onto it until the truth does come out. If you take it to her prematurely, your sister will just convince herself it's not as bad as it looks. Trust me. I know women."

Owen nodded and said, "Yep. Spot on assessment, Adelaide. Good thinking."

"Yeah, but Heather is my sister, and I don't want to see her get hurt. Maybe we can send it to her from a number she can't trace. That way it won't be coming from me, and she won't have any reason to be skeptical about the source of the information."

"You can't protect everybody from everything," Addie replied sagely. "Even if it comes from a different number you still have to contend with the power of the brain in love to delude itself."

The truth hurt, but she was right. "Know what, though? I want to let him know we've seen him, and watch him squirm a bit." At that moment, Steve seemed to get a sixth sense that someone was watching him. He looked around the restaurant and suddenly zeroed in on Derek and his table. The disgruntled expression that flitted across his face was priceless. Derek smiled smugly and mouthed, "Got you, motherfucker."

Steve saw Adelaide recording them with her cellphone, and he pushed away from the table so fast that his chair tumbled over. "Oops!" Libby laughed. "Watch it, honey! Bathroom emergency?" She peered at him curiously.

"Uh, why don't we try another restaurant? There's a bistro a block away that I'd love to take you to. Come on. Grab your purse." Steve pulled out Libby's chair, but she clung to the seat with eyes wide as saucers and a startled gasp.

"Well, wait a minute! We just got here," Libby replied, looking confused. She peeked over her shoulder and caught Steve's scowl. "I don't see what all the fuss is about! What is it? Is the menu overpriced?"

"No!" He made the mistake of darting a glance in Derek's direction as he tried to smooth his features into something less honest. That's when Libby finally spotted Derek, as well. A smile split her face. Steve grumbled, "I just really think we'll have a better time somewhere else. I hate to rush you, darling, but we really want to hurry if we want to get in before the lunchtime crush."

"Fine, fine, we can go. But, look, that's one of my co-workers. Let me just go say hi before we leave."

"Your c-co-worker?" Steve blanched. He ran a hand over his quivering mouth. "No, no, Libby. I forgot I'm allergic to garlic, and this place is really making me feel uncomfortable. I feel a bout of hives coming on."

"Mercy! That's terrible. Oh, well, you're right. I guess I'll speak to Derek another day." Libby wiggled her fingers in Derek's direction and followed Steve out of the establishment.

"Got it!" Adelaide had the whole incident on record. Unfortunately, not much of it was as incriminating as what had occurred before Steve realized they were there. She stopped filming and put her phone aside.

Derek sighed. "Now, I have to let Libby know the man of her dreams is…"

"More like a nightmare," Adelaide finished.

"And, that's why I don't do relationships," said Owen. "People don't know what they want. They think they want one thing, but the minute something new comes along that looks interesting, they go after that. Even me. I'm guilty."

Derek chuckled wryly. "That's a fallacy. People think because they believe something or they behave a certain way, then that behavior or belief is widespread. No, most people don't engage in relationships, not knowing what they really want." Although, he was guilty, too.

Addie shrugged and said, "In my opinion, Owen's assessment sounds about right to me. Sure, there's no such thing as absolutes. Everyone may not be like that, but whether most are or not doesn't really matter. Enough are."

Derek tried to explain, "I think it's more like some people misrepresent what they want. Steve never wanted to marry my sister. He couldn't convince me of that if he tried. Heather laid out an ultimatum, and he complied, rather than being upfront with her and telling her he wasn't marriage material."

"For once in my life I'd like to meet a man who is exactly who he says he is and says exactly what he wants, so that there are no misunderstandings."

Derek kept his mouth closed on that one. He could say he was that kind of man, but there were plenty of potential misunderstandings currently in the works, since he hadn't yet said what he wanted. He didn't think Adelaide understood how much he was into her. He didn't think she realized that Owen had some serious feelings for her, too.

Likewise, he had no way to know exactly how serious she was about either of them. So, it definitely wasn't the time for him to chime in with how he was the man for her. Maybe he was.. Maybe not.

Adelaide shrugged and dismissed the topic. "At any rate, I think I want fettuccini."

"Ohh, the fettuccini is nice," Owen replied. He pointed at

something else on her menu, and Derek peeked over her shoulder. They began discussing what they'd eat and then the server came over to take their orders. Eventually Steve and his cheating ways were put on the backburner. It wasn't enough to ruin a meal over.

Derek knew he would have to deal with it later, would have to come up with a way to guide his sister to the truth about her husband. He'd also have to be the one to break Libby's heart with the news.

CHAPTER 36

DEREK WAS DREADING going in to work. He rolled out of bed Monday morning and puzzled over exactly what—if anything—to tell Libby about Steve, but that was the last thing he needed to be thinking about. It was his first day as the head of his own team, and all his attention should have been focused on how not to flop. Harry was counting on him to fail spectacularly.

"Good morning, Mr. Cornwell!" Libby greeted him when he stepped out of the elevator.

Derek's eyes widened and he shoved his coffee cup to his mouth, mumbling around it, "Can't talk now, Libby. In a bit of a hurry!" He sped down the hall to his cubicle and put on his most serious face as he stared at the blank screen of his Mac, willing the computer to hurry up and power on already. Libby hadn't followed him to his desk, but she was shooting him curious looks. Derek groaned.

"If I tell her, it'll break her pretty little heart," he muttered. If he didn't tell her, he'd be as much the bad guy as Steve.

Mr. Clancy materialized at his desk later in the morning. "Mr. Cornwell?"

"Good morning, Mr. Clancy!"

"Have you met your new team yet?" asked the middle-aged gentleman. He rested a hand on Derek's shoulder, and Derek grinned up at him gamely.

"Not yet, sir, but we have a meeting in a bit."

"D'ah, well, I look forward to seeing what you and Harold do this time!" Mr. Clancy pointed at him with both hands and smiled, ambling away. Derek gulped apprehensively and turned back to his computer.

"Friendly competition," he muttered to himself. Nothing to get all worked up about. Derek fired off a multi-party text to Addie and Owen: "Wish me luck. I'm about to meet the new team."

Adelaide sent back a thumbs up and lots of hearts. Owen called him. Derek stuck the phone to his ear as he gathered up what he'd need for the quick meet-n-greet with his rookies. "Talk quick. I'm on my way to a conference," said Derek.

"Yeah, I know, busy guy. Just calling to remind you not to let Gensler get to you. You're not in competition with anyone but yourself, alright?"

"Right. Oh, on the off chance he knows what he's talking about, though, how do I handle any mouthy newbies who want to slay me and usurp my position as king of the castle?" Derek grinned and nodded a greeting to a passing coworker in the hall. Owen laughed on the other end of the line.

"Chin up, shoulders squared. Get in there, tiger."

Derek hung up the phone and stepped into the conference room. "Ladies and gentlemen, welcome aboard. Have a seat, everyone. We've got a lot to cover, but I don't want to tie up everyone's morning." Derek heaved a sigh and looked around at the bright, new faces. There were seven other people in the room, all looking young and overeager. He returned the smiles as they turned toward them. He was going to like this. It really wasn't so bad. "I'm Derek Cornwell, and I'd like to get to know each of you better because we're going to be spending a lot of hours at the drawing board together."

A red-haired guy in a navy blue blazer and seersucker trousers half-rose from his seat with his hand raised. "Mr. Cornwell, I just want to say that it's a pleasure to be a part of your team, sir. Everyone's talking about how you set the bar way high last week with your Wonder Man ad. I can't wait to see what, together, we can do next."

Derek smiled and peeked down at his list of names. "Thank you, Mr...."

"Willis Beauchamp, sir." Willis Beauchamp's neat strawberry blond hair was parted to the side, and he looked Ivy League, fraternity material, but if he could create designs, Derek didn't care how dissimilar their backgrounds were.

"Thank you, Mr. Beauchamp." He took a moment to peek through the digital portfolios of each of his new team members, starting with Willis Beauchamp, as the rest of his team introduced themselves. Katelyn Wells was a brilliant young woman with an impressive list of accolades to her name. Billie Jasper was equally talented. Nate Cordon, Chiang Li, Alydia Short and Bethany Viet. Judging by the information flitting across his tablet screen, Derek had nothing to worry about. He had a talented brood.

"Well, well, well! I think we're going to have a lot of fun together, Team Noob," said Derek with a wide smile. "First up, we'll be putting together an ad for a new razor from a well-known company. But, there is a catch. We will be competing with another team from Ad Ent, and only one ad can win. Are you guys up for the challenge? I'm sure you all know…we're the underdog."

"Hoo-hah!" Billie Jasper hooted. Chiang and Bethany giggled. Derek moved from the table to pace and give his rallying speech. The energy in the room was high.

"Now, because none of you have ever done this before, we'll be taking things nice and slow, but we'll still be making some aggressive plays. I'd like everyone to click over to the next module where I've outlined a plan we'll try to stick close to, while we brainstorm and navigate this process together."

"Oh, um…" Willis Beauchamp threw a hand up. "I also took the liberty of doing a little homework last night. Here, I'll sync this over to you."

Derek looked down at his device in surprise as a file upload notification chimed. His eyebrows came together as he looked up at Beauchamp. "Mr. Beauchamp, I'm impressed!" He clicked the upload and watched the file open. It was a remarkably detailed spreadsheet about the product they'd be working on. Overkill to an extent, but Derek appreciated the young man's initiative. "Now, that's the kind of go-for-it spirit I like. I just want to let everyone know the table is always open for fresh, new ideas. Everyone's input is welcome."

He meant the words he'd spoken at the close of the meeting, but it took not a good thirty minutes after the conference was adjourned for Harold to come over and plant seeds of doubt in his head. "Hmmm," the older ad man hummed speculatively as he passed Derek's desk. "I hear you've got that show-off Beauchamp on your team. Good luck with that."

Derek glanced up from the work he was doing. "Yes, as a matter of fact, Harold. And, I'm pretty pleased to have him on my side. Don't you have some poor sod's career to ruin or something?" He chuckled as he went back to what he was working on.

Harold smiled a smarmy smile before leaning close to whisper, "Just watch your back. That one sounds like he's coming out swinging."

Derek tried not to let it get to him, because he knew that's exactly what Harold wanted. By lunchtime, however, he had to consider whether or not there was merit to what Harold was trying to get him to believe. Historically, he could think of two or three others at the firm who had been let go after a more ambitious designer came aboard. Generally, when Clancy fired someone however, it was for better reasons than simply that someone new had come along.

Derek blew out a breath and shook his head. "Got nothing to worry about," he muttered. On the other hand, he had just come off of probation and almost had his job terminated for his previously lackadaisical approach to design…he'd have to be on top of his game. And, he'd probably better pay close attention to Beauchamp in the meantime.

Derek hurried into the elevator and took it down to the ground floor, intending to have lunch in his car. Although he had made up his mind to tell Libby what a prick Steve was, he wasn't ready to do it just yet. The last thing he wanted was to ruin her workday with bad news. He ate his cold cuts and drank his water in solitude and what should have been peace, but he had gotten used to the vivacious, somewhat nosy design floor secretary, and he kind of missed her company.

Derek had a thought. He pulled out his cellphone while it was fresh on the brain. Adelaide answered, laughing softly and talking to someone else in her background. He wondered who she was talking to but tried not to let jealousy creep into his tone. "Am I interrupting something?"

"No, I was just telling the nurse about the time George grounded me for wearing black lipstick. What's up?"

"Oh, how's your Dad doing?"

"Much better today. They've upgraded his diet. Did you need anything, babe? I was just thinking of you, by the way."

"Well, that makes me feel all warm and tingly on the inside," Derek smiled. "Listen, I've been considering this situation with Libby and my suck-ass brother-in-law. You know what would be great? If we could find her a better dude."

"I see where you're going with this, but exactly where do you propose we find said knight in shining armor? I think I got the last two in the city."

"Mmm, a woman after my own heart. Flattery will get you everywhere. But, think about it. I'm sure you have a friend or two who'd be willing to go on a blind date with her. Right? You said before that you had some male friends."

"Now, why does that sound like you're probing?" Addie said with a laugh. "I'll put out some feelers and see if anyone bites the bait. From what I recall from Saturday, she was quite a cute chick. Hey, how come you didn't date her? You said she's a coworker, huh?"

"Ick, I don't date co-workers," Derek replied, grimacing. Well, he had once, and it had ended badly. That taught him never to mix business with pleasure. Anyway, by the time Libby had taken a passing interest in him, he was deeply enamored with Adelaide. The rest, as they say, was history in the making. "Besides, Libby needs someone who's adventurous to her predictable. She's such a secretary." He pulled a face. Adelaide giggled over the other end.

"See? I told you opposite personalities add excitement. You didn't believe me when I said you and I could be..."

"What? Could be what?" he pressed softly.

"Ha! Never mind. I have to go. They're about to wheel Dad out for his first therapy session. I'll shoot you a text if I can find a guy friend who's single and interested."

"Perfect. I'll talk to you later," he replied. Derek hung up the phone and checked the time. He had been hiding out long enough, but if he could keep a low profile until Adelaide found Libby a suitable mate,   that   would   be   perfect.

CHAPTER 37

DEREK WAS IN a transitory phase of life. It took him only a few more trips to his parents' house to retrieve the rest of his earthly belongings. He was settling into sharing space at Owen's house well, and the two friends sank naturally into an easy cohabitation routine.

They got up in the mornings and got ready for work together, shared coffee in the breakfast nook, chatted about the news. Most of the weekdays were spent away from the house with Owen doing his sales gig and Derek working at Ad Ent. Then in the evenings, they would hang out by the pool or play video games. Simple shit. Derek, normally a casual cleaner, learned Owen's fastidious ways. Owen, normally a recluse, found himself coming out of his shell and talking to Derek about more than the superficial stuff the old friends had become accustomed to talking about.

There was something about knowing each other nearly a lifetime that made it easier to communicate, but harder to talk about anything of substance. That was changing because they were no longer 'just friends'. Derek had caught Owen staring at him when he didn't think he was looking. There were times when they couldn't keep their hands off of one another.

And, it wasn't necessarily anything sexual because if Adelaide wasn't around, there wasn't anything kinky going on between them. It was quick shoulder massages after a long day. Brief hand holds after handshakes. Hugs that lingered. Whatever burgeoning attraction between them was growing.

Derek strolled into Owen's bedroom late Tuesday evening, with a box of caramel corn and a rental. "Got time for this?" he asked.

Owen glanced up from the book he was reading. "Can we talk?"

Derek stilled. It sounded serious. He sat gingerly at the foot of Owen's bed and nodded. "What's on your mind?"

The room was quiet and heavy for a brief period, the only sound the whooshing of the ceiling fan blades. They shared a loaded look before Owen sighed and broke the silence. "I think we need to start preparing for the possibility that Adelaide might not want to keep this up."

"What do you mean?"

"Let me ask you something. How many times a day do you talk to her?"

Derek gave it a thought. "She calls me around lunch time or I call her. We text on and off through the day, chat on my way home from work. Why?"

"You know, she and I only ever talk when she's here with you." Owen delivered the comment quietly and stared down at his hands as he said it. "I'm not jealous." He shook his head and repeated it. "I'm not jealous...but you have to understand that I'm not made of stone. I look at you and her together, and the same way you seem to think she and I would make the perfect couple, that's what I see for you. Derek, I don't want to do this anymore. People could get hurt."

Derek lowered his gaze. "I'm not going to hurt you," he murmured. Owen looked up sharply. "I've thought of nothing else ever since the night I moved in with you, Owen. I know feelings are getting involved, regardless of what either of you say."

"She's going to choose, and her choice will be you. Point blank."

"What if I said I can't picture my life without the both of you now?"

"I'd tell you you're crazy. That's not how love works...and we're not gay..." Owen muttered. He grabbed his book and tried to get back into the story he'd been reading, but he didn't look convincing enough for Derek to let things go. He slid closer to Owen and touched his knee, forcing him to meet his gaze.

"We wouldn't be the first people in history to engage in a polyamorous relationship."

"I don't want a relationship," Owen replied instinctively.

"Then, why do you even care?" Derek shouted. He sighed and shoved up from the bed, ready to walk out. Back turned, he felt Owen's gaze burning his skin. He looked over his shoulder. "You could be with anyone, anywhere. Yet, you keep choosing to be with me," he whispered.

"Derek…"

"Either you hold onto me, or you let me go."

"It's not that simple."

Derek turned around. "It never is. But, those are the only options. I've been wracking my brain trying to figure out where this will go next, and I don't have any answers because none of us—not a one—seems to be willing to say what we really want. Well, let me clear the air. I want you. I want her. I want us."

"I want…"

"Say it," Derek urged. His long legged stride quickly consumed the short distance between his exit and the bed, and he sat next to Owen, facing him. Owen set aside his book again. His face was serious, as if he was trying to fix his mouth to say what Derek needed to hear. There were years behind them, memories tangled so tightly into the fabric of each of them, that cutting ties wasn't even an option. Unraveling the tangle would be impossible. There was love there.

But was it the kind that was brotherly or the kind that would keep them up at night for years to come, wondering what if?

"I want you. I want her," Owen confessed. He growled in frustration and snatched off his glasses, tossing them to the bed. His large hand scrubbed at his eyes as he tried to bury his face in his hands. "I never imagined I could want anything love-related so much."

Derek reached tentatively out for his best friend. "This scares me, too."

Owen looked up with a tortured expression. "And, yet the fact remains that Adelaide said herself the heart only has room for one. You know what she thinks. You say you won't hurt me, but you may not be able to help it, Derek. Because if one of us chooses, then we all have to live with that choice."

"I'm going to tell her," Derek replied resolutely. His lips firmed as he bolstered up the courage to do exactly that. The weeks of just messing around, keeping things chill had to come to an end. It all hinged on his ability to convince Adelaide that her fragile heart wouldn't break if she let them both in. But, there was a part of Derek that worried about the things he couldn't control. Like Addie's response. Like Owen's steadfastness. At any given point, the train of his love life could hurtle off track again.

CHAPTER 38

HE WAS IN the middle of delegating assignments to his new team members later that week when his cellphone jangled in his pocket.

"Alright, guys, click to the second page of the module and let's quickly go over it before we get started storming our brains," Derek replied, ignoring the call. Derek sighed as he adjusted his tie and dove into discussing the schedule he had painstakingly set up for brainstorming sessions, presentations, and reviews over the course of the next month.

He was only another ten minutes into his spiel when Libby rushed into the conference room with a worried look. "I hate to bother you, Mr. Cornwell," she stage-whispered.

Derek obligingly pulled away from what he was doing to meet the normally bubbly, now somber design floor administrative assistant he had been avoiding all week. "Is something wrong? What's up?" His brows came together over his forehead. He hoped it wasn't something related to Steven and Heather. He still hadn't figured out how to tell his coworker that the guy of her dreams was really a sleaze ball cheater.

Libby shoved a bunch of hand-written messages into his hands. Derek looked down, surprised. "Adelaide's been calling all morning," Libby whispered. "I didn't know who she was at first, so I told her I would deliver the message to you when you were out of your meeting. She just called again. She sounded upset."

"What?" Derek unfolded the crumpled messages and scanned over each one. There was almost no information other than an x-mark next to the box stating the caller would call back. "Did she tell you what she was calling about?"

Libby shook her head. "All I could gather was something about her father. Then, she hung up on me."

She wasn't done speaking, but Derek moved away from her mid-sentence to hastily dismiss his team. "Meet me back here after lunch," he had the presence of mind to state, as he gathered up his devices, folders, and briefcase. He flew past Libby, calling over his shoulder, "If anyone asks, I'm taking an early lunch. I had a family emergency."

"Of course," the shapely secretary nodded smartly. "You go ahead. I'll cover for you."

As soon he was down to the parking garage, Derek wrestled his cellphone out of his pocket to give Addie a call back. The whole time the phone rang, he prayed nothing terrible had happened to her foster father. It would destroy her if it had. Adelaide could only hide her feelings so much, and Derek knew that she was attached to George.

She finally answered the phone and Derek could hear she was crying so hard that she could barely speak. His heart dropped into his stomach. "Addie, Addie," he said soothingly. "Calm down. Tell me what's happening."

"My Dad's not in his room. I've been calling and calling all morning, and I couldn't reach him. I left a message for the nurse to find out where they could have taken him, but no one is returning my calls! What the hell kind of hospital do they run?" she agonized.

Derek inhaled deeply, relieved. "I'm sure there's some reasonable explanation," he replied, climbing into his car. "The nurses probably haven't checked their messages yet. Like me. Libby just so happened to interrupt my meeting after your last call because she said you sounded upset, and she knows you and I are dating."

Adelaide sniffled on the other end. "Wait, what?"

Derek waved his hands dismissively. "That doesn't matter right now. Where are you? I can head to you or I can call the hospital and see what I can find out."

"I'm sure they won't tell you anything. I'm on my way there but I didn't want to go alone in case…in case the news is bad. I'm sure they wouldn't have told me over the phone if he…Oh, god!" She sucked in a breath. He pictured her beautiful face marred by mascara tears, and wished he could fly instead of fight through traffic to get to her.

"Shh, don't think like that," Derek admonished. He cranked up his car and eased out of his parking spot. "I'm leaving work and heading straight for the hospital. Adelaide, I'll meet you there. You don't have to go alone. You don't have to go through any of this alone."

"Derek, why is any of this happening? Gah! I feel like a weakling, coming apart at the seams, and I hate you having to see me like this. I'm already in the car. I've been sitting here in the parking lot at my apartment, going through every worse case scenario possible. I couldn't move." She sighed. "Thank you for being here when I need you. Don't judge me."

It broke his heart to hear how relieved she was to know he was going. He smiled to himself. "Why would I judge you? You're having an emotional response to a troubling situation. And, you're on edge because you care about someone, and you want the best for him. Sounds like contrary to your own personal assertions, you know exactly how to love."

She didn't respond, and Derek didn't press. He told her to call him when she made it to the hospital, that he'd be waiting for her. Within the hour, Adelaide had made it across town and was tapping on his window after finding his car in the crowded hospital parking lot. Derek looked up in surprise.

"You made it here fast," he stated. She held up a ticket. He winced. "Ah, yeah, the cops out here really love their job." She smiled tightly.

"Come on, let's go. I'm getting antsy again. I need to know where he is and how he's doing."

They entered the lobby. Adelaide's mood was obvious. Her fingers twitched restlessly as they waited at the elevators. Her gaze darted around the room until the buzzer dinged. Derek put a hand to the base of her spine and ushered her inside. "Let me handle it when we get up there," he said cautiously, but she shook her head. Her riotous nimbus of golden hair swished around her face.

"No, like I said, they're not going to tell you anything. You're not family. It's HIPAA and all that."

"Right," he muttered. "All the same..."

The doors hissed open on the appropriate floor. She broke from Derek's grasp and flew across the waiting room in a huff. "Addie, wait!" he called after her. Flashing eyes turned his way, but Adelaide didn't stop. She barreled through the double doors. The first nurse in the hallway caught her wrath.

"Where is he?" Adelaide shouted.

The flustered nurse stammered soundlessly. Derek caught up to the pair and put his arm protectively around Adelaide's shoulders. "I have no idea who you're talking about," the nurse finally got out. The gray-haired grandmotherly woman straightened her scrubs and frowned sternly. Derek nodded apologetically.

"I'm sorry. We're looking for her foster father, George Bradley," said Derek. "He was a patient here on the neuro ward, but he's been released. We need to know where he was taken."

"I'm not sure how I can help with that," said the nurse, recovering her aplomb and now frosty after Adelaide's brusque approach.

Derek looked contrite. "Well, you can at least point us in the direction of the person to ask," he said.

"Maybe if your manners were a little bit better…"

Addie growled with frustration and jetted off down the hall toward the main desk. Derek clutched his head and gazed skyward. "Addie, wait up!" he called out. He quickly followed behind her. When he got to the desk, the charge nurse, a woman with a name badge that read Clarissa, was patiently explaining something to his frantic girlfriend.

Derek dropped his hands on Addie's shoulders and gave them an encouraging squeeze. "…Yes, I understand your concerns, but we did try to contact you, and once the room became available, we had to move on it while we could," said Clarissa.

"Fine, fine, I get it! Now, tell me where you moved him to."

Here, the charge nurse looked down. "I'm sorry, but George expressly asked us not to relay that information."

"What?" Adelaide screeched incredulously.

"Well…to be more accurate, his son asked us not to tell you anything more about his medical treatment."

"That's impossible. He doesn't have a son." Adelaide covered her mouth, shaking her head.

The nurse looked uncertain. "Are you sure? Because, George seemed to recognize him."

"No. He doesn't! What the hell do you mean, 'George seemed to recognize him'? My dad just had a stroke! He's not in any condition to recognize anybody!" She turned to Derek, hands to her forehead in a panic. He gripped Adelaide's arms and pulled her close. "I have to get to the bottom of this," she whispered to him.

"I'll have to call in a caseworker to help. She was the one to verify the familial relationship. Ms. Ingles, if there has been some kind of mix-up, we'll get this resolved." Clarissa immediately picked up a phone, but Addie stared daggers at her.

"Some kind of a mix-up? Honey, if you've made a mistake and released my father to some stranger, a mix-up is the understatement of the   year,   and   there   will   be   hell   to   pay!"

CHAPTER 39

"I'LL SEE WHAT I can do," said Owen. Derek nodded appreciatively.

"She wouldn't say a word the whole drive here. I think she's on the verge of a nervous break-down," Derek confided. The two men were in Owen's living room while Addie was in the kitchen, sipping a hot mug of chamomile tea that Owen had made for her.

"So, you're telling me they released her foster father to someone claiming to be his son? How did that even happen?"

"No clue. But, Addie is upset, and we have to get her calm before we let her contact the rehab center where they took him. The caseworker gave me a phone number and someone to speak with over there. The only problem we'll run into is the fact that whoever this mystery man is, he expressly forbade the medical center from talking about George to Addie."

"Like I said, I'll see what I can do about that. I'm having a hard time understanding the motives. Why would anyone cut Addie off from finding out information about George's health? What could they stand to gain from this? All of this sounds…personal."

Adelaide stepped into the living room and set her empty mug on the coffee table. "It is," she stated. "I think I know who this mystery son is. I hope I'm wrong. He's a con-man and a consummate liar." She looked a little more refreshed for the tea. With a blanket wrapped around her shoulders, she appeared vulnerable and waif-like.

"Who?" asked Derek. He led her to the sofa and put her feet up. His cool fingers pressed to her cheeks to soothe her.

Adelaide grabbed her purse as she sat and pulled out her phone. "Remember when I told you that George and Gloria fostered a lot of kids before they got me? Sometimes the duration of fostering overlapped, and shortly before I arrived, the Bradley's had taken on another foster child named Rayford Carlsbad. Here, I found a Facebook picture of him. I want to show this to the administrator at the rehab facility tomorrow to see if anyone recognizes him."

She showed Owen and Derek a picture of a guy about their age. He had unremarkable brown hair and a forgettable, but friendly looking face. He was smiling out from a profile picture. Derek took the phone and scrolled through the man's timeline. Addie wasn't actually one of Rayford's friends on the social media website, so she could only access what he had made public.

Derek saw a convoluted mess of inspirational memes and ranting status updates, lamenting unlucky breaks and bad hands. From what he could gather from his page alone, Rayford seemed a man with a grudge. Life hadn't given him what he expected, and he simultaneously wanted to encourage others that there was better out there, and tell them that he deserved to have it. He showed the posts to Owen.

"Why do you think he would step in and claim to be George's son if he's not, Addie?" Owen asked, accepting the phone. He glanced through the timeline, too.

"The Bradleys had a lot of money when we were with them. I mean, they were never millionaires or anything, but they were definitely upper middle class. If Ray thinks George is still well off, he might be positioning himself to use my dad's feebleness against him.

"It makes so much sense to me! Pretend to be the old man's son, then get him to hand over whatever assets are available. Even if I wanted to contest it—which I don't have the time or the resources to do—I'd be hard pressed to prove that my Dad wasn't in his right mind when he made the exchanges.

"After all, if Ray can convince experienced medical personnel that I'm the threat, then what else can he do? Those nurses knew I had been coming in to sit with George every day from the evening he was admitted."

"Right, I get it," said Owen. "Wow, this sounds like heavy stuff."

"You say you can help," said Addie, "but what exactly can you do?"

Owen shrugged, lifting his brows. "Well, in my line of work, I have a really good rapport with the higher ups at these various medical facilities. Pharmaceutical sales. I'm rubbing elbows with doctors, administrators, medical lawyers, you name it. My presence will maybe get some doors opened that might be blocked to you otherwise."

"Oh my gosh, you have no idea how much this means to me, you guys." She finally crumpled. Her face dropped and her shoulders slumped forward. Addie had to rest her elbows against her knees. Derek sat beside her on the couch and rubbed her back. Owen took the other side and held her hand.

"I told you we'd get through this together," Derek whispered. He looked up and caught Owen's eye. He was so grateful to be able to call such a nurturing, loving man his best friend. Something tugged in Derek's heart that felt suspiciously like falling deeper in love, and he quickly looked away. The more time the three of them spent together, the closer they got. It was a good thing and a bad thing at the same time.

Because, Derek still hadn't had time to talk to Adelaide. He didn't know if she would feel the need to choose. The variables were still up in the air, and he couldn't be so selfish as to put that over what she was going through with her sick foster father. Some things would just have to wait.

◇◇◇

Friday morning Derek left for the office, but he was so preoccupied that he didn't get much done at the cubicle. Libby showed up at his desk a short time after he made it in.

"Excuse me, Mister," she greeted him with a grin and sideways glance. "Why do I get the feeling you've been avoiding me?"

Derek looked down. He hadn't seen her approach. Otherwise, he would've ducked away as he had all week. "I, uh…"

Libby pulled up a rolling desk chair and crossed her legs. "Alright, spill it. What is it? Is it Adelaide? I thought I saw the two of you and some other guy out to dinner over the weekend. Then, I figured it wasn't you because you didn't mention it when you came in to the office. Now, I'm starting to think that it was you, and that there's something you need to tell me."

"Geez, Libby, you should've been a reporter," Derek chuckled nervously.

"Spill it," she repeated, this time with more insistence in her voice. "Come on, Derek."

"The guy you were with…"

"I knew it. You know him? What's wrong with him? Is he gay? Did he murder someone? Ugh! Why do I always pick the losers?"

"No," Derek scoffed. "How did you even leap to those conclusions?" He laughed.

"I know it has to be something for you and him to completely stop talking to me all after that one lunch date."

"So, he stopped talking to you too, huh? Count that a blessing." Derek loosened the collar of his shirt. He didn't want to say it, but he would have to. "Steve is my brother-in-law, Libby. I was going to tell you, but I was trying to wait for the right opportunity."

"He's married? When's the right opportunity, Derek?" she groaned.

"I was trying to find…I wanted to hook you up with…" He sighed. Suddenly, it didn't seem to make sense to withhold the information until he had found her a potential new suitor. "I don't know, Libby. The opportune time should be never, and I wish you didn't have to go through this. I knew how amped up you were when you told me you had met the guy of your dreams."

"Oh," Libby's face dropped. For five seconds, she looked like everything made sense. He could almost see the epiphany's going off one by one behind her glassy eyes as she gazed off. Probably explained a lot. Derek nodded glumly.

"Yep," he muttered ominously.

"Oh," she said softer. Her eyes dropped and her shoulders slumped. She buried her face in her hands and immediately started crying. It was like a dagger to Derek's heart.

"No, no, no, Libby, don't cry!" He leaned over to rub her knee and console her. "I'm sorry. I'm so sorry, honey." She sniffed bravely, quickly dashing the tears from her face.

"Like I said," she hiccuped, "I've got terrible luck with men."

"It's not you. It was Steve. I know what kind of guy he can be. Look, he used to date Adelaide. When she broke things off with him, he was a total dick to her. He's a liar and a cheater, and I have no idea what my sister sees in him. But, had I known he was the person you were talking about, I would've warned you off of him.

"As it is, I'm in a bit of a tough spot. I mean, you're my co-worker. He's my brother-in-law. I still haven't told my sister, yet. But Libby, I want you to forget about Steve because Addie and I may have a new friend for you to meet soon."

"Really?" she asked tearfully. "Ah, Derek, I don't think I'm in any place to meet anyone new." Libby shook her head.

"Don't give up hope yet." His phone rang, and Derek looked at it with regret. "I'm sorry, Libby, but I have to take this call. I know it's Addie or Owen calling with news about her Dad in the rehab facility."

"Okay. Well...we'll talk later I guess." She stood reluctantly and shuffled away, sniffling quietly.

CHAPTER 40

DEREK WISHED THERE was something he could do to fix the situation. It seemed he was being pulled in multiple directions all at once. There was Heather to worry about, Libby, Steve to handle eventually, Owen, and Addie. He heaved a weary sigh as he snatched up the phone, and he noticed Willis Beauchamp heading in his direction at the same time.

"Addie?" Derek answered distractedly.

"Yeah, we found him," she said.

"Oh, Mr. Cornwell, is this a bad time?" Beauchamp smiled apologetically. He held up a file folder. "I wanted to show you my own personal ad design I knocked up. I know it's a bit premature—"

"Hang on, Addie—Mr. Beauchamp, a moment, please? This is kind of an important call." Derek frowned. He turned his back to his teammate, but Willis Beauchamp waited patiently to be addressed. "Okay, is he alright, Adelaide? Is Owen still with you?"

"No, he's talking to the cops about Rayford now. The administrator called them in. Is this a bad time? You sound harried. Know what, I'll just call you back when you're off work."

"Wait, Addie!" Derek tried to stop her, but she had already hung up the phone. He growled, and swiveled around in his chair to talk to his subordinate. "Mr. Beauchamp. I'm a fairly open guy, but in the future if you see me on a call, please respect my privacy. Now, what can I do for you?" he asked huffily.

Beauchamp extended the folder, smiling smugly. He was so

pleased with him himself that he didn't have the decency to look contrite. "I'm sorry," he said glibly. "I was excited and this couldn't wait. I stayed up all night working on this."

Derek examined the work— it showed. The ad his newbie had created was eye-catching and error-strewn. He could see the gist of what the young man was trying to do however, and he had to applaud that. "This is a good draft, Mr. Beauchamp. Hold onto it until we do our next brainstorming session, and we'll see what we can use of it."

"Right, of course," Beauchamp finally looked chastened. Derek knew he couldn't have thought he had created the final ad. He handed the folder back to him.

"Hey, look, your enthusiasm is refreshing, but I want you to know that no one man runs this show. That's why we work in teams."

"No, no, I was just trying to show you what I can do!"

"I'm seeing that. I'm taking note. Thank you for showing me. In the meantime, work with the team. Their fresh ideas matter, too." Derek winked and turned away, effectively dismissing Willis Beauchamp. He had some calls he needed to make, some research that couldn't be put off another second and plenty to fill his time until his shift was over, and he could check in with Adelaide and Owen.

Of course, that's exactly when Gensler would decide to stop by his desk. "Dog-eat-dog," he muttered.

"This borders on harassment, or it would if you were actually getting to me. Goodbye, Harold," Derek said without looking up. He was feeling more in control of his group by the day, and neither Gensler's taunts nor Beauchamp's antics would throw him off his game. Harold Gensler walked away laughing, but Derek was too engrossed in his work to notice.

But, as Derek was checking his emails, tweaking his notes and gearing up to go to the conference room, he happened to look up. "Heather?" he said in surprise. His sister was marching across the design floor with Libby running behind her with a distressed look on her face.

"Ma'am, I'm sorry, but you can't just barge in here like this!" Libby hissed.

Heather whipped around. "You stay out of this. This is between me and my brother."

"Your b-brother?" Libby stammered, eyes widening. She put two and two together. "So, you're Steve's wife?" Thankfully, Heather didn't hear her last question. She was too busy glowering at Derek.

Derek rose, swallowing thickly. He groaned inwardly. By the scowl on her face, Heather wasn't in the best of moods. "I've got it, Libby. Sis, why don't we step outside and talk." He grabbed her arm before she had the chance to protest and gently ushered her out of his place of business. The conversation they needed to have couldn't be had in front of his coworkers.

He rushed her into the elevators. "Why didn't you tell me?" she sobbed when the doors closed behind them.

"You found out about Steve?" Derek said grimly. Heather nodded. Her nose was red and her eyes were bloodshot, but she looked more angry than sad.

"Why didn't you tell me you had seen him out with another woman?"

Derek dropped his head. "Because it wasn't my place," he said quietly. "And, the last time I tried to let you know what sort of a prick he was, you shot me down. I didn't know how to tell you, Heather, but I'm truly sorry."

"I don't want another apology," she whimpered. "I'm sick of I'm sorries. I just wish I had never wasted my time with him, and I wish you would've been straightforward with me, even if you thought I wouldn't listen to you about it."

"Well, how would that have made me look, Heather? Be reasonable," Derek pleaded. The elevator doors opened and she stormed out ahead of him. He hurried after her. "Heather, there are just some things you have to see on your own."

"That men are greedy, selfish bastards. I get it, Derek. I really do!"

"No, that *some* men are. That some *people* are. I know that you're upset, and I know that your feelings are hurt, but look at the bright side. You guys have been married for what—a couple of months? You don't need him. You haven't wasted any time. Just cut him loose and start over."

Heather spun around and jammed a finger into his chest. "Everyone isn't like you, Derek. We can't all take a loss like that without giving things a fighting chance! I'm used to accomplishing the goals I set for myself, and I set a goal to be married. I want this to work."

He threw up his hands. "Then, far be it for me to tell you otherwise."

"Fine!" she shouted, crossing her arms. They were in the downstairs lobby, and there were enough clients milling around for her raised voice to draw attention. Growling, Derek grabbed her by the arm and dragged her outside.

"You don't know how badly I wish I could back down and let you win this round with your stubbornness and pride, but I can't, Heather. Not this time. Like you said, I'm usually able to take a loss and give up. I'm not giving up on you! You're my sister. I want to see you happy, not settling for someone like Steve. You can do so much better than that."

She breathed raggedly, swiping tears from her face. "Maybe it's my fault, you know? Maybe I didn't pay enough attention to him."

"You are not to blame for his behavior. You're only at fault if, after recognizing that he's not the man he pretended to be, you stick around hoping to change him. The truth is, you can't. I know. A person can only change if he or she wants to change."

"Oh, when did you become such a walking success story?" she groaned. She sniffled, but she forced herself to smile with the words. She was in a bad spot, emotionally, and again Derek wished he could take away the worry. He was also grateful he had followed Adelaide and Owen's advice, because they had been right. Had he been the person to deliver this news to her, she might not have taken it to heart. This way, she had no choice but to confront the truth.

He dug his hands into his pockets and rocked back on his heels. "So, how'd you find out?" he asked.

Heather ran the back of her hand under her nose and scowled. "He told me. Well, it wasn't that easy. I found text messages in his phone, and when I asked him about it, he finally broke down and told me the truth. Some witch named Libby. Ugh!"

Derek scratched the side of his eye. "She, uh, isn't a witch. She's one of my co-workers...small world," he finished apologetically as Heather glared at him.

"What do you think I should do, Derek?"

"You know, a wise man once told me that the key to success was expecting and going after the best. You can't take a bad apple with you.

It'll spoil the bunch. Don't let Steve spoil you with bitterness and distrust. Life's too short for that. Take my advice and let him go."

"I can't believe I used to think you'd never get your shit together," she laughed tearfully. Derek laughed too. "Hanging out with Owen is working wonders on you."

"Yeah," he conceded. "It's a little of that. But, it's also the fact that I'm finally taking responsibility for who I am and what happens in my life. It's different, but different is good."

"How are things between you and your girlfriend?" she asked sarcastically.

Derek shrugged. "Honestly, I'm not really sure. I can tell you that, for the time being, I'm happy. I can also tell you that Adelaide isn't the bad guy like Steve made you believe. You think maybe now that you know the truth about him, you can give her another chance?"

"It'll be tough. She never should've crashed my wedding," Heather griped.

"When you think about it, she did you a favor."

"Oh, really, wise guy?"

"Yep. She set the tone. Years from now you'll be laughing about this and saying, 'I should've known it wasn't going to work when his ex-girlfriend crashed the wedding. She was trying to warn me,'" Derek said with a grin.

She fired back with a laugh, "Ha! Well, you tell her the next time to finish the warning instead of skipping off with my brother!"

CHAPTER 41

AT THE END of the day, he rushed home to Owen's house. The place was quiet. Derek eased out of his blazer and tiptoed upstairs to peek into Owen's room. No one seemed to be home. So, he took a shower and got dinner started before placing a call.

"Where are you guys?" he asked when Owen picked up.

"I just dropped her off at her place. I'm headed home now."

A few minutes later, he heard the car in the driveway and peered through the slats of the blinds to see Owen trudging to the front door. Derek threw it open with a smile. "I was worried," he replied. Owen, to his surprise, stepped into his arms and hugged him.

Derek held Owen close in trembling arms. The brush of Owen's beard induced shivers of arousal as their lips briefly met and separated. "You didn't have to worry. I was coming home to you," Owen murmured.

Hard bodies meshed together like fragile flowers pressed between the pages of a book. They walked backwards together from the front door and collapsed onto the cool, plush pillows of the couch, which felt like an oasis after the desert of desire they found themselves stumbling feverishly through. Owen disposed of his shirt and rested on his elbows in a semi-reclining position on the sofa. His body was buff and almost too beautiful to look at, but Derek forced himself to drink in the sight of him, because he didn't know when or if he would get this chance again.

With bold hands, Owen cupped Derek's groin and explored. An airy sigh escaped his mouth as his lips glided over Derek's. His feet slid along the carpeted floor, trying to gain purchase. Derek felt like he was falling. To where, was the question. Owen's questing tongue lit stars behind closed eyes. Pleasure like butterflies skittered through his body. He was overwhelmed by the urgency in Owen's touch.

"Wait a minute," Derek gasped, gripping the edge of the seat.

"Don't," Owen swore softly. His teeth nibbled at the corner of Derek's mouth as he stroked up and down his erection, fingers fumbling with the clasp of Derek's pants. Owen's raspy, labored breathing told tales of shared desire. Derek inhaled sharply as his manhood was pulled free of restraint and expertly masturbated to maximum arousal.

A sigh whooshed from Derek's lungs in an admission of defeat. No point in protesting. This was happening, and there was no stopping it. He didn't want to stop it. Owen's thumb and forefinger curved around beneath the swollen head of Derek's erection as he fluidly coaxed him to higher heights of rapture.

The veiny, turgid shaft pulsated with indescribable need. It was agonizing and fulfilling at the same time to be stroked and caressed. Derek helplessly thrust into Owen's palm. His whimpers of pleasure sounded vulnerable. "Ah!" Derek groaned. He couldn't hold back his ecstasy.

"What is this?" Owen growled against his cheek. "What do you do to me?" Owen planted his nose against Derek's racing pulse and sucked. To the rolling pressure of his insistent tongue, Derek's pulse sped up even more.

"I…" Derek swallowed thickly, squeezing his eyes shut as another tremor wracked his tense body. He gritted his teeth and groaned through the shockwave. His hips danced to the tug of Owen's hand. Perspiration beaded along his hairline as he struggled to contain himself. He was on the verge of an explosion, and the fireworks had only just begun. "I don't know! But, it's the same thing you do to me," he whispered raggedy

Gripping Owen's wrist, Derek slowed down the pace and what was happening between them became a wrestling match for domination. He tore at the waistband of Owen's jeans, diving into his boxers and caressing his erection in return. They battled for supremacy, but the victory was for the both of them as things skated dangerously closer to mutual completion.

Panting breaths mingled in another steamy kiss. Derek wriggled out of his clothes, and Owen did the same. It was dark, but by the moonlight through the picture window, they were two perfect silhouettes of male wonder. When they came back together after getting undressed, it was a collision to rock the world. Derek pushed Owen back to the couch and held his hips pinned to the seat as he kissed down Owen's chest.

He kneeled between Owen's legs as his best friend laid back, thighs gapped. Nosing through chest hairs laden with the smell of Owen's cologne, Derek felt like he was in a smoky woods, on a journey to uncharted territory. Owen's fingers dove into his hair, and he eased Derek lower, his bottom half rising from the couch to press his cock to Derek's face. As another heated moan escaped into the darkness, suddenly, there was a knock at the door.

Derek's head snapped up. Owen stilled. "Shit," he whispered.

"You expecting company?" Derek asked. Owen shook his head. He frantically jerked his jeans up off the floor and yanked them up his legs.

"Get to the room," Owen commanded.

Derek scrambled to get the rest of the discarded clothes. He was jogging up the stairs, skipping every other step, by the time Owen got to and opened the door. And, that's when he heard Adelaide's voice. "Surprise!"

"Addie? What are you doing here?"

Derek paused on the landing to ease back into his pants and tug his t-shirt over his shoulders. He crept downstairs when he was presentable and found Addie talking quietly with Owen. Owen looked concerned. Adelaide wore a brave face, as if she were fighting tears.

Derek gravitated toward the couple. "What's going on?" Derek asked.

"Oh, hi," Addie chuckled, brightening. She came over to him with arms outstretched, and it warmed his heart to see her reach out for him. Derek ambled over and pulled her into his embrace. He kissed her forehead.

"You're okay?" he asked.

"Yeah, I was just in the area. I thought I would stop by." This time she chuckled again, nervously, and Derek could tell something was wrong. On the phone Owen had said he had just dropped her off at home. To get here so quickly she had to have left immediately. "Actually, I couldn't sleep. I've got too much on my mind. Guys, I hope I'm not becoming a burden." She walked into the house.

Owen closed the door behind them and gestured over to the sofa. "Of course not. Our place is your place. Make yourself at home, Addie. Want something to drink? Derek?"

Derek nodded. Addie shrugged, and Owen disappeared into the kitchen to play host as the couple settled on the sofa together. "I'll be George's power of attorney from now on, and we won't have to face anymore hospital mix-ups," said Addie. "Not sure when, now. Oh, damn, I hope I wasn't interrupting anything? Is this a bad time? I was thinking only of myself." She winced, but Derek shook his head hurriedly.

"No, not at all. So, you say he'll be released from the long-term care facility? Do you feel better now that you know he's okay? Is he ready to live on his own again?"

"I'm not sure." Adelaide put her hands to her face and shoved them through her hair, looking up again with teary eyes. "I don't want him to live alone, but I'm not in a position to do much for him. That kills me. I don't want to send him into the wilderness alone."

"Then, let's talk about how to make things easier on the both of you."

Owen reentered with drinks for the both of them. He sat down on the couch on Derek's side instead of Adelaide's—a minor distraction to the conversation at hand. Owen's fingers grazed Derek's thighs as he handed him his drink. "Anything we can do to help, we're available," Owen volunteered. Adelaide breathed a gusty sigh.

"Just hold me?" Her voice cracked when she said it.

They both reached for her at the same time, but she turned to Derek. Owen's facial expression didn't change at all, but his eyes...his eyes misted up before he could look away. And, Derek knew they were at the point where she would soon choose, and one of the men would be left   behind.

CHAPTER 42

DEREK INSTINCTIVELY REACHED for Owen with one arm as the other wrapped around Adelaide, but Owen pulled back. "Don't. She needs you right now."

Addie looked over her shoulder. "I need you both," she murmured, confused. "I want to be surrounded by people who don't care if I'm happy or sad. Who know I can be beautiful, and intelligent, and dorky at the same time." She sniffed, wiping her eyes, and reached for his hand. Owen uncomfortably allowed her to hold it, but his face was wooden. His gaze flew to Derek's. Adelaide picked up on the tension and sighed.

"What's this about, guys?" she asked.

Owen shook his head and rose to his feet. "It's nothing."

"It is," said Derek.

"It's not the time," said Owen.

"What is it?"

"You know what you really need, Addie? Something to take your mind off of things," Owen perked up, changing the subject. "How about a game?"

She looked skeptical. Derek shrugged. "It's worth a shot. We haven't had a good laugh all day. All of us have been worried. What do you say?" He hated to admit it, but Owen was right. It wasn't the time for heartfelt conversations about love and relationships, and Addie wasn't in any position to be put on the spot. She looked emotionally drained.

"What kind of game?" Addie asked.

Owen tugged his phone out of his pocket, carefully hiding the fact that his pants were still unzipped. He handed it to her. "Pick something. I've got tons of apps."

That brought a smile to her lips. "Okay." Adelaide scrolled through his selection of games, and Derek disappeared into the kitchen to check on dinner. Owen ambled after him a few minutes later, while he was fixing plates.

"Look, I don't think we should force Adelaide to choose," said Owen.

"I never said I would do that."

"No, I mean…there's no need for any big discussion or to ask any deep questions. Let's just keep rolling like we're rolling. Humph! I was the one telling you to keep your feelings out of things, and here I am, a mess. She doesn't need that drama."

Derek paused in his preparation of the food. "I do think it's something that needs to be discussed, just not right now. So, don't bail on me. Don't harden that thick heart of yours, either." He smiled, half-teasing but more serious than not. He could tell Owen was getting skittish about the vulnerable position falling in love left him in. He turned to him and kissed his lips gently.

"What was that for?" Owen asked. His lips glided over Derek's again. Owen inhaled deeply and wrapped his arms around Derek's waist as he deepened the kiss. As their bodies came together, the fire from moments before Adelaide had arrived, reignited. Derek's pelvis strained against Owen's, his cock getting rigid from the contact. He groaned deeply, not wanting to stop.

At that moment, Adelaide walked into the kitchen. She took one look at them and smiled seductively as she tossed her hair over her shoulder. Holding up Owen's phone, she shook the device side to side. "I found one," she said.

Owen and Derek broke apart guiltily. "Ahem, what'd you find?" asked Derek. He wiped his lips and looked down. Owen moved a step away from him to put more distance between them.

"The 'How Gay are You' quiz," she answered mischievously. Laughter erupted from Owen. Derek smiled incredulously.

"Wait, what?"

"The 'How Gay are You' quiz! How about it, guys? You want to

NICOLE STEWART

answer the questions and see where you fall on the Gaydar meter?" She parked her hip on the edge of the table and eyed them until Owen finally said he'd be willing to take the quiz.

"Alright. If he will, I will," Derek consented.

Adelaide began asking the questions, with choices creatively written for humor and wit. Yet, each time it came to them answering, Owen would pick the most ludicrous option available. It was clear he was trying to make Addie laugh. Derek chuckled as he brought their plates over to the table, and the three of them settled down to eat.

"My turn," he stated.

"K, Derek, would you say your sense of style is rugged, fantabulous, or so great it borders on being a sixth sense?"

"Well, I do see chic people, sooo..."

Adelaide giggled and scrolled to the next question. "Here's the deciding factor. Owen...if you had to choose between me and Derek, who would you choose?" She peeped at him over the phone. Owen looked at Derek and looked back at Addie, at a loss for how best to answer.

He finally opened his mouth and admitted, "I wouldn't be able to choose."

"Wise answer," she said, grinning.

Derek couldn't help but point out, "Yeah, but you said that there's no way for someone to be in love with more than one person."

"Who said anything about love?" Owen quipped. He looked down at this plate and pushed the food around, avoiding eye contact. Derek could tell he was still feeling a little wounded after Adelaide had turned to Derek for support back in the living room.

The smile on Addie's face wavered. "I dunno, guys. I'm pretty sure I love being with both of you." She shrugged one shoulder as she nibbled a bite off of her fork. Suddenly, she slumped in her seat and threw her fork down. "This is so stupid," she whispered, crossing her arms. Addie turned her head and stared at the wall as she giggled mirthlessly, mumbling something to herself. The abrupt change in emotion made Derek and Owen halt and study her with concerned, confused expressions.

"What? What is it, Addie?" Derek asked.

She snorted, laughing self-deprecatingly as she straightened her face. "No, it's just that...I mean, I don't talk about love like that. I mean, we're all good now, but who's to say how things will be in a week or two, right?"

Derek reached across the table and rubbed her hand. "Humans need love."

"Yep. And, things are all good now. Who's to say they won't be even better in a week or two?" Owen added.

"Ah, c'mon! You're just like me," Addie scoffed at Owen's comment. "You don't believe in love."

He replied softly, "I don't believe in everything that calls itself love, you're right. But, I believe in love."

"Wow. How did we even get on this subject? Listen, guys, all my life I've been the chick people put up with for as long as they had to before cutting loose. When it comes to dating, I've learned not to push my luck. I like to bail before the party is over. Less mess to clean up," she chuckled.

"Yet, you said you love the both of us," Owen pressed.

"I was going with the flow of the conversation!" she protested, laughing.

"Nah, I don't think you were," said Derek.

Adelaide pushed away from the table. "Hey, I didn't make the rules of this game, and the both of you know exactly what this is. It's just sex."

"You're just scared," Derek muttered, shaking his head sadly. She'd never admit that her broken little heart still had the capacity to feel.

"You want sex?" Owen interrupted, pushing back from the table as well. He marched around and grabbed Addie's hand. "Just sex. Fucking, screwing, the whole nine. I can give you that. So can Derek. You're right. You didn't make the rules. But, what do you say we enjoy the game, hmm? I'm in the mood. You?"

"What—now?" she asked incredulously.

Owen pulled her through the kitchen archway to the stairway beyond, and Derek left the table to follow. With his libido in high gear, having been interrupted twice already, what Owen was saying sounded right up his alley. "I think we all could use a little no-strings-attached right   now."

CHAPTER 43

OWEN BACKED QUICKLY up the stairs, and Adelaide's hands raked at his slacks, popping the buttons. He shrugged out of his jacket and tossed it over the landing. Derek followed in hot pursuit, untying his drawstring pants and reaching for Addie's skirt at the same time. The three lovers spilled onto the second story and Adelaide fell into Owen's arms. The two of them hit the wall, kissing passionately.

Derek dropped to his knees behind her and dove beneath her skirt, ripping her panties down with a combination of his hands and teeth. As he shoved her legs wider to gain access, he eagerly opened his mouth against her womanhood. Addie moaned excitedly. Owen's hands rubbed up and down her back. He tore her shirt off and tossed it aside. Grunts of exertion flowed from his mouth as he hungrily kissed his way down her shoulder to her cleavage. Addie threw her hands out to brace them against the wall, legs spread, chest thrust into Owen's face.

Derek sampled her delectable vagina before tearing her away from Owen and dragging her into the room. She gasped, "Yes!" He threw her wanton body down upon the bed and pressed between her legs, his throbbing cock searching for entrance. Owen quickly climbed up and exposed his erection to her receptive mouth. Adelaide's slender fingers closed around him, stroking him with sure, firm tugs of her hand. Owen groaned as he grabbed a breast and squeezed.

Derek's hand rested at the base of her stomach as he moved in and out of her body with slow, long thrusts that spread pleasure through her erogenous zones, yielding sparks of ecstasy that made her body dewy for more. He reached up to fondle the other breast. Addie's erotic hums and whimpers for more encouraged him to keep pounding the spot she seemed to love the best. She writhed sinuously, rolling her body like a dancer.

Golden hair spilled across the mattress. Her dusky skin glowed in the soft light of the bedside lamp. Derek was staring at her in wonder when Owen suddenly grabbed him by the back of his neck and pulled his face close. Their mouths locked together with a fierce growl of surrender. Owen, trembling as he held himself in check while Addie worked her magic, whispered Derek's name against his lips. Their tongues clicked together. Derek moaned.

Derek knew. There was no choosing. The choice was already made. Even Adelaide knew what she wanted, though she fought it tooth and nail. Well, maybe it was time to show her how marvelous this relationship could be if she just let go of her fears.

He pulled out of her body. She was dripping wet, and the silky sliding sound of his cock pulling free was a reminder. They weren't done yet. He ended the kiss with Owen to lean down and kiss her. Addie released Owen's dick and whined with pleasure as she connected with Derek's lips. He braced his arms aside her face and poured his heart into the embrace.

"What's not to love?" she moaned deliriously. "There's nothing to not love about this." She pushed her fingers through his hair and locked them behind his neck, deepening the kiss. Derek rolled her onto her side, and Owen lowered himself to the bed behind her. They both held her. Owen eased his swollen staff into her sheath as Derek plundered her mouth with his tongue.

She gripped her thighs tight to squeeze him deeper into her body. Owen grimaced at the ecstasy that rippled through him. He held her hips steady, pounding, harder, deeper. Derek stroked her face and reached behind her to clutch Owen's neck. His fingers traced along Owen's jawline and came back to Owen's lips.

Owen kissed Derek's fingertip as he trembled, ready. Adelaide's nimble fingers skated down Derek's torso to bring him to nirvana, too. She rubbed his cock, and he was pulsating with a need to climax. Their mingled breaths, moans, and sighs filled the room. Faster, the carousel of desire swirled.

When the passion reached its zenith, they came together in a domino effect—first Adelaide, then Owen, then Derek. They were tangled. There was no beginning or end to the knot. They could not be taken apart.

"What's not to love about this?" Owen whispered, kissing the back of her neck. "What's not to love?"

"Can I tell you the truth? I've been abandoned all my life. Not even my own parents wanted me. I've spent much of my adulthood trying to foster a sense of intimacy that wasn't there."

"But, it doesn't have to be that way with us," Owen replied quietly. She looked at him as if she wished it was true, but she couldn't be certain, and Derek didn't know how to convince her. He could show her better than he could tell her.

That night Derek dreamed there was no such thing as goodbye for the three lovers. Mornings, they woke up next one another. They worked together and pooled their financial resources, living comfortably. They were friends and family. It was such an easygoing reality that he didn't even realize he was dreaming until he woke up.

He blinked his eyes in the darkness. When he reached out, he could feel Owen beside him. He thought he heard the sound of someone crying. "Addie?" he whispered. She sucked in a quiet breath.

"Did I wake you?" she whispered back. "I'm sorry."

"What's wrong?" Derek sat up. His eyes adjusted to the dark room and he noticed she was sitting at the foot of the bed with her knees up and her chin resting on the platform of her crossed arms.

"Do you think I'm selfish?" she asked. Silence reigned. "You care about me, Derek?" She looked over her shoulder at him. Derek smiled.

"More than I think you'll ever know."

"I probably will know someday. It'll probably be too late."

"It doesn't have to be."

"I don't like needing people."

"I know the feeling. It's even worse when you need someone who doesn't need you back." He looked at her pointedly. Adelaide didn't respond. They were dancing around the subject but getting closer to the point. "Do you care about me?" he asked.

Addie nodded. "I care about you, and Owen."

"Then, why do you keep us at arm's length? You know what I think? I think the three of us need each other. Owen gives me guidance and support and unconditional friendship. You give me excitement, adventure, the opportunity to share this big heart I've got. Owen needs us because he was getting jaded. He didn't used to be so cynical about love. And you? Well, you need us because we're the family that won't give you up."

She pondered that for a moment in the quiet darkness that permeated the room. The world seemed to slow its dizzying spin, and everything seemed to fall into place. Owen stirred, and Derek realized he was awake, too. He reached out a hand and Derek grabbed it. Adelaide lay down in his arms, resting her head on Owen's chest. Derek took the other side and stared across Owen's chest at her.

"You said before that the heart only has room for one," he whispered. "I don't believe that's true. I believe our hearts have an infinite capacity to love. And, I know that my heart has room for the both of you."

Nothing more was said as the three of them sat, pondering where their relationship was headed. Soon, Addie's eyes drifted shut, sleep finally claiming her like a much-needed salve on an emotional wound that just wouldn't stop bleeding. Owen followed soon after, the long day having finally sapped him of any vestige of energy. Derek was left awake to think about what he had said to her. It felt right. It *was* right.

CHAPTER 44

"YOU GUYS NEVER did tell me how things went at the rehab facility," Derek said the next morning over breakfast. Adelaide had spent the night. The three of them sat together in their favorite spot by the picture window, the breakfast nook.

"Essentially, Rayford made everyone believe he was George's son, but the charade could only last as long as my Dad was out of it on his meds. By the time we got to the rehab facility, he was raising a fuss, calling for me," Adelaide replied. "It did my heart good to hear him trying to get his point across."

"You could hear him in the halls. His speech hasn't cleared up yet, but he certainly knew how to say Addie."

She smiled. "I never mentioned it, but he was the only one to call me that into my teen years. You guys brought back so many memories when you started using that nickname."

"Aww, that's nice to hear," Owen gushed, grinning. It was obvious, he was smitten. If Adelaide couldn't see that, she was blind.

"Excellent," Derek replied with a smile. "Glad to hear that everything is going as it should be. I just have one question for you."

"Oh, yeah? What's that?"

"Once all this is settled—the power of attorney, your Dad out of the long-term care facility and all that—where's it going to leave us? I hardly think we're just casually sleeping together any longer. Never mind last night."

"No, I don't suppose it was very casual, was it?" she said softly.

◇◇◇

Derek sat in his cubicle, staring at the blank computer screen, thinking about Adelaide. He and Owen had gone with her on Sunday to get her foster father settled in at the facility, and it had been a memorable experience. George Bradley, who was only just re-learning how to talk, had looked at him sternly when he walked into the room. "My Addie," the old man said. He repeated it again, and the implication was clear: "Don't mess with my Addie. Don't hurt her."

"Poppy, you want me to read to you?" Addie asked.

"Mmm," George grunted and nodded his head. Adelaide pulled a big book of fairytales out of her purse. Derek eyed her with wonder.

She explained, "I came down with a bad case of mono in high school, and do you know he actually read this to me while I was getting over it? At the time, I couldn't appreciate it. I felt like him and Gloria were treating me like a baby. She kept coming in with warm chicken noodle soup, and there he was, reading at the bedside. Now…it's one of my fondest memories. It was the first time anyone had cared enough about me to truly take care of me."

She flipped over the faded, old book and turned to the first page. Adelaide smiled as she began to read, "Once upon a time there was a girl named Ella…"

The three men listened to her lilting voice bring the fairytale to life. Derek and Owen shared a look from the two chairs by the bedside, and Adelaide sat on the side of the bed next to George. She read until the old man fell asleep, and she softened her voice to finish the story until the very last Happily Ever After. Seeing this tender side of Adelaide was enlightening.

When she was done, she held the book in her lap and studied her foster father with misty eyes. Her gaze drifted over his lined face. He looked peaceful in rest, and some of the worst of the twisting of his handsome features relaxed away. Owen rose to his feet and stood behind her, placing his hands on her shoulders. Adelaide looked up with a sad smile.

"He's going to pull through this," Owen reassured her.

She nodded. "He's resilient like that. He won't have to go it alone, either. Now that I have him back in my life, I wouldn't dream of losing this connection." She sighed, thinking things through. "I'll have to get a bigger apartment. I want him to move in with me."

Adelaide pushed away from the bed and put the book back in her purse. The curtain of her golden hair fell over her face as she composed herself. When she stood up and pushed her hair back, she blinked at Owen and Derek, remembering something. "You know Rayford had the nerve to call me earlier and tell me he would've cut me in on the deal if I had kept my mouth shut? The loser... a guy like that could never understand that the people in our lives are more important than money."

"Yeah, well, he'll think twice next time he tries to con someone. He's lucky the facility didn't press charges."

Derek suddenly had an epiphany. "Hey guys, how do you three feel about all of us living together?" he asked out of the blue.

"What?" Owen looked up with quirked brow. "I mean, technically we already do. Adelaide knows she's welcome anytime."

"Right," she replied. "Although, I'm sure the frequent visits are about to get fewer and farther between until George is on his feet again. Like I said, I want him to move in with me."

"That's what I'm saying. The four of us." Derek thought of the dream he had had the night before and shook his head. "What I mean is, what if we all pool our resources and buy a bigger house? Then, when George gets out of here, he can come live with us, too."

Adelaide looked surprised and pleased by the suggestion. Owen nodded carefully. "It's a big commitment," he pointed out. He looked at Adelaide specifically. "I don't want you to feel like you have to stick around just because, you know?"

Addie shrugged. "I dunno. I think I like having you guys around. Think about it. Even if we 'break up,' so to speak, we're all great friends. I'm sure we'll be able to manage. I can hire a home health nurse for George. We can be one big, happy family."

Derek nodded eagerly, and Owen smiled, completely on board as well. Adelaide pulled out her phone and started scrolling through links to real estate agencies. "This is so unorthodox," she admitted with a grin.

"Well, we're rather unorthodox people," Derek replied, laughing.

By the time they left, George was settled in and quite content. They had a plan in place for how to have a future together. They were all aware that it might not remain sunshine and roses, romance and hot, steamy sex, but it was destined to remain friendship and camaraderie. What had started as a one-night stand had turned into the kind of partnership not even a broken heart could compromise.

Derek sighed as he shook out of the memory of the day before and tried to get back to work. The solution would have to do, even if it didn't come with promises of eternal love. He was happy with it. Now, it was time to focus back on his career. All the pieces of his successful life story were back in place, and Derek was confident his days of being a born loser were over.

He had a brainstorming session with his crew during which he intended to set the record straight that he wasn't looking for anybody to be a one-man band. He wanted to kill the notion that competition was about one-upmanship. In this game, it was about working together aggressively to deliver quality content. There was never any way to know exactly what ad would catch a client's eye or what they were looking for, so the best bet was to put your all into whatever you produced and hope it stood the test.

Derek pushed away from the desk as the clock registered the final hour of work. One loose end to wrap up, and the rest would be solid.

CHAPTER 45

DEREK STROLLED INTO the conference room with confidence and headed straight to the presentation screen. He yanked it down out of the ceiling and set up his tablet with the wireless HDMI projector. The rookie teammates who had been chatting amiably before he walked in straightened up and went silent, like a classroom waiting to be lectured.

Before Derek could say anything, Beauchamp instantly threw a hand up. "Oh sir, I have that ad we said we'd show the team."

Derek raised his palm to halt the other man. "Before we get started on this brainstorming session, I'd like to tell you all a story. It's mine, actually. You see, when I first came to this company, I came bursting with ideas. Many of them were shot down by the higher ups."

He paced away from the table and hit the remote to bring up a picture of him a few years back when he was a ruddy-faced newbie like these guys. Derek smiled as his team chuckled good-naturedly. Beauchamp looked like he was bursting to show off his work, but Derek ignored him for the time being. This was more important.

"Well, you can imagine how that felt for me. I learned my lesson. No bright ideas. No gleeful suggestions. I learned to keep my head down and go with whatever everyone else was doing around me. Inevitably, flash forward a few years and where did that track lead me? To almost getting fired."

Derek put his hands behind his back and turned to his team. He clicked the remote so the slide could transition. His Wonder Man ad popped up. "I was called in by Mr. Clancy and told he had selected me

275

as a new hire solely off the merits of my portfolio. It was good body of work. It just didn't carry over into what I was doing here, keeping my head down and going where everyone else wanted to go.

"You guys probably know some of this story. Mr. Clancy gave me another shot, and I went up against Harold Gensler's team while simultaneously working with them. Why would he do that? Because, our supervisor understood that not only would we have to be personally great, we would have to know how to work with others.

"That's the message I wanted to bring to you guys." Derek turned away and sat back at the table. He pulled up the information for the ad they were currently working on and locked his fingers together as he gazed out at his team. "We're working as a unit. I will never shoot your ideas down. You will never have to worry about voicing a stupid suggestion, because there are no stupid suggestions.

"Our job is to create marketable content, and that requires some out-of-the-box thinking. Fortunately, our very newness is what makes us the best ad people for the job. The only thing that can hinder us is in fighting. If we can't work together, then we can't do this job."

He looked pointedly at Beauchamp, who had stopped fidgeting around and was paying closer attention to him. The other members of the team were also all eyes and ears. Derek smiled, glad to see his point was getting across.

"Now, let's start this brainstorming session, and I want everyone's input. Each of you brings something unique to the table. Let no voice be unheard, and let no voice try to outshout the others, alright? See, Harold Gensler warned me that this job came with the dog-eat-dog mentality. That some of the people in this room would inevitably be out to take my spot in the company."

"But, I don't believe that. Because, there's enough room at this table for all of us. I do hope that someday each one of you goes on to do something greater. I have no need to keep anyone down. So, we should shine. We should shine very brightly. But, we should also remember that a sky with one star wouldn't be as magnificent as a galaxy in the dark night. Are you guys with me?"

They sent up an office-sized cheer, and Derek laughed and got to work. When he looked up an hour later after the meeting was over and his crew was filing out, he noticed Mr. Clancy in the doorframe. "Can I do anything for you, sir?" Derek asked.

Mr. Clancy shook his head and waited for all of the others to leave before strolling over to the table and sitting down with Derek. "That was some speech," he said.

Derek blushed. He hadn't known anyone was listening, much less his very own supervisor. "Yes, well, I just wanted everyone to know that this job didn't have to be as cutthroat as people think it is," he said, clearing his throat nervously. "I mean, not that it's cutthroat or anything. I'm very happy to have this position…"

Mr. Clancy chuckled and lifted a hand to stop his rambling, apologetic backtracking. "I know what you mean, Derek. You know, you never cease to amaze me. When I almost fired you, I was certain there was no way you would ever take this career seriously. Yet, here you are, shining in the night sky with a constellation of your own."

"I am forever indebted to you for that, sir," Derek replied sincerely.

Mr. Clancy waved away the statement dismissively. "Word around the water cooler is…" Derek immediately thought of Libby when Mr. Clancy said that. "…Harry Gensler has given you some trouble lately."

He said guardedly, "Nothing I can't handle, sir."

"All the same, I'll have a word with him myself. What you're doing here with this team is revolutionary stuff, as far as this company goes. Here's to hoping it inspires others to try the same approach." Mr. Clancy got up from the table and exited.

Derek stared after him, feeling a surge of happiness at how things were working out for him.

A month ago, he had been struggling to hold onto his job, juggling one failed relationship after another, disappointing his parents and himself by not maturing into the man he could be. Now, he had a home, and a future with his two best friends. He had a secure spot on the job. He had everything he could have asked for.

They say lightning never strikes the same place twice. He had been double-struck, however, with both love and luck. And, while there was still no telling exactly what the future would hold—whether he and Owen and Adelaide would work out in a relationship or end up being just friends—he was sure that his success story would end with a Happily   Ever   After.

EPILOGUE

STREAMERS SWAYED FROM the hotel ballroom ceiling, and the glamorous space was transformed by the party atmosphere. Music pumped from the speakers as the DJ mixed things up with classic rock and the most popular tunes. The guests were all casually dressed, mostly young, single women. Derek and Owen stood back and watched the mass of people gyrating on the dance floor and drinking too much at the bar.

"Some turnout, right?" Heather passed them and shouted. She threw up two thumbs, and Derek threw up his in return. "Better than at the wedding!"

A banner draped across the longest wall, written in what looked like lipstick, boasted, "HAPPY NOT ANYMORE-VERSARY!"

A solid year had passed. It had taken that long for the divorce to finalize because Steve had done everything in his power to stall the process, and Heather had chosen to celebrate her divorce with a party unlike any other. A massive cake topped with a guillotine and a little groom with his head lopped off, red icing blood oozing from the stump, took up a table across from the bar. Instead of a wedding dress, Heather was dressed in all black, as if 'mourning' the loss.

Really, she was getting a kick out of things, and it showed. "Down with love," Owen replied cynically, raising his glass. He chuckled to himself and Derek laughed along with him.

"You know, there was a time I could picture you being someone's husband," Derek confided. Owen hit him with a skeptical look.

278

"Me? Now, why would you ever wish a thing like that on me, of all people? You know I prefer a full bed to a ball and chain," he responded cheekily.

"Yeah, well, once upon a time," Derek trailed off. Neither of them discussed how intimate things had gotten between them back in the day. In fact, for all outward appearances, nothing had ever changed in their friendship.

They were still roommates. Derek was still going strong at Ad Ent, where his newbie team had quickly risen in the ranks as the go-to ensemble when clients wanted hip, hot ads. Owen was prevailing as a pharmaceutical sales associate. Success was something they could both claim. And, as far as love went?

Libby hurried over to Derek's side, holding up a flute of champagne. "Word around the refreshment table is they're about to cut the cake," she said gleefully. She looped her arm through Derek's. "I'm so glad you invited me to this shindig. Your family is a hoot!" Owen smiled warmly at her.

Derek chuckled and patted her hand. "Glad you're having a good time. I was kind of worried a divorce party would disturb your sense of romanticism."

"Ha! Honey, after the year I've been through trying to find the right guy for me? I'd celebrate anything that disses chumps like Steven!"

At that moment, a woman strutted to the entrance into the ballroom, catching the eye of every male in the vicinity. She paused at the threshold, as if her presence alone could stop the world. She was tall. She was stacked, and she had blonde hair that glistened in the light of the chandelier. Her long legs ate up the distance, as the crowd parted to let Adelaide pass.

It had shocked the shit out of Derek when his sister had invited Steve's ex-girlfriend, but upon finding out what a no-good scumbag he was, Heather no longer seemed to have any hard feelings toward Addie. When a well-dressed gentleman stepped through the door behind her and followed in her wake, the faces of disappointment from the men who had been entertaining thoughts of pursuing her were comical. At least one or two of them were married, a fact Derek was privy to.

He shook his head in amusement. "There she blows," Owen muttered. He swallowed a big gulp of his cocktail and tried to tear his gaze away but was unsuccessful in ignoring the one woman who had ever stolen his heart. Both Derek and Owen stared, as she and her plus-one made their way across the dance floor.

Libby watched, too. She went from being excited about the party to a fidgety, nervous wreck. Upon noticing this, Derek squeezed her hand reassuringly. "It won't be as bad as you think," he whispered quietly.

Adelaide and her friend came directly up to them, and she paused in front of Owen and Derek with a toss of her golden hair. "Owen, Derek, I'd like to introduce you to my friend, Kevin," she said with a smile. Kevin looked like the luckiest man in the building. Derek tried not to be jealous at Addie's connection with the new guy, but knowing how potent her love was, it was hard to keep the envy at bay.

"Nice to meet you, Kevin," he stated coolly. "Addie, Kevin, this is my friend, Libby."

"Yes, we've met," said Adelaide. She and Libby knew each other quite well.

Libby replied shyly, "Well, it's good to see you again, but Derek and I were just about to go for some cake." Libby had always found the buxom blonde somewhat intimidating. Libby didn't need to be intimidated by her, however, because Adelaide had brought her sexy looking male model escort best friend to meet *her*.

Addie's flawless face broke into a strikingly beautiful smile. She scooted in between Derek and Owen. "Oh, Kevin, why don't you and Libby go for cake instead? I haven't seen my besties all day!"

"Of course, Adelaide," the gentleman murmured quietly. To Libby's surprise, he genteelly extended his arm to her. Her rosy cheeks went crimson at being catered to as the handsome man whisked her away to the refreshment table, leaving Adelaide, Derek, and Owen behind.

Derek leaned in familiarly and kissed Addie's cheek. "I've missed you cupcake," he whispered into her ear.

Owen was less openly affectionate, but his fingers traced down her back and he stared at her with a half-smile. "Ditto for me. What took you so long?"

She giggled. "I had to school Kevin on how important it was for him to give this one girl a chance. He can be shy with his heart, but everything I know about Libby tells me this could be a great match."

They had already introduced her to three others who hadn't turned out to be the one.

"It's not an exact science, playing matchmaker," Owen replied thoughtfully. "I mean, look at the three of us? No one would've ever guessed a year after a one-night stand, we'd be here. I'm damned glad for happy endings, however."

"Right on," Derek chimed in. The two men bumped glasses in a toast, and Adelaide laughed as she snuggled up closer to Derek, one leg rubbing intimately against Owen's as well. The three of them stood in a corner watching Heather's divorce party play out, and gossiping about the guests. It was a decidedly irreverent event.

As they watched the singles try to pick up dates, the married pretend at faithfulness, and the jilted gamely soldier on, they shared inside jokes about how the world would be so much better if everyone did like them, and gave up the ridiculous notion of monogamy. Of course, no one else at the party knew the exact nature of their polyamorous situation—not even Libby—but perhaps that was the best part. There were no expectations from others about how their relationship should play out. How different would people's expectations of love be if everyone started loving outside the box? Their matching rings glinted in the light of the chandelier, and Adelaide took notice.

"Promises made, promises kept," she replied to herself.

"What was that, honey?" Derek asked. She tossed her hair out of her eyes and stared him boldly in the face, shifting her perspective to look at Owen, too.

"I said I love you two," she whispered.

Made in the USA
Columbia, SC
17 January 2020